PENGUIN
Until Next Weekend

Until Next Weekend

RACHEL MARKS

PENGUIN BOOKS

PENGUIN BOOKS

UK | USA | Canada | Ireland | Australia
India | New Zealand | South Africa

Penguin Books is part of the Penguin Random House group of companies
whose addresses can be found at global.penguinrandomhouse.com.

First published 2021
001

Copyright © Rachel Marks, 2021

The moral right of the author has been asserted

Set in 12.5/14.75 pt Garamond MT Std
Typeset by Integra Software Services Pvt. Ltd, Pondicherry
Printed and bound in Italy by Grafica Veneta S.p.A.

The authorized representative in the EEA is Penguin Random House Ireland,
Morrison Chambers, 32 Nassau Street, Dublin D02 YH68

A CIP catalogue record for this book is available from the British Library

ISBN: 978-1-405-94009-2

www.greenpenguin.co.uk

MIX
Paper from
responsible sources
FSC® C018179

Penguin Random House is committed to a
sustainable future for our business, our readers
and our planet. This book is made from Forest
Stewardship Council® certified paper.

For my mum and dad, Paula and Mike – the best parents a girl could ever ask for

CHAPTER ONE

One day, I will learn that turning up to work with a stinking hangover is a terrible, terrible idea.

'Mr Carlton, there's something stuck up my nose.'

'What is it?'

'My finger.'

'Well, take it out then.'

'Mr Carlton, Mr Carlton, will you open my banana?'

'Yes, but can you ask Mummy to teach you to open it yourself?'

'And me, and me.'

It's like stepping on a wasp's nest. Multiple bananas are shoved in my face and I spend the first ten minutes of my working day splitting open overly ripe fruit and wiping banana goo on to my chair. Where did it all go so wrong?

It does make me laugh sometimes – to think of the years of studying – and now I spend the majority of my working life teaching children how to take off their jumper (just pull it over your head) or drink their milk without spilling it or how to tell the difference between the fruit bin and the paper one (the fruit one has a *lid*, people).

I say *sometimes* it makes me laugh. Most of the time it makes me want to jump into a large pit with no method of escape. I didn't exactly 'fall' into teaching. I'm well aware of the expression, 'Those who can, do. Those who can't, teach.' And it probably does apply to me in some respects.

I'm not sure there is anything else I'd be very good at (not that I'm particularly good at teaching). But it was an active decision. I do really like kids – their innocence, their honesty. I'm just not so keen on thirty of them, all trapped in a confined space, badgering me relentlessly.

'Right, enough. Everyone sit down. If you need your banana opening, you will have to wait. I need to do the register.'

The obedient ones sit down, but there are still a few persistent pests that need swatting away – metaphorically, of course. Once they're all finally sitting on the carpet, I clap my hands and they all clap back, out of time, and then this wonderful silence descends on the room, bringing with it the feeling of intense calm I imagine you would experience walking into a Buddhist temple.

It doesn't last long. I'm only a few names down the register when Harley starts his usual morning routine of being a complete pain in the arse. First comes the jigging, the shaking, like an aeroplane with a major fault before it starts its catastrophic descent to the ground. Then the poking of anyone nearby (accompanied by over-the-top squeals from the victims).

I try to ignore as many of these misdemeanours as possible. In part because it's a strategy we were taught at teacher training college, and in part because my head is pounding so hard that engaging in a heated confrontation with Harley, where he will only deny all wrong-doing, is not at the top of my current to-do-list.

I didn't *plan* on coming to school with a hangover. I *planned* on taking my boys for a rare mid-week outing to the cinema to see the new *Spiderman* film, but then Kate rang to say they'd been fighting since the second they got home from school and that she felt it was important we gave them a consequence (the consequence being no cinema trip with me). She said it with the inflection at the end of the sentence, pretending it was a question, but we both knew it wasn't. So, with a disappointment in the pit of my stomach that made me feel a little queasy, I decided to go to the pub. And now here I am deeply regretting that decision as I face another battle with the bane of my current working life.

'Right, Harley, come and sit by my chair because I can see I can't trust you to sit nicely with the other children.'

I don't know why I waste my breath. I know he won't. That he'll use the other children as hurdles on his rampage across the carpet and then bolt for the door – Mrs Watson, my world-weary teaching assistant, preventing his escape with a subtle clothes-line manoeuvre before manhandling him back to the carpet.

That's pretty much what happens, although Bailey saves Mrs Watson a job, grabbing Harley's trailing leg as he leaps over his head and sending him flying, head first, on to the classroom floor.

There are shrieks, not just from Harley, but also from timid little hamster-like Annabelle, who is squashed beneath him. Mrs Watson glances over but chooses to ignore it, despite the fact I'm only halfway down the register and I've still got the joyous task of taking the dinner choices to contend with.

'Uh, Mrs Watson, I think you might need to take Harley and Annabelle here and just give them the once-over to check they're both OK.'

Mrs Watson looks at me like I just asked her to shovel shit and I make a mental note to print out a copy of her latest appraisal and pop it into her pigeonhole as a little reminder of her areas to work on, predominantly contributing more to the role than piercing the straws into the milk cartons at fruit and milk time. With a pointed sigh, she comes over and grabs both children by the arm, pulling them up to a standing position and removing them from the carpet area, the ringing in my ears gradually dissipating as she moves them further away.

I finish the register. Sadly the only child that's away is the one you couldn't pick out of a line-up anyway. And all the wondrously big characters (teacher code for little tykes) push on through, inflicting their snotty noses and diarrhoea episodes on the rest of us.

'OK, dinners.' I utter an internal 'yippee' that's soaked in sarcasm and paint on my happy clown face. 'So the options today – remember to listen so I don't have to say them again, you know how it puts Mr Carlton in a grumpy mood to have to say the options lots of times' (at this, a grimace dressed up as a smile) '– are beefburger, Spanish omelette or that old trusty favourite, jacket potato with cheese or beans.'

James raises his hand – well brought up, but full of inane questions.

'Yes, James?'

'What's a Spanish omelette?'

For once, it's actually a perfectly reasonable question. I have no idea what a Spanish omelette is, but the thing that's served in the canteen by our very talented mid-day supervisors (formerly known as dinner ladies) will

4

bear no resemblance to it anyway, so I won't bother to google it.

'It's made of eggs, maybe some tomato.'

'It sounds disgusting,' Layla says, wrinkling her nose like she's detected a nasty smell.

I can't help but laugh. 'I'm sure it's delicious,' I say with absolutely no conviction. 'So, Darcy, let's start with you.'

Darcy stares at me, and it's like her eyes are open but there is no discernible brain function. I repeat the options, for the second time of what will undoubtedly reach double figures, but she just continues to stare. I'm tempted to wave my hand in front of her face or tap my knuckles against her skull, but instead I try my most supportive smile.

'Darcy, you need to choose something or you'll be very hungry at lunchtime, and we wouldn't want that, would we?'

Nothing. Just a world of blankness. I choose her a jacket potato, as it's the least likely to offend, and move on.

'Tommy?'

'Last night, Mummy and Aunty Jo took me to the pub and then we went back to Aunty Jo's but her and Mummy had an argument so then we had to walk home and . . .'

'All fascinating, Tommy, but the question was, what do you want for lunch?'

Tommy doesn't take a breath, ignores me completely and continues talking.

'. . . then we went back to Aunty Jo's and Nanny came over and . . .'

I mentally turn down Tommy's volume and lean my head against the back of the chair. And just as I vow not to drink again on a school night, Harley comes bounding back in and I immediately know that I will be pissed by six o three.

*

'Jerry Sedgeway here. Who's calling, please?'

It's at times like this I wish I lived in some supernatural television series, where you can send a poisonous signal through the telephone wire that kills the recipient on answering. Who answers the phone by stating their full name anyway? I'll tell you who. Tossers like Jerry.

'Kate's not answering her phone. I want to speak to the boys.'

'Noah. How are you?'

The tone of his voice is always so smug. It's like everything he says is underlined with *ha ha, I'm sleeping with your ex-wife*.

'I'm fine. Now please can I speak to the boys?'

'They're all in the bath together, I'm afraid. That's probably why Katie didn't pick up.'

The combination of him calling her Katie (she's been Kate for the entire twenty-eight years of her life) and the image of her naked in his house makes the highly nutritious meal of pie and chips I stuffed myself with earlier rise in my throat. He's been with her for what, just over a year, and he thinks he can just waltz in, give her a new version of her name and erase everything we shared, like I never existed. I was with her for eleven years. *Eleven years.* I know everything there is to know about her. And her name is Kate.

6

'Get them to call me when they're out, please. I promised I'd find out what the class thought of Gabe's Lego model and Finn had his first full day today – I wanted to see how he got on.'

'He was fine. He had a great day. He was full of it when I got home and Gabe said they thought his model was awesome.'

'I want to hear it from them. I wasn't asking you to tell me.'

'Of course. I get that. Sorry. They'll be out of the bath in ten. Once Katie's got them all ready for bed, I'll get her to call you.'

I hate it when he pretends to understand. He has no children of his own. How can he possibly know how it feels to have some other man hearing your children's exciting news before you, sending your children off to school with a kiss in the morning, having them climb into *his* bed in the night when they have a bad dream?

'Right. Make sure they call me.'

'I will. Bye, Noah.'

*

Kate doesn't call for at least another hour, and I spend the time productively, torturing myself with images of Kate and the boys in Jerry's bath. When they used to share a bath at our house, I'd light candles and put them on the bathroom shelf, and take Kate a glass of bubbly. The boys always wanted to join in the fun so I'd pour them apple juice into plastic prosecco glasses and they'd all sit in the tub, which was overflowing with bubbles, and clink their glasses together like they were three girl-friends at a spa.

I open a bottle of beer, down it, open another one and then, finally, the phone starts ringing.

When I answer, Finn launches straight in.

'Daddy, I stayed all day today. We did PE in the afternoon and I got to go on the big apparatus. It was so much fun.'

The sound of Finn's voice down the phone always gets me. It's like someone's got me in a chokehold and I'm tapping out, but they won't release their grip.

'Sounds brilliant, buddy. You're such a big boy going to school all day.'

'I know. I'm four.' He says it like he's announcing the title he's just won.

'Daddy's proud of you for being so brave. Daddy misses you.'

'Miss you too, Daddy.'

The grip around my neck seems to get that little bit tighter and my next words come out as a splutter.

'I'll pick you up on Friday from after-school club, OK, buddy? Only two more days.'

'One, two.'

'That's right. One, two. Now put your big brother on. Love you, monkey.'

Finn doesn't remove the phone from his mouth when he shouts for his brother and it batters my already sore head. There's some shuffling, an argument about a toy of some sort and then Gabriel's voice.

'Hi, Daddy.'

'Hey, little man. How are you?'

'I'm OK. I'm really busy on the PlayStation so I can't be long or I won't finish the level before bed.'

Rationally, I know his eagerness to get off the phone doesn't mean that he doesn't love me, but my neurotic heart is determined to make me think otherwise.

'Who lets you play on the PlayStation before bed?'

'Mummy said it was OK, just for thirty minutes.' Then a pause. '*You* always let me.'

Fair point.

'OK, well just make sure you're still doing lots of other cool stuff, building dens and kicking a football around, you know, that sort of thing.'

'Don't worry, I am.'

'So tell me then, what did the class think of your awesome shark mech?'

'They loved it.' I can hear the happiness in his voice and picture his face, his blue eyes sparkling.

'Did you tell them you made it at Daddy's house?'

'No, I forgot. Anyway, I've got to go.'

'Oh, OK. Don't forget I love you, will you? And look after your little brother for me, OK? I'll see you Friday. We'll do tons of amazing things together, I promise.'

'Can we stay up late and have film night?'

'Film night, popcorn, sweets, pancakes for breakfast, soft play . . . whatever you want, we'll do, OK, buddy?'

When Kate and I were still together, there was this 'dad' advert on the TV that really annoyed me. It depicted all these different family situations and one of them was Weekend Dad. He was this super-cool fun guy who took his kids to all the best places and they looked up at him like he was some kind of god. I'd sit there – this grumpy git who stomped around the house telling the boys to put their shoes on the rack and go to bloody sleep and stop leaving their foot-piercing Lego on the floor – and I hated Weekend Dad, getting all of the good bits and none of the crap, and being put on a pedestal because of it. I used to shout at the TV, 'Be responsible, make them do chores, don't always take them to Pizza Hut and the cinema like every weekend is a holiday,' and then one day, suddenly, I became him. I'm now Weekend Dad. And it's like you put on a costume and no longer are you nerdy Clark Kent, you're fricking Superman and every weekend they stay with you has to be extraordinary. No more rules, no more Mr Miserable, just fun, games and their fortnightly sugar allowance exceeded in one fell swoop. But when I drop them off and return home, I feel more like Batman at the start of *The Dark Knight Rises* – decrepit, washed up, alone.

'Awesome. Love you, Dad.'

It's a recent development – this occasional dropping of the -dy – but even though he's only recently turned eight, I can't help feeling that bit by bit, syllable by syllable, I'm losing my little boy and he's being replaced by someone altogether more knowing, more autonomous and far less dependent on me. And what's worse, I'm missing so much of it.

'You too. Hand me over to Mummy, will you?'

'OK, she's in the kitchen. I'll just take the phone down to her.'

I listen to the sound of his footsteps, the change in his breathing, as he charges down the two flights of stairs in Jerry's glorious three-storey mansion to their modern, spacious, open-plan kitchen.

'What's up, Noah?'

'Don't I even get a "hello" these days?'

'Hello. Now, what's up?'

'I just wanted to check you've remembered it's my weekend with the boys this weekend?'

'Really? You know it's on the calendar, that I would never forget and that the typical reason plans change is because *you* ring up to cancel them.'

'That's not fair.'

It's actually totally fair because it's a fact. The truth is that sometimes, because it hurts how much I miss them, I don't show up. I know. It makes no sense. Report me to the logic fairies. I always intend to go, I want to go. I adore my boys. When I'm not with them it feels like my internal organs are in a vice that just keeps tightening. I wish I understood the dark, confused place that is my brain, but I don't. Maybe it's just easier to pretend they don't exist sometimes. Because then I don't have to face the fact that they're getting on with their lives so happily without me.

Kate lets out a long sigh. 'They're looking forward to it, Noah. Make sure you're there at half past four on Friday, OK?'

'Of course I will be.'

'Good. Have a lovely weekend. Oh, and actually whilst I've got you on the phone, Gabriel mentioned that he saw a woman in your flat the last time they stayed with you. If it's something serious, great, but please introduce her to the kids properly rather than them being faced in the middle of the night with a strange naked woman.'

'He must've dreamt it. You know he's got a vivid imagination.'

'So there wasn't a naked woman in your flat when they stayed?'

'Well, there was, but she was in my room the whole time with the door shut and I made sure she left before they woke up.'

'Well, perhaps you need to tell your girlfriend to be careful when she's having her naked night-time bathroom trips. It was a bit scary for a sleepy little boy going for a wee to be faced with that.'

'Trust me, it wouldn't have been an unpleasant sight.'

Could I be any more of a dick? Is it possible?

'Oh grow up, Noah. Just try to think of them, OK? It's confusing for them.'

'And seeing Jerry's hairy arse walking around the house isn't?'

'For your information, he doesn't walk around naked. And besides, it's different. We love each other. He loves the boys. They love him.'

I always thought that being heartbroken was just an expression, a state of being, but it's not. It's a physical thing, a real pain, like something in your chest is actually cracking.

'That's not what they tell me.'

Actually, it is. Not in so many words, but more and more often I hear it in the way they talk about all the great things he does with them, the homework he's helped Gabe with, the exciting bedtime story he's reading them both. But I don't want Kate to know that. For a while I hoped (and maybe a tiny, stupid part of me still hopes) that this 'getting divorced and Kate living with another man thing' was just a blip. A pretty big blip, I'll admit.

But we've had several breaks over the years, Kate telling me she's done and taking the boys to live with her parents for a few days, but I always managed to win her back in the end. I thought our love was powerful enough to last forever, to overcome anything. And I know *my* love's still that strong, but I think perhaps I destroyed hers – chipped away at it bit by bit until there was nothing left.

'Cheerio, Noah. I'll see you on Sunday. No later than six. I need to get them sorted for school.'

'Kate.'

'I'm going, Noah. Take care.'

She puts the phone down and, to fight the desire to ring her back, I open another beer.

CHAPTER TWO

Harley's mum has been late every day this week. It's Friday. Using my exceptional ability with numbers, that means that for the last five days I have had to stand outside the classroom door, shivering my tits off, engaging in riveting conversation with my favourite pupil.

The clock hits twenty-five to four. Enough is enough. I bundle Harley out of the playhouse, through the classroom and march him down to the office.

'Sit just there a second. I'll get them to ring Mummy and find out where she is.'

Harley clambers up on to one of the shabby grey fabric chairs that sit outside the office. It makes him look tiny, like a Playmobil person placed on a high chair. 'She's probably asleep.'

'No, it's not bedtime, Harley. It's just the end of school.'

'She sleeps in the day too, not just bedtime. She's poorly so she has to sleep a lot.'

I rack my brain for anything I've read in Harley's notes that mentions his mum being ill. For a class of thirty, particularly at *my* school, there's a lot of paperwork to get through but there definitely wasn't anything serious, like cancer. I would've noticed that. He joined us about a month ago, just as I was naively celebrating what a lovely class I had this year. Mum reportedly told our head teacher that she hadn't been happy with the previous school, but now I wonder if it was more that the school hadn't been particularly happy trying to manage Harley.

I sit down on the chair beside him. 'What's wrong with Mummy? Has she got a bug?'

Harley shrugs. 'I don't know. She just says she doesn't feel very well and goes to bed. Not all the time. Some days we go to the park or the cinema. Mummy lets me have as much pick 'n' mix as I want. It's so much fun.'

'That does sound fun. And what do you do when she goes to bed?'

'Watch TV. Play with my Power Rangers. Play on my DS.'

I nod, my child protection antennae flashing steady amber. It's not enough to fill in a form about, but it's worth keeping an eye on. Often he doesn't bring his book-bag in, or a coat, Mum's listening to him read is sporadic, little things like that, but he's certainly not the only one. Sometimes I wonder if teachers said similar things about me and Ben, or whether all the things our mum did for us when she was in a good headspace were enough to stop them being concerned about the lack of care and attention when she wasn't. Every so often, I contemplate whether things would've worked out differently if someone had noticed and raised the alarm, but in my experience as a teacher, external agencies getting involved usually just makes things worse. I think sometimes we report stuff for our own benefit, so we feel like we're doing something, even though we know it probably won't make a positive difference for the child involved.

'Right. Well, I'll give Mummy a ring. See what's going on. She's probably just stuck in traffic.'

'We don't have a car.'

'Oh, OK. Well, I'm sure she'll be along in a minute. Just hold on there for a sec, will you?'

Harley plays with the Velcro on his bookbag and I go into the office to ring his mum. Just as I pick up the phone, she appears, walking through the glass doors at a pace that suggests she's early rather than half an hour late. She's dressed in joggers and a hoody, no make-up, her hair tied back in a messy bun. She looks exhausted, as if the process of putting one foot in front of the other is using up the last of her strength.

'Come on then, H. Let's go.'

Harley climbs down off the chair and I step out of the office. His mum glances up at me, but then looks back at her son. No apology. Nothing.

'See you tomorrow, Mr Carlton,' Harley says, walking underneath his mum's arm, as she holds open the door.

'It's Saturday tomorrow, Harley, but I'll see you on Monday. Bright and early, OK?'

I.e., get him here on time for once, Mum.

'OK, Mr Carlton,' Harley says, and they walk off down the school drive, Harley chatting away animatedly whilst his mum stares off into the distance somewhere.

*

Heading back to my classroom, I bump into Dan and Jack. They're the only other male members of staff so we've kind of been thrown into this arbitrary friendship based solely on gender. I mean, Dan's actually a pretty decent bloke. He's in his mid-twenties, engaged to the girl he met at university. But Jack's a bit of a twat. Since he hit thirty, he seems to feel the need to constantly prove that he's still wild, crazy. When you ask him if he's all right in the morning, he always grabs his head and moans about his 'killer hangover'. His weekends are always 'insane', his phone's always beeping (I swear he purposefully puts it on its loudest setting) with messages from 'clingy' girls.

'You coming to the pub, mate?' Jack says, swinging his rucksack on to his shoulder.

I check my watch. 'I better not. I've got to get the boys in a bit.'

'You've got time for one, haven't you? Come on, don't be a Larry Lightweight.'

I often wonder how it would feel to put my fist through his face. I imagine it would be intensely cathartic.

'Yeah, come on. I'm buying,' Dan chips in. 'Don't leave me with just Jack for company.'

Jack guffaws, but I get the sense Dan's not joking.

As much as I tell my kids not to give in to peer pressure, I'm terrible at saying 'no' and, besides, the thought of a drink is like the promise of a million-pound lottery win. I feel my willpower dwindling. It never has been very strong.

'Oh, go on then. Just one.'

'That's the spirit,' Jack says, slapping me on the back. 'Meet you in there?'

'Yeah, cool. I'll just grab my stuff.'

I go back to the classroom, unplug my laptop and put it into my bag, then leave school, avoiding the route past the head's office so she doesn't see me sneaking off early. When I get to the pub around the corner, Jack and Dan are sat propping up the bar with three pints lined up in front of them.

'Ah, here you go, mate,' Dan says, pushing a glass towards me.

A freshly poured pint is a thing of beauty. The way the light shines through it, making it glow, the deep amber colour, the glisten of the condensation on the glass. I take a very large swig, the tension in my shoulders easing almost immediately as the liquid runs down my throat.

'Ah, that's better. Thanks, mate.' I put my glass back on the bar. 'I swear that boy is going to be the end of me.'

'The wonderful Harley?' Dan raises his eyebrows.

'The one and only.'

'Try being in year six,' Jack chips in, running his hand through his long hair. I think he's going for Chris Hemsworth in *Thor* but his thin, lank hair isn't quite achieving it. 'I had to do sex education today. *Sir, what is a wet dream?* Seriously, it was excruciating.'

Dan and I both laugh.

'Yeah, but at least you don't have to mop up piss,' I say. 'I couldn't believe Sam today. He was literally stood right next to the toilet and yet proceeded to go in his trousers. And there was so much of it. How can a child that size contain that much wee?'

The conversation continues in this vein, all of us trying to outdo each other's tales of woe. We've downed our drinks by ten past four and Jack buys the next round without asking if I want one. I figure I can get a taxi to the boys, or a lift with one of the other teachers that live near them. I'll drink this one in five and then head back to school and sort something in time to get to them.

But after the second beer on a relatively empty stomach, I get that wonderful heady feeling where you feel like anything is possible and simultaneously that nothing really matters. Drinking is like eating Pringles: you try to put the top back on and walk away but you can't help reopening them and having a few more until, before you know it, the whole tube is gone.

I text Kate.

I'm so sorry. I'm stuck in a meeting at work. Do you mind getting the boys? I'll grab them from yours in a bit x

And, despite all evidence to the contrary, as I write the text, I really believe it. I believe I will pick them up from Kate's and that just being a little bit late isn't really a big deal.

After a few minutes, my phone starts buzzing. It's Kate calling, presumably to have a go at me, so I ignore it, mentally preparing the excuse that I couldn't answer my phone in a meeting. I buy the next round and, as usual, Jack starts ribbing me about my sex-life or lack thereof. I let him believe I'm still going through a serious drought despite the fact I'm probably getting more sex than him and Dan put together. It's not something I want to shout about. I don't see anything particularly impressive about having sex with some stranger you feel nothing for and then spending the rest of the night drowning in self-loathing. The rounds keep coming and I don't realize the time is passing, but when I check the clock, it's six p.m.

It comes over me sudden and intense – the longing to call a taxi and get it to take me to Kate's house so I can pick up the boys. But when I get down off my stool to go to the toilet, I'm unable to walk in a straight line and I know

I can't turn up there like this – and with that knowledge comes such a horrific sense of regret that I feel like my legs might give way beneath me. I use the backs of chairs to support me and manage to reach the toilets, then sit in one of the cubicles and call Kate. She doesn't answer so I call her again and again, getting more and more frantic as I listen to the dial tone.

I ring her home phone and Jerry answers.

'I want to speak to Kate. Why isn't she picking up her phone?'

'You don't need to shout at me, Noah. I'll get Katie for you, but not if you're going to shout.'

'I'm shouting because she won't answer her effing phone.'

Kate must grab the phone because it's her voice that comes stomping down the line. 'I'm not answering because you're drunk again, Noah. The boys are gutted. They love their weekends with you. They make me count down the days on the calendar. Do you realize that? I won't let you keep hurting them like this. I just won't.'

Kate's crying now and my throat feels so tight that I can't manage to say a thing. When I don't respond, Kate puts the phone down and I sit on the toilet with my head in my hands.

It's at times like this that the desire to rewind my life is so intense I don't know how to go on. When bad things happen *to* you, it's sad and it's hard, but you can come out stronger, fighting, knowing you survived it and that you aren't going to let it ruin you. But when you caused the bad things, when it's all your fault for making stupid fucking decisions and never ever learning from them, the pain and regret is crippling. It's so much harder to walk away from intact, because you're constantly thinking *if only*.

I steady myself and head back out to the lads. I order more drinks, moving on from beer to shots because I might as well get absolutely wasted now. I've got no reason not to. It's OK for a while, the alcohol making things feel better than they really are. But then I get sick of the empty conversation, the fake laughter, so I track down an Uber, make my excuses and head home. Except, when I'm nearly there, I can't face the thought of going into my flat knowing that the boys should be there – making a mess, fighting over the PlayStation, hassling me for more treats – and instead opening the door to stark and empty silence. So I lean forward, poking my head through the two front seats.

'Drop me at the Bear, will you, mate?'

The driver gives me a quick once-over, an automatic reaction to my heavily slurred speech, then he nods, a sense of resignation in his movement. 'Sure.'

*

'Same again, please.'

I push my glass towards the barmaid and she looks at me as if I just asked her to jump on the bar and give me a striptease. I've not seen her here before. It's usually cheery, middle-aged Mandy who gives me a drink free at the end of the night with a wink and a 'This one's on me, darlin'.' But tonight's barmaid is probably in her mid-twenties, bright-red cropped hair, wearing a loose-fitting black Jack Daniel's T-shirt that falls off her shoulder (is it supposed to be ironic?). Her lipstick is the same shade as her hair and she gives the impression that she'd give you what for if you crossed her.

'You sure you've not had enough?' she says, her hand paused on my glass.

'What's it to you?' I pat my pockets to show they're empty. 'I'm not driving.'

She shrugs. 'Okey doke. Another double JD and Coke coming straight up.'

She puts a definite emphasis on the word 'another', like I'm reaching double figures when actually this is only my second drink of the night, or at least the second drink that she has witnessed me consuming. She releases a measure of Jack Daniel's into my glass, repeats, then starts squirting in the Coke.

'That'll do, thanks.'

She removes her finger from the button and pushes the glass back towards me. 'Enjoy.'

I take it off her with a smirk. What's her problem? She's supposed to be a barmaid, not my bloody AA sponsor.

'Where's Mandy, anyway? Is she poorly?'

She shakes her head and wipes the bar with a cloth. 'Left for better climes. Admin, I think. Got sick of watching people drinking themselves into an early grave, perhaps.'

Her lips twitch, as if to suggest she's joking, but it's clear from the way she says it that it's what she thinks.

'So you thought you'd step in on some kind of noble crusade to stop us, did you?'

'Oh yeah, modern-day Mother Teresa, me.' She laughs and her whole face softens. 'No, I'm here for the big bucks and the numerous career perks, obviously.'

Despite myself, I feel a smile forming on my lips.

'To be honest,' she continues, 'I was just trying to save you from the epic hangover you're heading for.'

I shrug. 'I've only had two drinks. But thanks for your concern.'

She nods but there's more than a hint of scepticism on her face and it dawns on me that I must be less accomplished at appearing sober than I first thought.

'No problem.' She starts taking glasses out of the dishwasher and stacking them in the cupboards underneath the bar. 'Anyway, I'm closing up in five minutes. *You* might not, but I need my beauty sleep, so drink up, yeah?'

I look around. The place is empty. And it feels suddenly tragic, sitting here, all on my own at the end of a Friday night, surrounded by dingy paintings on the dirty cream walls, the flashing lights of a fruit machine, miserable dark-stained wooden tables and stools with grimy, dated fabric on the seats. Before kids, Kate and I would often spend our Friday nights in pubs like this. She hated fancy bars – finding them pretentious – much preferring to while away the hours in a spit-and-sawdust establishment, drinking reasonably priced drinks and playing the selection of board games they stocked. Places like this didn't feel tragic then. They felt cosy and warm and safe. And afterwards, we'd stumble home putting the world to rights, Kate snuggled in under my jacket. Once kids came along, we didn't go out as much but we'd always mark the fact it was Friday night, ordering take-out and sharing a bottle of wine and laughing at crap on the telly. It was always my favourite day of the week.

And now Friday nights look like this.

I down all the liquid in my glass in one. 'I can certainly do that. Well, nice to meet you . . .'

'Amelia. Mimi for short.'

'Nice to meet you, Mimi. I'm Noah. It's impossible to shorten. I'd end up being No or Er. Neither is particularly desirable.'

She humours me with a smile, but I'm well aware I'm talking crap. 'I get the feeling I might be seeing you again, Noah.'

I try to put my arms through the sleeves of my coat, clumsily missing one of the holes, the alcohol impairing my spatial awareness. 'Only if your luck's in.'

She laughs, a deep, hearty laugh that mocks me, as I stumble out into the cold, dark night, still not wanting to go back to my flat, but with nowhere else to go. I reach into my pocket and pull out my phone, going to my recent calls and pressing on Kate's name. I only let it ring for a second before ending the call. As I'm walking, I check my phone every minute or so, just in case I miss it vibrating in my pocket. But she doesn't call back. She never does any more. For the first couple of months after we split up, she would. Sometimes she'd leave it half an hour or so, but she'd always call back in the end. And then one day she stopped. And that's when I started to wonder if she was serious this time – if perhaps it really was over for good.

CHAPTER THREE

'Let them down again and this arrangement's finished,' Kate says once the boys are deep enough into my flat that they can't hear us.

Kate and I are standing at my door, her passing me bag after bag full of stuff she thinks the boys will need. The truth is most of it will stay in the bag, but Kate likes to be super-prepared and I'm not sure she really trusts me to cover the basics on my own. Despite the fact the boys have everything they need here, she still puts in things like toothpaste, pyjamas, a hairbrush (OK, I might not have one of those). Sometimes she even includes pieces of fruit in snack boxes, as if she's worried the boys will get scurvy from spending a weekend with me.

'I won't let them down again. I'm really sorry, Kate.' I try to secure eye contact, but her eyes flit back and forth, not wanting to connect with me. Her shoulder-length blonde hair is straight and neat, how she always has it these days. If she's wearing any make-up it's not obvious, but then she doesn't need to. Her face seems to have its own inbuilt luminosity and her large blue eyes stand out of their own accord.

'You're lucky Jerry had planned us a weekend away or the boys wouldn't be here.'

'So I'm just glorified childcare, am I?' I joke.

'Seriously? You're going to play that card? Are you sure? Because I can still change my mind and take them with us.'

'No, I'm sorry. Thank you for letting me have them.'

I know I messed up. I know I deserve her animosity, but I still hate the sound of my voice, *thank you for letting me have them*, like I'm borrowing one of her belongings.

'Don't be late tomorrow. Six o'clock.'

'Of course.'

'Do you need me to write it down somewhere?'

No, I'm not a total idiot.

'I'll be there at six o'clock on the dot, I promise.'

'Right. Good.' Kate's face looks like it's on the verge of softening and I wish that I still had access to that Kate, *my* Kate, the Kate who held me while I wept until my throat was raw when my mum died. I see glimpses of her occasionally, but it seems to be becoming more and more rare. But then that's probably because I keep screwing up.

'Take care of them.'

'Of course I will. And have a lovely weekend away.'

'Thanks.' Kate looks almost embarrassed, her eyes dropping to her shoes, and I get the sense that behind the veneer of anger there's a whole world of hurt she's trying to keep at bay.

She turns to leave but I reach for her hand, gently guiding her back to face me. 'I really am sorry.'

'I know you are, Noah. That's the saddest thing about it.'

She gives me a downbeat smile then pulls her hand away and heads back towards Jerry, who is waiting for her in the car.

*

So far, we've had ice cream with Smarties on top for breakfast, two hours destroying monsters on the PlayStation, sweated our way around soft play (where I narrowly avoided a fight with a tween who insisted on running *up* the slide we were trying to come down) and now it's Happy Meals at McDonald's.

'Mummy said you love Jerry. Is that true?' I put on my best nonchalant voice, like I couldn't care less if it was true or not, despite the fact the state of my mental health rests entirely on their answer.

I wish I had the maturity to deal with this whole 'another man living with my kids roughly eighty-six per cent of the time and me getting only a measly fourteen' thing, but it's like I'm Benjamin Button – emotionally I'm getting younger each day.

'Yeah, he's really fun. We play Nerf guns and we have to shoot the target. He's really good. He always gets it in the middle,' Finn says, chuckling at the memory.

I try to disguise the hurt on my face, but I clearly fail because Gabe says, 'But he's not as fun as you, Daddy. We love you more.'

I should feel proud of my eldest son – already, at eight, an accomplished mediator – but I hate that it's a skill Kate and I have forced him to acquire. And despite the touching sentiment, I find little comfort in Gabe's words. I don't want them to love me more. I want them to love me only.

'Well, of course he's not as fun as me. I bet he doesn't let you have ice cream for breakfast and I'm certain he doesn't have gherkin sunglasses.'

I close my eyes and stick two slices of the circular pickled vegetable to my eyelids. They attach for a moment, then slip down my cheeks, landing with a plop on the table. The boys giggle, but they look a little nervous, like they're not sure if their dad has officially lost the plot. If it was a date, it'd feel like I was trying too hard.

'Soft play was good, wasn't it? We had such a great time, didn't we, boys?'

Gabriel nods, his mouth full of chicken nugget, but Finn is too engrossed in the plastic Minion from his Happy Meal to grace me with a response, jumping it across the back of the seat.

Scraping the remains of the ketchup out of the sachet with his final chip, Gabe stares over my shoulder and I know a tricky question is looming. I can always tell when one's coming: there's a certain look to his eyes, a particular crease of his forehead.

'Daddy?'

'Yeah?'

'Do you think Mummy will stay with Jerry forever now? Will they get married and have a baby?'

'No, of course not. Well, no, I don't think so.' I'm suddenly not sure what the right answer is, what he wants me to say. I know what *I* hope the answer is. I know she's living with him, but they're not right for each other. He's, well, he's *Jerry* – dull and strait-laced, whereas Kate is fun and sparky. He's your typical rebound candidate – safe, secure – but there's no way he's enough for Kate for the rest of her life.

'Do you *want* Mummy and Jerry to get married?'

Gabriel rips open the plastic bag containing his Minion, turns it over in his hand and then passes it to Finn, who greets it with a gigantic smile. 'Maybe. I'm not sure.'

'Have you asked Mummy if she's going to marry Jerry?'

He nods. 'She said she doesn't know. It depends if Jerry asks her.'

Due to the panicky feeling in my stomach, my voice comes out several octaves higher than normal. 'What does she mean by that? That she'd say yes if he asked her?'

Gabe shrugs in a how-the-hell-am-I-supposed-to-know-you're-the-adult gesture that makes me realize I need to try harder to put on my responsible-parent hat and reassure him.

'Well, I think it's a bit soon for all that. But one thing's for certain, I'll always be your dad and I'll always be here for you.'

Listening to myself, I still can't believe I'm having to say things like this. The divorce only came through a couple of months ago, the handwritten brown envelope unceremonious in its arrival on the doormat. I used the paperwork as a beer mat, purposely, finding a comforting satisfaction in the appearance of the circular stain cutting through our signatures. I thought that maybe making it official would bring some closure, help me to move on, but it just made me feel even more intensely that my life was over.

I try to gain eye contact with my eldest son but he seems to be focused on something beyond me.

'Can we have a McFlurry, Daddy?' Finn blurts out, bashing his two Minions against each other in an epic battle.

'Yeah, yeah, please, Daddy,' Gabe joins in, suddenly distracted from his previous thoughts, a tag-teamed attempt to tap into my immense absent-parent guilt.

'Why not?'

Finn throws his arms around my neck, knocking me off balance. 'Thanks, Daddy. I love you.'

Weekend Dad strikes again.

*

On Sunday, a slight dent in my Super Dad performance: we have a visit from the cousins. Finn doesn't mind, but Gabriel's reached an age where he's much less willing to accommodate Little Miss Perfect and her equally flawless younger sister. I'm totally with him. Unfortunately, they're miniature replicas of their mother – definitely not something the world needs, and my brother's fault for procreating with The Worst Woman in History. OK, there are worse women in the *whole* of history, like Rose West or Myra Hindley, but she's definitely up there. Nothing good was ever going to come out of my brother and Claudia having sex. But I gave him his fair share of warnings. I tried my best to get him to explore his options before committing, suggesting nights out with a few of the women from work, little things like that, but he remained irritatingly loyal and Miss Claudia Lechlade became Mrs Claudia Carlton, destined to ruin every future family gathering.

'Do you think maybe they should be seeing someone about their anger? The school nurse or something?' The disgust slips from Claudia's eyes, down her sharp nose and lands on Gabriel and Finn, who are engaged in a particularly violent altercation about a certain Lego figure.

'They're boys. You wouldn't get it.' I glance over at Lucy and Rosie, carefully colouring fairies and princesses in the books Claudia brought with her, never venturing outside the lines, passing each other the colours with a genteel grace I have never witnessed between my sons.

'They're boys, Noah. Not alien creatures. I understand brothers play-fight a bit, but look at them.'

It doesn't look good, I'll admit. Gabe now has a handful of Finn's blond curly hair grasped tightly between his fingers and Finn is kicking him in the stomach with a force likely to rupture internal organs.

'Come on, boys. Break it up.' I pull Gabriel off his brother, a clump of Finn's hair travelling with him, accompanied by piercing screams from my younger son.

I deposit Gabriel on the sofa next to his cousins (they cower, holding on to each other and moving as far away as possible, as if I've just thrown an unexploded bomb on to the leather beside them) and pick up Finn in my arms. He clings on to me like a limpet, rests his head on my shoulder and channels his screams directly into my earhole. Gabe crosses his arms, clearly feeling unfairly wronged.

'We used to fight like that, didn't we, Ben?' I say, punching my brother playfully on the arm, hoping to encourage some kind of sibling loyalty but knowing that, inevitably, he will disappoint.

'Well, we'd have a bit of a ruckus, yeah, but not quite like that.' I sometimes wonder exactly which day Ben lost his ability to think for himself. Was it the day he mistakenly took brainwashing for love, or was it a more gradual process, slowly squashed out of him by the force of Claudia's thumb?

'Perhaps my fists to the head were so powerful you've just forgotten.' I laugh.

Ben allows himself a half-smile and Claudia looks over at us with a cross-teacher frown.

'Well, I'm going to go and make everyone a drink. The girls are thirsty.' She says it in a way that implies I'm negatively affecting her children's health, like they're dehydrated puppies wilting in the boot of a car on a swelteringly hot day. 'Do you want anything, Noah? Something that doesn't require fermentation, perhaps?'

'Oh, no thanks, Claudia. I can only stomach yeast-based drinks. I'm on a reverse gluten-free diet.'

Claudia gives me a look that could curdle milk. 'Come on, you lot. Let's go into the kitchen and see if we can find something to eat and drink amongst the microwave meals for one.'

She lifts my supposedly starving child from my arms and the other children follow her into the kitchen in a line like she's the Pied Piper.

I jab Ben with my elbow. 'Jokes aside, want me to grab you a beer?'

He looks at his watch. 'Better not.'

I laugh. 'Alcoholic beverages must not be consumed before seven thirteen p.m. precisely.'

'Fuck off, Noah.' It's more weary than aggressive, Ben lowering himself on to the sofa and kicking off his Timberland boots.

'I'm going to grab one for me. I'll be back.'

I stalk into the kitchen and open the fridge, Claudia's eyes like a CCTV camera catching an illicit steal, then take the beer back into the lounge and sit on the sofa next to my brother.

'So, how's the exciting world of computer analysis?'

'Surprisingly interesting and well paid. How's wiping the bums of four-year-olds? Still changing the world one child at a time?'

'Of course.' I tilt my beer towards Ben.

There was a time when Ben and I were inseparable. Two years his junior, I'd follow him around like an infatuated groupie. Everything he did, I wanted to do better. Everything he had, I wanted it too. I'd always end up sleeping in his bed and when I'd lie in, he'd lie opposite me, his face so close it was touching, willing me to wake up so we could start the day's adventures – building dens, re-enacting *Power Rangers* episodes, creating elaborate traps for Mum and Dad involving large balls of string.

At secondary school, we inhabited different circles. He was sciencey. I attempted to adopt an artistic persona although I wasn't very good at art. Whilst he was solving algebra equations, I was writing poems about love and loss. But, although we skirted around each other at school, at home we were still close. As things with Mum got worse, and Dad didn't seem to be around all that much, Ben distanced himself from the family a bit, staying at friends' a lot. But when he was there, we'd spend a lot of time in each other's rooms chatting and beating the crap out of each other on the console. We were always each other's safety net.

When we both left home for university, him first, choosing the studious Exeter, and me, two years later, on a mission to embrace my inner socialist in Manchester, months would pass when we wouldn't see each other, but we spent a lot of time on Facebook Messenger. He was still the person I would choose to confide in. Then when

Mum died, we made this silent pact to meet up once a week, without fail. Neither of us ever missed it (except for the summer holiday after Kate left when I only surfaced from my bedroom to eat, shit and get more alcohol). But lately, the excuses have started popping up, on his side not mine – mismatched schedules with Claudia, a persistent cold – and we tend to only catch up when we get the kids together.

'And how are things with my favourite sister-in-law?'

Ben shrugs. 'It's a marriage, Noah. Ups and downs. We're currently in an "up", so it's good. The girls are going through a nice stage. We're enjoying our time as a family. They've just learnt to use their bikes without stabilizers so we're spending a lot of time cycling in the Forest of Dean. Not quite as rock and roll as your life, I know.'

I raise my eyebrows in a what-can-I-say gesture, whilst wondering how walking around with a permanent hangover and a barely functioning heart is very rock and roll.

'So are you seeing anyone yet? For more than a night, I mean.'

I take a large gulp of my beer and shake my head, then start rolling off a very well-practised spiel. 'I'm not sure why I ever thought having a relationship was a good idea. I mean, no offence, but it's just not worth the hassle. I get sex on tap and no one telling me what to do. If I want to have a beer for breakfast, I can. If I want to have a weekend away to Ayia Napa, all I have to do is throw a few clothes in a case and go.'

Ben nods slowly. 'I guess you did miss out on all that, getting together with Kate so young. So have you had any weekends away to Ayia Napa, then?'

'Well, no, not yet. I was talking hypothetically. I mean all my options are open. I'm as free as a bird and it feels amazing.'

Ben looks reassured by my answer and I realize I must be getting good at playing the part if even my own brother can't see that I'm lying.

'Good. I'm happy for you, bro. I was worried about you for a while back there.'

He's referring to a number of events that occurred in the first year after Kate left. In fact, there are too many to list, but key highlights include turning up at Ben's house at four a.m. in only my boxers because I'd fallen asleep on a park bench and someone had thought it hilarious to remove my clothes and run off with them, and a frantic phone call from Kate begging him to come and get me when I'd turned up at Jerry's house when they first moved in together and drunkenly threatened him with a knife (it was a plastic picnic knife, I was clearly never going to hurt him with it. I was just making a point – what point I'm still not quite sure).

'No need to worry about me. It's you with the old ball and chain I worry about. Can't be good for your blood pressure.'

'Married men live longer, don't they? We've got to have some perks, I guess, what with all the entrapment and constrictions.' Ben smiles. 'And how's Kate? Still with Jerry?'

'Yeah, I'm not sure she's that happy with him, you know, but I guess it's easy to become dependent on the security of it all, now that they're living together and everything,' I say, not sure who I'm trying to fool, myself or Ben.

'I guess so. And the boys? They're doing OK?'

'Yes, despite Claudia's fears for their humanity, they're doing great. They miss me, of course, but that's to be expected.'

Ben gives me this look, like a doctor whose terminal cancer patient is arguing that they're going to fight this evil disease despite having only weeks to live, and I wonder if actually he knows me a lot better than he's letting on.

*

'You're late.'

I check my watch, as the kids rush past us and charge up the stairs without a backward glance. 'It's ten past. We were watching the end of *Star Wars*.'

'I was getting worried.'

'Oh come on, Kate. I know I messed up on Friday, but now I'm ten minutes late. You can't be mad at me for that.'

Kate sighs and steps out of the porch, putting the front door on the latch and closing it. She sits on the front step and pats the concrete. Obediently, I sit beside her. She still smells the same, a mixture of Toni & Guy hairspray and Armani perfume. They say smell is the sense that's most closely linked to memory and it certainly applies now, sitting here drinking in Kate's scent, because it hurtles me right back to when we were still living together. Evenings reading a book or watching a film, Kate resting her head in my lap whilst I stroked her hair. Mornings watching Kate getting ready in our en suite, wondering why it took so long when she looked beautiful just as she was on waking up.

'I hate being this person.' Kate runs her hand through her hair, two small dents appearing above her nose. 'But you make me like this.'

I reach out and put my hand on her knee, her skin warm underneath her joggers, and I'm glad when she doesn't remove it. 'I'm sorry. I'll be better.'

Kate shrugs. 'I hope so.'

I can tell how badly she wants to believe me and it makes me feel even worse than I already do. She deserves so much better than me. If I was more selfless, I'd be glad that she came to her senses and left.

'London looked romantic.'

Kate crumples her face in confusion, moving her knee away from me so that my hand slips and drops to my side.

'I see everything on Facebook, remember?' I continue. 'We're still friends on there, even if we're not in real life.'

Kate brushes some rogue gravel off the step. 'It was nice, but I missed the boys. It's ridiculous. They drive me mad half the time but it just doesn't feel the same when I do stuff without them. I still can't get used to not seeing them every other weekend. I thought it would get easier but it's not. Well, not yet, anyway.'

Try only *seeing them every other weekend.*

'Sorry, that's really insensitive of me,' she continues, as if reading my mind. 'I know it's much harder for you.'

For a short time, we sit in silence, looking out at their large, neatly manicured front garden, my mind busy. When we first discussed custody arrangements for the boys, Kate argued that it made sense for them to stay with her the majority of the time, as she was at home and Finn hadn't started school so he needed full-time childcare, and we both felt it would be disruptive for them to keep changing houses all the time. And, although it wasn't spoken, I think we could both see the state I was in, that the boys were better off with her.

I pull my sleeve over my hand, take off my glasses and wipe the lenses with my jumper. 'I'm not going to let them down again, Kate.'

But even as I say it, I'm not sure if it's true and I wonder for the thousandth time how I can allow myself to hurt them like that when I love them so entirely. As much as I'd love to see them more often, I know I still can't be trusted, and I hate myself for that more than anything.

'You need to stop drinking so much.'

'I'm not drinking much any more. Friday night was a one-off,' I lie.

'It was not a one-off. We were together eleven years, Noah. Like it or not, I know you like the back of my hand.'

'OK then, tell me, how many different freckles make up your birthmark?'

'Very clever. You know what I mean.'

"It's seven – well, almost eight, but two parts of it are just about joined together so they only really count as one.'

Kate holds out her hand and studies her birthmark. I count each freckle, touching each one in turn.

'See, told you. It's seven.'

Kate looks at me, her eyes narrowing. 'I can't believe you know that.'

'I can still surprise you. You don't know everything about me after all.'

A gust of wind blows and, as Kate shivers audibly in her thin, long-sleeved top, I feel angry with it for breaking the moment. We have occasions like this sometimes, very rarely, when I wonder if perhaps there *is* still something on her side, whether she regrets asking for the divorce, but then the moment always passes too soon and I wonder if I've just imagined it.

'I'd better be getting in. I'll see you in a fortnight, OK?'

'OK. Can you just call the boys down to say bye?'

'Of course.' Kate pushes herself up. 'And, Noah, we are still friends, you know? Not just on Facebook. You drive me mad sometimes, but I'll always be your friend. I'm always here if you need me.'

I know I should be comforted. That I should be glad that, despite our disagreements and my failures, we're not the sort of divorced couple who can't stand to be in the same room together. But it feels like a consolation prize.

I shrug and shake my head. 'I'm fine. I'm great. Things are really good.'

'Good.' Kate smiles, but it's the kind of smile she used to give me when she'd find me passed out on the pavement somewhere and I'd try to crack a joke. 'I'll just get the boys.'

CHAPTER FOUR

If someone were to film me trying to get my class changed out of their PE kits and back into their school uniforms, it would be the kind of thing that pops up on my Facebook timeline causing me to sit there creasing myself. But actually being in it – taking the leading role in the utter mayhem – it's nothing short of insufferable.

'Tommy, you need to put your trousers on before you do your shoes.'

'Sam, you need to keep your pants *on*.'

'Well, tell Jasmine that Mr Carlton says it's not OK to lift up her vest and shove your head underneath.'

Lola rushes towards me holding up a pair of tights, crumpled up and inside out. I infer she wants me to turn them through the right way so I put my hands down through the legs. When I reach the toes and grasp them with my fingers, I stop abruptly. It's a repulsive sensation. They're wet. Why are kids' socks and tights always wet? Surely four-year-olds' feet should not sweat that much?

'No, I'm sorry. I just can't do it. Mr Carlton is now installing a firm no-handling rule for tights and socks. You are just going to have to learn to sort them out for yourselves, I'm afraid.'

Mrs Watson looks at me as if I've just announced I can't do the washing-up without my Marigolds, and wearily comes over, grabs the tights and turns them through with the efficiency of a school nurse doling out injections. 'Right, who's next?'

'Mr Carlton, I'm not sure which item to put on first?'

'Well, surely it's obvious, Olivia.'

But in her defence, when I turn around and look at the pile of clothes on the floor beside Olivia, it's not obvious. She has come to school wearing a vest, a T-shirt, a long-sleeved top and a woollen cardigan underneath her school T-shirt and jumper. No wonder the poor girl's always the last to finish getting changed. I accept our classroom is not the warmest of places but even so, she must be losing weight by the second. I hand her her vest then clap my hands.

'OK, everyone, once you're changed, please hang up your PE bags and then sit on the carpet with a book.'

The floor of clothes, kids and bags slowly starts to clear, like ants when the dropped cake crumb has been removed, until I'm left with the stragglers. Poor Olivia is on layer three, Darcy is pushing a peg back and forth along a mini washing line that's used to display the 'sounds of the week', and Harley has put his trousers on his head and is standing in the corner of the classroom in his pants doing the floss.

'Harley, as wonderful as your flossing is, can you please stop now, take your trousers off your head and put them on properly?'

Harley's face breaks into a huge grin and he takes his trousers off his head, stops flossing and starts dabbing instead. I'm unable to stop a smile creeping across my lips.

'Very good. Come on, mister, trousers on, time for assembly.'

Harley gives me a mischievous look and I'm concerned for a moment that I'm going to have to manhandle him into his uniform, but then, surprisingly, he begins getting dressed at speed.

The same cannot be said, however, for Darcy.

'Darcy, can you please get changed?'

She looks at me, directly in the eye, and then returns to pushing the peg along the line.

'Darcy, we are going to celebration assembly in five minutes. You need to get changed now.'

She stares at me again and then takes her trainers out of her PE bag, pulls on the Velcro straps and sticks them back down before discarding the trainers on the floor.

I point to her school T-shirt and skirt. 'Uniform, Darcy.'

No response. Sometimes it feels like I've landed on a different planet filled with strange alien life forms who have no idea what I'm saying. Like, to the children in my class, my voice is just a garbled radio signal or a repeating beep.

So I try a different tack and start singing 'time to get your uniform on' to the tune of 'Time to Say Goodbye' in true operatic style and the whole class start to giggle, even though they don't get the Sarah Brightman reference. Even Mrs Watson's face displays a flicker of amusement.

Darcy still doesn't get dressed, however, poor Olivia has only just got to her school T-shirt and I'm sure I just spotted Ethan poking out of the sandpit in the outdoor area. I check the clock. Once again, I'm late.

'Mrs Watson, I need to take the class to assembly. Could you please round up the remaining few?'

Her eyes unmistakably shout 'fuck you' so I add my most appreciative smile then herd my class into assembly.

As the few switched-on ones stop as they reach the edge of the hall, the daydreamers walk straight into each other, tripping up before finally forming a wiggly caterpillar-like line in front of our bemused head teacher, Mrs Jackson. Just before I gesture for them to sit down, I notice that Tommy clearly has someone else's trousers on (as they stop mid shin), Lola has her T-shirt on back to front and Annabelle has her shoes on the wrong feet. Not for the first time, I wonder how long it will be before someone realizes I have absolutely no idea what I'm doing and politely gives me the push.

*

'So, do you have a job?'

'Yes. I'm not a complete waster, thank you.'

Mimi holds up her hands. 'I didn't say you were. It's just the regular week-night drinking, the late-night rendezvous, it doesn't scream career man, that's all. So, what is it that you do?'

'I'm a primary school teacher.'

Mimi looks as if she's choking on an invisible grape. 'Yeah, right. Seriously, what do you do?'

'Why is that so hard to believe?'

'I don't know. I suppose when I picture a male primary school teacher, I picture Mr Tumble, not . . .' She moves her hand up and down to signal me in my entirety.

'A hot young thing like me?'

'That's not quite what I was getting at. Someone more . . .' she screws up her face whilst searching for the word. 'Wholesome, I guess.'

Now it's my turn to offer a spluttered laugh. 'I'm wholesome. I'm an excellent role model.'

Mimi tucks her sweeping fringe behind her ear. She has a very striking face – strong cheekbones, large, surprisingly green eyes. Usually when people say they have green eyes, they're more of a muddy grey, a slightly greeny blue, but Mimi's eyes are really green, like emerald.

I seem to be spending many of my evenings here, chatting crap to her whilst drinking away my blues. She doesn't give me any free drinks like Mandy did, but it turns out she's actually quite funny when she's not berating me for my alcohol consumption. And it's better than sitting at home on my own.

'Well, I'm impressed. At least you're doing something worthwhile. Perhaps you're not quite the dick I thought you were.'

'Oh, no, I am. I only went into teaching because it seems to attract the ladies. Turns out nearly all women have some kind of hidden teacher fantasy.'

'Nearly all.'

'So what about you? Did you always want to be a barmaid?'

'Oh, yeah. I remember as a four-year-old girl, sitting, dreaming of the day I'd get to pull pints for a living.'

'Fair enough, but I couldn't exactly say, "So what do you really want to do rather than the crappy job you're doing right now," could I?'

'Tact and a meaningful job. You really are blowing my mind tonight.'

'You're avoiding the question. So what did you dream about as a little girl?'

44

Mimi rolls her eyes, as if mortified by the memory of her childhood aspirations. 'I wanted to be a singer.'

'Wow. So can you sing? Go on, sing me something now.'

'No way. Never going to happen.'

'Go on. Just a few lines. I promise not to laugh.'

Momentarily, the usual amused glint that resides in Mimi's eyes disappears and what's left is something raw and almost melancholy. 'I used to sing a lot, in pubs just like this, and then I looked around and realized that no one was listening. Not one person. In fact, the more I belted it out, the more they all shouted to be heard over me so, one day, I just stopped singing.'

'Not even in the shower? Like Ariel after doing a deal with the Sea Witch, never to be heard again?'

Mimi reaches across the bar and pushes me in the chest. 'Sod off.'

She surveys the pub. It's pretty empty: a couple chatting over a bottle of wine in the corner, two blokes with eyes fixed on the football on the tiny screen on the wall and a group of twenty-something women, steadily getting louder as they get the drinks down them.

'So who's going to be your poor victim tonight?' Mimi tilts her head towards the group of women.

I follow her line of sight. 'You know what? I was having so much fun talking to you, I'd actually forgotten about sex for once. Unbelievable, I know.'

'Nothing like chatting to me to quell all sexual desire.'

I put my hand on top of hers. 'Don't be so hard on yourself. If there was a zombie apocalypse and there was only you and me left on the planet, I'd do you.'

45

Mimi gives me a look of contempt.

'And not just to procreate, you know, for the survival of the entire human race. I'd even do it just for pleasure.'

'And just when I thought you couldn't get any better, you shower me with such beautiful compliments. You're just too good to be true.'

'That's what all the girls say.'

Mimi comes out from behind the bar and collects the empties from the unoccupied tables. She's wearing skinny black jeans and a black-and-white-striped figure-hugging top. I try my best not to stare, but she has an unbelievable body. For someone so slim, she has a size-able bum, but firm, like she spends all her spare time doing squats. It wouldn't surprise me to find out she'd had one of those bum implant operations. I've never been much of a bum man before, but Mimi's has the power to convert.

When she returns to the bar, I feel my face flushing at the thought that she might be able to read my mind, but although her eyes settle on me for a bit longer than normal, she doesn't say anything. Then to detract from my self-consciousness, in typical man fashion, I decide to say something arrogant and stupid that makes me sound like a prick.

'I was thinking I might just go for all of them.'

She takes a sip of her lemonade and raises her eyebrows. 'Do you ever think that maybe less is more?'

I drink the last of my JD and Coke and give her my glass to make me another. 'Who are you? My wife?'

Mimi emits a spluttering noise from her lips. 'God for-bid. No, I was hoping for her sake there wasn't "a wife"?'

She hands me my drink and I take a large swig. 'Well, you're right. There's not. So doesn't that mean I can sleep with whoever I want?'

'I guess. But I still think one at a time would be more pleasurable.'

'Had a lot of threesomes, have you?'

'Nah, I don't like sharing the limelight. Like to be star of the show.' She smiles, her eyes full of mischief. 'How about you? Had many?'

Although it would probably come as a surprise to her, my sexual past is about as vanilla as it gets. Kate and I got together when I was seventeen. She was the person I lost my virginity to. I never cheated on her, despite some of the lads at uni trying their best to persuade me to – *Doesn't it get boring? How do you know it's any good if you've got nothing to compare it to? She'd never find out.* Occasionally, when I compared myself to them, I'd wonder if I was settling down too young, if one day I'd regret it. But then I'd drive home to see Kate every weekend and, as soon as I was with her, I knew for sure that none of the girls at uni could come close. A few months after Mum died, I shocked everyone by proposing to her and a year later, me aged twenty and her only eighteen, and still living apart, we got married. Everyone told us not to rush into it, that there was plenty of time, but after what happened with Mum I didn't want to wait.

For a year after Kate left, I couldn't even look at another woman, so at age twenty-nine, I'd only slept with one person. And now I have crappy one-night stands where we only ever do it in the missionary position because (a) I'm too pissed to manage anything more adventurous and

47

(b) I can bury my head in my poor companion's shoulder and not have to look at her, or have her look at me. Where I spend the whole time lamenting how our bodies just don't *fit*, whereas with Kate, it sounds ridiculous, but it's as if we were made exactly for each other, as if every curve of her body fit every concave of mine and vice versa.

I open my mouth to offer Mimi some bravado about having had too many threesomes to count, but then I say, 'No. Looks far too complicated, to be fair. I think satisfying one woman's needs at a time is enough work for me.'

'Well, you're certainly getting enough practice at it.'

'I do not sleep with that many women.'

'Oh, come off it. It's got to be at least one a week. I've been watching you.'

I nod slowly and give Mimi a wink. 'Tempted to get in on the action, aren't you?'

'Absolutely. I can't stop thinking about it. I've always wanted a good STD.'

I wag my finger. 'No glove, no love.'

She laughs, a genuine laugh that somehow makes me feel good about myself. 'I'm actually seeing someone.'

'Oh, do tell,' I say, unwittingly adopting the vernacular of a gay best friend.

'He's called Liam. He's in a band. I went to see him at this gig a couple of months ago and we got chatting afterwards.'

'He sounds like a twat.'

'Why?'

'Blokes in bands are always twats.'

Mimi polishes a group of wine glasses. 'I have to say I did worry about that at first but he seems pretty nice so far.

It's nothing serious but it's fun for now. I don't like to look too far ahead. Live in the moment and all that.'

'Good attitude to have.'

Except if your 'moment' is anything like mine.

Mimi takes a tiny bow. 'Thank you.' Then she looks along the bar. One of the women from the group is standing at the end with her purse raised in her hand.

'Better go and assist getting those ladies inebriated so they don't have the horror of remembering you in the morning.'

'So which one should I go for, do you reckon?'

Mimi nods her head towards the table of women. 'Definitely the brunette. She's been eyeing you up since she got in here.'

'Ah, is that right? Clearly has great taste.'

'I was thinking more "desperate". Enjoy.'

I climb down off the bar stool and pick up my drink. 'I will. Night, Mimi.'

'Night, Noah.'

Then she goes to serve the buxom blonde of the group and, with a sinking heart, I slink over and position myself next to the eager brunette.

*

It turns out the brunette is called Hannah. We're both fairly drunk so it all happens quickly (both the process of getting from the front door to the bedroom and, a little embarrassingly, the sex itself). The sex is mediocre at best (my fault) – she says she came but I'm not convinced. We chat a bit afterwards, not much. I find out she does

49

admin for a recruitment company, she likes peanut butter mixed into her scrambled egg (random fact – don't for the life of me know how we arrive at it), she tells me she's never been married, no kids. I tell her I'm a teacher, that I like ketchup on my scrambled egg and I don't tell her about the ex-wife or kids. And then she says she's tired and turns away from me and I position myself safely on my side of the bed, adhering to the invisible line, and we both go to sleep.

*

In the middle of the night, I wake up sweating, my heart banging against the inside of my chest like a prisoner thumping his fists on the wall of his cell. It's always Mum's face and the same feeling, a desperate panic, a race against the clock, as if there's a simple way to save her, but my hands are frozen and however hard I try to move them, they won't do what I'm telling them to.

On automatic pilot, I reach for my phone on the bedside table and press on Kate's name. As I listen to the dial tone, I notice the body in the bed beside me. It startles me at first and, in my still slightly drunken haze, it takes me a while to remember who it is. And when I do, I wonder if it should feel like a comfort – that, mid panic attack, I'm not entirely alone – but it doesn't. It just makes the loneliness and the anxiety feel more intense.

'Hello?' As soon as I hear Kate's voice on the other end of the line, sleepy and slurred, it's like piercing a blood blister. Suddenly the pain seems to disperse and my heartbeat starts to slow.

'Hey. It's me. Noah,' I whisper, gently manoeuvring myself out of bed and creeping along the corridor until I reach the lounge, where I slump on the sofa.

'What time is it, Noah? Is everything OK?'

'I'm fine. It's late. I don't know what time it is. I'm sorry. I didn't know who else to call.'

I hear a voice in the background. Jerry's. Kate whispers something to him and then I hear a ruffle of the covers and the sound of Kate getting out of bed. 'Let me just put my dressing gown on. I'm just going to pop the phone on the side. One second.'

'OK.' It still makes me sick to think of her naked in bed with another man. And, like every emotion you feel in the middle of the night, it's magnified to something that feels unbearable to cope with.

'Right, I'm sorted now. Do you want to talk about it or do you just want me to sit on the other end of the line for a bit?'

'I don't want to talk about it.'

'OK.'

We sit in silence for a little while and I listen to her breathing, using its uniform rhythm to steady my own. As the heat from the panic gradually leaves my body, I find myself shivering, so I curl my body into the foetal position.

'Do you think she'd be proud of me, Kate? If she were still alive?'

Kate's answer is immediate. 'Absolutely.'

'But I've made nothing of myself. I've messed every-thing up.'

'She'd be proud of the way you love our boys. And you're a good person, Noah. You don't always make the best decisions, but you are a good person. She'd be proud of that.'

Tears catch in my throat, the all-too-familiar regret making my stomach churn with a sense of panic. How could I have thrown someone so wonderful away?

'Thank you.'

'No problem. Now try to get some more sleep.'

'I'll try. And Kate?' I hold my phone in front of me for a second and then bring it back to my ear, desperate to tell her how I still feel about her, but knowing that she'll just dismiss it as me being silly, or worse, that she'll ask me to keep my distance. 'Nothing. Don't worry. I'm sorry for waking you.'

'It's OK. You ready for me to go now?'

'Ready as I'll ever be. Night, Kate.'

I put the phone down first so that I don't have to listen to a dead line then head back to my bedroom and climb into bed, careful not to touch Hannah, and spend the night tossing and turning until morning comes around.

*

Usually when a girl stays the night (it turns out eighty per cent do, maybe eighty-five even) they don't stay long in the morning, getting dressed quickly before letting themselves out. I should possibly be offended that they're so desperate to get away from me, but I'm just glad to avoid the awkward small talk, knowing that neither of us is interested in what the other has to say because we're never going to see each other again.

This morning when I wake up, Hannah's not there and I'm hopeful she's already gone home but then I notice her jeans on the floor beside the bed. I force myself to get up, grab some joggers and a T-shirt and follow the clinking sounds to the kitchen. Hannah's put on the shirt I was wearing last night and is helping herself to cereal from the cupboard. On seeing me, she looks up and smiles, and with a sinking feeling in my stomach, I can tell from the look on her face that she is going to be one of the few girls who is looking for more. The type who doesn't just stay for breakfast but suggests we meet for a drink after work.

'I hope you don't mind me grabbing some breakfast. I'm always ravenous in the morning and I wasn't sure what time you'd wake up.' Hannah holds up her bowl. 'Do you want me to get you some?'

She looks so keen to please, so sweet, and she's a pretty girl, even prettier without the heavy make-up she was wearing last night. I don't want to hurt her. I'm not like Jack or all those other twats who think it's OK to string a girl along and then suddenly disappear. I try to make it as obvious as possible from the get-go that I am not relationship material. I never take girls out, I never see them more than once, I don't feed them corny lines or make them promises I can't keep. And most girls understand that because they met you in a bar and slept with you on the first night, it was never going to be anything serious. It was just sex. In my experience, most women are surprisingly on board with that. They're not looking for anything else from me either, but there are just a few, like Hannah, who mistakenly believe they are going to meet Mr Right sitting in a dingy bar, on his own, drunk, and whose opening gambit is, 'I was wondering if you wanted to come home with me.'

'No, it's fine. Thank you. I'll grab something.'

I get myself some cornflakes and make a coffee with the water Hannah has recently boiled. Then we go through to the lounge (I have no table to eat at – yes, I am still a child) and sit on opposite ends of the sofa with our breakfast. For a moment, neither of us speaks, focusing intently on the food we are spooning into our mouths, but then she stops, looks up at me and, as predicted, says, 'Do you fancy doing something later? I finish work at six. We could go for a drink or some food or something?'

I consider which of my potential responses will cause her the least pain. It takes guts to ask someone out and I don't want her to feel embarrassed but I don't want to give her false hope either. 'Look, Hannah, you are really lovely, but I'm just not looking for a relationship at the moment.'

She wipes at the droplet of milk that is currently trickling down her chin, her cheeks pinkening as if the rejection has slapped her round the face. 'Well, no, nor am I particularly. I'm not saying we're going to get married and have babies . . .' (an awkward laugh) '. . . I'm just saying let's spend a bit of time together, see if we get on.'

How can you tell someone gently that you know, just by the pitch of their voice, the fact they put your shirt on without asking, the feeling you had in the pit of your stomach when you woke up in the middle of the night next to them, that there will never be anything between you? And that even if they were, by chance, perfect for you in every way, you don't want to test the water, to see if you can feel anything for anyone, that the thought of ever being in love again makes you want to run screaming as if being chased by a hitman who has you firmly in his sights?

'I'm really sorry. It's not you. I just don't want to date anyone. It was just about sex. I'm sorry if I didn't make that clear.'

Hannah puts her bowl on the carpet, brings her knees to her chest and covers her bare legs with her arms. 'Oh, OK. Well, perhaps I could just use your shower to freshen up then I'll get out of your hair?'

The look on her face, a guilt-inducing mixture of disappointment and shame, makes me want to backtrack and say we can go for a drink after all, but it'd only be prolonging the inevitable. 'Of course. Take all the time you need. I've got an early morning meeting so I'd better get ready and rush off. Help yourself to whatever you want though, and just pull the door to when you go.'

Hannah nods and I give her a kiss on the cheek then quickly get dressed and sprint out the door, feeling horrible and wishing I hadn't gone home with her in the first place. I don't even know why I do it. Do I actually enjoy the sex? I think sometimes you can feel so full to the brim with emptiness that you just need to feel something, *anything*, else. It seems strange to think you can be *full* of emptiness, but sometimes that's how it feels, like it could spill over.

CHAPTER FIVE

Finn stands up off the bench and takes a step forward, holding up a yellow painting that I can just about make out is of a group of people. He loves yellow. He won't use any other colour, regardless of what it is he is depicting. We have yellow Santas, yellow Superheroes, yellow monsters. Right now, Finn's face is hidden behind the large piece of sugar paper as his teacher clicks her fingers in front of her to try to get his attention, but he begins to talk from behind the paper so no one can hear what he is saying.

'Finn, pop your paper down, sweetheart,' his teacher says in a hushed voice.

Gradually, Finn lowers the paper to reveal a slightly daunted-looking face. His eyes search the room and then he spots us, his face breaking out into a huge smile that makes my chest physically hurt.

He puts his paper into one hand and waves enthusiastically with the other. 'Hi, Mummy and Daddy.'

A ripple of laughter travels along the rows of children and through the parents seated around the edge of the room. I look over to Gabe, who is grinning widely at his little brother.

'Do you want to say your line now, Finn?' his teacher asks softly.

'Oh, yeah, I forgot.' Finn gives an awkward little head wiggle. 'In Bolt class, we have been painting pictures of ourselves and our family. This is me and Mummy and Jerry and Gabe.'

His teacher gives him a thumbs up and I force my mouth to adopt the position of a smile whilst trying to breathe normally, but it feels like my airways are constricting and I'm running out of oxygen.

Suddenly, there's a hand on my knee, squeezing it gently, and my eyes trace along Kate's arm and up to her shoulder, but I can't bear to see the apologetic look in her eyes, the sympathy, as if she understands how it feels to be the other parent, the one always on the outside looking in. She's the essential. I'm just an added extra.

At the end, the other classes filter back to their classrooms and parents are allowed to take photos of their little stars. Finn runs up to us and we both crouch down, Finn putting one arm around each of our necks, pulling us together in a circle.

'You were amazing, little man. I'm so proud of you.' I kiss him on the forehead and then Kate releases herself from his grip, stands up, picks him up and twirls him round. 'You're a superstar.'

Finn's face beams. Kate is such a wonderfully natural mother. Always has been. So often, the nitty gritty of parenthood felt like such a challenge to me, but straight away Kate took it in her stride with a calmness and patience I was never capable of. Whereas I seemed to be constantly craving some time to myself (oh, how I wish I hadn't now), Kate was happy to sit with the boys for hours when they couldn't get to sleep or play game after game long after I'd got bored and walked away.

'Mr Carlton, have you got a minute?' It's Finn's teaching assistant – a short, stout woman with a kindness in her eyes that makes you feel you want her to take care of you, and a deep chuckle that suggests there's a little more naughtiness to her than originally meets the eye. Like maybe underneath the mother-hen exterior, she has a bit of a penchant for the old *Fifty Shades*.

'Sure. Is everything OK? Do you need my . . . Finn's mum to join us?'

'No, just you. Follow me. I just want to show you something quickly.'

She leads me into the classroom and rifles through a pile of paintings on the drying rack. I notice, reassuringly, that like mine, the classroom is a mess – books scattered across the floor, folders piled high on every surface, a wide variety of toys all thrown into one big muddled box in the corner.

'Ah, here it is.' She pulls out a large yellow painting and hands it to me. It's almost identical to the one Finn showed in assembly, except there are only three people this time. 'He was absolutely adamant that he be allowed to do two. He got in quite a state about it.'

I stare at the painting and bite my lip. At the bottom, an adult has written, 'Me, Gabriel and Daddy'.

'I just thought it was important that you saw it.'

I nod, wanting to envelop her in my arms, but instead I stand there motionless and no sound comes from my lips.

'Anyway, I'll let you get back to Finn.'

'Can I keep this?'

'Of course. It's yours.'

'Thank you. Really. Thank you so much.'

She places her hand between my shoulder blades and then leads me back to the hall.

'Everything OK?' Kate says when she sees me return.

'Yeah, fine.'

'What's that?' She gestures to the rolled-up painting in my hand.

'Oh, nothing. Just some ideas for my class.'

Kate draws her head back and narrows her eyes.

'Probably a ploy to get some alone time with me. Haven't you noticed that cheeky glint in her eyes whenever she's talking to me?' I joke, covering the true emotion I'm feeling with bravado.

Kate rolls her eyes. 'Oh yeah, the Noah effect. I remember it well.'

We go and say our goodbyes to Finn (lots more cuddles and telling him how wonderful he was) and then watch him skip back to the classroom, holding hands with another boy from his class.

'Sometimes I wonder how we made something so incredibly beautiful,' Kate says, staring wistfully at Finn as he disappears out of the hall.

I put my mouth next to her ear. 'I can tell you in detail how we made that one. I'll never forget that saucy little rendezvous in the sand. In fact, my knee's never quite been the same since.'

Kate elbows me in the side. 'You know what I mean.' Suddenly, a film of sadness seems to slide across her eyes like a cataract. 'Our boys are so perfect. It must've been right for us to have babies together, mustn't it?'

'Of course it was right.'

'But it didn't turn out to be right. Us, I mean, in the long term.'

I nod, enough to acknowledge I understand what she means, but not enough to suggest I agree with her.

Then Kate shakes her body, like a dog coming out of a lake, as if she's trying to shake off what it is she's feeling, and I wish that she'd allow herself to consider it further – the idea that we're meant to be. 'Have you got to go straight back to school or do you have time for a coffee?'

'It's my prep time. I'm all yours until after lunch.'

'Great. I'll take you to my new favourite place.'

Kate links her arm through mine and guides me to her chosen café, and it's ridiculous how excited I am at the prospect of being alone with her for an hour or so.

*

I can see immediately why this is Kate's new favourite place. The coffee is reasonably priced, the cakes are massive, the sofas are comfy and there are bookshelves on every spare bit of wall filled with novels of every genre.

Kate takes out a well-thumbed copy of *One Day* and sits down on the sofa with it, flicking through the pages. 'Oh, the wonderful David Nicholls. Still my all-time favourite novel.'

'Except for the ending?'

'Well, yes, I will never forgive him for that, but it's just so brilliant. Listen to this, "*Loss has not endowed him with any kind of tragic grandeur, it has just made him stupid and banal. Without her he is without merit or virtue or purpose, a shabby, lonely, middle-aged drunk, poisoned with regret and shame.*" Oh, it's just so heartbreakingly beautiful.'

The passage rings a bit too true for me, but I smile at her enthusiasm. She's like a kid in that way. She's never become numb to the world around her. She still gets ridiculously excited about Christmas, she cries at building society adverts . . . I guess it was one of the things that brought us together – our tendency to feel things intensely – but somehow, unlike me, she managed to avoid the fear that went along with that, the crashing lows.

'Can you believe Jerry doesn't even read?' she continues, putting the book back on the shelf and then sitting down and taking a sip of her coffee. 'I mean, he'll occasionally pick up the autobiography of some sports star or other, but that's not proper reading, is it?'

In the early years of our marriage, before kids monopolized all our time, we used to spend a lot of time in cosy B&Bs by the sea, tucked under the covers reading. We had different tastes. I've always been partial to a bit of fantasy and dystopia, and Kate would always mock my ability to accept a world where goblins roamed the fields or you were in danger of being picked off by a zombie on a random trip to the supermarket. She couldn't see how I could buy into that stuff, but to me it was no more unrealistic than the happy-ever-afters she was so fond of. Either way, I loved those times.

'I've already told you he's not right for you.'

Kate smiles, but there's a sadness in her eyes. I'm not quite sure of the origin. 'So how about you? There must be someone you're interested in for more than just a one-night stand?'

I want to say no, how can there be when you put my heart in a grinder and shredded it, when the fragments that remain are still so full of love for you, but, instead, I play the part of Mr Billy Big Bollocks.

'Turns out one-night stands are really fun. It's like the edited highlights, no adverts, no slow plot development.'

Kate nods, but she looks hurt and I regret my comment immediately, because of course to her it sounds like I'm criticizing what we had; and I guess, in my pig-headed defensiveness, that's exactly what I'm doing.

She finishes the last of her carrot cake, scraping the plate with a fork, then reaches into her bag. 'Well, I suppose the real reason I invited you here is to give you this.'

She hands me an envelope and I look at my address in her handwriting and the stamp in the corner.

As if following my line of vision, she says, 'I was going to post it, but it didn't seem right. I wanted to give it to you in person.'

I slip my finger underneath the flap. 'Well, it isn't my birthday, so I know it's not a card. What is it, Kate?'

Her eyes are dewy, serious, and I have a sinking feeling in my stomach that causes a bubble to rise up into my throat. I reach into the envelope and pull out the card – the words 'Wedding Invitation' hitting me like a bullet.

'Please tell me your sister is getting married.'

Kate bites the tip of her thumbnail.

I open the card, my eyes skipping the formalities and landing on the names of my ex-wife and new husband-to-be.

'I want you to be there, but I'll understand if you don't want to be. You're welcome to bring someone with you if you want, if you do decide to come, that is.'

I look at the date. 'It's in a couple of months? Are you going for world's shortest engagement?'

Kate's face flushes and I know immediately that she's been keeping this from me for quite some time. 'We didn't tell anyone. Not even the kids. We thought we'd get all the details sorted first.'

I suddenly wonder if Gabe overheard something, if that's why he asked me about it a couple of weeks ago in McDonald's.

'And you're sure about this?'

Kate nods, killing me with the tiniest movement of her head.

'Have a nice life, Kate.'

I know it's a ridiculous thing to say – that I'll see her again on Sunday when I drop off the boys, that I'll always have to see her, at least until our children have grown up, that I want to see her, despite everything – but I don't know what else to say. I storm out, the invitation in my hand, feeling like it's coated with poison, filtering its way up through my arm into my heart.

CHAPTER SIX

'So are you going to come to Mummy and Jerry's wedding?' Gabe asks, frantically pressing the X button on the PlayStation controller.

The baddy on screen is fading fast, blood squirting out all around him, the bar that shows his health almost empty. I move my character towards him, attack him with a killer blow and watch him fall to the ground with a thump.

'Nice one, Daddy. Let's quickly find a "save the game".'

We search around the dingy caves. Finn is sitting next to us putting his Imaginext figures in and out of the walled prison of his Batcave, muttering each character's dialogue.

'Did Mummy say I was coming?'

'She said she didn't know. She said she hoped you would. Please come, Daddy. They're having a chocolate fountain.'

'Yeah, it's going to be so cool,' Finn chips in.

I don't want to hear the details of their special day because it makes it real and therefore harder to push to the corner of my mind (for it to have a little party there with all the other stuff that's too painful to face up to). Not that I *can* push it to the corner of my mind. Ever since Kate told me, it's infiltrated my every thought, even my dreams (nightmares).

Our wedding was very low-key. We got married in church – Kate wouldn't have it any other way. It felt right to me too. I'm not sure I believe in God, but I'm not sure enough that I don't either, so I was happy to grant her her wish. Somehow it felt more 'proper' saying our vows there, more long-standing, not realizing at the time that I'd go on to screw it all up. The reception was held in a small rustic barn near Kate's parents' house. We lit candles everywhere, adorned the walls, tables and chairs with greenery we'd gathered on our walks, and the centrepieces were made up of simple silk wild flowers. Kate planned it meticulously, considering every little detail to ensure it was the perfect day. And it was. We had a winter wedding and in the evening just after our first dance, as if by magic, a few light flakes of snow began to fall outside the door. I can't believe she's planning to do it all again with someone else. And with Jerry of all people.

'Me and Finn are going to be page boys. That means we follow Mummy down the aisle and she said I'm the only one she trusts to hold the rings.'

'I want to hold them,' Finn says, crossing his arms.

'Well, you're too little. I'm the big boy.'

Finn sticks his tongue out at Gabe and returns to his superhero adventure re-enactment.

I press the buttons on the PlayStation controller with such force I'm either going to break it or my fingers, but I just keep going. The baddies are slaughtered one after the other. It's satisfyingly cathartic to see them defeated.

'Are you OK, Daddy?' Gabe asks, peering around to try to make eye contact.

'Yeah. Course.' I continue to stare at the screen and then there's a pause as the console loads the next level. 'Do you guys want a drink?'

'Coke,' they say in unison, so I go into the kitchen and open the fridge. On the worktop, I notice a bottle of Jack Daniel's and find myself drawn to it, hoping it might numb me just for a while, but I manage to resist and grab myself a beer instead. A lunchtime beer is acceptable, isn't it? Then I get the boys a can of Coke each, open them and take them back to the lounge where Gabe's eyes are glued to the television screen as if he's been hypnotized, and Finn is lost in his own world smashing figures together. And I know that I should be doing more with them. Taking them to museums, getting them out in nature, climbing trees, making rafts, teaching them about dinosaurs or space, *anything*; but, despite knowing that, all I have any desire to do right now is drift away into a world where I'm the hero and it's easy to overthrow the monsters.

*

At bedtime, I lie in between the boys on the bottom bunk. I don't know why I bothered to buy them a bunk bed because they always choose to sleep in the same bunk, sometimes the top one, sometimes the bottom, but always together. I'm reading them Harry Potter, each boy clinging on to one of my arms, the heat of their bodies like being swaddled. And for a moment I feel calmer than I have in a long time but then all of a sudden a wave of panic comes over me and it feels like I'm in *A Christmas Carol*, the spirit of what's yet to come showing me my future, and in the future it's not me lying in the middle of them, it's Jerry, and they're looking up at him like they look up at me and asking for 'one more page, Daddy' as if I never even existed.

I try to keep reading but I keep stumbling over the words, so I finish the page I'm on then put the book down on the floor.

'Can we just have a bit more?' Gabe begs, but I shake my head, suddenly feeling too hot and finding it hard to catch my breath.

'Sleepy time now, boys. I love you both so much. I'll see you in the morning.'

Ignoring their protests, I turn off the under-the-bed lamp, slide out from in between them, kiss them both on the forehead and then head to the lounge. And without the boys in it, it feels so empty that it's stifling. I go into the kitchen and pour myself a JD and Coke, but it's the last of the bottle and the thought of a night at home with all these tormenting thoughts and nothing stronger than a couple of beers to dull them is too much to bear so I reach for my phone and call Ben.

*

Ben closes the front door and removes his shoes as if he's a burglar not wanting to be heard.

'You're lucky. Claudia was supposed to be out with work friends tonight but one of them cancelled at the last minute. Tummy bug,' he whispers. 'They're asleep, aren't they?' He nods his head towards the boys' bedroom.

'Yes, don't worry. You don't have to look after my insane children.'

Ben does little to disguise his outward breath of relief.

'Help yourself to beer in the fridge.'

'You going straight out?'

I look at my watch. 'Well, I could have a quick one here first, I guess.'

'Great. Grab me one whilst you're at it.'

I go into the kitchen to get us both a beer. I don't really want an inquisition from my brother right now. I want to get wasted, find someone to bring home, and engage in some angry, meaningless sex in the hope that it might take this fucking ache away, if only for a second, but Ben's given up his Saturday night to babysit for me and I know it won't have been easy getting a pass from Claudia.

Sitting down on the sofa beside him, I hand him a beer and he clinks it against mine. 'Cheers, bro.'

'What are we toasting to?'

'I don't know, fresh starts.'

I take a large swig of my beer, feeling the mixture of alcohol finally having some effect. 'Good one. I'll toast to that.'

Ben looks me up and down, assessing something – I'm not quite sure what. 'So how are you feeling about Kate and the upcoming wedding? Are you OK?'

Ah, so he was checking my mental stability, deciding whether I was in a suitable state to raise the topic of my ex-wife's planned nuptials to a man that isn't me, or whether it'd send me running off in the direction of the next passing train.

'Yeah, I'm cool. I mean, I think she's making a mistake but that's for her to discover the hard way, I guess. It's not my place to try to convince her otherwise.'

'No, of course not.'

We sit in silence, the sound of us slurping our drinks somehow magnified by what we're not saying, both knowing full well that the other is holding the words they really want to say tucked into the side of their mouth like a boiled sweet.

I finish my beer, get up and put it on the fireplace. 'I said I'd meet a friend at half nine,' I lie. 'Are you OK with Netflix if I go now? I'll try not to be too late.'

'Yeah, go. I've got a night of *Stranger Things* lined up. Just make sure you come home, OK?'

'Don't worry, I will.'

I pick my jacket up off the sofa and start to put it on.

'And I'm always here, you know, if you want to talk about anything. In a manly way, of course, with beer and grunts.'

'I know. I'm fine though, honestly. Don't worry, I'm not going to lose the plot like I normally do. I think I've put you through enough of that over the years.'

'True. But it'd be OK if you did.'

I force my lips into an appreciative smile and feel glad of the alcohol in my system, like a covering of sticky-back plastic, an impenetrable skin.

*

'Line up the shots, Mimi. It's Saturday night, I'm young, free and single, and ready to mingle.'

I throw my jacket towards the bar stool in an attempt at some kind of smooth James Bond gesture, but it misses and lands on the floor.

Mimi raises her eyebrows. 'Are you OK?'

'It's the question on everyone's lips, Mimi, but I can assure you, like I assured them, that, yes, I am absolutely splendid.'

Mimi screws the top back on to a bottle of wine and puts it in the fridge. 'I'm guessing this isn't your first drink of the night?'

I scoot myself up on to the bar stool. 'You're far too intelligent to be working behind that bar, young lady. Your skills of deduction are being wasted.'

'So what's your weapon of choice? Tequila? Sambuca?'

'You choose. Just line them up and keep them coming.'

'Your wish is my command.'

She lines up a row of shot glasses and starts filling them, in the way they always do in drinking establishments, at such a height that if I tried it, I'd end up with nothing in the glass and a sticky mess on the surface of the bar. As she does, it's like inhaling nail polish remover, and I cover my mouth as the fumes make me cough.

'All yours. Although if you change your mind about obliteration by sambuca, you could always tell me what's up. I'm stuck here all night anyway. I've got nothing better to do.'

'Why do I have to keep saying it? Nothing's up, OK?' A few of the people nearby turn to look in the direction of my raised voice.

Mimi looks startled, even a little scared. 'Right. Sorry.'

I drag my hands through my hair, pushing it back off my face, and let out a loud sigh. 'I'm sorry. I didn't mean to shout.'

'It's fine.'

She goes to the other end of the bar to serve another customer. It's a young guy, good-looking in a stuck-up twat sort of way. He leans over the bar, whispering something in Mimi's ear, then pulls up a bar stool and beckons his friend over to join him. They sit with their pints, chatting away to Mimi, and every now and again she does this coy smile, pushing her fringe behind her ear and pushing out her chest.

I raise my hand but she takes no notice. 'Um, drink needed here. You are working, you know?' I shout down the bar.

Mimi glares at me, apologizes to the men and marches over. 'Look, you want to drink yourself into a stupor, go ahead, but don't you dare speak to me like that, do you understand?'

She's right. I'm being an arsehole, but I'm on the slippery slide to self-destruct and I'm not sure how to get off. 'You're not seriously won over by that prick, are you?'

Mimi's shoulders rise and fall slowly as she lets out a pained breath. 'He's the prick, is he? It doesn't look like that from where I'm standing.'

I slam my shot glass on the bar. 'Whatever. Same again, please.'

'Sure.' Mimi pours me another row of shots, both of us purposefully avoiding eye contact. Then she turns to go back to her new acquaintances, but I reach out and grab her hand.

'My wife, ex-wife, is getting remarried.'

Mimi nods but doesn't say anything, like she's waiting for me to say more before she decides whether or not to keep walking in the opposite direction.

'It's a shock, I guess. It feels too soon, like an insult to our marriage, you know? Like I wasted the best years of my life on something that meant nothing.'

I can feel tears in my throat and bite down on my thumb to stop them. There's no way I want Mimi to see the state I'm in.

'How long since you split up?'

I shake my head. 'It's been just over two years, but that's not exactly a long time in the grand scheme of things. It doesn't feel long. Not long enough to reach a point where you are ready to marry someone else. I mean, I've not even liked someone . . .' I pause, suddenly feeling like I'm on the verge of blurting out the truth and needing to reel myself back in. 'Well, you know, it just seems a bit quick, that's all. It's not like I'm not over her. She can be with who she wants. It's a respect thing, you know what I mean?'

The look in Mimi's eyes suggests that, no, she doesn't know what I mean. Or, more accurately, that she knows exactly what I mean, but that it's not contained in the words bumbling out of my drunken mouth.

'Do you want me to come home with you?'

I jolt my head back in surprise. 'What?'

She downs one of the shots she poured for me. 'Let's just say you're not the only one in need of some meaningless sex.'

My breathing suddenly feels more laboured, the anticipation of sex with Mimi causing my heartbeat to accelerate. I mean, Mimi's stunning. She's well out of my league. 'What about the singer?'

'He's a guitarist, actually. A cheating guitarist, it turns out.'

'Oh, sorry.'

'It's fine. I'm not bothered.'

I raise my eyebrows. 'But you want to have sex with me because . . .'

'A girl has needs too, you know?'

'So why don't you just go for Mr Big Shot over there?' I tilt my head towards one of the two lads, feeling his eyes boring into the side of my face.

'Because he'll keep calling, wanting to take me out on dates. Either that or he'll never call and I'll obsess about why. I know with you it'll just be tonight and you probably won't even remember it in the morning, let alone call me.'

I can't argue with that. And yet the thought of sex with Mimi feels odd, like overstepping an invisible boundary.

'But . . . is it going to ruin our friendship?'

Mimi laughs. 'So we're friends now, are we?'

'You know what I mean. I don't usually sleep with people I . . .'

Have said more than a handful of words to?

'Don't worry. I promise it won't be weird between us. Purely sex. Unless you'd rather choose someone else in here to go home with. I won't be offended, well not *too* offended, anyway.' She smiles, but she looks less sure of herself than normal.

'If you're OK with it, I'm OK with it. When do you finish?'

'In about half an hour.' She takes the shot glasses down off the bar. 'No more of this, though. I'd like a half-decent performance.'

'Oh, you don't need to worry about that. It'll be better than half decent,' I say, even though I'm utterly terrified now.

'Well, I'll be the judge of that. Now, like you said, I'm working, so can I get on with my job, please?'

I nod. 'I need to make a phone call anyway. I'll meet you back here.'

It's freezing outside and I sit on a bench and shiver whilst I wait for Ben to answer his phone.

Finally, he picks up. 'Don't tell me you've fallen into the river and need rescuing?'

'No, actually I need a favour. I'm bringing a girl home.'

'So you need me to do my usual disappearing act?'

'Thanks, bro. I'll text you when we're just around the corner so you can make a swift exit. And could you just tidy away any really obvious kid stuff. Just throw it in a cupboard. I'll sort it out tomorrow.'

'OK. Although I'm sure these girls would still want to sleep with you if they knew you had kids. You could just tell her.'

I knew as soon as I started bringing different women home that I didn't want them to know about the boys. I have no intention of them ever becoming part of each other's lives and it just feels wrong talking about them – like revealing a hidden scar. And yeah, maybe I want these women to think I'm just this carefree guy up for a bit of fun rather than a divorced dad trying to forget about the gaping hole in his chest.

'I find it easier to keep my two worlds separate.'

'Up to you. Roughly how long do you think you'll be? Just wondering whether it's worth starting the next episode.'

'About half an hour?'

'Perfect. Catch up soon, yeah? And have a good night.'

'Oh, I'm pretty sure I will. You should see this girl's arse. It's ridiculous.'

I don't even know why I say things like this. It's like I feel that if I act like a misogynistic twat then no one will cotton on to the fact that I'm hanging on to my sanity by a very thin thread.

Ben laughs, but I can tell he (rightly) thinks I'm an idiot. 'Night, brother.'

*

When we first get back to mine, it's a little awkward. We enter the hallway, remove our jackets, I offer Mimi a drink and she declines. Having already verbally agreed what's going to happen, it's hard to know exactly how to start things off.

Luckily, Mimi isn't backwards in coming forward. 'So are you going to show me where your bedroom is?'

I take her hand and then release it, rubbing my clammy palms on my jeans before taking it again. I lead her to the bedroom, going in first, surveying it quickly for incriminating items before turning the light on.

Mimi squints her eyes. 'Have you got a lamp? That light is a bit intense.'

'Of course.' I turn off the ceiling light and lean over the bed to switch on my bedside lamp.

'Much better.'

I sit on the bed and she positions herself beside me then we start kissing. I feel oddly shy, like I'm seventeen again and having sex with Kate for the first time (not knowing what the hell to do, where the infamous clitoris is located,

75

when and how to put a condom on). At the time, Kate had guided me so calmly, so gently, with so much more confidence than I had, despite it being her first time too.

Mimi is much the same, taking my hand and putting it on her waist, slowly unbuttoning my shirt and then pulling her own top over her head and removing her jeans so that she's sitting in just her underwear, a plain black bra and a pair of Superdry boxers peppered with pink stars.

'Sorry, I haven't got my best underwear on. Although it might not seem like it, I didn't plan on having sex with anyone tonight.'

'Don't be silly. You look amazing.'

Mimi gently removes my glasses in a gesture that feels so tender, I'm tempted to hand her her clothes and send her packing. But then she slips her hand down the back of my boxers and squeezes my bum and I can't resist copying the gesture. And after that, there's only one direction this is going to go in and it doesn't involve Mimi getting into a taxi.

When we're done, we lie on my bed like stickmen, covers kicked off, naked and both glistening with sweat.

'You're right. That guy would've been buzzing your phone the second he got home with sex like that.'

Mimi laughs and turns on to her side so she is facing me, pulling the cover up and tucking it under her armpit in a touchingly self-conscious gesture. 'Thank you. I feel much better.'

'You're welcome. I feel much better too.'

Mimi scans the room. 'So this is where you live.'

I follow her gaze, taking in the lack of curtains or blind on the window, the faded bedding, the pile of clothes in the corner, the empty beer bottles lined up on the window-sill. 'Yeah, sorry, it's a bit of a shithole. I've not really got round to sorting it out yet.'

Mimi laughs. 'Two years, didn't you say?'

'Well, yeah. But teaching is a full-on job. I don't have much free time.'

'It's OK. I still live with my dad so I can't really talk.'

'Oh, how come?'

'Well, my mum died when I was eight. Brain haemorrhage. So it's always just been me and Dad really. I've never had the heart, or the money, to move out.'

I nod. 'I'm sorry about your mum.'

'It's OK. These things happen, right? In a way I think maybe it was better that way. Sounds odd, but I think losing her as an adult, after all those years of being so close, might have been harder. I don't know. It would've been nice to have a mum through my teenage years, though. I think that's when I felt it most. Dad was great, but it's not the easiest talking to your dad about periods and breasts and boys.'

I wonder if she's right. Whether it would've been easier to lose Mum before I understood what it meant, before I'd had the chance to develop such a deep love for her. My thoughts must be clear on my face because she looks at me and says, 'Shit, you lost your mum as an adult, didn't you?'

'Don't worry. You couldn't have known.'

'But I need to learn to think before I speak. I'm always doing this. Saying insensitive things without realizing it.'

It's actually one of the things I like about Mimi, that she just says what she thinks instead of filtering it.

'Seriously, it's fine. Like you said, it's life, right? We all have to lose our loved ones eventually. It was eleven years ago now.'

'What about your dad? Are you close to him?'

'No. He was hardly ever around. He'd say he was working but I think he spent most of his time at the pub. And then when Mum died, he buggered off and didn't contact my brother or me for two years.'

'Wow. I'm sorry.'

'Don't be. We were better off without him. He's an arsehole.'

'But still, him leaving you after your mum died. That must've been really hard.'

I shrug, as if it didn't really bother me when in fact it broke my heart.

'So I'm guessing you're not in touch now?' Mimi continues.

I shake my head. 'He tried to grovel his way back in but we told him he could stick his reconciliation. It's been nine years now since he got in touch and we've not spoken a word to him.'

Mimi doesn't say anything further and we lie in silence for a while, both seemingly lost in our own thoughts. Then she props her head up on to her elbow so that her eyes can meet mine. 'Well, that was a cheerful conversation. Want to have sex again?'

'Um . . .' She must hear the fear in my voice because she starts laughing.

'I'm joking, Noah.'

'Good. For a moment there, I was worried about my manliness. I'm sure some men must be able to manage immediate repeat performances, but I'm definitely not one of them.'

Mimi smiles. 'Right, well, I suppose I best call a taxi.'

It feels so easy. I wonder what the catch is.

'Do you want a coffee or anything before you go?'

She sits up and supports herself against the headboard. 'No, it's OK. I'll grab a glass of water on my way out.'

She leans over the side of the bed and picks up her jeans, reaching into the pocket and pulling out her phone. Just as she's finished her call, I hear the pitter-patter of feet coming down the corridor. Shit. I push Mimi down the bed and pull the cover over her. 'Quick, hide.'

Before I have the chance to explain, Finn is in the bedroom.

'Daddy, I had a nightmare. There was a monster,' he says, half-asleep, and climbs up on to the bed into my arms, laying his head on my shoulder.

Mimi lies motionless and I try to imagine what she might be thinking whilst also feeling slightly uncomfortable that she is down there, under the covers, her face very close to my naked appendage. Within minutes, Finn is asleep again so I struggle to put my boxers on, get up and carefully carry him back to bed, lying him next to Gabriel, and then return to my bedroom where Mimi is getting dressed.

'I'm sorry about that.'

'Your private life is your private life.' She's acting nonchalant, focused on the task of pulling on her socks, but I can tell she thinks I'm a dick for hiding the fact I have kids from her.

'I wasn't trying to be duplicitous. It just never came up in conversation, I guess. I have two boys. Finn is four and

79

Gabriel is eight. I have them every other weekend. This is my weekend.'

'And yet you're out drinking with me?' She says it with a smirk and I know I've dropped even lower in her estimation than I already was. And, weirdly, that bothers me. I don't want Mimi to think I'm a total scumbag.

'They were asleep when I left. I didn't sacrifice any of my time with them. And my brother was babysitting. He left a second or so before we arrived.'

'A well-oiled machine, hey?'

I shake my head. 'It's not like that. I was . . .'

'You don't need to explain, Noah,' Mimi cuts me off. Then there's a beep from a car horn outside. 'Right, well, thanks for tonight. It was very enjoyable.' She grabs her bag and then kisses me on the cheek before heading out the door.

CHAPTER SEVEN

A couple of weeks later, I am sitting in the staffroom enjoying my delightful school dinner (I think it said beef hotpot on the menu but it's hard to tell) when one of the midday supervisors, Tracey, peers around the door. I look down at my phone, hoping beyond hope she's not looking for me.

'Mr Carlton, have you got a minute?'

I hate the way the lunchtime staff address us using our surnames, as if having gained a teaching qualification makes us somehow superior, but however many times I ask them to call me Noah, they won't.

'Yep. Just on my last mouthful. One second.'

I know before Tracey says anything that it's going to be about Harley. It's always about Harley. I put my tray on the side, go over to her and, sure enough, when I glance over her shoulder I see Harley, arms crossed and red-faced, sitting on the chair outside the office.

'What's he done this time?'

'He bit Cody on the shoulder. There's a pretty big mark. Cody's in first aid at the moment. Do you want me to bring him up?'

'No, it's OK. I'd like to have a little chat with Harley on his own. Leave him with me.'

'OK, thanks,' she says, the relief at being able to pass him on written all over her face.

I take a seat next to Harley. 'What happened?'

He wraps his arms more tightly around himself and dips his chin. He has two dents at the top of his nose and his bottom lip protrudes like it's been stung by a bee.

'I'm going to talk to your mummy in a minute and I'd like to be able to explain to her why you bit Cody, but if you won't tell me anything, I'm going to have to say that you were just being unkind for no reason.'

The dents at the top of Harley's nose deepen. 'I just wanted to.'

'So Cody didn't do anything to you?'

'I don't like him. He's stupid.'

'But did he do anything to you, Harley?'

Harley snaps his head away from me.

'Right. You need to stay here until I get hold of your mummy. You are not allowed back into class this afternoon.'

I pop into the staffroom where Mrs Watson is sitting eating a bulbous cream cake. 'When lunch finishes, do you mind just having the class for a bit? I need to get in touch with Harley's mum. He's bitten Cody.'

Mrs Watson wipes the residual cream from her mouth with the back of her hand. 'And what exactly do you want me to do with them?'

Use your initiative.

'I've got the instruments out ready. You could put that "Dinosaur Stomp" song on and get them to try to tap a steady beat in time with the music.'

The colour visibly drains from her face. In her defence, I know what I'm asking her to do is not as easy as it sounds – that I am setting her up for an afternoon of painful, discordant noise and tantrums over instrument alloca-tion, but Harley injuring the other children is becoming a daily occurrence so I can't keep letting it pass.

'I'll try not to be long.' I leave the staffroom and return to the office before Mrs Watson has a chance to devise one of her many ingenious excuses for why she can't do what I've asked of her.

After six phone calls to Harley's mum and two left mes-sages, I give up.

'Do we have another number on record for Harley?'

Our school administrator, Verity, a tall, spindly woman with definite power issues, glares at me as if I am not, in fact, asking her to perform one of the duties that her job requires.

'It'll be in the file. Top drawer.' She doesn't even extend her finger into a full point, instead flicking her arm in the general direction of the filing cabinet.

'Thanks so much for your help.'

She smirks, evidently picking up on the sarcasm that I don't bother trying to disguise.

I find the file and locate Harley's details. His second contact is listed as Amelia Thomas. In brackets, it states 'Aunt'. It's not ideal, but perhaps 'Aunt' will give me more than the usual grunts I get from Mum.

Just as I pick up the phone and start to dial, there's a crash from outside the office and I peer through the screen to see that Harley has removed his shoes and is launching them at the glass panel in the hall door.

'I need to deal with Harley. Give his aunt a ring, will you, and see if she can come in now. Just say there's been an incident with Harley and another child.'

Verity pushes a puff of air through her lips and I take on the joyous task of calming an irate Harley.

*

It's not until she's halfway through the door that I recognize her. She's wearing a jacket with the hood up, rain dripping from the fur trim on to the floor.

'Mimi?'

'Noah?'

'What are you doing here?'

And then the penny drops, albeit a little bit slowly. Amelia Thomas.

'I came here to pick up my nephew, Harley. The office rang and said his teacher wanted to see me. There's been an altercation in the playground or something.'

'I'm Harley's teacher.'

Mimi looks me up and down as if she's trying to make sense of the information I've just given her. 'Oh, right. Well, this is a bit awkward.'

I feel Verity's beady eyes spying on us through the screen into the office so I usher Mimi and Harley into our school Nurture Room, the comically titled cage where we put the kids who are trashing the classroom or attacking staff.

Whilst Harley throws himself on a beanbag in the corner, I sit on the chair on one side of the desk and Mimi sits on the other – an uncomfortably formal configuration considering the last time I saw her she was naked.

'I haven't seen you in the pub for a while.'

'No. I've just been busy, with work and stuff.'

Mimi nods, a smile on her face that says I-know-you're-talking-shit. And she's right. I am. It just seemed simpler to find a new watering hole rather than tackle a slightly embarrassing 'let's pretend we haven't had sex' conversation. Thanks to the Fates, I've got to face that now instead, in my place of work, stone-cold sober. Some might call it karma.

'Right. Busy sorting out my nephew here by the looks of things. Emma mentioned he's not had the easiest time settling in, but I'm surprised he's getting into fights. He's a caring boy, you know?'

I nod, reluctant to shatter her rose-tinted glasses. 'Does his mum work? I've left messages on the home phone and the mobile but she's not called back. We don't have a work number for her.'

'No, she doesn't work. She . . . she's had a tricky couple of years, but she's getting there. She's doing much better.'

'Harley mentioned something about her being in bed a lot. Anything we need to know about? Does she need some support from the school?'

Mimi furrows her brow. 'She went through a bad patch . . .' She looks over at Harley, who is rolling around as if wrestling with the giant beanbag, and then turns her mouth away from him and lowers her voice to a whisper. 'When Harley's dad walked out, she struggled for a while, but she's doing much better now on her own. She loves Harley to bits. She doesn't need any help.'

I wonder whether Harley's interpretation of events isn't accurate or if Mimi just isn't aware of what's going on with her sister, but it doesn't feel fair to say much more without speaking to Harley's mum first.

'Well, I think it would be best for today if you took him home with you, if that's OK? There's only about an hour or so left until home time anyway. I think he'll just get himself into more trouble if he comes back into class.'

'Of course, no problem. And I'm sorry he's causing you such difficulties. I'll have a chat with him on the way home. Aunty Mimi will sort him out, don't you worry.' She gives Harley a faux-cross stare and his face breaks into a smile.

I'm not sure it's quite such an easy fix, but I nod encouragingly. 'Please tell his mum that my door is always open if she wants to discuss anything.'

Mimi waves my concern away. 'She's fine, honestly. I'll talk to Harley.'

'OK.'

Looking over at Harley, with his wild, unbrushed hair and permanently snotty nose, I suddenly have the strangest desire to put my arm around him. I'm sure it'll soon pass. That my usual inclination to throttle him will return with force. But looking into his eyes right now, he doesn't look so much malevolent as scared shitless, and I know just how that feels.

'So is there anything else?'

I realize I've gone quiet. 'No. Sorry. You're free to take him home.' I look at Harley. 'I'll see you tomorrow, little man, OK? Best behaviour, yeah?'

I know I'm wasting my breath, that asking him to behave is, like most of the tools in a teacher's arsenal (sticker charts, missed playtimes, clouds, rockets and rainbows), entirely ineffective.

'Harley? Answer Noa— I mean, Mr . . .'

'Carlton.'

'Answer Mr Carlton, please.'

'Yes, I'll be good tomorrow.'

It rolls off the tongue so easily. I imagine he's said it a thousand times before and then broken his promise within seconds. I give Mimi a weak smile and I wonder if she can tell that I don't believe a word of it.

'So, I'll see you around? Perhaps you'll stop hiding from me and come back to the pub?'

I feel my cheeks flush. 'I'm not hiding. I . . .'

'It's fine, Noah,' she interrupts, and I'm glad because I have no idea what I was going to say. 'I'm just winding you up.'

'Well, it was nice to see you again.'

'You too. Right, come on, trouble. Let's get you home.'

I hold the door open for her, trying to avoid our bodies touching as she walks out.

*

In a strange moment of mirroring, just after sending Harley home, my phone buzzes in my pocket with a message from the boys' head teacher asking if I could pop in to see her about Gabriel. My initial reaction is panic (what has my child done to humiliate me?) but then I remember it's Gabe we're talking about. He's a model student. The only thing his teachers ever want to see me about is to tell me how amazed they are by his work ethic or his exceptional attainment, the little creep. If it was Finn, I'd be more concerned. He's more like I was at school. The class clown. A follower. Desperate to be liked. But Gabe's like Kate, moral to a fault and far too headstrong to do something he doesn't think is a good idea just to fit in with the others.

I walk past the office, on to the field, and call Kate. It rings for ages before she picks up.

'Hi, Noah. I'm guessing you've also had a call from the school?'

'I missed it. Mrs Newman left me a message. What's going on?'

'She said she'd rather talk to us together and in person.'

'Sounds ominous. But he's never been in trouble for anything. He's the kid you dream about having in your class.'

'Well, let's wait and see what she has to say. Maybe there's a simple explanation.'

'Maybe.' I pace the field, feeling my rage building. How could anyone have a bad word to say about Gabe?

'And, Noah, please don't go in there all guns blazing. Listen to what she has to say first.'

'I won't. But I will stick up for him if he's being unfairly judged.'

'OK, but just remember what it's like to talk to the parent who thinks the sun shines out of their child's arse.'

'But it does. He's a superstar kid.'

Kate laughs. 'I know he is. Look, meet me in the car park, OK?'

'OK. See you soon.'

*

Mrs Newman has that uncanny ability to make you feel ten again, called into the head's office because you flooded

88

the boys' toilets. She's in her early sixties and everything about her appearance is sharp – her tightly cropped dark grey hair, her pointed nose and pinched cheeks. When she smiles, it always looks like it's an effort, like she's having to force her face into the expression.

'Thank you both for coming in. I recognize it can't have been easy for you to get away from school at such short notice, Mr Carlton.'

'Oh, it's fine. You got me out of a staff meeting so I owe you one.'

She utters a clipped laugh. 'So. Gabriel.' As she talks, she rearranges the pencils in her desk organizer. If she were one of the children in the school, I bet she'd be told to stop fiddling and focus. 'As you know, he's usually one of our star pupils, which is why his most recent behaviour is worrying us. He seems to have had a distinct change in attitude. Refusing to participate, being quite rude to staff. He seems very angry. Have either of you noticed that?'

I immediately jump to his defence. 'No, not at all. Are you sure you've got the right boy?'

Mrs Newman smiles at me as if to say 'Yes, I'm not totally incompetent,' and then she looks at Kate.

'How about you, Mrs Carlton, sorry, Miss . . .?'

'Just call me Kate.'

'Right. Kate. Have you noticed a change in Gabriel at home? I gather he spends the majority of his time living with you?'

Mrs Newman's opinion of our muddled surnames and fractured living arrangements is written clearly on her face.

Kate doesn't immediately respond and I join Mrs Newman in looking over at her questioningly. She rubs her right thumb down the length of the fingers on her left hand, one by one, and, like being pricked by a needle, I notice the sparkling engagement ring that she must've been hiding in a drawer somewhere up until now.

'He has been a bit angrier than usual. I figured it was just a stage he was going through.'

I swiftly turn my body towards her. 'News to me.'

'Oh, come on, Noah. It was nothing major. He's just been snapping at me more, answering back a bit, storming off to his room. Just kid stuff. I would've told you if I thought it was anything serious.'

Mrs Newman smiles at us both, like a marriage counsellor trying to ensure a productive session. 'Have there been any changes at home? Anything that might have caused him to feel angry?'

Kate shakes her head.

'Only the fact you're rushing into another marriage. It can't be easy for him to understand.'

Kate's cheeks flush. 'It's been two years, Noah. I wouldn't exactly call it rushing. Anyway, Gabriel is really excited about the wedding so I don't think it could be that.'

Mrs Newman straightens a pile of papers by tapping them on the desk. 'Well, maybe you could both just have a chat with him. See if there's anything bothering him. It would be such a shame for this to have a negative impact on his otherwise excellent academic performance. I'm afraid he will have to miss his playtime tomorrow for refusing to finish his story today.'

'We understand,' Kate says, like we are still a cohesive 'we' when actually she chose to shatter that, to break us apart into two stand-alone beings.

'I'll go and speak to him now. I'd like regular updates, please,' I say, adopting the role of serious educational professional when it suits me. 'Can you let me know how his behaviour is tomorrow?'

'Of course. I'll call you at the end of the day.'

'Thanks.'

'And please keep school posted about how his behaviour is at home, Kate,' Mrs Newman says, giving Kate a gentle smile.

Kate nods weakly but doesn't say anything.

When we get outside the head's office, Gabriel is sitting in the library with Finn showing him a book about space. When he sees us, his chin falls towards his chest and he looks up at us through his fringe with sad-dog eyes.

'Right, out to the car, please, boys. I want to speak to your father for a second.'

Kate's disciplinarian voice is so much more effective than mine and the boys respond immediately, Gabriel putting the book back on the shelf and then walking out of the school with his brother following closely behind, heads hung and in silence, towards the car. I'm not sure Finn realizes he's not even the one in trouble.

When the boys are far enough ahead of us that they can't hear anything, I'm expecting a tongue-lashing for embarrassing Kate in front of Mrs Newman, but instead, she turns to me with an almost childlike fear in her eyes.

'Do you really think it's the engagement? I thought he really loved Jerry. That it would feel more secure for him if we were married, so he knows Jerry's not going anywhere.'

And this is one of the many reasons my ex-wife is an infinitely better person than me. Not only does she turn the lens on herself instead of blaming other, much more obvious targets (i.e. me, flaky dad), she does it openly, in front of the person who just humiliated her. She makes me want to be a better person. And I almost manage it. I feel the comforting words she deserves tiptoe across my lips, but I can't quite bring myself to say them.

'Maybe he was just saying he liked him because he knew you'd be upset if he didn't? He's a sensitive kid like that. It wouldn't surprise me.'

'Has he ever said anything to you about not liking him?'

I'm so tempted to lie, but even I'm not quite that morally unsound. 'Well, no, not in so many words, but he knows I'd tell you so he might not say anything to me either.'

It's not officially a lie, but I know I should have told her all the good things Gabe says about Jerry.

Kate's face is full of anguish. 'I hope it's not that. I don't think it can be, can it?'

I can see she's on the verge of tears and feel the guilt seeping through my bones like the cold on a frosty day. 'Let me talk to him. I'll try to get to the bottom of it. We'll sort something out, don't worry.'

I place my hand in the dip of her lower back but she barely notices me. I can see on her face how terrified she is at the prospect that something she's done has upset the boys, and I hate myself that it makes me feel slightly hopeful – that maybe this could be the catalyst for the demise of her relationship with Jerry. She catches up with the boys and leads Finn to the car whilst I take Gabe to sit on a nearby bench.

'So, what's going on, buddy?'

Gabriel shrugs, his eyes focused on his feet.

'I'm not cross. I just want to know how you're feeling. Why you're feeling angry. Do you know?'

He nods, but doesn't speak.

'Is it about Mummy getting married?'

Waiting for his answer is like waiting to hear the results of a critical blood test.

Finally, he says, 'I'm angry with Mummy for saying yes when Jerry asked her.'

I nod, hoping he might elaborate, but he doesn't.

'Do you like Jerry?'

It shows what an awful person I am just how badly I want him to say no.

Instead, he says, 'I do like him. I'm really excited about the wedding. Well, sort of.'

'So what's up?'

Gabriel lifts his head and looks me right in the eyes. 'I'm angry with Mummy for making you sad.'

Not knowing what to do with my face, I search for an alternative focal point and settle on a red car with a number-plate that spells BUM. It's the only thing that stops me from blubbering like a baby.

'Why do you think I'm sad?' I ask, still not looking at him.

'I can just tell. I'm very wise, you know, Daddy.'

I put my hands on his cheeks – my beautiful, sensitive, insightful little boy. 'You are very wise. But you don't need to worry about me, OK? Of course it's a bit strange for me

93

that Mummy is getting married again and, you're right, I did feel a bit sad at first, but I'm fine now.'

Gabriel pulls away from me and sits up straight. 'Will you come to the wedding? Please, Daddy.'

I can't think of anything worse than watching Jerry's self-satisfied face as he makes his vows to *my* wife (for that is still how I see her). But how can I say no when my son is reaching out to me?

'Sure. We can bust some moves on the dance floor together and make ourselves sick with the chocolate fountain.'

Gabriel's face breaks into a smile for the first time since we picked him up. 'Can I tell Mummy you're coming?'

'Yeah, fine. Now be kind to her, OK, buddy? She's an amazing mummy and you're very lucky to have her. I'm fine. I'm happy for her.'

Before I have a chance to give him a kiss, Gabe runs to the car and climbs in. I give Kate a thumbs up and gesture with my hand that I'll call her. She mouths 'Thank you' and then they drive off, and I stand there wondering what the hell I've just agreed to.

CHAPTER EIGHT

'You're back?' Mimi puts her hands on her hips.

'Yeah. They hired this judgemental barmaid at the other pub I started going to who kept giving me grief about getting drunk and going home with a different woman each night, so I thought I'd sack it off and come back here.'

Mimi smiles. 'She sounds like a total pain in the arse.'

'She was.' I climb onto the bar stool. 'Plus, I thought perhaps you fancied coming home with me again?'

I'm breaking my rules, I know. But watching Kate drive away with my kids, back to her fiancé . . . right at this moment, sex with Mimi is what I need. I don't want to analyse it. It's like needing to scratch an itch or needing to eat when you're hungry. You don't think about it. You just do it.

'And I thought you were a safe bet. Don't tell me not even you are immune to my sexual prowess?'

'It would seem not.'

Mimi runs her hand through her red hair, her fringe immediately bobbing back across her eye. 'I enjoyed the other night, Noah. I really did. But, honestly, why do you want me to go home with you? Besides the obvious.' She smiles.

Because I'm scared of sitting in my flat alone with only my thoughts for company.

'I don't know. A bit of fun, that's all. Meaningless sex, that's what you called it, wasn't it?'

Mimi screws up her face. 'It's just the kids, the issues with your ex-wife . . . the one time was nice, don't get me wrong, but it's all a bit complicated for me. And I don't think you really want to have sex with me either. I mean, no more than you want to have sex with any of the women in here.'

We both look around the pub. There's a group of what looks like the school mum brigade on one table and an elderly woman sat with her husband at another.

I tilt my head towards the octogenarian. 'Well, maybe a bit more than with her.'

Mimi laughs. 'I'm doing you a favour really. Men have this horrible habit of falling in love with me and then when I tell them I'm not looking for a relationship, it always breaks their hearts.'

'Is that right?'

She pours me a JD and Coke and pushes it towards me.

'So how come you're so anti-commitment, anyway?' I ask, taking a large sip.

'With you? Well, where shall I start?'

'Very funny. You know what I mean.'

Mimi reaches into her pocket and gets out her phone, tapping on something before holding it out for me to see. It's a travel app showing the countdown of 156 days until a trip of some sort. 'I'm going travelling. I've only booked the first bit so far but I'm going to start in India and then explore more of Asia. Depends how much money I can save by then if I travel on to Australia or not.'

Despite there being only about a five-year age gap between us, at times like this Mimi seems so much younger than me.

'Sounds good.'

'Did you ever do the whole backpacking thing?' she asks.

I shake my head. 'I got married young. We knew we wanted kids pretty quick so all our money went on getting a mortgage. There wasn't really a chance.'

Mimi looks thoughtful, and I wonder if she pities me. I've not exactly made it sound very exciting. But in reality it was. Saving up for our very own house together, getting the keys and eating chips out of the paper on the kitchen floor because we didn't yet have a table or tableware. Finding out Kate was pregnant and ruminating on what our child would look like, which of our personality traits he or she would have.

'Do you regret it at all? Settling down so young?' Mimi's question cuts into my thoughts and I must take longer than expected to respond because she adds, 'I don't mean do you regret having your kids or anything, just that you were so young when you did it. You don't hear of it much these days, do you?'

'No, I don't regret it.'

I regret fucking it up.

Mimi nods, her eyes looking into mine and, for a moment, it feels like she's looking into my soul, seeing all the bits I try my best to keep hidden. Then she seems to shake it off, putting her hands on her hips as if she's ready to make an announcement.

'Do you know what I think you really need?'

'No, but I'm sure you're going to enlighten me.'

'I think you need a friend.'

'Because I don't have any already?'

Mimi shrugs. 'You spend a lot of time drinking alone.'

Although I try not to show it, her comment stings. Because she's right. I don't have many friends – not real ones. After Kate and I split, all our couple friends seemed to side with her. And the blokes at work don't really count. There's no way I could have a proper conversation with them.

'I've got plenty of friends, thank you,' I lie.

'OK then. Well, maybe you just need a friend like me.'

I raise my eyebrows. 'I've never really had a female friend before. They always struggle to keep their hands off me.'

Mimi laughs. 'I think I'll manage.' She takes my empty glass and puts it behind the bar. 'In fact, I'm not working on Saturday, if you fancy a coffee? Unless you've got the boys?'

My initial reaction is to turn the offer down. But actually chatting to Mimi is quite often the highlight of my day.

'It's Kate's weekend. Coffee sounds good.'

'You can always sneak in a hip flask if you can't cope that long without alcohol.'

'Actually, you'll notice I'm only having the one drink tonight.' I take my coat off the back of the bar stool and start to put it on.

'Not going to hit on someone else now I've turned you down?'

'No. Thank you. I'm going home to my book and a cup of cocoa.'

Mimi smiles. 'So, should we exchange numbers then, friend?'

'I suppose so. As long as you can resist calling me every second.' I hold my hand out and Mimi gives me her phone. I type in my number and click 'add contact', labelling it 'Naughty Noah' before handing it back.

She looks at the screen and laughs. 'You're a dick.'

I put some money on the bar. 'I know. See you Saturday.'

*

There are times when I'd like to give the school curriculum to the wise, distant authority figure who devised it and ask them to teach it to a group of children as yet unable to wipe their own backsides. Today's wondrous R E circletime talking point is: what fascinates you about the natural world? I've prompted them with a slide show about amazing animals, given my own excellent example (driving to work noticing how birds all fly together). Even Mrs Watson contributed something valuable for a change (about tides being pulled in and out by the moon) so we should be good to go. I get the Talking Tiger (he doesn't talk – it's a soft toy I pass round with the instruction that only the child holding the tiger is allowed to speak – basically a more humane version of a gag) and give it to the child nearest me.

'The way the birds fly together,' Jasmine says, then passes the tiger on.

'Great, yep, you think that's fascinating too.'

'At the seaside when the sea comes up.' Tommy this time.

I can see a pattern forming. At least they must've been listening.

The tiger continues around the circle to Darcy. 'Let me guess, the birds or the sea?'

Darcy stares at me as if I've suddenly morphed into a zombie.

'Anything you find fascinating about the world around us, Darcy?'

Darcy's eyes seem to look straight through me, as she sits in silence.

'The sea, perhaps? Do you like the waves at the seaside, Darcy? Or the animals? Which one's your favourite?' I point to the pictures on the board and Darcy nods, almost imperceptibly, but I take it as a response to one of my questions, remove the tiger from her hands and pass it on to Harley.

'Mummy got me a Transformer and it's a Bumblebee one . . .'

Now Harley has the opposite problem. Once he's given the floor, there's really no shutting him up.

'That's great, Harley, but we were talking about what fascinates us about the world.'

'Transformers are fascinating how you change them because first they're a car and then a robot.'

'Yes, well, I suppose they are, but we were thinking more about the natural world, like trees, animals, that sort of thing. Never mind, though. Can you pass the Talking Tiger on now, please?'

'And she got me another Transformer. It's Optimus Prime. He is so cool. You can do battles with him and flips and . . .'

'Time to pass the Talking Tiger on now, Harley.'

'. . . he turns into this awesome truck and you can smash it into other cars. It always . . .'

The only solution, as unprofessional as it may be, is to have a tug of war with Harley, wrenching the Talking Tiger out of his hands and passing it on to the next person.

'I think rainbows are fascinating because they're lots of different colours but it's always in the same order.'

I nearly drop my whiteboard pen on the child sitting next to me.

'Exactly, James. That's exactly what I'm talking about. Rainbows are fascinating.'

I feel like doing a little dance around the room, but then Charlie grabs the tiger. 'My mummy went to hospital and she pushed my baby brother out of her belly button.'

'Great example, Charlie. Moving swiftly on then . . .'

Rescued from the brink of awkward conversations 101, I'm happy when the suggestions return to the tried and tested birds, tide and newly approved rainbows, and the introduction of that good old nature's miracle: the remote-control car.

*

Harley has been kept in yet again, this time for gouging a chunk of flesh out of another boy's face, so lucky old me gets to enjoy my coffee and KitKat with Harley for company, despite the fact I've got a load of observations to input on to the computer that were due at least a week ago. We sit in the classroom and he rocks back and forth on his chair.

'So how's Mummy at the moment?'

'She's not poorly now so we went to the toyshop and got the Transformers like I said.'

'That's good.'

'Well, I think she might be poorly again today because she didn't wake up for breakfast.'

I hold Harley's chair still, the repetitive noise of it hitting the floor like a constant punch in the temple. 'Did you have any breakfast?'

He shakes his head.

'Do you want some?'

'Yes, please.' He says it in such a way, as if I'm offering him a brand-new Xbox, that I feel immediately guilty for despairing of him ninety-five per cent of the time.

Once I've poured some of the cereal that I keep in the cupboard into a bowl and added some milk from one of the school cartons, I hand it to Harley and he tucks straight in. When I was with Kate, she'd always cook me a proper breakfast, adamant that I needed the energy for a day in the classroom. But now I rarely even bother to put myself a piece of toast on, instead keeping a box of cereal in the cupboard at school for when I'm absolutely ravenous by break time.

'Did Mummy bring you to school?'

'Yes, I tapped her and tapped her because the clock said nine and I know that means we're late for school, but she wouldn't get up, but then she did in the end.'

'Good.'

Watching Harley shoving the cereal into his mouth like a starving orphan takes me back. Ben and I soon learnt how to make our own breakfast. Some days Mum would be there with croissants or pancakes, anything we asked for, but other times she couldn't even face getting out of bed. By about age eight, when Dad being home of an evening became a lot more sporadic and Mum's ability to manage a full day reduced, Ben could even make a simple evening meal. Depending on what was in the freezer, the three options were always pizza, fish fingers or chicken nuggets, but we were happy with that. Sometimes, there was a tub of ice cream in the freezer and we'd help ourselves to huge bowls and eat it until we felt sick. Occasionally, the freezer was empty so we'd have to search the cupboards. We attempted baked beans on toast once, but we couldn't get the tin of beans open so we ended up with crisps on toast. It was a reasonable alternative. Looking at it as an adult, I can see it wasn't ideal, but those memories are still strangely surrounded with a fuzzy warm glow. It was like being in *Home Alone,* except I had a partner in crime to enjoy the freedom with and no burglars trying to break into the house.

I turn my attention back to Harley, scraping the last of the cornflakes from around the side of the bowl. 'Shall we have a special signal for days when you haven't had any breakfast? How about if you put your thumb down, I'll know and you can help yourself to some of my cornflakes?'

Harley holds out his hand and points his thumb to the floor. 'Like this?'

'Exactly. Now come on, we better go and get the others from the playground. You can be my helper, OK? Check they're all in a straight line and being quiet.'

'OK, cool.'

I put my coffee cup and Harley's bowl into the sink and head out to get the rest of the class, whilst Harley skips beside me, taking hold of my hand.

*

After school, I'm just about to take Harley down to the office when I spot Emma heading towards the classroom, her eyes barely leaving the ground.

'Come on, Harls,' she calls.

I put my hand on Harley's head to stop him running off and try to buy myself some time to talk to Emma on her own. 'Harley, just go and find that picture you did earlier. The one of the pirate ship so we can show Mummy.'

'OK.' Harley skips off, pride lighting up his face, and it makes me feel immediately guilty for not praising him more often.

I turn to Emma. 'Look, I hope you didn't mind me calling Mimi in the other week. We couldn't manage to get hold of you and Harley was in a bit of a state.'

She doesn't look up at me. 'I didn't have my phone on me.'

'It's fine. I just hope Mimi told you that my door's always open if you need anything. If you're struggling with Harley at home, we could put things in place together that might help.'

'I'm not struggling with him.'

'Right, OK, well . . .'

Harley comes running out with his picture. 'Look, Mummy, do you like it?' Emma gives it a very quick glance and then nods. 'It's great. Come on now, we need to get home.'

'Can I take it with me to put on my wall?' Harley asks me.

'Sure.'

'Thanks.' He gives me a big smile and Emma puts her hand on the back of his head and guides him out the playground, and I head back into the classroom, a niggling feeling in my stomach that's hard to shake, like I'm not doing enough. Sometimes when I look at Harley, it's like looking at four-year-old me and I, for one, know how long-lasting the effects of a home environment like that can be. But maybe I'm just projecting. It's easy to jump to false conclusions in this job, and besides, Mimi seemed to think Emma was doing fine.

I go to my desk and start to upload photos of the class to the parent communication system, but soon lose the will to live, shut my computer down and head home, wishing my boys were there so I could give them a big hug and tell them how much I love them.

CHAPTER NINE

The café Mimi's chosen is annoyingly busy so we're queuing out the door and people keep bumping into me to get past, even though I can't imagine where they're going as I'm standing in the queue, in front of them. It's one of those slightly too cool places that I tend to avoid now I've got kids, knowing they'd only show me up, shouting and fighting over what cake they wanted, holding up the queue of people who are yet to have any awareness of what being a parent is really like.

'Do you want to share a cake?'

It's only a casual suggestion – I'm being friendly – but Mimi glares at me as if I've just proposed killing a small furry animal in front of her whilst we wait.

'OK. I'm guessing you really like cake?'

'It's my one vice.'

'Really? Cake is your only vice? Come off it. There must be something worse than that?'

'Like your sex and alcohol addiction?'

'Maybe.'

'Seriously, I really don't have one. Just cake.'

Mimi's a funny one – on the one hand, she's super-chatty and open, no holds barred, and yet, when the spotlight's on her, she seems to shut up shop and I can't help wondering if she's hiding something behind that happy-go-lucky exterior.

We finally reach the counter and, under strict instruction from Mimi, I order two cappuccinos and two slices of cake. Once our coffees are finally made, I carry the tray and we search the café for somewhere to sit down. After a few more bumps on the arm, causing me to spill some of the drinks (*am I invisible today?*), we spot a young couple leaving and swoop in on their table in the corner.

'So, tell me more about the singing stuff. Do you write your own songs?' I ask, settling into my chair and wincing as I burn my tongue on my drink.

'Steady on, Noah. Are you actually trying to get to know me?'

'I thought that's what friends did.'

'Ah, I was seeing my role more as rescuing you, to be honest. I didn't foresee you asking questions about me.'

'Firstly, I don't need rescuing.'

Mimi holds up her fingers in a pincer position to gesture 'a little bit' and I lightly kick her under the table.

'And secondly, I am interested in the world beyond myself, you know.'

'Really? OK then, but there's nothing to tell. Yes, I used to write my own songs, but as I said, no one was listening so I gave up.'

'So how long were you performing for? Did you have a manager or anything? Maybe you just needed someone to get you better gigs.'

Mimi picks up her coffee and takes a slow slip. 'I had a manager. It didn't work out. I'm just not good enough.'

'I bet you're great. You should try again.'

Mimi puts her coffee cup down with force, causing it to clunk on the table. 'Noah, please. Can we just drop it, yeah?'

It's unlike Mimi to appear riled, so I decide to leave it. 'OK. Sorry, just asking.'

Mimi sighs. 'I know. Thank you for asking.' She tucks into her cake, breaking off large bits and shovelling them into her mouth.

'Good cake?' I ask, in an attempt to change the subject and release the tension.

Mimi's face softens and she nods, her mouth full.

Then I try some of mine. To be fair, it *is* delicious. 'You were right. This cake's not for sharing.'

'Told you.' Mimi licks the icing off her fingers. 'So how's Harley doing now? I spoke to Emma about what you said and she said things are good at home.'

I nod, conscious that I shouldn't say too much, but also keen to check up on Harley. 'He's doing OK. Could just be teething problems. So are you close then? You and your sister?'

'Yeah, we see each other a couple of times a week. And I adore Harley. I never realized how much you could love a nephew.'

Although I don't share quite the same level of fondness for my nieces, it's a relief to hear that Mimi's so closely involved. Makes me a little more optimistic that perhaps I've been unduly worried about him.

'He's a good kid really,' I say, and I mean it. As much as he exhausts me, there's something very likeable about him.

'He really is. I can imagine him being a bit of a monkey at times but he's so loving. His heart's definitely in the right place.' Mimi scrapes up the last few crumbs of her

108

cake, putting them in her mouth before dropping her fork on her plate with a clunk. 'Anyway, talking of kids, do you fancy going to the zoo?'

'The zoo?'

'Yes, the place where they have all the animals in cages for people to stand and guffaw at.'

'I know what a zoo is. I just wonder why you want to go there, and with me, of all people?'

'It's just around the corner. I like animals. I have no answer for the "with you" bit.'

I consider the alternative – going back to the flat, eating junk and watching *Game of Thrones* repeats. 'OK. Let's go to the zoo.'

*

I seem to have a habit of always sitting down to watch an animal enclosure just as said animals start mating. It's happened to me twice with the kids, cue lots of questions about 'Why is that animal attacking the other one?' or 'Look, he's clinging on to the other one's bottom and it's trying to run away,' (much to the amusement of unaccompanied adults around me) and it's happening to me now, sitting in front of the gorilla enclosure with Mimi, trying to enjoy some lunch.

Mimi raises her burger to her mouth but then lowers it again. She gawps at the gorillas, her mouth hanging open. 'Oh. My. God. He is actually doing what I think he's doing, isn't he?'

'Yes. Yes, I think he is.'

'Look at her,' Mimi continues, fascinated. 'She's like, "Get on with it, love. It's bloody uncomfortable down here." Ha. Isn't it brilliant?'

'Absolutely.'

It was bad enough with the kids, but watching the act of sexual intercourse next to someone you recently slept with is nothing short of excruciating.

Mimi takes her eyes off the gorillas for a second to look at me. 'You're actually embarrassed, aren't you? Cocky sex machine Noah is turning red at the sight of a perfectly natural act?'

The more she focuses on my face, the hotter it seems to burn.

Mimi laughs, slapping me on the thigh. 'Don't worry, I'm not comparing your style to his.'

I cover my face with my hands. 'Seriously. Stop. I cannot have this conversation sober.'

'Ah, shy Noah. It's actually quite cute.'

I try to ignore Mimi's mocking, focus on looking straight ahead and wait for the heat in my cheeks to dissipate. After what feels like hours, the silverback is done and he strides away, hunts down a stray banana and starts eating.

'Show's over. Come on, let's go and see what other animal porn we can find.' Mimi takes my hand and pulls me towards the reptile house and I stumble along after her.

*

On the way home, we walk across the Downs. It's a beautiful day. One of those rare days you sometimes get in

March – when it's warm enough not to need a jacket. We sit on a bench with take-out coffee and I turn my face to the sky, enjoying the feel of the sunshine on my skin. It's weird, but during the winter you forget how good it feels, the warmth, and then when it returns it feels like a gift, a blessing.

Mimi points her coffee cup towards a family walking along, the parents storming off and leaving their little one crying and waving his arms around. 'Poor little mite. Why would you treat your kid like that?'

'Clearly said by someone who doesn't have kids.'

Mimi turns her head to look at me. 'Seriously? You treat your boys like that?'

I shrug. 'When they deserve it, yeah. Perhaps he's being a little brat.'

'Oh, come on, look at that face. Does he look like a brat?'

He's a cute kid, I'll give her that. All big blue eyes and pouting lips. He looks a little bit like Gabe did when he was a toddler.

'Yeah, just wait until that cute little face is waking you up at five a.m. and screaming at you because he wanted Shreddies, not cornflakes, you incompetent fool. Suddenly it doesn't seem so cute.'

'I don't know. I think he'd always look cute to me. Look, even covered in snot and tears, he's gorgeous.'

'Your children would be hideous, though. Look at the gene pool.'

Mimi looks down at her hands and when she looks up all the earlier humour from her eyes has vanished.

'What's wrong? I was only joking.'

Mimi shakes her head. 'I know. I'm fine.'

She looks anything but fine, but before I have a chance to delve any deeper, a dog comes hurtling over to us, immediately shoving its head into Mimi's lap. She cowers towards me as if she's just been approached by a tyrannosaurus rex rather than a sappy-eyed beagle, then crosses her legs and holds her coffee in the air. 'Go away. Seriously, Noah, get it off me.'

I stroke the dog's head and encourage it to come towards me, but it's persistent in its pursuit of Mimi.

She scours the area for the owner, a cheery-looking middle-aged man heading towards us carrying a tennis-ball launcher in his hand.

'Oh, don't worry, he's really friendly,' the man says with a smile.

Mimi moves further towards me. 'Yeah, a bit too friendly if you ask me.'

The man looks at her as if she just swore at him, and not just one of the tame ones like 'bloody' or 'shit', but one that, when you write it down, you have to use an asterisk to replace the vowel. Then he grabs his dog by the collar and storms off.

'What is it with bloody dog owners? They think the whole world loves their four-legged friends as much as they do. How would he feel if I sauntered over to him and started sniffing *his* crotch?'

'He'd probably be delighted.'

Mimi shoots a look my way and her anger softens into amusement.

'Is this the wrong time to tell you I have a Great Dane hidden in the basement underneath the flat?'

'Looks like I won't be coming over to yours ever again then.'

I smile, but then it occurs to me that the day is nearly over and that soon Mimi will leave and I'll have to go home alone, with nothing to look forward to, haunted by thoughts of Kate and the boys in their happy home. 'In fact, do you want to come back to mine? Not in a dodgy way, of course. We could get take-out, watch a video or something?'

Mimi furrows her eyebrows. 'How old actually are you, Noah? Even the DVD is pretty archaic now – a video?'

'A digital file, is that better? We could watch a digital file together.'

Mimi laughs. 'OK, as long as I can choose.'

*

After we've eaten curry and watched a film, some pretentious art-house thing that Mimi kept trying to convince me was 'actually really powerful', I take our plates through to the kitchen and come back to the sofa with two glasses of wine.

'Is that your mum?' Mimi bows her head towards a framed photograph on my fireplace.

I nod and take a sip of my drink, hoping it signals the end of the conversation.

'She was very pretty.'

Another nod.

'How did she die, if you don't mind me asking?'

Usually, I find Mimi's inquisitiveness refreshing. But with this topic of conversation, I just want to shut her down. 'Cancer.'

It's an easy lie. Cancer is so often the cause of death that it tends not to even muster a 'Which one?' and when it does, again it's an easy selection – breast, bowel, ovarian. No more questions asked.

'Sorry.'

I shrug.

'And is that your ex-wife and your children with you in that one there?'

I look at the photograph of the four of us in Sweden. We stayed in this little hut in the forest. We found it on Airbnb and, when we arrived, it felt like being in authentic Sweden. There wasn't even a working toilet, just a hut in the garden with a hole in a bench and two buckets of earth to throw over what you'd produced (which the boys thought was hilarious, of course). It was so peaceful out there among the trees. The weather was unseasonably hot for May and we spent the days foraging in the forest and taking the neighbour's boat out on the lake. It's still my favourite-ever holiday.

'Yeah. I suppose I should take it down really. I'm not sure you're meant to have a photo of your ex-wife on your mantelpiece, but it just reminds me of a really happy time.'

'I don't think you're breaking any divorcee laws,' Mimi says with a smile, but I wonder what she really thinks – whether she thinks it's a bit tragic. 'She's very beautiful, by the way. And your boys are gorgeous.'

'Thanks. As you can see, they take after their mum.'

She gives me a knowing smile. 'So I'm guessing your anger the other night about her marrying someone else – it wasn't just a matter of respect?'

I scratch my scalp. 'Do you want the honest answer or the "I'm a bloke, nothing bothers me" answer?'

'Oh, why don't you go crazy and hit me with a bit of honesty.'

I take a deep breath. 'I feel like if she marries him, I'll lose my family forever and my whole life will be over.'

'Blimey, I didn't mean *that* honest. So why did you split up anyway?'

In a way I wish one of us had had an affair, fallen for someone else, because then it would be easier to explain. It's not so easy to convey the rationale behind the Houdini Great Escape moments that eventually caused the demise of my marriage.

The first time it happened was when I came to the realization that if I lost Kate, I would shrivel up into a ball and die. It seems a little dramatic now, but that's how it felt at the time. So very young and so madly in love that we stayed on the phone to each other all night just so we could hear each other breathing. Mum nearly killed me when she saw the phone bill, but I don't think it was really the money she was bothered about, more having to share me with someone else. I understand how she felt a little bit more now, but back then I couldn't work out why I kept hurting her or how to stop.

On the day in question, Kate and I had taken a picnic down by the weir and were perched on a rock with our feet dangling in the water. She started talking about when we were older and who we'd end up marrying and how many kids we'd both have. She joked she'd marry a bloke in a rock band and I'd probably marry a model, and I'm sure I had what can only be described as a panic attack. I started sweating. I felt dizzy. I thought I was going to pass out or throw up or both. I didn't say anything, just chucked the remains of my sandwich into the water, watching it travel down the river with the current and ignoring Kate's questions about whether I was OK. I dropped her home and made my excuses to leave. I called Mum and told her I was staying at Kate's house, but instead I drove all the way to Exeter to see Ben. He took me out clubbing, we got wasted – well, he got sensibly drunk and I got completely off my face and spent the early hours throwing up in his dormitory sink. I blanked each and every one of Kate's fifty-seven calls and didn't reply to any of her numerous texts asking me what the hell was going on.

A few days later, when we were lying on Kate's bed, my fingers twiddling her long, wavy hair, I told her everything and she explained she'd only said all that stuff about marrying someone else to test the water, to see if I was feeling what she was feeling, which it turned out I was. I think she thought once we got married, once I had the security of the ring on my finger, the running away would stop, but it was never that simple for me. And then when Mum died, the feelings, the fear, it all just intensified, and the blowouts got more extreme, longer, their effect more damaging. Until Kate seemed to grow immune to it all. She didn't bother to keep calling. She barely batted an eyelid when I returned, stinking and bruised. I guess I knew deep down that was the beginning of the end.

'I wasn't a good enough husband. Or father, for that matter.'

I get the sense Mimi wants to ask me more but she seems to brush it off, like an insect that lands on her shoulder.

'And you're sure there's no chance of getting her back?'

'She's marrying someone else, isn't she?'

Mimi shrugs.

'I mean, we've had breaks in the past,' I continue. 'But never for this long and there was never anyone else. I don't think Jerry's right for her, not by a long shot, and we have the kids, but . . .'

'So why don't you fight for her?' Mimi says, looking suddenly animated. 'If she means that much to you?'

I shake my head. 'I'm pretty sure she knows how I feel. Besides, she knows where I am.'

'I'm sure the alcoholism and sleeping around is really appealing.'

I roll my eyes.

'Look, I don't know exactly why your marriage failed,' she powers on, 'but you said you should've been a better husband. A better father. So why don't you show her how you've changed? Make her see what she's throwing away? Looking at that photo of you guys, you obviously had something pretty special.'

I thought so.

'Oh, I don't know. She probably *is* better off without me.'

'So make yourself better. So that the best thing for her *is* to be with you. You've got two kids together. You were obviously very happy once upon a time. It's got to be worth a try.'

It feels like she's drip-feeding me steroids, slowly making me feel more pumped up. Maybe she's right. Maybe I should fight for Kate. I was the one she chose all those years ago. Not Jerry. I was her first love. Maybe things could be different this time.

But then I have a thought that's accompanied by a sort of nausea, slowly rising in my throat.

'What if I make myself better and she still chooses him?'

Mimi looks at me as if I'm a child first discovering that the world isn't quite the wonderful place I thought it was. 'Then you move on with no regrets.'

I raise my eyebrows.

'OK, with fewer regrets.'

'So what do I need to change?'

Mimi's face forms a what-don't-you-need-to-change expression but she says, 'Well, what did you do that makes you think you weren't a good husband?'

It's hard to look back on a relationship, particularly one that lasted eleven years, and be objective about it. It's always the really big highs and the crashing lows that you remember, not the humdrum day-to-day stuff. When I wasn't buggering off for the night, or the weekend, I think I was an OK husband, maybe even better than OK. I could be grumpy sometimes, after a tough day at work when I'd come home to find her cuddled up in her pyjamas watching a film with the boys – the house a complete mess around them – piles of washing-up by the sink, toys on every surface, various garments scattered across the floor. Sometimes I'd say things like, 'You're at home all day, surely you could do something?' or 'Why are you so tired when you've just been sitting around having coffee mornings with your friends?' But I'd always apologize before the day was out. I'd tell her that I recognized how hard it was to look after the boys, how she was doing an amazing job, how proud I was of her.

I think I was quite romantic. I'd write her heartfelt or cheeky notes and leave them in various places in the house, like in the fridge or in the little pot where she kept her car keys, so she would find them throughout the day. Once, I made the mistake of putting one in the toaster. In my defence, it was sticking out a mile, but she must have been half-asleep or distracted by the boys, as she put a piece of toast in the other slot and pressed the lever down, then wondered why the hell the toaster was suddenly on fire.

I'd buy her gifts from the supermarket on my way home from work on a Friday. It was only little stuff: a book she'd been looking at, a mug, a magazine, a cupcake with a heart on top, that sort of thing. She knew when she married me there were never going to be trips to the Bahamas or meals at those fancy restaurants where they don't even put the prices on the menu. But I tried my best to make her feel special.

We managed to laugh at most things. Not always, of course. But often. Like when one of the boys was having a huge tantrum – I'd stand behind him and imitate his behaviour and Kate would struggle to maintain her cross-parent face. Or when we were blaming each other for forgetting to put the recycling out and we'd stop mid-argument and say, 'Are we seriously arguing about the recycling?' and then she'd wrap her hands around my neck and kiss me.

So maybe I shouldn't say goodbye to my marriage so easily. Because, to me at least, a lot of the time it seemed like such a good one.

'She felt she couldn't trust me.'

'Why? Did you cheat on her?'

'Oh, God, no. Never. It wasn't that she couldn't trust me with other women. She couldn't trust me not to bugger off for the weekend when things got too much. Or to miss parents' evening because I was a drunken mess somewhere. Or to not come home after work some days.'

Mimi looks confused. 'So why did you do those things?'

I shake my head. 'If I knew that, Mimi, I wouldn't be here, regretting losing the love of my life.'

Mimi nods slowly and I get the sense she feels like she's signed up to more than she bargained for, like agreeing to a bank card that gives you free insurance and cinema tickets and then realizing you have to pay a monthly fee.

'Well, I think you need to show her she can trust you, then. That you're dependable. Start small – get the flat straight, cut down on the drinking, help the boys with their homework, that sort of thing.'

That doesn't feel very small, but I nod enthusiastically. 'Will you help me? I could be your improvement project.'

Mimi looks me up and down. 'I do love a project, I suppose. But I usually like to go for something more achievable.'

I shoot her a look.

'OK then. I can't promise it's going to work though, Noah. But it's got to be worth a try, right?'

'I guess.'

'So how long have we got? When's she getting married?'

'May the fifth.'

Mimi pulls out her phone and starts scrolling through the calendar. 'OK. So we've got six weeks. That's achievable, I think.'

I'm not entirely convinced but, after Mimi's gone, I lie in bed and think about what she said – the thought of getting my family back like a lottery win, the odds solidly stacked against me. But in the same irrational way you feel a burst of excitement at filling out your numbers, I automatically feel better at the thought of at least holding a ticket.

CHAPTER TEN

'What do you mean, you've bought him a bike? Why didn't you ask me? It could've been a joint present.'

I tuck my phone between my shoulder and my ear so that my hands are free to open another beer. I *am* going to cut down on the drinking but right at this moment I need beer number two.

'It was all a bit last minute. He went over to one of his school friends and had a go on his bike and became obsessed with it. Jerry chose him one at the weekend. He's good with that sort of thing. I guessed you'd already got him something.'

Come off it. She knows I wouldn't be that organized.

'Well, I've got a few ideas, but I was going to pick something up after school tomorrow.'

'Noah, it's our little family party for him after school tomorrow. You have remembered, haven't you?'

'Of course I have. I'm going to get it on the way.'

'Nothing like leaving it until the last minute.' Kate lets out a somewhat derisive snort.

I can almost hear Mimi whispering in my ear to let it go, rise above it, be understanding, but I'm not sure I'm capable. I don't want her making these sorts of decisions without me. It just makes me feel like I'm being pushed further out.

'You could always get him a bell for it or something?' Kate continues.

Now it's my turn to snort. 'Great. What did Mummy get you? A bike. What about Daddy? Oh, he got a bell.'

Kate laughs. 'Look, I'm sorry. I didn't mean to piss you off. Get him whatever you want.'

I'm tempted to buy him his first car, just to make sure I get in there first.

'You don't get it, do you? Your first bike is a big deal. It's a rite of passage.'

'Look, give me some money and we can say it's from both of us, OK?'

'No, forget it. It's too late now. It's the principle.'

'Stop being silly. Just bring me seventy pounds tomorrow. We'll go halves.'

Seventy pounds? What's this bike made out of? Gold? Is it diamond-encrusted?

'No. I'm going to choose something myself. Something awesome. Something that blows your bike out the water.'

Kate laughs again. 'I look forward to seeing it. I'll see you after school tomorrow. Finn's really excited you're coming.'

'Of course I'm coming. It's my son's fifth birthday.'

I can almost hear Kate's exasperation. 'See you tomorrow, Noah. Try to wake up in a better mood, yeah?'

Operation 'Get Kate Back' has not started well.

*

I'm late (again, not a great start but it's because it took me ages to choose the perfect present) so I miss out on the party food, but get there just in time to see Finn blowing out the candles on his cake with gusto, showering the product of hours of Kate's hard work and dedication with his germ-ridden spittle.

'My baby is five.' Kate picks Finn up and covers his face with kisses. 'How did you get to be five?'

'I growed,' he says, matter-of-fact.

Everybody laughs. 'That you did, my darling. You did grow.'

She puts him down and he runs off to the lounge to play with Gabe, leaving me stuck in the dining room with Kate, Jerry, and Kate's parents for company.

I'm pretty sure Kate's parents were delighted when we split up and she found good old dependable Jerry. I think they liked me at first. You never really know, I suppose. But after a few times of me going AWOL, their demeanour changed. Her dad no longer bothered to get me the beer I like when we went for Sunday lunch. The banter with her mum became a bit more pointed, a bit less affectionate. It's fair enough. Their instinct is to protect their daughter. I just sometimes wish I'd had more of a chance to explain, not that I'm sure what I would've said.

'Good to see you, Noah.' Kate's dad, Ted, shakes my hand firmly. 'You're looking well.'

'Come on, Dad, don't lie. He looks like crap,' Kate says, ruffling my hair (which, to be fair to her, is in need of a cut).

I wonder if the ease and warmth with which we still tease each other pisses Jerry off. If it does, he doesn't show it. Instead, he laughs in a carefree manner at his fiancée's joke.

'Hello, Noah.' Sue, Kate's mum, gives me a tentative kiss on the cheek.

'Nice to see you, Sue. Now you really do look great.'

She smiles. 'Always the charmer.'

'I mean it.'

She takes my hand in hers and taps it. 'Thank you.'

'Right, shall we go and join the birthday boy?' Jerry says and everyone picks up their drinks and follows him through.

In the lounge, the boys are fighting over the big helium balloon that Kate's parents have bought for Finn.

'Hey, it's my birthday,' Finn says, yanking the ribbon from Gabe's hand.

'But I had it first.' Gabe pushes Finn over so that he bashes into the sofa and starts crying, holding his head as if he's got concussion.

'Too rough, Gabe,' Jerry says, putting his hands on my eldest son's shoulders.

And although he's right, it was too rough and Gabe was out of line, it still makes me want to punch him in the face.

Kate picks Finn up and sits with him on the sofa, Finn snugly cradled in her lap. She wipes the tears from his cheeks and pushes his wild, curly hair off his face. 'Shall we open some presents?'

Finn's face changes immediately and Sue passes him their gift. He climbs down off Kate's knee and takes his present to the carpet, ripping off the wrapping paper.

'What is it?' He holds up the box of brightly coloured modelling clay and wrinkles his nose.

'It's Fimo,' Kate says. 'You can use it to make things for your figures and then you put them in the oven and they go hard.'

'Oh, cool,' Finn says, but there's more than a hint of disappointment on his face. 'Can I have another one?'

Kate looks at me. 'Noah, do you want to give him yours?'

It's a tricky decision. If I go first, there'll probably be a short spell of him loving it, but then when Kate reveals the bike, it's highly likely my gift will be overshadowed and quickly forgotten. However, if Kate goes first, he might be so wrapped up in trying out his bike that he's not even bothered about opening mine. I decide on option two. He can't ride a bike without stabilizers yet so, once the initial excitement passes, he'll soon tire of it and I'll be able to sweep in, the awesome-present-yielding hero.

'No, you go first. I'll give him my present later.'

Kate eyes me suspiciously, like she suspects foul play. 'OK then. Well, we need to go outside for ours, Finn. Do you want to come and see?'

Finn looks up at Kate expectantly. 'Is it a bike?'

Jerry puts his hand on top of Finn's head. 'Why don't you come and see?'

It takes all the willpower I've got to stop myself from reaching out and chopping off Jerry's hand. Instead, we all follow Kate outside and there in the front garden, adorned with a huge bow, is Finn's first proper bike. He and Gabe both run towards it and Finn jumps on, ready to pedal off down the drive.

Jerry races towards him and grabs the handlebars. 'Hold on, buddy. We need to teach you to ride it first,' he says, laughing.

And there it is again, like when you eat a piece of cake where you've burnt the chocolate, the bitter taste in my mouth.

'Let's put your helmet on,' Jerry continues. 'Then we can give it a go.' Jerry looks over to me, as if he's just remembered that I, the provider of the sperm that brought Finn into creation, am there. 'Your dad will hold on to the back to keep you steady.'

'Yeah, come on, mister. Let's get you cycling,' Kate says, putting Finn's helmet on. Then he starts to pedal, me running along behind holding his saddle.

His feet keep slipping off the pedals and it's hurting my back to keep stopping him from falling over, but we continue to do it because he wants to and it's his birthday. Besides, I'm trying to prove to Kate that I'm not completely useless. So when I'm tiring and would usually have thrown in the towel, persuading Finn to come in with the promise of sugar or screens, I keep going, but I can't help thinking that Jerry might have done a better job. That he would've been more proficient at teaching Finn the techniques to effectively ride a bike without falling off. More patient.

Finally, Finn gives up. I click my back into place and we go inside for my glory moment. Once we're all sitting back down in the lounge, I hand Finn his present.

'Well, it's not quite a bike, but I hope you like it.'

Finn opens the present and immediately starts tearing at the box. 'I love it!' he shouts, jumping up and down, battling with the excessive packaging. You'd think it was a real gun, it's that hard to get out. I take it off him and use the keys from my pocket to slice at the plastic fasteners.

'A gun?' Kate says, shooting me a look.

'What? You let him have those mini ones.'

'But look at it, Noah.' Luckily, her expression is one more of amusement than anger and, after looking over at Finn's outright joy, she gives me a smile that says '*Touché*'.

'It's awesome,' Finn says, circling the room pointing it at everyone. 'Let's load the bullets.'

Kate's parents stand up. 'Right, well I think that's enough excitement for one day. Nice to see you, Noah.'

I stay sitting on the sofa and accompany my wave with a weak smile.

Jerry stands up, ever the gentleman, tapping Ted on the back and then embracing Sue in a hug. 'Lovely to see you as always.'

'You too, Jerry. See you on Sunday for lunch,' Sue says, kissing him on the cheek.

'Looking forward to it.'

I wonder if he's really looking forward to it or if he moans to Kate about going like I used to. If he's not being genuine, he's a very good actor.

In turn, Sue and Ted give Finn a cuddle. 'Happy birthday, handsome.'

'Say thanks for your present, Finn,' Kate says.

'Thank you,' Finn says, like a puppy in training, then returns his focus to loading the foam bullets into his gun.

Gabe stands up and gives each of his grandparents a hug and then races upstairs before charging back in to the lounge, his tiny Nerf gun held to his cheek like he's seen on TV, and I can't help but laugh at how ridiculously puny it looks next to Finn's magnificent killing machine.

'Blimey, Gabe. He's got no chance against you with that,' I tease.

'Daaaad.' Gabe wrinkles his nose and pouts his lip, but then he starts giggling, and I feel at once happy and sad that he's reached an age where he gets the joke too.

*

I pick Kate's glass of wine up off the bookshelf next to Finn's bed and pass it to her. In honour of his birthday, he asked us both to read him stories and sit with him until he fell asleep, so we agreed. It still feels weird seeing his bedroom at Jerry's house – the dinosaur wallpaper that I didn't choose, the new toys I've not even seen yet, and maybe even worse, the stuff that used to be in our house, looking out of place in a new setting. When we sold our family home, I remember doing a last-minute hoover, the new owner waiting outside in her car desperate to get in, and suddenly noticing the lines on the wall where the kids had made us measure them over the years. I dropped the hoover and wept. With no one else there, I didn't hold back, just let the tears fall until the sleeves of my jumper were wet from wiping them away.

Although I'm not about to break down into a whimpering mess, I feel something of the same emotion now, sitting next to my ex-wife at the end of our (not so) baby boy's bed in a house that's not my own.

I get the sense Kate's quite tipsy because she puts her hand on my thigh. 'Do you remember the night we had him and I kept trying to wake you up to tell you I was

129

convinced he was on his way and you just kept rolling over and telling me to go back to sleep?'

'I thought you were just being dramatic.'

'We were lucky we got there in time.'

I finish my bottle of beer, but hold on to it, not wanting to move and lose this moment of close contact with Kate. 'I remember you even managed to make that hospital gown look hot.'

Kate elbows me in the ribs. 'Seriously, Noah, how could you have been thinking about sex when I was trying to push a baby out of my vagina?'

'I wasn't thinking about it during, just after, when you were all mellow and sexy from the gas and air and the new-baby euphoria.'

Kate shakes her head. 'You're insatiable.'

'Only with you.'

'Yeah, I suppose one thing our relationship did have going for it was passion.'

'Certainly did.' I pinch Kate's thigh and she giggles. 'Come on, though. It had more going for it than just that.'

Kate takes a deep breath before sitting up straight and turning to look at me. 'You know, don't take this the wrong way, but sometimes I wonder, if your mum hadn't died . . . well . . . whether things would've turned out differently between us?'

I look away, her eyes suddenly feeling too intense. I'm sure she's thought about it, but she's never voiced it before. Despite us being so close, we never talked much about Mum. I think she was always too scared to say something that might send me running, and my childhood was a topic I just never felt able to open up about.

Kate puts her hand on top of mine. 'Sorry. I didn't mean to upset you by mentioning your mum.'

Then suddenly, without thinking, I lean towards her and attempt to kiss her, Jerry entering the room just as my lips touch hers.

'Is Finn asleep?'

I know exactly what he's saying – 'What the hell are you still doing here?' – and I take the hint and push myself up off the bed, trying to slyly glance at Kate to see if I can read what she's thinking, but she's looking down at her hands.

'He's just gone down. I'll call a taxi.'

'No, it's fine. I'll give you a lift.'

'Seriously, it'll take ten minutes. It's not a problem.'

'I'll drive you.' I realize it's not an offer. There's no choice involved here.

'Great. I'll just get my stuff.'

*

I suddenly have a horrible feeling that Jerry is about to drive the car into a tree with the aim of killing me on impact. My only reassurance is that he doesn't seem suicidal, and planning a car crash that only hurts me is probably a fairly challenging feat.

Either way, we're going at quite some speed down narrow country lanes and he doesn't look happy.

'So Katie says you're coming to the wedding?'

'Yep.' It comes out at a squeakier pitch than intended as he doesn't slow on reaching a particularly sharp bend.

'It means a lot to Katie for you to be there. You're still a very important person in her life.'

I'm waiting for the 'but'. Surely the aim of this slightly terrifying lift home isn't to shower me with compliments?

'Well, of course. We have two kids together. It's only natural.'

'So you realize she'd never forgive you if you messed up our special day?'

'Uh, well, of course I wouldn't mess it up. I mean, other than showing you both up with my awesome moves on the dance floor.' I laugh in a slightly strained way, more like a cough.

Notably, Jerry doesn't smile. 'I was thinking more like a wild declaration of love during the service.' Now he smiles, but ironically; it's painfully apparent he's deadly serious.

'Why would I do that?'

At this point, terrifyingly, Jerry takes his eyes off the road and looks directly at me. 'Because you're still in love with her.'

I screw up my face and shake my head, as if this is the most absurd thing anyone in the world has ever said. 'Don't be ridiculous. What makes you think that? I love her as a friend, you know, as the mother of my children. But not like that.'

'Is that why you were just trying to kiss her?'

The laugh-cough again. 'No, you've got it all wrong. She was just showing me those new earrings you bought her. They're lovely, by the way.'

'Noah, I haven't bought her any earrings.'

'I mean the necklace.'

'Look, I don't think we need to continue this conversation any further. I think you know what I'm saying.'

'I promise I'm not a threat to you, Jerry. You're her fiancé. I'm just the lowly ex-husband.'

'I know you're not a threat, Noah. I just want *you* to know that.'

Who does he think he is? I *am* a threat. I'm North fucking Korea.

'I do. Of course.'

Jerry pulls up outside my house. 'Good.'

He holds out his hand. At first, I think he's going to punch me, but then I realize he's expecting me to shake it.

I do, weakly, and then release my seatbelt. 'Right, well, thanks for the lift.'

'Anytime.'

I search for my house keys in my pocket and then open the car door.

'She's really happy, Noah. I love her with all my heart. I take care of her. You might not get it. I know you think I'm not good enough for her. But she loves me. We're happy.'

I open my mouth to speak even though I'm not sure what I'm going to say, but Jerry's clearly not looking for a response, as he quickly shuts me down. 'Take care, Noah.'

I nod. And then get out of the car, my breathing taking some time to return to normal.

*

Lying on top of my quilt, I text Mimi.

I tried to kiss her x

Her reply is almost instantaneous.

WTF ?! How did she react?

133

I start to type but then realize that I don't know. How *did* she react? It all happened so fast. If Jerry hadn't walked in, would she have stopped me?

Jerry walked in.

OH.

Yes, oh indeed.

CHAPTER ELEVEN

We dip the newspaper into the bucket of gloop (which I can't help noticing looks decidedly like semen). I don't think I've got the ratio of glue to water quite right because the newspaper turns to mush and starts breaking into tiny pieces.

'Do you think we need more glue, Dad?' Gabe says, peering into the bucket with a face that suggests it contains rotten soup.

No shit, Sherlock.

'Yes, I was just about to do it. I've got this thing under control.'

'Why do we have to do it anyway?' Gabe says, looking and sounding more and more like a teenager every day.

'Your homework is about volcanoes so we're making a volcano.'

'Loads of the other kids just brought in books from the library. Can't we just do that and go and play on the PlayStation? We're nearly at the big baddy.'

'No. Those children . . .' – *don't have fathers on some insane crusade to win back their mother* – 'are just being lazy. We're being creative. It's fun, isn't it, Finn?'

My youngest son stirs the mixture like he's baking a cake and nods. I pour in more glue and he continues stirring.

'I want to mix it,' Gabe shouts, trying to wrench the spoon out of his brother's hands.

'No, I want to do it,' Finn yells, grabbing on with both hands.

They have an animated tussle over the spoon until Gabe manages to release it from Finn's hands and it flicks up, sending a glob of glue flying towards me. As if in slow motion, I watch it hurtling across the room before it lands right between my eyes, the texture of it sliding down my nose utterly repulsive.

'Thanks, boys.'

They stop fighting immediately and collapse into fits of giggles. Nothing like their dad's misfortune to encourage solidarity between brothers.

I wipe the glue off my face with my sleeve. 'Right, shall we get papier-mâchéing now?'

The boys start dipping great big pieces of paper into the glue and I show them how to rip the paper into strips first and then stick it around the plastic Coke bottle. It seems to take an age to cover and when it's done, there's no getting away from it, it just resembles a giant penis.

Finn holds it up and furrows his brow. 'How are we going to get it to look like a volcano?'

Gabe snatches it off him. 'It needs a structure, made out of card or something, to make it look more like a pyramid shape.'

I wonder when my son's intelligence surpassed my own. I take a photo of the bottle and send it to Mimi along with the message: *In craft hell. Please rescue me.*

Five minutes later, her reply comes through.

It's an awesome rocket. Keep going!

It's supposed to be a volcano . . .

Oh. I'm actually not far from yours. Do you really want some help?

Do birds fly?

After I've sent it, I realize it's probably not the best question to elicit a definitive yes. What about penguins? Or emus? Or ostriches? But hopefully she'll get my intention.

'Good news, boys. My friend Mimi is going to come over and help us turn this into the best volcano ever in the whole world.'

'Can we play on the PlayStation whilst we wait?' Gabe says, ever resourceful.

'No. She'll only be a few minutes.'

'But when can we play on it? You normally let us.'

'There's more to life than the PlayStation, kiddo.' I ruffle Gabe's hair and he sits and sulks until there's a knock at the door. 'That'll be Mimi. Let's go and let her in.'

The boys always get so excited when there's someone at the door. It's actually quite hurtful, as if any visitor is preferable to spending the whole day with just me. They rush past me and open the door to a slightly startled-looking Mimi.

'Can you help us make the volcano?' Finn says, still unaware of the function of social graces.

'Of course. I'd love to.'

'Come on in. Welcome to the mayhem.' I guide Mimi through to the lounge. 'Can I get you a drink?'

'A coffee would be great. Thank you.'

'Right, look after Mimi, please, boys. By the way, the big bossy one is called Gabriel and the little scraggy-looking urchin is Finn.'

'I'm not an urchin,' Finn says, creasing his forehead, even though he has no idea what an urchin even is.

I go through to the kitchen to make Mimi a drink, listening to the ripping and scrunching of paper, the boys' fights for Mimi's attention (*Look, Mimi, I've cut out the base. Look, Mimi, I've made three balls of paper. Well, I've made four.* And so on and so on), but she sounds like she's taking it all in her stride, calmly and enthusiastically doling out praise to both of them for their achievements.

When I get to the lounge, the creation already looks more like a volcano. A circular stand has been cut out of cardboard and scrunched up balls of newspaper have been stuck around the bottom of the bottle to give the volcano a wider base.

'Right, now we need to do some more papier mâché on top of these balls,' Mimi says, ripping off strips of newspaper and handing them to the boys. She's a complete natural and the boys happily follow her every command.

'How do you even know this stuff?' I ask, handing Mimi a coffee.

She puts the coffee down on the hearth and pulls out her phone from her pocket, showing me the screen. Step-by-step instructions with photos.

'If in doubt, google, hey?' I say, smiling.

'Well, having my skills and intelligence help too. Right, come on, get your hands dirty.'

I kneel down beside them at the coffee table and help with the papier mâché. I have no doubt that our masterful creation will end up in the teacher's bin by the end of the week, but it's nice to see the boys working as a team, to be creating something instead of destroying things.

When we've finished the basic structure, we leave it to dry and decide to head out to the park.

'Do you want to come with us, Mimi?' Finn says, tapping her on the arm. It's strange to see him with an adult who's not family or a teacher. He's such an open child. Immediately warm and accepting.

'Well, I'm actually walking that way to work so, yes, I could join you for a bit, I suppose.'

'You don't go to work on a Saturday,' Finn says, laughing at Mimi as if she's made a really stupid mistake.

Mimi smiles. 'Unfortunately, I do have to work on a Saturday sometimes. Rubbish, isn't it? But I've got time for a quick play first.'

We walk along to the local park. It's a dull day, but it's not too cold and the boys have fun climbing around on the play equipment whilst I pretend to be a monster and chase them, grabbing at their limbs from the ground and making growling noises.

'They're adorable,' Mimi says, as I take a breather from my role as children's entertainer and sit down on the bench next to her.

'Thank you. They have their moments. And they clearly loved you.'

'Ah yeah. Emma sometimes calls me the child whisperer. One of my many skills. In fact, maybe that's why I get on with you. Same mental age.'

'Maybe.'

Mimi checks her phone and then puts it back in her pocket. 'So how are things with Kate? Have you spoken to her about the kiss yet?'

'No. I haven't spoken to her at all since. I wonder if I'll be able to gauge how she's feeling when I drop the boys off tomorrow.'

'And how are *you* feeling about it?'

'I don't know. It felt right at the time, like there was something still there between us. More than just our shared history, but it's hard to tell with Kate.'

'The volcano is a nice touch. I'm sure she'll be impressed.'

'Thanks to you, yeah. Hopefully she will be. To be honest, it felt good to do something worthwhile with them. Even if Kate decides she doesn't want me back, I'd like to be a better dad.'

'Good for you.' Mimi glances at her watch. 'Right, sadly work is calling. Keep telling myself it'll all be worth it when I'm off on my travels.' She stands up and wipes some debris from the bench off the back of her jeans. 'I'll see you soon though, yeah? In fact, I'm taking Harley to this kids' mindfulness session tomorrow. It might impress Kate if you wanted to bring the boys along? Unless it's a bit weird with Harley being in your class and everything?'

I'm not sure if there are any hard and fast rules about seeing children out of school, and taking the boys to a mindfulness class certainly would surprise Kate. She was always quite on board with that sort of stuff, buying herself one of those mindfulness colouring books and talking about taking time to just 'be', whereas I always just mocked it as a hippy fad.

'I think it'd be OK if we happened to turn up to the same class, wouldn't it?'

'OK, great. I'll see if there are any spaces left and give you a text later.'

'Sounds good. And thanks for today. I do really appreciate it.'

'Not a problem. It was fun. Right, I'll just go and say bye to the boys.'

I nod and Mimi heads over to where the boys are hurtling down the slide, Gabe hanging on to Finn's legs to pull him down quicker. She says goodbye and they both wave and then she leaves the park.

When we get home, the boys paint their volcano and, when it's dry, I take great pleasure in showing them the exciting bit, pouring vinegar into the bottle and then spooning in the bicarbonate of soda and watching it bubble and hiss down the edges.

'That's awesome, Daddy,' Gabe says, looking up at me like I'm a magician.

'Yeah, do it again, do it again,' Finn says, jumping up and down.

So I do it a couple more times until the volcano is looking a little worse for wear and then I put it on the front step to dry out.

In the evening, we order in pizza and cuddle up in front of a film, one boy under each arm. I love our film nights, the nostalgia of watching kids' movies, the feel of my boys snuggled in next to me.

When it looks as if the main character (a dog with superpowers) is going to be captured, Finn starts shaking and buries his head in my chest.

'What's up, little man? You know he's going to be fine, right? Kids' films always have a happy ending.'

Finn peers up at me, looks back at the screen (where the dog is being dangled by one of his back legs) and then hides his face again.

They've always been sensitive, my boys. I mean, they can be as lively and boisterous as the next kid, but they seem to feel things deeply. A lot of things that go over other kids' heads have a more long-lasting effect on my two. I suppose I was the same when I was little. I remember crying when the teacher read us a story about an evacuee – none of the other kids batted an eyelid over it, some even joking about how amazing it would be to get away from their parents, but I felt every ounce of the boy's loneliness and fear. I was quite clingy too. I never liked saying goodbye when Mum dropped me at school or going to parties on my own.

In fact, I used to have to carry around a 'magic' stone. Of course, it wasn't really magic but my dad told me it was. He said if I kept it in my pocket it would bring me good luck and keep me safe. I'd hold it tightly every night to help me get to sleep, stroke it whenever I was feeling scared. I got a bit obsessed with it in the end, freaking out if I ever forgot to take it somewhere. Even when I went to secondary school, I always kept it on me, more secretly of course, putting my hand into my pocket to touch it rather than bringing it out.

Remembering the comfort it used to give me, I reach into my pocket to see if I can find anything that would do the trick, and underneath a random receipt I feel some coins. I dig out two one-pence pieces and hand one to each boy. 'These are magic coins. If you keep one in your pocket, then you never have to feel scared. It'll always keep you safe.'

Gabe flips his coin over, a slightly sceptical look on his face, but I notice he then tucks it into his pocket. Finn has none of the same bravado, smiling broadly and clutching his penny tightly. Gradually, he allows himself to look at the screen again, then after a few minutes he turns back to me with a look of wonder on his face. 'It works, Daddy. I don't feel scared any more.'

It helps that the dog's now got the upper hand in the battle, but I'm chuffed nonetheless.

'I love Daddy weekends,' Finn says, wrapping his free arm around my tummy and squeezing it tight.

'Me too,' Gabe says, taking his eyes off the screen for a second to look up at me.

And it dawns on me that maybe I didn't fight hard enough before because I thought my family were better off without me. That I was only dragging them down. But hearing my boys makes me wonder if I *can* be a positive influence in their lives, in Kate's life even. Maybe I'm not a total waster. And one thing's for certain – I don't want this to be my once a fortnight any more. I want this to be my every day.

*

The kids in the mindfulness class are pretty much what you would expect – long-haired, knitted rainbow jumpers and baggy linen trousers, with names like 'Tarquin' and 'Indigo'. Harley, in particular, stands out like a sore thumb. But I can tell he's super-excited to have me here and I can't help but find it endearing.

Our first activity is to make superhero poses, noticing how strong and brave they make us feel. Unfortunately, it's one of those kids' classes that requires full adult participation so I'm currently stood on one leg with one arm out in front of me like Superman. I don't feel particularly strong or brave – I feel like a numpty – but the boys seem to be enjoying it, giggling away with Harley, as they become Spiderman and Thor and Captain America. I'm concerned that perhaps we'll be seen as the naughty contingent, not taking it seriously enough, but as I look around, all the other children seem to be giggling and having fun too.

Our next activity is to use our 'Spider-sense' (I get the feeling they've been given the feedback to make the course appeal more to boys) where we have to sit in a space, still, and just observe all the things our different senses are picking up. I can tell this one's going to be harder for Harley and, within seconds, he's wriggling around and making silly noises with his lips. But to be fair to the teacher, she's really good with him (perhaps I need to take a few tips back to school with me), putting her hand gently on the top of his head and taking deep breaths with him until he's stiller and then helping him to notice all the things he can sense.

Then she stands up and moves around the room. 'Think about what your fingers are touching, the sensation of it, what you can smell – is it sweet, is it bitter – what you can taste, what you can see. Just look straight ahead of you, and what can you hear? Because even in the quiet here there are tiny noises.'

My tummy rumbles, embarrassingly long and loud, and Mimi glances over at me, biting her lip to try to stop herself from laughing.

After that, we finish the session with a drawing activity where we have to pair up and draw the person in front of us, just their face, but trying to include as many details as possible. The boys decide to make a three, Harley taking on the challenge of drawing Finn *and* Gabe, and poor Mimi's stuck with me.

'Be kind,' I say, suddenly feeling horribly self-conscious as she picks up her pencil and starts drawing the outline of my face.

She just smiles and continues drawing and I start to draw her, noticing for the first time that she has a birthmark above one eyebrow – a slightly paler India-shaped patch of skin – and that one of her eyes is a slightly brighter green than the other. When we're finished, I'm mortified to find we have to show each other. Mimi shows me her drawing first. It's not flattering. With my dark hair and glasses, I always hope I've got something of the Robert Downey Jr about me, but she's made me look more like Woody Allen.

'Is my nose really that big?'

Mimi laughs. 'I'm not a great drawer, OK?' Then she grabs my drawing out of my hands. 'Let's see your depiction of me, then.'

I cover my face, scared of her reaction, but when I peer out from behind my hands, she looks happy. 'You can actually draw. And you've even made me look quite pretty.'

'You are pretty.'

She looks unusually shy at the compliment and then the boys charge over, shoving their pictures in front of our faces for us to praise. Before the class finishes, we have to go around the room, shaking hands and thanking each other for coming, and then we're free.

When we get out, I ask the boys if they enjoyed it, expecting a 'No, it was boring' but instead they are full of smiles.

'It was really fun. Can we go again?'

'I guess. I'm glad you enjoyed it.'

Mimi ruffles Harley's hair. 'How about you, trouble? Did you enjoy it?'

Harley jigs up and down. 'Yeah. Especially seeing Mr Carlton on a Sunday.'

I smile at him. 'It was nice to see you too, Harley.' Then I turn to Mimi. 'And thank you for suggesting it.'

'No problem.' She moves towards Gabe and Finn, who have started wrestling on the grass, the whole calm mindfulness spell having clearly worn off already. 'Listen, boys. Remember to tell Mummy all about your new class, yeah?'

They stop fighting for a second and nod, and Mimi gives me a sly wink.

'Right, I better get this one home. See you soon though, Noah, and you, boys.'

Then we wave Mimi and Harley off and head back to the car.

*

'Here you are. On time. Homework done.' I push the boys out in front of me, Gabe holding out the slightly deformed volcano for Kate's approval.

'Wow,' she says, eyeing our creation then looking back at me. 'You have been busy.'

'It actually erupts,' Gabe says. 'Can we show you?'

'Of course, but perhaps we could do it in the garden. I'm not sure Jerry wants the house covered in lava.'

'We've just been to this mindfulness session at the community centre, haven't we, boys?' I slip in as casually as possible, as we walk through the house.

'Yeah, it was really fun, Mummy. Can we go again?'

Kate ignores them and turns to me. 'Mindfulness?'

'I thought it might be good for them, that's all. And they seemed to enjoy it.'

'It sounds great! I'm just surprised. I didn't see you as a mindfulness kind of guy.'

'Well, people change.'

Kate looks at me, a mixture of suspicion and intrigue. 'Well, anything that gets them off screens is a winner in my book. Thanks for doing that, Noah.'

'No problem.' I try not to show her how chuffed I am, playing it as nonchalant as I can.

When we reach the kitchen, Jerry is standing at the stove, moving vegetables around in a pan, and I try not to let the sight of him dampen my good mood.

When he hears us come in, he turns around, a big (forced?) smile on his face. 'Oh, hello, Noah. Hi, boys. Did you have a good weekend? Wow, what's that you've created?'

I'm not sure if I imagine the mocking tone in his voice or if it's really there. I think maybe I want it to be there so I have further excuse to hate him.

'We made a volcano at Daddy's house. Come and see how it works.' Finn takes Jerry's spare hand and pulls him towards the glass doors and I try not to cry at the sight of Finn's tiny little hand against Jerry's rough manly one. I know how awful it is of me but I can't help feeling slightly betrayed.

Jerry and the boys go out into the garden whilst Kate gets some vinegar and bicarbonate of soda out of the cupboard (unlike me, knowing automatically how to make a volcanic eruption).

'So what's all this in aid of?'

'What do you mean?' I say, as if I have no idea what she's referring to.

'First the mindfulness thing. Then homework. You've never done their homework with them before.'

'That's not fair.'

Kate widens her eyes.

'OK, but Gabe's only eight. It's not like I've been idly avoiding homework for years.'

'I'm not complaining. It's nice.' She gathers the two ingredients and takes a little bottle of something else out of the drawer. Whilst she's busy and not looking at me, I brave raising the topic of 'the kiss' or 'the not-quite kiss'.

'Look, Kate. About the other night . . .'

Kate waves her hand. 'It's fine. It was an emotional night. I know you didn't mean anything by it.'

It feels like she's reached inside my chest and is crushing my heart in her hand. I'm not sure what I expected her to say with her husband-to-be on the other side of the patio door, but I thought there might be something, some hint of emotion in her expression. Maybe she's just hiding it really well, but I can't see anything.

'Right. Shall we go and make this volcano erupt?' she asks, as casually as if we'd just been discussing the best way to cook sprouts.

I force my head to nod and follow Kate into the garden. The boys gather around the volcano and Kate puts the ingredients into the bottle, adding what I now realize is food colouring and, after a few seconds, the red mixture spews down the sides of the volcano.

'Wow, it looks like real lava now,' Gabe says, his face full of glee.

Kate smiles at me and I fake a smile back. It's completely stupid and irrational, but it just feels like another way in which she doesn't need me, in which she's succeeding and I'm failing.

Kate must read something in my expression because she says, 'Thanks to the awesome volcano Daddy helped you to make, it does look real. You've all done a great job.'

The boys push out their chests proudly and I know I should be thankful to her for making sure I come out the winner, but I just feel even sadder that it's come to this, that I'm having to try and win her back, that I lost her in the first place.

'I better get back. Come and give me a cuddle, boys.'

'You can stay for a beer if you want?' Jerry says. Despite our conversation last week, he clearly wants to pretend we're still the best of friends, even though we never were and never will be.

'No, thanks. I need to go and tidy the flat before work tomorrow.'

'You, tidy the flat? Has the real Noah been abducted by aliens?' Kate teases, and I know she's only joking, but I wish I'd not allowed myself to become such a mess so that I didn't have so far to go to show her that I could still be good for her.

'Turning over a new leaf.' I smile half-heartedly.

I give each of the boys a kiss and a cuddle, and head back through the house and out to my car, deciding to make a detour to the pub on the way home.

*

'Why did she have to come along and steal my thunder? Why won't she let me have anything? First the bike and then this. I bet she spends her life slagging me off to them.'

Mimi hands me the shandy she's just poured me. 'Do you really think that?'

'Well, no, but I'm just sick of being Deadbeat Dad Noah, the blotch on her otherwise pristine family. Jerry acts like he's so fucking perfect, standing there at the stove cooking his cordon bleu meal. He was even wearing an apron, for fuck's sake. Who the hell wears an apron?'

'I bet you make a mean beans on toast.' Mimi taps my hand but I pull it away.

'See, now you're doing it. Presuming I'm rubbish at everything.'

'Come on, Noah. I was joking. For what it's worth, I thought you seemed like a great dad.'

I sigh. 'I couldn't even make a sodding volcano.'

'But you tried. And you went to that class and made yourself look like an idiot posing as Superman.'

I take a sip of my drink and then slump back on my bar stool.

'Did you get a chance to ask her about the kiss?'

I shake my head. I can't face telling her about how Kate totally dismissed it. It's too humiliating. 'Jerry was there the whole time.'

I lean forwards on to the bar and prop my head up on my elbow. Mimi bends down and pinches my cheek, giving it a wiggle, like you would to a child. 'Don't be sad. You're almost making me feel sorry for you.'

I narrow my eyes.

'Look, my shift finishes in about quarter of an hour. I go to yoga on a Sunday evening. Why don't you come with me?'

'Yoga and mindfulness in one day? What are you trying to do to me?'

'It's actually really good for the soul. I used to think it was a load of hippy mumbo-jumbo, but it's calming and it makes you feel better and it'll also give you a bod like mine.' Mimi winks whilst running her hand down her abs.

'I'm not sure I can trust anyone who uses the words "good for the soul".'

'Just give it a go. Think of it as part of the improvement project.'

*

Mimi picks me up an hour later. I'm not sure what you're supposed to wear to a yoga class so I'm dressed in

151

running shorts and a sports vest and, when I get into the car, Mimi looks me up and down with a cheeky glint in her eyes.

'What?'

'Nothing.'

When we arrive at the yoga centre, it's exactly how I expected it to be. Joss sticks burning away on the window-sill, a small bamboo tree in the corner, rows of mats lined up on the wooden floor. The instructor is typically lean, her skin glowing as if she's lit from the inside, and rather than walk around the room, she floats, calmness exuding from her every pore. To be fair to her, she's a great advert for yoga, but I expect she probably also treats her body as a temple, existing on halloumi, chickpeas and spin-ach smoothies. There's no way I could ever take things that far.

She rings a little bell and the groups of people chatter-ing immediately stop and everyone heads to a mat, lying down and closing their eyes. Mimi gestures for me to copy so I lie down on a mat next to hers. And then for a good five minutes, nothing happens. Not a movement, not a peep from anyone. And it's amazing how hard it is to just lie there, in silence, completely still and alone with my thoughts, without any of my usual distraction techniques to turn to.

Finally, everyone stands up. There didn't seem to be a signal asking them to, unless I missed it, more an inter-nal timer. But I copy them all and stand. And then the class properly begins. My body is stretched and bent into positions I didn't even know were possible, Mimi giggling every time my bones crack or my balance wobbles.

Then at the end, they all lie down again. But this time the teacher talks everyone through a relaxation exercise and as much as my cynical brain tries to fight it, to mock it, as much as I wish it weren't true, I feel my muscles relax and my brain calm.

*

'See, you enjoyed it, didn't you?'

'I think "enjoyed" is a bit excessive, but it wasn't too painful, well, not mentally anyway.'

Mimi smiles. 'Yeah, I did notice there was a fair bit of creaking coming from your mat.'

We reach my flat and Mimi pulls up outside.

'Now, I was thinking,' she says, lifting up the hand-brake, 'I've got next weekend off. How about we tackle your flat? Clean it up, give it a fresh lick of paint? It'll be like *DIY SOS*. Divorced dad improves home in attempt to win ex-wife back.'

'You don't want to spend your weekend off doing that.'

'Honestly, I'm never happier than with a paintbrush in my hand.'

'Really? I suppose it would be good to get it straight. If you're sure you don't mind?'

'Absolutely not. I'd love to help. Now remember – this week, stay away from the beers and women. And keep your chakras in line.'

'Yes, boss. You're relishing this role, aren't you?'

'Maybe.' Mimi smiles.

I open the car door and climb out. 'See you next week-end then.'

'Looking forward to it. I'll bring my colour cards.'

I shut the door and head inside. And I'm not sure whether or not it really was the cleansing effect of the yoga, but I notice I feel a hell of a lot better than I did when I left Kate's.

CHAPTER TWELVE

'No, no, no, no. Don't listen to him. He pushed me first.' Harley reaches out and puts his hand over Ethan's mouth.

Ethan starts to cry and Harley pushes his face away. 'He's lying. He's lying.'

I take Harley's arms in my hands and move them away from Ethan. 'Look, Harley, I'm not listening to you until you keep your hands by your sides and stop shouting at me.'

Harley jigs up and down, Ethan's tears intensifying beside him. I wonder what would happen if I did a runner, just slipped through the door into the outdoor area and hurdled over the wooden fence.

'But he's lying. He's lying.'

'I'm not lying,' Ethan splutters through his tears. 'He threw a car at my head.'

Automatically, Harley's hand returns to cover Ethan's mouth and I gently remove it again. He yanks it from my grip and starts flapping his arms by his sides. He's like a boiling kettle. It's like you can physically see the bubbles, the pressure building, looking for a way out. I remember that feeling. I didn't lash out at the other kids when I was at school, but I remember trashing the book corner once, and quite a few afternoons sat with the cushions over my head because I didn't want to talk to anyone. I don't remember what the triggers were. I'm not sure you even know what they are at that age, just that your tummy is burning with rage and you don't know how to make it stop.

I take a deep breath and lift Ethan's fringe off his face. My heart sinks when I see the angry red mark on his forehead.

'Mrs Watson, please can you take Ethan to get an ice-pack for his head and note that he's had a bump in the accident book?'

Mrs Watson is trying to look busy in the corner, doing the highly useful job of sorting pieces of sugar paper into colours, and she makes a song and dance about having to stop what she's doing before slumping over and taking Ethan's hand.

As the noise of Ethan's crying disappears down the corridor, the tension in my shoulders eases. 'Right, Harley, sit down on this chair beside me and tell me what's going on.'

Harley screws up his face and crosses his arms. 'I don't want to sit by you.'

'Well, then, I can always take you to sit by Mrs Jackson and you can explain things to her instead?'

Harley blows air out his nose.

'Your choice, buddy.'

Although we both know no one's going to *choose* to be sent to the head teacher.

Reluctantly, Harley sits on the chair beside me. 'He wouldn't let me have the car I wanted. He pushed me away.'

'So you launched your car at his head?'

Harley nods.

'Do you realize that's not the way to deal with things? Can you think what might have been a better way to deal with the situation?'

Sometimes when I'm having these conversations with the children in my class, I realize what a monumental waste of breath it is. They are four. They are not going to stop mid-disagreement, ponder for a moment and think, 'Oh yes, we were taught to walk away, to tell the teacher, to breathe in and out whilst counting to ten' (most of the children in my class couldn't even manage the counting, let alone the self-regulation). They are unable to stop and consider how it might make another child feel if they launch a hard object at their skull.

'I wanted the car and he wouldn't give it to me.'

And, in Harley's world, it's as simple as that.

'But you have to share, Harley. I know it's tricky, but when you're at school there are lots of other children and you can't just have what you want.'

'I don't want to share.'

'Well, in school it's not a choice. You have to.'

Harley turns around in his chair so he is facing the opposite way. 'I'm not listening to you, stupid head.'

It may be coming from an agitated four-year-old, but being called 'stupid head' is surprisingly hurtful.

'Then you can sit there until you will listen.'

I stand up to walk away and Harley starts rocking his chair so that it bashes noisily on the floor and then, just to make sure it's impossible to ignore him, he starts shouting 'La la la la' at the top of his voice.

Suddenly, I'm surrounded by children.

'I can't concentrate.'

'He's making my head hurt.'

'Mr Carlton, it's too noisy. I don't like it.'

Taps on my leg, pulling on my shirt, my name repeated not quite in unison, tears . . . I feel like covering my ears with my hands, falling to the floor and screaming 'Stop'.

'OK, enough.' It's a little louder than I was going for. Annabelle cowers in the corner and starts sniffling. Even Harley shuts up for a nanosecond.

'Right, you, out we go. I can't have this in the classroom.' I take Harley's hand, as gently as possible, conscious of the fact I forgot to renew my teachers' union membership, and try to pull him out of the classroom.

'No, no, no, please. I'm sorry.' He anchors his feet by spreading his legs wide and pulls against my hand.

'It's not a choice, Harley. You've taken it too far. Come on now, don't fight me.'

Harley grabs on to a cupboard on wheels and it starts sliding across the room with him, toy dinosaurs crashing off on to the ground.

It takes every fibre of my being to not just let him off, leave him in the classroom and ignore the protests of the other children, but I know I have to follow through now.

Finally, Harley stops pulling back. 'I'm sorry.' He wriggles his hand free from mine, falls to the floor and starts sobbing. The anger seems to have dissipated and what's left is a raw sadness that's even harder to know what to do with.

I crouch down beside him and put my hand on his shoulder. He flinches and at first I worry he's going to punch me, but then he stands up and throws himself at me, wrapping his arms so tightly around my neck, it makes it hard to breathe. My initial reaction is to try to squirm away, but then he rests his head on my chest and his breathing starts to calm, so I just hold him until the tears have soaked my shirt and I'm pretty sure there are none left.

*

Finally, in what feels like painful slow motion, pick-up time rolls around. I send the majority of children off to their parents. Harley, still here of course, swings his bookbag around in a circle, slightly clipping Annabelle's shoulder and causing a dramatic switch-on of the water-works timed immaculately for the very moment her mum appears at the gate. If I were more cynical, I might believe Annabelle walked into the circling bookbag on purpose.

'Oh, darling, what's happened?' Annabelle's mum picks her up, cradles the back of her neck and pulls Annabelle to her chest.

'Harley hit me again,' she screams, squeezing every last drop out of the moment like an *EastEnders* cast member in her final scene before being killed off.

'I didn't. She's lying,' Harley shouts.

'I'm sick of this. If this matter isn't sorted out immediately, I'm going to take Annabelle to another school.'

What a horrifying loss – a child so full of life and charm.

'He didn't hit her. It was an accident. He was swinging his bookbag round and it accidentally caught Annabelle lightly on the shoulder.' Annabelle's mum shoots me a look that says are-you-calling-my-child-a-drama-queen so I add (in a sick-makingly saccharine tone), 'I think she's probably tired and in need of Mummy cuddles after a busy day at school.'

My faux-affection has little to no effect on Mrs Sampson's mood. 'Well, it's not the first time, is it? He needs to think about what he's doing. He's out of control.'

She says it in such a way that I picture Harley as a rabid beast, on the loose with intent to kill. By contrast, he is standing next to me with his bookbag placed sensibly over his shoulder, the stillest I've ever seen him. I want to high-five him behind my back.

'With all due respect, Mrs Sampson, he doesn't exactly look out of control now, does he? Harley had a few problems settling in, I recognize that, but we have put measures in place and he is working hard and making good progress.'

The image of the bump on Ethan's head flashes through my brain but I push it to the side. The truth is, I wouldn't really want Finn in a class with Harley either, but Annabelle's mum gets right on my wick. And, much to my surprise, I feel protective of Harley, like he needs someone fighting his corner sometimes.

'Well, I'll be keeping a close eye on things and if he hurts Annabelle again, I'll be in to see Mrs Jackson.'

Ooh, I'm trembling in my shoes.

'Of course. Have a good evening.'

Mrs Sampson storms off, still cradling Annabelle, and glares at Emma who is now walking towards us.

'How's he been today?' she asks, for the first time ever making eye contact.

I hate telling parents when their children have been in trouble, especially when I sense they're as fragile as

Emma, but I know I have a responsibility to keep her in the loop about his regular outbursts.

'He got into an altercation about a car and unfortunately he did end up hurting the other little boy with it.'

I can almost see Emma's defences coming up. 'He's fine at home. I don't know why he's playing up so much at school.'

It's a common parent approach – 'Well, he's great for me so it must be something you're doing wrong' – but I get it. It's much harder to admit you might be partly responsible.

'He just seems to see red quite easily and it feels like he's not sure how to handle it. Does he not get angry at home, then?'

'Not really. I mean, he has tantrums sometimes, but what child doesn't?'

I nod, proceeding gently. 'Is there anything going on that might be making him feel angry? Even if you don't see it much at home?'

Emma shrugs. 'I don't think so. I mean . . .'

But just as it feels she might be about to lower those walls, just an inch, Harley comes running over and starts tugging on her sleeve. 'Mummy, can we go to the park now, please? I've been waiting ages.'

I put my hand on his head. 'One minute, buddy. Just go and build me a quick sandcastle, will you?'

He looks at his mum for an alternative answer but when he doesn't get one, he sidles over to the sandpit.

'Is Harley's dad in the picture?' I ask, pretending that I don't already know that he's not.

Emma shakes her head. 'He buggered off when Harley was three and hasn't seen him since.'

I look at Harley – now happily digging a hole in the sand – and I wonder if he feels it, or if he's lucky enough to be too young for it to really sting. That feeling that your dad doesn't want to know you. Doesn't miss you like you miss him.

'I'm sorry.'

'Don't be. He wasn't worth having around anyway. But it could be why Harley gets angry sometimes. He worshipped his dad for some strange reason. I've never been able to compete.'

The hurt is clear in Emma's tone and I want to explain to her that Harley's longing for his dad is not a negative reflection on her, but I'm not sure how without revealing too much of myself.

'Mimi mentioned you've had a tricky couple of years. Is everything OK now? Is there anything we can support you with?' I drop in, as tactfully as possible.

Emma snorts. 'Mimi's told you about her messed-up little sister, has she?'

'No. Not at all. I just mean, single parent, it's not easy. It's perfectly natural to need a little help sometimes.'

Emma shakes her head. 'We're fine. We don't need any help. I'll make sure Harley stays out of trouble.' Then she shouts across to Harley, 'Come on, mate, let's go.'

Harley comes running out of the sand and I watch them leave, knowing I've unwittingly pushed Emma even further into her shell and wishing I could find a way to encourage her to let me in.

*

'So who is this Mimi?'

This phone conversation with Kate started with an exchange about something trivial. So trivial in fact that I can't even remember what it was. Most of our conversations go like this, like peeling back the layers of an onion before we get to the core – the real reason one of us called the other. On this occasion, it was Kate that called me, and I can see now that it was to quiz me about the woman the boys told her helped them with their homework and went with them to mindfulness class.

'She's a friend.'

'A friend?' She says it like she would've said 'You only had two?' when I used to get home late from work.

'Yes. I can imagine it seems hard to comprehend that a woman could cope with just being friends with me and not want to jump my bones.'

'I was thinking more the other way round.'

'Well, you're wrong. We are just friends.'

'So you haven't slept with her then?'

I feel backed into a corner. Although the irony isn't lost on me that she's the one planning on marrying another man. 'Well, yes, I have, but it was only once. We're not sleeping together any more.'

Kate laughs, but it's filled with bitterness. 'God, it must've been bad then.'

I'm not sure why but I feel strangely protective of Mimi, and slightly angry towards Kate.

'If you must know, it was great. But we decided we'd both rather have a friendship than meaningless sex.'

Because I want you.

'Well, I'm glad the sex was so good.'

And, all of a sudden, it occurs to me that Kate isn't being judgemental, she's jealous. And, however hard I try not to get carried away, I feel a rush of hope.

'Sorry. I didn't mean that. I'm not having a good day.' I hear Kate swallow something and I'm fairly sure it'll be wine. The only time Kate is truly open with me these days is when she's been drinking.

'What's up?'

'It's nothing. I mean, it's stupid.'

Your life with Jerry isn't as perfect as you thought? You're having doubts?

'You know you can tell me anything.'

There's a pause and I can hear her taking another sip of her drink. I imagine her running her finger around the rim of her wine glass, like she always does when holding one, as if the repetitive nature of the act helps her to clarify her thoughts. 'Jerry got me an interview at his work.'

I feel my breathing becoming more strained. Before having the boys, Kate worked for a graphic design company as an illustrator, drawing logos. She loved it, but she was always adamant that once she had children, she wanted to be a stay-at-home mum and that even once they started school it was a non-negotiable that she be there to take the boys to school, pick them up, go on school trips, watch assemblies, et cetera, so she chose to do a bit of freelance work from home. And I was fine with that. Yes, it meant we struggled for money, but it was important to both of us that she be there for the boys. It was what we chose together for our family. How dare Jerry think he can waltz in and question it?

'What about the illustration? I thought you wanted to work from home? He's not forcing you to get a job, is he? If you need more money, we can sort something together.'

'No, it's nothing like that. It's just with Finn starting school full-time I've been feeling a bit lonely sometimes. I wanted something where I could socialize a bit, something I felt passionate about, where I could meet like-minded people. He found this admin role that I could do in school hours. He was trying to be helpful.'

'Oh.'

Why couldn't he have just been being an arse?

'But admin for an insurance company? Something I felt passionate about? Does he know me at all?'

This conversation is like being on a rollercoaster, one minute I'm hurtling towards the ground and the next it feels like I'm on the top of the world.

'Do you know what he got me for Christmas?' Kate continues, the wine clearly loosening her tongue. 'A mixer. I mean, seriously, me, baking? It cost a fortune and it just sits unused on the side.'

I feel almost manic – the thought that Kate might be realizing Jerry isn't right for her causing my heart to thump in my chest. I daren't speak in case she stops talking or I say something that changes her mind.

'I'm sorry. I probably shouldn't be talking to you about all this. I bet I sound like an ungrateful cow, don't I?'

'No, God, no. I'm with you. Working for an insurance company? Shoot me now. And a bloody mixer? He might as well have bought you a pair of rubber gloves.'

Kate laughs. 'He thought it would make it easier when I bake with the kids.'

'What, once a year for the Comic Relief cake sale?'

Kate laughs again, but when she starts speaking, her tone is sad. 'I know his heart's in the right place but sometimes I just wish he knew me a bit better, like . . .'

She stops herself before she says any more but she doesn't need to finish her sentence. We both know exactly what she's thinking and I just pray that she realizes how significant it is, that she doesn't just brush it off as her being silly or tipsy.

'Look, I'm sorry for being a bitch about Mimi,' she continues. 'It just felt odd hearing that there was some other woman spending time with the boys when I'm not there. I suppose it gave me a tiny insight into what it must be like for you with Jerry. And I'm sorry. It's quite hard, isn't it?'

Isn't she the master of understatement?

'Yeah. It is.'

'Anyway, it meant a lot that you'd done such valuable stuff with them. Thank you.'

'You don't need to thank me. That's my job. I'm their dad. I'm supposed to do things like that with them. I'm sorry I've not been the best since we split up, and probably before that, but I promise I'm going to be better from now on.'

'That's good to hear. Just be you, Noah. The real you. Because when you're not drinking yourself into a ditch or sprinting in the opposite direction, you really are wonderful.'

As she says it, a feeling of desperation runs through me. It feels like I'm racing against a ticking clock. Like a bomb is about to explode if I don't figure out a way to defuse it. I've got just over four weeks. I have to make things right. I have to change our ending.

'Look, I better go,' Kate continues. 'Jerry will be serving up our dinner any minute now.'

'OK. I'll see you in a week and a half. And Kate?'

'Yeah.'

The words form in my mouth and I nearly manage to spit them out, to send them flying across the ether to her, but I can't quite do it. 'Nothing. Have a good evening.'

'You too. Bye, Noah.'

CHAPTER THIRTEEN

We walk up and down the aisles of B&Q like a married couple. I've already told Mimi that I think we should just go for Brilliant White and be done with it, but she's determined to get me to branch out.

'It's a fresh start. A blank canvas. Come on, you could choose anything.'

I stop at a tin of bright yellow paint. 'Let's go for this. Finn's favourite colour.'

Mimi screws up her face.

'You said I could choose anything.'

'But it'd be like living in a tub of butter.'

'And what's wrong with that?'

Mimi guides me towards the 'Neutrals' section, which is basically just lots of shades of white, as I originally suggested.

'I like this one,' Mimi says, picking up a tin and holding it out to me.

'*Strong White*, seriously? So it's better to be strong than brilliant, is it?'

'In the paint world, yes, it seems it is. I promise, this is going to look great.'

I look at the price label under the space on the shelf where the pot of paint was. 'Thirty pounds? For a small pot of paint? Is it made of crushed plutonium or something?'

Mimi laughs. 'Why plutonium? Why not gold or diamonds?'

I laugh too. 'It was the first thing that came into my mind. Random, I know.'

'Right, well, let's take two tins to start with. We can always come back and get some more if we need it, but it should cover the kitchen, the lounge and the hallway. Your flat's not that big.'

'What about the bedroom?'

'Oh no, I was thinking a deep red for that.' Mimi's eyes twinkle when she's teasing me. I can imagine she was the kid at school who could always get away with being cheeky because she was adorable with it.

'Like the Red Room of Pain? *Fifty Shades?*'

'I don't know. If that's what Kate's into?'

'It was your idea.'

'I was thinking romantic. You were the one that had to take it somewhere dirty.'

I grab another pot of Strong White and we take the paint over to the cashier. Once we're home, Mimi rummages around in her bag, locating an oversized shirt, already covered in splatters of paint, which she puts on over the top of her T-shirt, and then she pulls two paintbrushes out of her bag, handing one to me. I put it on the side, slip my jeans off and pull my T-shirt over my head.

'What are you doing?' Mimi looks at me as if I've just stripped off in the middle of Tesco.

'I don't have any painting clothes so I'm going to paint in my pants. I'm sorry, is that going to be too erotic for you?'

Mimi looks me up and down. 'No, definitely not.'

'Good.' I use a knife to pop open the tin of paint, grab the paintbrush and we both get to work.

Mimi's right. There is something quite therapeutic about the task of painting, the way it's mindless and repetitive, the way it immediately makes the room look better, brighter. We listen to the radio. Occasionally, I catch Mimi singing along, but she's too quiet for me to really tell what her voice is like. At the odd song, I stop painting and dance around the lounge, Mimi pretending to be disgusted, but I can tell that, quietly, she's impressed by my killer moves.

Before we know it, it's seven o'clock and Mimi wraps up her brush and collapses onto the sofa. 'I don't know about you, but I'm starving.'

I finish the last edge of the wall, wrap up my brush and put it next to hers. 'Bacon butties?'

'Perfect.'

I go into the kitchen and plop some bacon in a pan. As I cook, I google local bars with a karaoke night on my phone and fortunately find one within walking distance. When I've finished making us both the best ever bacon butties – the key is in adding maple syrup to the bacon right at the end and using both ketchup and mayonnaise on the bread (*I may not be the next Gordon Ramsey, Jerry, but try beating that*) – I take them through to Mimi and hand one over.

'Right, eat up. I'm taking you out to say thank you.'

'Where?' Mimi says before stuffing a load of food into her mouth.

'You'll see.'

*

As we arrive at the bar, I feel a flutter of excitement in my chest. I've always liked surprising people. Every year, on Kate's birthday, I'd think up somewhere new to take her. One year, I did a treasure hunt around Bristol, hiding clues around the city that eventually led her to The Ox – a swish restaurant she'd always wanted to go to. Another year I took her paintballing, one time we did quad bike racing, one year we went to the circus. For her twenty-fifth birthday I arranged with her parents for them to have the kids for the weekend and I took her to Paris. It always made me so happy to see her face when she realized what we were doing, to watch her enjoyment at trying out something or somewhere new. And I feel something of the same emotion right now.

That is until we go down the stairs into a dingy room with some woman stood on the stage, mic in hand, caterwauling in the guise of Mariah Carey, and Mimi looks at me as if she is planning how she is going to kill me.

'I'm not singing,' she says, shaking her head vehemently.

'Have a few drinks. See how you feel then.'

'Nope, no way, nada, never, not happening.'

'Don't beat around the bush. Tell me what you really think.'

Mimi surveys the room, the crowd cheering far more enthusiastically than the performance deserves. Then she leans into me slightly. 'Thank you, though. It was a lovely thought.'

Finally. The recognition I deserve.

'It's OK. Come on, let's go and get a drink.'

We walk to the bar and Mimi orders a cocktail (at nine pounds a pop) and I get the feeling it's a subtle attempt at payback. I order a JD and Coke and then hand over the cash, feeling a little sick at the thought of the forty-five minutes I had to spend dealing with the woes of four-year-olds in order to earn it.

We find a table in the corner, far enough away from the speakers that we can just about manage to have a conversation by shouting into each other's ears. I still miss quite a lot of what she says and there are a few of those awkward moments when I've pretended to hear, but then it's evident from the fact she's staring at me that she's asked me a question and I have no idea what the answer is supposed to be. If I'd known she wasn't going to sing, it would've been easier to go to a normal bar where our attempts at conversation wouldn't have to compete with a bunch of *X-Factor* rejects.

The conversation's not exactly deep – to be fair I miss half of it – so instead we get through the drinks pretty quick and by the time it gets to last orders, we're both what could only be described as rat-faced. Mimi excuses herself to go to the toilet, and my inebriated body walks up to the guy sorting the karaoke and manages to persuade him to put Mimi's name down for the last song. I know nothing about her musical taste so I scan the menu in the hope something jumps out at me. It does, although I'm not sure it's for the right reasons. I point it out to the guy and he jots it down in a notebook. Rushing back to our table, I wrap my hand around my glass and try to look relaxed.

When Mimi walks towards me, smiling and carefree, it suddenly dawns on me that this might not have been my best idea.

'Right, shall we drink up and go?' She sits down beside me, picks up her vodka and Coke (thank God she moved on from cocktails after the first one) and downs the last of it.

I sip my drink slowly, stalling for time. 'Yeah, won't be a minute.'

The current song finishes, a tall, lanky white guy's attempt at 'Rapper's Delight' and he hands the mic back to the compere.

'Now, sadly, we've reached the last song of the night.'

The pissed crowd let out a loud groan.

'But it's a corker. So, everyone, put your hands together for Mimi Thomas with "Let it Go".'

The crowd erupt into rapturous applause and Mimi gives me daggers.

'"Let it Go"? Seriously? Do I look like a six-year-old girl?'

'It was the first song that jumped out at me. The kids sing it in the car. Go on, it'll be fun. I want to hear you sing.'

Mimi pushes herself further back into her seat. 'No way.'

The compere searches the room. 'Mimi Thomas, are you out there?'

'Go on, it's an experience. You'll enjoy it once you get started.'

'There will be no getting started, Noah. If you think it's such fun, why don't you go and do it?'

'Come out, Mimi, come out, wherever you are. Otherwise I'm going to have to sing it and that won't be pretty,' the compere shouts into the mic. He doesn't seem to have grasped the idea that a microphone amplifies the sound of your voice, taking away the need to project quite so strongly. Then he spots me. 'Ah, there you are. It was you that put your name down.' He looks down at the name and looks at me, his expression suggesting he's not sure whether to openly question it or whether he might offend someone in the process of gender reassignment. 'Come on then, mate.'

When I stand on the stage, I'm confronted with a mass of confused faces. The music starts up and I'm not sure what's worse – the fact I'm going to have to sing a song from *Frozen* to a crowd of strangers or that they all think I'm identifying as a woman despite the fact my face is covered in a fairly thick layer of designer stubble.

The lyrics flash up on the screen and I begin. This bit's not too bad. It's that sort of breathless talk-singing people do when feeling deep emotion. I can just about manage that. Then I'm supposed to sing something about me looking like I'm a queen (an apt lyric at this particular moment if ever there was one) and I want to shrink into myself.

I can feel the music building towards the bridge and my throat feels dry, my heart pounding in my chest. Here we go. Here comes the real singing.

And then the cheers from the crowd and the alcohol take over, and I'm back in my living room with the boys performing in front of the television and I start belting it out. I even sweep my hand across my body and perform a dramatic air grab.

When the chorus finally arrives, the whole crowd sways their arms in the air and sing along, and then suddenly

Mimi appears, taking the extra mic off the compere and joining in.

At the sound of Mimi's voice, the crowd stops singing, stops swaying, and just stares at her, dumbfounded.

It's all right for her. I did all the hard work. It's easy to jump in, give it the old Whitney Houston and get all the glory.

For a little while, I continue to sing along with her, a mismatched duet, but like Batman and Robin, it's clear who the star is here, and after a lot of irritated glares from the audience, I take a step back and hand my mic to the compere.

When Mimi's finished singing, the crowd erupts in whoops and cheers and Mimi gives a shy bow, her face flushing pink as she does. And I'm glad I brought her. It's very rare I do anything that makes me feel good about myself these days, but right now I don't feel half-bad.

*

When we reach the taxi rank, Mimi leans up and kisses me on the cheek. 'Thank you for tonight. Despite my initial reservations, I had a great time. I hope I didn't embarrass you too much with my singing.'

'Well, you did kind of rain on my parade a little bit, but I'm glad you enjoyed it.'

Mimi smiles. 'I didn't realize how much I'd missed it. Thank you. Seriously. I never would've done it without you forcing me to.'

'You're very welcome. It was the least I could do after all your help with the flat. You were right. It does feel much better getting it sorted.'

'Good. Now, just make sure you invite Kate to pick up the boys from yours next weekend so that she can see it.'

*

In the morning, I paint a second coat on all the walls and then grab a black bin liner and have a huge clear-out. Old clothes I never wear any more, receipts, bank statements, empty bottles of shampoo and shower gel that were lining the bottom of the shower, magazines I'm never going to look at . . . I take all the recycling to the tip – it's got to the point where it needs its own room because I never remember to put it out on recycling day. On the way home, I pick up some polish and a duster from the shop and, when I get back, I polish all the surfaces (who knew the TV picture was that clear?) and run the Hoover round. I tidy the boys' room, putting their toys away in the cupboard and Blu-Tacking some of their pictures to the wall. And when I'm finished, I sit down with a microwave curry, a beer and an episode of *American Horror Story* feeling decidedly cleansed.

CHAPTER FOURTEEN

'Right, good morning, everyone. Tommy, can you please stop sticking your carrot up your nose and, Jasmine, I don't think James wants you licking his cheek, although I'm sure you're only being friendly. Now, this morning we've got a special treat because Ethan has decided to bring in his new puppy.'

A cacophony of excitement ensues and I'm just trying to settle the class down when I notice Harley skulking in with his hood up.

'Morning, Harley. Can you take your hoody off, please?'

Harley crosses his arms and shakes his head.

'Well, Ethan is bringing his puppy in to meet us all in a minute. If you want to join us on the carpet, then you're going to have to take your hoody off.'

I'm not sure why. Because it's an arbitrary school law that children all look like clones of each other, perhaps?

Harley shakes his head again, remaining standing.

'Right, Mrs Watson, if you could get the class in a circle and calm for the imminent arrival of Ethan's delightful puppy, I'm just going to have a quick chat to Harley.'

Mrs Watson scowls at me, deservedly so on this occasion. The children seem to have no concept of a circle, however many times I ask them to sit in one, and trying to get them calm, with the prospect of a small, supposedly cute and cuddly animal joining them in the classroom is a seriously tricky task. Which is why I'm avoiding it, using Harley as my excuse.

'Thanks,' she says, with a bitter twitch of the lips.

'No, thank *you*,' I say, mirroring her gesture.

Then she enters the lion's den and I steer Harley out into the corridor and sit down with him on the mini chairs that cause my knees to stick up in the air.

'So, what's up? I thought you'd be jumping up and down at the news a puppy was going to be coming into class.'

Harley looks at his feet and pulls his hood down further over his face. Sitting close to him, I can see his cheeks are blotchy like he's been crying a lot. I reach over and gently push his hoody off his head. He screws up his face and gives me a death-stare. Then I see it, the angry bruise covering the side of his face next to his eye.

'What happened to your eye, buddy?' As I ask the question, I pray there's a simple and innocent explanation, that Harley's behaviour this morning is not linked to the cause of the bruise, but my instincts tell me that the bruise has everything to do with why Harley is acting out.

Harley doesn't speak, just pulls his hoody back down over his face. Then a flustered-looking Mrs Watson puts her head around the door. 'The puppy is here. I've asked Ethan's mum to wait by the back door just a sec, but the kids are going crazy.'

I can see that Harley isn't in the mood to tell me about what happened, and I don't want him to miss out, so I stand up and hold out my hand. 'Come on, Harley. Let's go and meet this puppy. We'll talk about this later.'

Reluctantly, Harley takes my hand and I lead him past the circle, well, gaggle, of very squealy, wriggly children to the back door where Ethan and his mum are waiting with a ridiculously over-excited puppy on a lead beside them. When I open the door, the little mutt jumps up at me, his muddy paws marking my trousers.

'Sit,' Ethan's mum says, but the puppy ignores her entirely, so she yanks on the lead and pulls him away, nearly dislodging his head.

I'm sure what I'm feeling is something akin to a panic attack, but I smile as sincerely as I can manage.

'OK, give me two seconds to calm the class a little bit. They are understandably very excited. And then you can bring him in. Does he have a name?'

'She's called Misty.'

'Oh right, sorry,' I say, apologizing for my misogynistic error, instilled in me from a childhood of books where the dogs were always male, like the doctors and the firemen.

I take an unusually subdued Harley with me back to the carpet and then attempt to calm the manic class. I did suggest to the head that perhaps the combination of a class of reception children and a sprightly puppy wasn't the most sensible idea, but she assured me it would be fine and said it was good to show the children that we valued the things that are important to them outside of school. I don't see why we couldn't do that with a photograph of Misty, but it's easy to sit in your ivory tower and inflict pain on other people, I suppose.

'OK, we must be silent, everyone, or we will scare little Misty,' I whisper. 'Let's see if we can be so quiet that she doesn't even notice we're here when she comes in.'

As if by magic, it works. The class are silent. Well, until the bloody puppy comes in, jumping up at them, licking their faces, swatting them with her wagging tail. It's like trying to control the riot when a group of young girls spot their adored boy band. All the shushing and holding my arms out as a barrier is never going to have the desired effect, so I sink back into my chair and pray none of the children tell their parents they spent the morning being mauled by an untrained animal.

Just as I'm looking on, as if the class belong to someone else, my eyes fall on Harley, now happily joining in with the class to smother the poor puppy, the bruise on his face shouting at me like a flashing light, and I know I've got no choice but to raise the alarm, even though I worry that if I do, I'm only going to make things worse for him, let alone the effect it will have on Emma.

*

'We're going to have to make a call to social services, Noah. There are too many red flags.'

'But Mum seems like a good person. I really think there'll be an innocent explanation.'

'It's often the quiet ones.'

'Let me do a home visit. If her explanation doesn't wash or if I feel there needs to be some kind of intervention, we'll make the call.'

Mrs Jackson takes a deep breath. 'I want a thorough check and a thorough report.'

'Of course. Absolutely. Thank you. I'll call her now and tell her I'm going over after school.'

'And try to get out of Harley what happened. Then you can see if their stories match.'

'Will do.'

*

All day, Harley refuses to tell me what happened, which makes me even more concerned about what I'm going to find when I get to the house. Following the satnav, I pull up outside. It's a terraced house at the far end of a large estate.

When I knock on the door, no one answers for a while, but I can hear Harley yelling about something on the other side. There's some banging and then Harley opens it.

'Hi, Mr Carlton. How come you're here?'

'I came to have a quick chat with Mummy. I just wanted to . . .'

'I'll be there in a sec,' Emma calls down and then she appears at the top of the stairs. She's wearing joggers and a cropped sports top, and her hair is pushed off her face with a hairband. She's so skinny I can see the bones and the sinew beneath her skin. She pulls on a loose-fitting T-shirt and heads downstairs.

'Do you want to come and see my bedroom?' Harley says, looking up at me expectantly.

I place my hand on his head. 'Not just now, little man. I need to talk to Mummy for a bit. Perhaps you could go and make something, then you could show me it?'

When Emma reaches the bottom of the stairs, she shoos Harley up and guides me through to the lounge, where I sit down on the worn-out leather sofa.

181

'Can I get you a drink? A coffee? Squash?'

I shake my head. 'I'm fine. Come and sit down a minute.'

'It's about his eye, isn't it?' Emma looks at the floor and I notice that her eyes look black too, except not with bruises, just exhaustion.

'Sort of. The school just wanted me to come and check everything is OK.'

I don't want to go in all guns blazing. Partly because she's more likely to cover up the truth if I do that, but also there could still be a perfectly innocent explanation.

Emma shakes her head and I think she's preparing for battle, but then I notice her eyes are filled with tears. 'I didn't mean to hurt him, I swear.'

As she says it, there's a sinking feeling in my stomach, because I'd so hoped she wasn't going to have been the perpetrator. I'd so hoped there was going to be some other explanation.

'He was just going on and on at me and I told him to stop, that Mummy needed him to stop, but he wouldn't. He just kept shouting at me and I pushed him to get him away from me, but I pushed him too hard and he hit his face on the TV unit.' She points at the MDF cabinet supporting the ridiculously large flat-screen TV. 'It was an accident. You believe me that I'd never hurt him on purpose, don't you?'

I nod because I can tell that Emma's not a bad person and we've all been pushed to our limits before. Sometimes you grab your kids a bit too hard, push them into their car seat a little over-zealously, but at the same time, there's something about Emma that makes me worried for Harley.

'Please don't tell the school,' Emma continues. 'I just have bad days sometimes. But I'm trying my best. I know I'm not a great mum but I do love him. I love him with all my heart.'

'I can see that. I just wonder if it would help having someone to talk to. What about Mimi? Could she help you out sometimes when you're having a bad day?'

'Oh, God, no. Please don't tell Mimi what happened. She thinks little enough of me as it is.'

'She really doesn't. That's in your head, you know.'

'Trust me, she despairs of me most of the time. If you tell her this, she'll take Harley off me and I'd die if that happened. He's all I've got.'

'I would never tell her. It's confidential. But of course she wouldn't take him off you. She knows you're a good mum.'

Emma shakes her head. 'You don't know her like I do. When it comes to stuff like this, she's very black and white. You mess up, you don't get any more chances.' She looks so drained I can't help but feel sorry for her. 'After a while, it takes its toll, you know, always being the black sheep, the lesser daughter, the failure. This would just be more fuel to the fire. I don't want her to know I'm still struggling. She thinks I'm doing better. And I am. Most days.'

The thing is, I know exactly how she feels. The desire to hide your perpetual mistakes from a sibling that never makes any.

'I just think . . .'

Then there's the sound of the door crashing open and Harley appears in the lounge. 'I've made a rocket to show you. Will you come up?'

He looks so desperate to show me his creation, I can't turn him down. 'Is that OK?' I ask Emma.

'Of course. Just ignore the mess. I'm going to have a big tidy-up tonight.'

'Don't worry, my flat is always a mess. It's no problem.'

Harley leads me up to his room and I search it for signs of neglect, but other than the fact I can't see any books, it's a perfectly adequate kid's room. There's a bed, a few toys, a large photograph of him and Emma on a canvas on the wall. And then, touchingly, I notice he's Sellotaped his drawings of Finn and Gabe to his wardrobe door.

'You put your pictures up?'

Harley looks at them and nods. 'They're my friends. And it was one of my favourite days.'

I feel a lump forming in my throat, then Harley pulls me on to the floor to show me the rocket he's made out of Lego. Like most of Finn's creations, it is basically just a base plate with four walls built up on it (it's amazing what that basic construction can masquerade as), but he flies it into the air and makes whooshing sounds to show it really is a rocket.

'Awesome rocket. Well done, you. And thanks for giving me some time to talk to Mummy.'

'What were you talking about?' Harley asks, swirling his rocket around in a loop-the-loop.

'Just checking you and Mummy are OK, and talking to Mummy about that baddy on your face.'

Harley drops his rocket and his eyes to the floor.

'You know, you can always talk to me about anything, Harley.'

Harley keeps his eyes fixed on the carpet. I notice it could do with a good hoover, but it's not exactly a child protection issue. If it were, I'd have been hauled straight in to the boys' school for a telling-off.

'Mummy told me what happened.' I put my hand on Harley's shoulder.

He looks up at me briefly then looks away again. 'I didn't mean to make her so cross. I just really wanted to try out my new scooter.'

I hear it in his voice – the fear, the shame – and it suddenly dawns on me that Harley hasn't been protecting his mum as I'd first thought – he's been protecting himself.

I can still remember it as clearly as if it were yesterday. It wasn't the first time Mum hit me, but it's the time that hurt the most, emotionally anyway. I was nine. It was a Sunday. I'd spent the day alone in my room. Ben had been at a friend's, Mum had been in her shed 'studio' and God knows where Dad was. Running away somewhere as usual, probably. Anyway, I'd spent all day on this painting of Mum – it was supposed to be a surprise for her. I'd copied the photograph of her on the windowsill, sitting in a field of bluebells, her long dark hair blowing in the wind.

When I was finally happy with it, after two or three attempts, I took it down with me and went to knock on the shed door. Mum hadn't answered at first and I'd wondered if she was asleep, but I was desperate for her to see my painting so I kept knocking. After what seemed like a really long time, she opened the door and before I even had a chance to speak, she slapped me right around the face.

'If I don't answer, it's because I'm working,' she said, her eyes full of rage, spittle erupting from her mouth and landing on her lips.

Then she slammed the door in my face and I ran back up to my room, ripped up the painting, buried my head in my pillow and wept. I was so ashamed I never told anyone what happened, not even Ben.

It's so clear to me now that Harley is feeling exactly what I felt. And it makes me surprisingly furious.

'You didn't do anything wrong, OK, buddy?'

Harley doesn't look convinced and it suddenly feels exceptionally important that I make him realize this is not his fault.

'You were not being a naughty boy. You have to understand that. It's OK to be really excited about something and find it hard to wait. It's OK to be . . .' I want to say 'a kid' but I know that wouldn't make any sense to him.

'I haven't been on it yet. It's really cool. It's blue. My favourite colour.'

'Do you want to go and try out your new scooter now?'

Harley circles his room and then slumps on his bed. 'Mummy said she's too tired.'

'That's OK. Mummy can rest. I'll take you out.'

The happiness on Harley's face makes me want to pick him up and hold him. And at the same time I feel guilty. For not doing more for him. For all the times I've failed with my own boys.

'Come on then. Let's go and get it.'

'It's in the cupboard under the stairs. I can't reach it.'

'No problem. I can do it.'

We go downstairs and I get his scooter out of the cupboard. It's full of crap and getting it out is a mission and a half, but I eventually manage it. Probably wondering what all the crashing is, Emma puts her head around the door.

'Harley wants to show me his new scooter. Is it OK if I take him out for twenty minutes?'

Emma looks like she's trying to work out the catch. 'Of course. Tea will be ready by about five.'

I look at my watch. Half four. 'Perfect timing. Come on then, Harley. Helmet on.'

I put the helmet on his head and fasten it, careful not to catch his skin. I remember when I did that to Gabe once. Four years on and he still won't let me do his helmet up for him.

Harley leads me to a quiet side alleyway and scoots up and down, giggling every time he reaches me, skilfully stopping just before he crashes into me and sends me flying.

'Look how fast I am,' he shouts whilst zooming along.

'You're amazing, Harley. A superstar.'

When it's time to go back, Harley's reluctant, but I persuade him with the promise of taking him out again soon. When we get in, Emma's putting tea on the table. It's lasagne and looks home-cooked and I feel guilty that I'd expected convenience food from the freezer.

'Right, Harley, eat up. I'll be one minute.'

Harley takes his food into the lounge and I hear him put the TV on before Emma closes the door.

'So what are you going to tell the school?'

I'm so confused about what to do. I don't think Harley's in real physical danger – Emma shouldn't have pushed him, but I believe she didn't mean to hurt him. There are no signs of serious neglect. He might not be given breakfast sometimes but Emma obviously cares for him. The majority of the time he's fed, watered, clean. His basic needs appear to be being met. And yet I feel uneasy. Because I see so much of my mum in Emma. I can see that she's struggling and trying to hide it from the world, and it feels like the littlest thing could tip her over from just about getting by to not coping at all.

'I'll tell them it was an accident.'

'Oh, thank you so much. It *was* an accident. I promise nothing like that will ever happen again.'

'If it does, Emma, I will have to report it and the head teacher might need to take it further. You understand that, don't you?'

Emma's head falls and when she looks up her eyes are full of tears. She looks so desolate I know I can't just walk away. I unclip the pen from my shirt and find a scrap of paper in my trouser pocket.

'Here's my number. I shouldn't really give it to a parent so please don't say anything to anyone, but if you're really struggling and need someone to come and take Harley out for a run around or whatever, please give me a call.'

Emma takes the paper from me, and I get the sense from her expression that she's not used to people doing kind things for her. 'Thanks.'

I'm scared that, being as fragile as she is, she might abuse it, but at the same time it feels like the right thing to do for Harley.

'And I'd really advise you to open up to Mimi or anyone else you feel close to. People want to help, not judge.'

Emma nods, but I'm fairly sure my advice is falling on deaf ears.

'I'll see you both in the morning, OK? Take care.'

Emma closes the door and I walk back to my car, feeling unsettled the whole way home.

CHAPTER FIFTEEN

'Wow! Finally, we can see your face.'

I smile at Mimi's reflection in the mirror, whilst the hairdresser puts the finishing touches to my cut. It's long overdue. I like it to be tousled, but it was definitely starting to look more 'tramp'.

'He's actually quite good-looking, isn't he?' the bloke doing my hair teases, then he turns on the hairdryer, blowing the clippings off my shoulders first and then running his fingers through my hair whilst he dries it. When he's finished, he puts in a bit of wax and I'm good to go.

'Ta-da,' he says, taking off my gown and spinning my chair so I'm facing Mimi, who starts clapping. 'A new and improved boyfriend.'

'Oh, he's not my boyfriend,' Mimi clarifies. 'He's not *that* good-looking.'

The hairdresser laughs and gives Mimi a high five. 'You go, girl.'

I smile and follow him to the counter to pay and then we head out along the river towards the pub, the early evening sun making Bristol Docks feel almost Mediterranean. En route, we pass an art gallery advertising an exhibition by a local artist, so I stop for a second to look at the poster in more detail.

'You know, I've never been to a gallery before,' Mimi says, pausing beside me.

'What? Never?' I almost shout.

'All right. All right. Don't make me feel like a philistine. It's not that I haven't wanted to. I've just never really had anyone to go with, I guess.'

I take her hand and pull her towards the doors. 'Well, now you do.'

'What are you doing? I thought we'd come out tonight to work on *making a better you.*' When she says the last bit, she adds quotation marks with her fingers.

'Isn't part of self-improvement doing things for other people?'

Mimi smiles. 'I suppose so.'

Inside, we circle the paintings, pausing at each one for several minutes, in keeping with all the other arty types next to us. Mum always used to do that, standing and staring for ages, as if she'd entered some kind of trance and couldn't be reached, shushing us if we dared to ask her a question. I never quite understood it. Surely once you've given it a good look, you've seen it. Time to move on. But maybe I'm missing something, a greater depth of experience I'm not capable of.

'Is it just me or does that one look like a vagina?' Mimi whispers into my ear. 'You should know. You've seen your fair share.'

'Very funny.' I take a more considered look at the painting. 'Can't quite see it myself, but you might be right.' Then I read the title listed on a plaque to the side. 'Look, it's called *Opening.*'

She looks like a kid – the thrill of getting something right. 'Told you so. Check out my interpretation skills. I might not have been to an art gallery before but I'm clearly a natural.'

I point to a poster advertising for a part-time gallery guide. 'There you go. Perfect job for you.'

She continues to look smug whilst we walk into the next section. It's the permanent exhibition, a lot of dark Surrealist stuff, some Pre-Raphaelite. It's not really my cup of tea, and when I turn to Mimi I'm glad to see she looks a bit glassy-eyed herself. 'Come on, I think I've had enough high-brow culture for one evening. Let's go and get that drink.'

For the first time this year, it's warm enough this late in the evening to sit outside, so we order our drinks and then find a table overlooking the water.

'So, we've sorted out your chakras, created some slightly phallic-looking homework, your flat no longer looks like you're a student, you're no longer rocking the whole homeless-chic look and you're not *quite* such an alcoholic.' Mimi eyes my beer. 'Now I think we should focus on your strengths. What do you think Kate loved about you?'

'Other than this face and this body?'

'Yes, as irresistible as they are, I'm guessing she didn't marry you based solely on your looks.'

I search my brain for reasons, then shrug. 'I can be quite thoughtful when I want to be. Romantic, I guess.'

Mimi's face lights up. 'Perfect! So what could you do that would remind her how thoughtful you are, without making Jerry suspicious?'

Before I have a chance to respond, there's a tap on my shoulder and I turn around to see Ben and Claudia, dressed up to the nines, standing behind me.

'I thought it was you,' Ben says.

'Oh, hey, you. What are you doing out? You both look very smart.'

'It's date night. We try to go out once a month.'

'Well, we go out more than that,' Claudia says, correcting Ben as usual. 'But we make sure we have a special night out each month, just the two of us, don't we, Ben?'

Isn't that what he just said?

Not daring to argue, Ben paints on a smile.

'We've just been for a meal at that fantastic new restaurant. You know, the seafood one. So we thought we'd follow it with a glass of wine.' Claudia looks at Mimi. 'Sorry, my rude brother-in-law here hasn't introduced us. I'm Claudia. This is my husband, Ben. And you are?'

'I'm Mimi.'

Claudia looks her up and down and then looks at me, obviously trying to work out what's going on between us.

'Mimi's my friend,' I clarify.

'Well, it's nice to meet you, Mimi,' Ben says, holding out his hand. It looks oddly formal, but Mimi politely shakes it.

'Would you like to join us?' I ask, although I hope they'll say 'No', not wanting to inflict Claudia on Mimi.

Ben looks at Claudia, as if searching for the right answer in her eyes. 'Well, we don't get much time to ourselves so I think we might pass, but . . .'

'Nonsense,' Claudia interrupts. 'Ben, go and get me a glass of wine. White, but not the house one. Something

193

fresh and crisp. Look at the menu, don't just ask the barman. They know nothing.'

'OK, I'll try my best.' Ben glances at Mimi, who gives him a slyly supportive smile. 'Do you guys want another one?'

'I'm fine, thanks,' Mimi says, putting her hand over her glass.

'I'll stick to this one. It is a school night after all.'

Ben gives me a shocked look and Mimi looks decidedly proud. Then Ben goes inside to get the Queen her drink.

'So Mimi, what do you do?' Claudia says, clutching her handbag tightly in her lap, as if she's scared someone might try to steal it.

'I'm a barmaid.'

'Oh right, so what are you studying?'

'Nothing. I'm not a student. I'm just a barmaid. You're right, we know nothing.'

Claudia looks like she's swallowed a particularly sharp bone and I feel a renewed admiration for Mimi. Anyone who's willing to take on Claudia is all right in my book.

'I didn't mean it like that. I just meant they're not always wine connoisseurs just because they work behind a bar.'

'Don't worry. You're right. All tastes much the same to me.' Mimi pushes her chair back and stands up. 'Anyway, I need a wee. I'll be right back.'

As she goes inside, she passes Ben who smiles widely at her. When he reaches the table, he puts the drinks down and sits opposite me, next to Claudia.

'So, tell us more . . .' Ben says, taking a sip of his beer.

'There's nothing to tell. Like I said, we're friends.'

Ben smiles. 'Oh, come off it. *You* are friends with *her*?'

'What do you mean by that, Ben?' Claudia says and I imagine the bollocking he is going to get when he gets home.

'I just mean . . .' Ben pauses, clearly trying to think of a way to dig himself out of the hole he's thrown himself into. 'I mean she's not a patch on you,' he puts his hand on Claudia's knee, 'but she's an attractive girl and, besides, I didn't think Noah would be *just* friends with a girl unless they were thirty years older than him or a nun.'

'I'm not saying I've *never* slept with her,' I say and Ben laughs.

'Oh, come on, Noah,' Claudia says, shifting in her chair like a bird ruffling its feathers. 'Don't you fancy something more serious now? She's not exactly marriage material, is she?'

I feel suddenly protective of Mimi. Although there's nothing going on between us, it's certainly not because she's not worthy. 'I told you we're just friends. But, for the record, why the hell not? Because she's *only* a barmaid? What about the fact she's kind, and funny, and I don't feel quite so crap when I'm around her?'

Ben looks concerned, like he thinks I might be about to make a scene. 'Claudia didn't mean anything by it, did you, love?'

'No, I just meant . . .' but she stops mid-sentence, as her eyes fix on something and I turn around to see Mimi walking towards us.

Mimi climbs on to the bench beside me. 'So, what have you lovely people been saying about me? I could feel my ears burning whilst I was in the toilet.'

'Just that we're glad Noah finally has at least one friend,' Ben says, smoothly defusing the tension around the table.

'It's a tough job but someone's got to do it,' Mimi says, slapping me on the back.

'Try being his brother.'

'All right, all right, enough Noah-bashing for one night, thank you very much,' I say, holding up my hands. 'So was your meal good?'

'Oh, it was exceptional,' Claudia says. 'I'd highly recommend it.'

'Looks a bit fancy for me. I prefer my fish with chips and mushy peas.'

Claudia gives me a look of despair. Sometimes I think I say things just to annoy her.

'So how about you guys?' Ben asks. 'What have you been up to?'

'Noah took me to my first art exhibition,' Mimi says. 'And I thoroughly enjoyed it.'

'Ah, yes, Mum's protégé.' Ben smiles. 'I think all those tedious gallery trips put me off for life.'

'I blame your mum for ruining my cultural social life. He wouldn't even go to see Monet's 'Water Lilies' when we were in Paris.'

'When you've seen one painting, you've seen them all. Now Maths, that's what you call beautiful.'

I laugh. 'Once a geek, always a geek.'

Ben smiles. 'Well, we can't all be as hip and trendy as you, can we, Noah?'

I suddenly have a vision of Gabriel and Finn when they're older, throwing warm-hearted banter at each other. Gabriel will be like Ben – settled, steady, logical.

He'll have savings, a secure marriage, a sensible job. Finn will be the one going to art exhibitions, falling nonsensically in love with unsuitable girls. I just hope he'll make fewer mistakes than me. That he'll be happier. I remember when Finn arrived and the midwife handed him to me, wrinkled and blue-tinged, there was a momentary flicker of disappointment that he was another boy. I'd wanted to experience a daughter – the different dynamic – but now I'm so glad we had two boys. There's something pretty special about brothers and I hope my boys will always have what Ben and I do.

'Right, come on, Claudia,' Ben says, picking up his beer. 'Let's leave these two in peace and go and discuss highly important matters like our children's education.'

Claudia gives a forced smile, but I can tell Ben's going to get an earful later for implying their lives are less glamorous than ours.

'Well, nice to meet you, Mimi,' Claudia says, leaning over and giving Mimi an air kiss on both cheeks.

'You too,' Mimi says. 'And you, Ben.'

Ben kisses Mimi on the cheek too, unlike his wife making contact with her skin. 'Keep him out of trouble for me, will you? Or at least make sure it's the good kind of trouble.'

'Will do.'

'Oh, and remember I'll pick you up at nine tomorrow. Can you manage to be up and ready that early?' Ben says to me.

'I'll be ready.'

They wander off to find a table indoors and I notice Mimi looks concerned. 'Did I say something to offend them?'

'No. Of course not. I think Ben knows I can only tolerate Claudia for very short periods.'

'She's nice. I get the sense she's just insecure.'

'Well, she's pretty confident in her criticism of me.'

'Clearly a good judge of character then.' Mimi smiles. 'Anyway, how come you're not going to work tomorrow?'

'It would've been my mum's birthday. Ben and I always go to the beach, because that was her favourite place.'

Taking me by surprise, Mimi looks like she's about to cry. 'Oh. That's really lovely.'

'It's become a sort of tradition really, like turkey at Christmas,' I say dismissively.

'Well, I think it's a really sweet way to honour your mum.'

'Thanks.'

We fall into a slightly awkward silence, both turning to our drinks. But then Mimi looks at me with a serious expression. 'How come you never want to talk about her? Your mum, I mean.'

I shrug. 'There's nothing much to say, I guess. She's gone. Talking about her isn't going to bring her back.'

'But don't you find it comforting to share your memories of her?'

I scrape my teeth over my bottom lip and shake my head.

'Fair enough.' Mimi eyes our empty glasses and then stands up, and I feel bad for shutting her down. 'I'm going to head home. Thank you for my initiation into the world of art galleries.'

'No problem.'

'And remember your homework for this week. Something thoughtful for Kate, OK?'

'I'll work on it.'

Mimi smiles, but she looks as if she's sitting on what she really wants to say. 'I hope tomorrow goes well. I'll see you soon.'

'Thanks.' I watch her walk away and then head home. When I reach my door, I have a sudden brainwave. *Something thoughtful for Kate.* I go straight to my laptop and look up the name of the gallery, navigating my way through the website until I find details of the part-time vacancy. I scribble down all the details, pop them in an envelope, write Kate's address on the front, add a stamp and then walk straight to the postbox at the end of the road.

CHAPTER SIXTEEN

I wonder if we'll always do this. Even as two old men, Ben driving an automatic electric car, me in the passenger seat, walking stick resting on my knee, our few wisps of hair blowing from one side of our heads to the other, as the air channels through the open windows. So far, we've not missed one of the eleven years since she died. Our employers seem to understand it's a non-negotiable and there's no way Ben or I would ever let each other down.

We always play the same CD on the journey down. The Cranberries. Mum's favourite. And we sing at the top of our voices even though neither of us can hit a note. When we're nearly there, we stop at the same bakery in Braunton, just like we always did with Mum. I wonder if it will still be here when we're old. Perhaps we'll all be eating rehydrogenated space food by then. We buy three jam doughnuts, one each, and we share one for Mum. We don't eat them until we get to the beach. Mum wouldn't have let us, however much we moaned at her. 'They have to be eaten overlooking the sea,' she always said and then she'd draw an imaginary zip across her lips to signal the end of the discussion.

When we reach the beach, we take our paper bag full of doughnuts and Mum's picnic blanket (she made it using the material from all our old baby clothes) down to the water's edge and set up camp. This year, the weather's not too bad. It's a bit cold, but bearable with a hoody on. We've had all sorts: pelting rain, glorious sunshine, severe winds. But rain or shine, we pitch up in the same spot and watch the waves rolling in.

'It's stupid, but I definitely miss her more on her birthday,' Ben says, wiping the sugar from above his lips. 'Well, all the big days, I suppose. My birthday. Mother's Day. The anniversary of her death. It's ridiculous really. It's just another day.'

I nod, but don't say anything. It's something I've never understood. The way everyone suddenly sends me messages of support on these days, as if every day isn't a struggle. I take another bite of my doughnut and the jam trickles down my chin so I stick out my tongue to reach it, and it returns to my mouth peppered in jammy sand.

'Do you remember that one time we came to the beach?' Ben continues. 'When she disappeared and didn't return until the sun was going down? I tried to make that spear with a stick like I was some sort of survival expert.'

Ben laughs and I smile, but it's not a happy smile. This isn't one of the memories we normally conjure. Usually, it's the good ones. Mum being crazy and running into the sea fully clothed, Mum helping us to build a sandcastle that looked like it belonged on the pages of *The Guinness Book of World Records*, Mum chasing the ice-cream van down the road and slamming on the back of it until it stopped because we 'must' have an ice cream when we're at the seaside. Part of me wonders if this is Ben's thinly veiled attempt to talk about some of the other stuff, the stuff we never talk about, but I'm not sure if I'm game. I don't think Ben ever knew what she said to me that night, once we'd finally got home and he was fast asleep in the bed next to me. There's a lot I never told him. Although I was younger, I felt the need to protect him. Mum tended to confide in me for some reason. I think Ben thought it meant she loved me more, but it always felt like it was because she loved me less.

'I'm sure you would've managed to keep us alive. You were always pretty good at looking after me.'

'Thanks. You were pretty easy to look after. Back then, anyway.'

I press my lips together. 'Yeah, I've made up for it in the past few years, I guess.'

'You seem to be doing better, though?' It's definitely more of a question than a statement.

'Yeah. Most days.' I force a small smile.

'I thought Mimi seemed lovely. She's the one from that night in the bar, isn't she?'

'Yeah.'

'I can see what you mean about her bum. Remarkable.'

'Isn't it? It's almost inhuman.'

'*Never* tell Claudia I said that, though.'

'I'll try to resist the temptation to split you up.'

Ben splits the last doughnut, handing one half to me then licking off the jam that's spilt on to his fingers before crumpling up the paper bag and pushing it into the outer pocket of his rucksack. 'She's not what you think, you know? She's a lot less sure of herself than she lets on and it doesn't always make her come across well.'

'Funnily enough, that's what Mimi said.'

'See, I knew she was a keeper.'

I smile.

'It's OK to move on and be happy, you know? Kate won't mind. Mum wouldn't mind.'

Except she would. For all the wonderful things about Mum, selflessness wasn't one of them. She hated it when I was happy without her.

'Do you really think my misery is some strange feeling of guilt for getting on with my life without Mum? Or Kate, for that matter.' I shake my head. 'I just miss her. Every day. And I keep waiting for it to get better, but it doesn't. Or it does for a while, but then it hits me again like a truck.'

'Mum or Kate?'

'I don't know. Both, I guess. I know everyone thinks I should just be OK by now. That I'm milking it, wallowing in my misery. But I am trying. If I could just get on with my life, I would.'

'You think I loved her less, don't you? Because I manage to be happy?'

I shake my head, but it has crossed my mind before. In my less rational moments, I feel angry at him. For not being as much of a mess as I am. 'Of course not. Everybody deals with things differently.'

'Come on, Noah. I know that's what you think. I know we weren't as close as you two, but I did love her. But I can't let what happened ruin the rest of my life and you shouldn't either. Give yourself a chance to feel something for someone.'

I pick up a shell and draw lines in the sand with it, wondering whether to tell Ben about the plan to try to get Kate back, but I know he'd just say it's a stupid idea and that I need to face the fact it's over. 'Right, shall we go for a walk? I'm sure no one's going to come and steal our stuff.'

We stroll along the beach, chatting about Ben's girls and my boys, about *Game of Thrones* and *Stranger Things*, about what we'd do with the money if we won the lottery. He, incidentally, would buy an even bigger house, a sports car and take the family to Disney World, then put the rest in savings. I'd quit work and travel the world (in my head, the kids and Kate would come with me, like one of those nomadic families). We reminisce about school and Mum, avoiding the memory he brought up earlier.

But in the car on the way home, I can't stop myself from thinking about it. Once she'd eventually found us, huddled by the rocks shivering, with the picnic blanket wrapped around us, she'd pretended that she hadn't abandoned us without telling us where she was going, and had taken us for hot chocolates at the beach café. As usual, I'd immediately forgiven her, won over by the treat, but Ben had sat sulking the entire time and refused to speak.

She'd driven home and I'd sat in the front beside her, both of us singing along to the radio, whilst Ben stared out the window. When we'd got home, she'd taken us up to bed and lain beside us, all of us squished on a single mattress, Ben against the wall, me in the middle and Mum just about squeezing on to the edge. Ben had fallen asleep in minutes, but I'd stayed awake talking to Mum. Then, I'm not sure what I said wrong, something about wishing we'd spent all day together, but, whatever it was, her face had suddenly changed.

'If it hadn't been for you and your brother fighting, I wouldn't have left today. I just had to get away from you both.'

'Sorry, Mummy. I didn't mean to fight.'

'Well, it's easy to say that now, isn't it?'

Often, I rack my brain for the fight she was referring to. But I'm becoming more and more sure over the years that there wasn't one. Or if there was, that it was something minor that wouldn't even constitute a fight between my boys. But at the time, I just wanted to rewind and not do whatever it was that drove her away.

'I promise I'll never do it again. Can we go to the beach again?'

'Well, I'll think about it. We'll see whether you boys deserve it.'

'OK.'

I never argued with what Mum said. Instead, I'd closed my eyes and tried to sleep. After a little while, Mum had started to stroke my hair and I'd felt her body shudder as she cried. I'd pretended to be asleep, scared to open my eyes, scared what she might tell me or ask me. Some of the stuff she offloaded on to me sometimes was frightening for a young boy. I didn't always understand it, and the look that accompanied her thoughts always made me feel panicky in my stomach.

'I love you so much, little Noah, my precious angel,' she whispered through the sobs. 'I love you so much.'

She never said she loved Ben, but I'm sure she did.

'I've been meaning to tell you something,' Ben says, bringing me back to the present with a jolt.

'What is it? Claudia's not up the duff again, is she?'

'No, nothing like that.' Ben smiles but he looks uncomfortable, his Adam's apple bulging as he swallows. 'It's to do with Dad.'

I turn my head to look directly at him, but he keeps his eyes on the road.

'I realized that it's not fair on the kids to miss out on a relationship with him,' he continues. 'It's time to bury the hatchet and all that. So we started FaceTiming him a bit. And I took the girls to meet him.'

I nod, forcing Ben into a very one-sided conversation. I haven't seen Dad since he abandoned us on the day of Mum's funeral. Sometimes it feels like yesterday. Sometimes it feels so long ago. But I'll never forget the sheepish look on his face when he came over, stinking of booze, and told us that he was moving away, he needed some space, and that we could sell the house and split the profits if we wanted, each buy ourselves a flat. He said it like he was doing us a favour, as if providing financial support was all a parent was needed for anyway. I went mental, screaming at him, but he just walked away with his head hanging and Ben held me back and wrapped his arms around me until I calmed down.

'He'd really love to see you. To meet the boys. I said I'd talk to you but that I couldn't promise him you'd want to.'

'Well, you got that bit right.'

Ben sighs and it feels like he's mocking me – that he thinks I'm pathetic and childish. 'Aren't you tired of being angry with him, Noah? I know I was. OK, he wasn't the best husband to Mum, and it was really shit the way he lost contact with us, but . . .'

'Lost contact with us? He abandoned us, Ben.'

'We were grown men, Noah. He was grieving and . . .'

'*He* was grieving? Perhaps if he'd been a better husband in the first place then none of this would've happened. If he'd looked after her properly. In sickness and in health, right?'

'He tried. He did try, Noah.'

'He was never there.' Within the confines of the car, the volume of my voice is quite shocking, but I feel like I've been sitting on my emotions since he started the conversation and, like sitting on a semi-inflated balloon, they can't help but spill out from beneath me.

'Calm down. Please. I'm not saying you have to have a relationship with him or even understand why I am. I just wanted to be honest with you.'

'Right, well, thanks for being honest. And you can tell him I'd rather jump out of a plane without a parachute than ever let him see my boys.'

For the rest of the journey home, the sound of the indicators, the squeak of Ben's brakes, the rattling of the items tucked in the door pockets, painfully highlight the lack of conversation between Ben and me. But I'm so angry with him. He's supposed to be on my side, an ally, and him seeing Dad again feels like a huge betrayal.

*

When I get home, there's a package on the doorstep. I pick it up and take it in with me. Inside is a wooden box with a gold clasp. I flick it up and open the lid. There's a piece of paper inside with a note from Mimi that reads: *You might not find it easy to talk about your memories, but you shouldn't keep them in. This is a memory box. Write down your memories and put them in here.*

It physically hurts to read it. Because she's right, but I don't know how.

When I lift up the note, there's a little book underneath called *Penis Pokey*. My initial reaction is confusion, the two gifts like clashing colours, but then I open it and on the inside cover, Mimi has written: *Just because it was all getting a bit serious! x*

I smile as I scroll through the pages, a range of pictures with a hole in each one. I text Mimi.

Thank you for the thoughtful gifts. Who knew my penis made such a convincing banana? Xx

Then, because I suddenly can't bear the thought of a whole evening on my own, thoughts of Mum whirring around my head like a tornado, I text her again.

Do you fancy coming over?

*

We don't talk about today. Instead, we watch *The Apprentice* whilst working our way through a bottle of Jack Daniel's (Mimi allowing me to ignore my excessive drinking ban for tonight). It feels good to forget about Mum, about my argument with Ben, about Dad, about Kate. It feels good to laugh.

When the programme has finished and I'm feeling quite drunk, I go through to my bedroom and come out with my guitar. I haven't played for years. I dabbled with it a bit at university, hoping playing an instrument would make me appear cool, but I was never much good.

'Play me something,' I say, handing Mimi the guitar. 'One of your songs.'

Mimi takes it, wrapping her arms around it like it's a child she hasn't seen in a long time. 'Oh, I don't know. What if you think I'm terrible?'

'I'll lie.'

Mimi rolls her eyes.

'I heard you at karaoke, remember? You are not terrible.'

'OK,' Mimi says, getting the guitar straight and putting her fingers on to the strings. 'But only because I'm feeling quite drunk. And you have to turn around.'

'Don't be ridiculous.'

'I'm not playing unless you turn around.'

I laugh. 'OK, boss.' I turn my body so that I'm facing the arm of the sofa and cross my legs. 'Go on then.'

Mimi clears her throat and then starts plucking the guitar strings delicately. After a few bars of a pretty introduction, she takes a deep breath and then she starts to sing.

And my immediate visceral reaction takes me by surprise. The tone of her voice is so beautiful. Without the distraction of the karaoke track and the cheering crowd, it's pure and clear and has a slight rasp that makes the hairs on my arms stand up. And the song she's written is brilliant. It's all about heartbreak and the desire to find a way out of it, to reach a place where things no longer hurt.

And I wish I'd never asked her to sing because it feels like my head's about to burst and I have a sudden desire to delve into her story, to pour out mine. I'm just glad she asked me to turn around because I can't help it, there are tears in my eyes, and I just about manage to blink them away before she stops singing and I know I'm expected to turn around and give her my verdict.

As she sings the final note, I steady myself and turn towards her, perfecting my best wow-that-was-amazing expression, as if I'm just impressed by her talent rather than on the verge of curling up in a ball and weeping in a way that feels like I'll never stop.

'So?' she says, and her face looks like that of a child, desperately seeking approval.

'It was beautiful.' I want to say more but I'm scared that if I do then I'll say everything and she'll look at me like I'm insane and run away as fast as her legs will carry her.

'Do you really think so?'

I nod, swallowing down the lump lodged in my throat.

'Well, thanks. I know you're probably lying but it's still nice to hear.'

'I'm not lying.'

We sit in silence for a moment, the raw emotion of the song still floating in the air between us, changing the atmosphere, like somehow it's stripped us naked and left us both exposed.

'So who's the song about?' I eventually ask. 'Who's the guy that broke your heart?'

Mimi shakes her head. 'It was a long time ago. I don't really want to talk about it.'

'You sound like me. Perhaps we're both emotionally stunted?'

She offers a weak smile. 'Maybe.' Then she pulls out her phone, scrolling through the calendar, and I get the sense she's desperately looking for a way to change the subject.

'So, only ten days to go until the big day. Do you think you're going to be able to put a stop to it?'

'I don't know. I'm not sure what else to do. How to convince her to choose me.'

'Well, why exactly did you split up? You said you've had breaks and stuff before. What made this time different?'

I shrug, letting out a noisy breath. 'To be honest, I think it was a build-up. When I got scared about how much I loved her, how much I needed her and the kids, I couldn't cope with it, the fear of losing them, so I'd go off drinking, miss important events like parents' evening or dinner with her parents. Eventually she got fed up of covering for me. I think I always felt like I wasn't good enough for her, that she didn't really love me like I loved her, and it kind of became this self-fulfilling prophecy.'

Mimi doesn't interrupt or ask questions, just listens intently.

'The day she finally left I hadn't come home until nine o'clock in the morning. It was the day after Gabe's birthday. The day before, I'd rung her at school just to tell her I was missing her and she'd hurried me off the line because she was at some pre-school music group with Finn. Just before she'd put the phone down I'd heard a man's voice and her laughing about something. Turns out he'd just been asking her to pass the tambourines, but by the end of the school day I'd managed to turn it into her having an affair. Needless to say, I got wasted, ended up on the sofa of some guy I vaguely knew who deejayed in one of the local clubs. I turned my phone off. Totally forgot it was Gabe's birthday. Missed the whole thing. By the time I got home she'd packed her bags. I thought it was an idle threat like all the other times, but she never came home.'

'I'm sorry, Noah.'

'Why? It's my fault, isn't it? I was the idiot.'

'Doesn't make it hurt any less, though.'

True. It makes it hurt more.

'So you need to prove to her that you've learnt,' she continues. 'That you'd never do anything like that again.'

I drag my hands through my hair. 'But how do I know I wouldn't, Mimi? What if it's just in me and I can't help it?'

Mimi looks as if she wants to say something but isn't quite sure if she should.

'What is it?'

'Nothing.' Mimi starts tapping on her phone and then she stands up. 'There's an Uber just round the corner. I've got work tomorrow so I better get some sleep.'

I stand up to walk her to the door, not really wanting her to go. 'Thanks for coming. And for the gifts.'

'No problem. Hope they come in useful. Well, the memory box anyway.'

I smile, but my heart feels heavy, the intensity of the day's emotions making me feel suddenly exhausted.

'For what it's worth, I think she'd be crazy to let you go,' Mimi says, as she puts her hand on the latch.

'Really? After everything I just told you?'

'It's not often you find someone who loves you like you clearly love her. That's all any girl really wants, if they're honest.'

I'm surprised how much it means to me to hear that. 'Thank you.'

'No problem.' Then Mimi leaves, closing the door behind her.

*

The next morning, I'm just getting out the shower when I get a text from Kate. I wrap a towel around me and sit on the bed to read it.

I got your note about the job. It made me cry! That's exactly what I was looking for. Thank you. I'm going to call them today x

Followed by another text.

Thank you for being you, Noah xx

And suddenly the hope returns with force and I get ready with a renewed spring in my step, like I'm walking on clouds.

CHAPTER SEVENTEEN

'Boys, it's Daddy's day. I am not going to let you ruin it.'

Another yearly tradition. On the closest Saturday to Mum's birthday, we have a family day out – family in this context meaning me, Kate, Gabriel and Finn, even though our real family is nowhere near that neat any more. Kate always chooses what we do, with the aim of the day being to take my mind off Mum and to try to cheer me up. I thought it would stop when Kate and I split up, but, testament to the fact she's a remarkably better person than I am, she still insists we do it.

'Sorry, Daddy,' the boys say in stereo, as they reluctantly stop tearing shreds off each other in the back of the car.

'Where are we going anyway, Mummy?' Gabe says in that whiny way kids do.

'I told you, it's a surprise. You'll like it though.'

'Is it somewhere Nana would've liked?' Finn asks, completely unaware of the emotional weight attached to his question.

Kate must notice me flinch because she reaches over and puts her hand on my leg. 'Yeah, I'm sure she would've loved it.'

Seemingly satisfied, the kids plug themselves back into their in-car DVD players. And for a strange moment, it feels like we're just a normal family again, off on a day out, and the anxiety that usually resides in my stomach, like some sort of parasite, isn't completely conquered, but it feels like its forces have been weakened.

Kate returns her hand to her lap. 'I'm so sorry that the wedding's so close to your mum's birthday. It was a complete oversight of mine. I feel terrible.'

I don't even want to think about the wedding. I'm praying there's not going to end up being one.

'You were busy planning the second most exciting day of your life. It's understandable.'

Kate smiles. 'I'd hate for you to think I don't care about your feelings, because I really do.'

'I know. You're here, aren't you?'

Kate studies the satnav for a minute and then takes the next turn. 'Oh, and I rang that gallery. I've got an interview next week. Thank you so much, Noah.'

'Oh, it was nothing.'

Kate looks over at me and I'm sure I can see it in her eyes – the way she used to look at me – but at the same time, I'm scared to allow myself to hope. 'It's not nothing. You're always surprising me, you know?'

I try to keep calm and hide my anticipation by changing the subject. 'So where is it that we're going today, anyway?'

'Like the kids, you'll have to wait and see.'

We see signs for a sculpture trail, but I don't mention it, pretending I still don't know where it is she's taking me. Mum actually brought us here once when we were teenagers, but I'm not sure we were the right age to really appreciate it, shuffling all the way round with our heads to the floor wishing we were with our mates. We park up and do the usual toilet stop, both boys insisting they don't need to go but then producing enormous wees when we force them to 'have a try'.

'Right, our session starts in half an hour, but we need to go and have our safety talk.'

I don't recall any of the sculptures posing a safety risk. 'What safety talk?'

'Mummy, where are we going?' Finn says, copied by Gabe.

'There,' Kate says, pointing to something up ahead in the forest.

Finn and Gabe run ahead and, as we get closer, I finally see the rope course suspended at a great height amongst the trees.

'You do remember that time at the Eiffel Tower when they had to call the fire brigade to get me down because I was literally paralysed with fear and couldn't move, don't you?'

'I thought that was because you were scared of the lift?'

'Well, I was, but I was also petrified of the fact I was that far off the ground without a large metal shell other-wise known as a plane surrounding me.'

Kate takes my hand and pulls me along. 'Come on, it's not that high. And it's good to face your fears. It's life-affirming.'

'That's one way to describe it.'

When we reach the course, the boys stare up at it in wonder, whilst Kate queues up to check us all in. I pre-tend to be Macho Dad, jostling with the boys about racing ahead of them, but inside I feel like a timid toddler wish-ing I had a leg to hide behind. Kate comes back over with our wristbands, which I struggle to put on with franti-cally shaking hands. Then there's a quick safety talk. Some cocky sixteen-year-old who's not scared of anything joking about how to raise the alarm if you get scared and he'll come and rescue you. Then, much to my despair, he says it's time to put on our harnesses and attach ourselves to the overhead rope.

Kate goes first, then the two boys, with me bringing up the rear. We climb the stairs, my heart in my throat, and then we're up on the balance beam, suspended ten metres above the ground, attached to trees with a feeble bit of rope. Only two people are allowed on a platform at a time, thank God, as they barely look strong enough to take my weight let alone several others, so I wait until Gabe steps on to the next obstacle before I join Finn. Then suddenly I notice this overconfident brat of about ten coming up behind me and about to step on to the platform.

I hold out my hand. 'Only two people on the platform at a time. Didn't you hear what they said?'

The boy gives me a look of contempt and, ignoring my instruction, steps on to the platform. I wrap my arms around the tree and practically push Finn off on to the next challenge.

'Quick, Finn, get off.'

Finn looks confused but steps on to the wooden stepping-stones, skipping across them like a lamb. I follow him, gripping on to the rope above me so tightly it starts to chafe my skin. Then the little shit behind me steps on to the first one, jumping up and down so that it makes the rest of them wobble. I try to turn around to give him my scariest teacher stare, but I'm too terrified to twist my body that far so I just shout.

'Stop jumping.'

I hear him laughing and he starts to jump harder. I reach the platform and climb on, noticing that the tree protruding through the centre of it looks like it might have some sort of disease. It's thinning at the top and swaying *a lot*, especially with twat features behind me rocking the bloody thing. Surely, it shouldn't be moving that much. I make a note to mention it to the guys at the bottom, that's if I make it down alive.

I quickly move on to the rope bridge, but that's not much better, rocking from side to side with each step I take, but I can see the end in sight, the stairs down. I just need to make it to the next platform, round the corner, and I'm there.

I make it, clumsily unclip, and we're back on the ground.

'That was awesome,' Gabe says. 'Can we do it again?'

I crouch down, afraid my legs are about to buckle. 'Well, no, but it was fun, wasn't it?'

Kate puts her hand on my shoulder. 'You do realize that was just the practice? To check we could get our latches over the transitions?'

I feel my heart rise into my throat. 'Oh, yeah, I was just teasing the boys. Can't wait.'

Kate bites back a smile.

'Right, ready for the proper course?' the teenage lad says. 'You boys looked great. Dad looked a bit scared though, hey, Dad?' He slaps me on the back and I have to resist the temptation to grab his arm and snap it.

'Me, scared? Never. Raring to get back up there.'

'Right, let's go then. Do you want to do the course with the guide ropes to hold on to at the sides, or the one without the ropes?'

I look at the boys, imploring them with my eyes – *please choose the one with the ropes, please choose the one with the ropes* – whilst trying to look as nonchalant as possible.

'Without the ropes,' they both say in unison and Kate and the teenage lad laugh. I laugh too. It just gets stuck somewhere in my throat.

'Right, come on then.'

I carefully position myself between Finn and Gabe so there's no chance of the brat being anywhere near me, and this time Kate goes behind the three of us.

The next forty minutes is so terrifying that I have to block it out. I expect it'll all come out as some kind of post-traumatic stress disorder, but for now I've squashed it deep down inside my ego or super-ego or id or whatever it is. When the end is near, of the course, not my life thankfully, I feel a moment of what can only be described as pure elation. It's how I imagine it would feel to survive a plane crash, a sudden appreciation of the beauty of life mixed with the feeling you will forever be deeply scarred by what has happened to you. But then I realize that the rope our harnesses are attached to does not join the path back to the stairs down to the ground. It goes one way and one way only. To the zip wire. Now, I like a zip wire. Often, I've been known to argue with a pre-pubescent child or two that it's my turn, not theirs, so back off. But this zip wire means launching yourself from a platform over ten metres from the ground along a wire that is over eighty metres long.

The four of us stand on the platform waiting for our turns. You're allowed four on that platform. I did double-check.

'I'm a bit scared, Daddy,' Finn says, wringing his hands together.

I put my hands on his shoulders, using him for support. 'You'll be fine. You'll love it once you jump off.'

The instructor beckons for Finn to come over and he nervously shuffles towards him.

'OK, buddy. When you're ready just jump off. Hold the rope here, not at the top.' He shows Finn where to grip. 'When you get to the bottom, try to land bottom first. And then Jenna down there will help to clip you off, OK?'

Finn nods.

'Whenever you're ready then.'

Finn walks up to the edge of the platform and I suddenly wonder what kind of responsible parent would encourage their child to jump into the abyss with only a thin rope holding them up.

'It is perfectly safe, isn't it? You haven't had any incidents where a child's been hurt, have you?'

I ask in the guise of concerned parent, but he and I both know I'm asking for me.

'Oh, the rope snapped once, but I think the guy was just a bit overweight.'

I'm about to reach into my pocket for my phone and call the fire brigade to get us all down when the lad laughs.

'I'm kidding. It's perfectly safe.' I'm not sure this is a time for jokes. I'll be sure to put it on the feedback form. 'Go on, Finn. Jump as high as you can.'

Finn takes a little run up and then launches himself off the platform, the tree shaking as he whizzes down to the bottom. When he lands with a bump, a young girl picks him up and helps to unclip his harness. He stands at the bottom and I think he's putting his thumbs up, but he's so far away, I can't quite make it out.

'Right, your turn.'

I know it's my bloody turn. There's no one in front of me. I get how turns work.

'Go for it, Noah. Fly like a bird,' Kate says, giggling.

I turn around and glare at her then walk up to the edge of the platform, close my eyes and, not wanting to look like a wuss, I step off. As I do, it's the weirdest feeling as the rope takes my weight and I'm flying through the air.

'Woo hoo,' I shout, as the fear turns to pure joy, and then within seconds I'm at the bottom and Finn is running over to me and hugging me. In no time at all, Gabe has joined us and we all turn to watch Kate.

As she hurtles towards the ground, her face is fixed in a wide grin and her arms and legs are wriggling like a baby who hasn't yet learnt how to control its limbs. She lands backwards, bark flying up all over her and sticking to her hair. She unclips herself and then brushes herself off and we all walk back to the entrance to collect our certificates, then wander over to the nearby playground and get an ice cream.

Kate and I sit eating ours whilst the boys take theirs on to the climbing frame.

'Thank you for this.'

'Don't be silly. I'm sorry. I didn't realize you'd be so scared.'

'I wasn't scared.'

Kate raises her eyebrows.

'OK. Just moderately terrified.'

Kate smiles. 'Has it helped a little?'

I nod whilst finishing my mouthful. 'It always helps. You turn the worst part of my year into the best. I'll always be grateful for that.'

'Good. It's my pleasure. I love spending time with you and the boys.'

I feel like bashing my head against hers. *Come on, Kate. Doesn't that tell you something?*

'They've turned out pretty well, haven't they?' Kate tilts her head towards the climbing frame where our sons are playing tag, then licks all round the edge of her ice cream.

'They're perfect.'

'Well, I'm not sure you would've said that when they were beating the crap out of each other over breakfast, but they're good boys really. They're kind to everyone other than each other. They're polite. They try their best. I think they'll be good men.'

'Like their daddy.'

Kate nods, a serious expression on her face that doesn't quite fit with my jokey comment. 'Just like their daddy.'

I wonder what would happen if I kissed her. I can almost taste the sweet caramel on her lips. But instead, I lift my hand to her face and wipe the ice cream off the tip of her nose with my thumb.

'You're messier than they are.'

I might be mistaken but it feels like she leans into my hand, like she's pleading with me not to take it away. And then she puts her own hand on top of mine and I know I'm not imagining it.

There's a sudden yell in the distance and instinctively we both know it's Finn. It's part of being a parent. There can be a hundred kids shouting and screaming around you, but you know your own in a second. We frantically search the playground for where he is. Then Kate stops looking and starts running over to the fireman's pole, a screaming Finn lying on the ground next to it. I follow Kate over and she picks Finn up and holds him out for inspection. Luckily, he's got away with just a bloody fat lip, but he's white with the shock.

'He fell right from the top,' Gabe says, rushing over, the concern on his face for the brother he's usually attacking warming my heart.

Finn is hysterical and Kate holds him in close to her, his bloody lip making a mark on the shoulder of her T-shirt.

I stand behind her and kiss Finn on the forehead. 'Come on, mister. Let's get you home.'

I take Gabe's hand and we walk back to the car, Kate carrying Finn and rocking him all the way, whispering 'shh, shh' repeatedly until he starts to calm down. Then we reach the car and strap in a child each, Kate wiping Finn's tears and kissing his swollen lip.

'I'm sorry your fall ruined a lovely day,' Kate says to him, her brow furrowed.

'It was still my favourite day,' Finn says, a smile suddenly appearing on his face.

'And me,' Gabe says. 'Best day ever.'

'Can we have family days even when it's not Nana's birthday?' Finn says, unaware, as only a child can be, that it's a delicate subject.

'Then it wouldn't be as special, would it? Like if we had Christmas every day,' Gabe says and gives me a knowing look that smashes me into pieces.

'Exactly,' I say, tapping him on the head.

But, like Gabe, I know that it's a lie. And as Kate looks across the car at me, I'm pretty sure that she does too.

*

As soon as I'm home, I ring Mimi, desperate to tell her about my day with Kate, the way she held my hand to her face, the look in her eyes when Finn said what he did.

'Hey, Noah. How did it go?'

'I think there's a possibility this plan of ours might work,' I say excitedly.

'Wow.' Mimi is unable to hide the shock in her voice.

'You thought it was a lost cause, didn't you? You've just been humouring me with the quest to get Kate back.'

'No, of course not. I mean . . .'

'It's OK. To be honest, I never thought it was going to work either. But maybe you were right. Maybe I just needed to remind her why she fell in love with me in the first place.'

'That's great,' Mimi says, the positivity in her tone feeling somewhat forced.

'Do you think I'm being stupid? That it's all in my head?'

'No. I mean, I've not met Kate, but if you think she's starting to see things differently then I'm sure you're right.'

'I hope so. I mean, right now, she's still marrying someone else next weekend. But I'm going to take your advice. I'm going to tell her I love her. I'm going to fight for her.'

'Good for you.' Despite her words, she sounds downbeat and I wonder if I've done something to piss her off.

'It's all thanks to you, you know? Without you, I would've still been drinking in the pub every night and lamenting everything I've lost.'

'No problem. Just don't tell my boss that though, or I'll be in trouble for losing custom.'

I laugh. 'Don't worry. I won't.'

'Right, well, I'm going to go and get some sleep. Let me know how it goes with Kate.'

'I will. And Mimi?'

'Yeah?'

'Do you think I'm doing the right thing?'

She doesn't answer straight away and there's a ruffling, as if she is moving her phone from one ear to the other. 'Of course. This is what we've been working towards, isn't it? Our mission is almost complete.'

But as she says it, I realize that, in a strange way, I don't want our joint quest to be up. Because Mimi has inadvertently become a highlight on an otherwise grey landscape, the piece of cake at a birthday party, and if our little plan does succeed and, by some miracle, I manage to win Kate back, I can't imagine I'll be seeing much of Mimi any more. And without her, the months ahead feel that bit less bright. In the same way that being around some people drags you down, Mimi pushes you up, like you're sitting on someone's shoulders and can suddenly see all these things you couldn't see before.

'We could still meet up one night this week if you want? How about some more culture? A poetry reading or something this time?' I joke.

'I've actually got a really busy week this week, but keep me posted on how it all goes.'

'Oh, OK. Is everything all right?'

'Yeah, of course. I'm just tired. Speak soon, yeah?'

And at this, she puts the phone down and I try to ignore the sense that something's wrong, grab a pen and paper and start to plan what I'm going to say to Kate. When I'm about halfway through my speech, my phone vibrates with a message on WhatsApp. Noticing it's from Kate, I feel my heart going crazy in my chest, hoping that maybe she's going to tell me that she felt it too today, that she's calling the wedding off, but then I open the message properly and see that it's a photograph of the boys in their wedding suits, huge smiles on their faces. She's followed it with a heart eyes emoji. And it feels like a gut punch. I know she didn't send it to hurt me. That she just wants me to see how adorable our boys look. And they do. But I can't help the sinking feeling in my chest. Does this mean that, despite everything – the almost-kiss, her reaction to me finding her the job, the look in her eyes when Finn talked about us being together as a family all the time – she really is going to marry Jerry after all?

CHAPTER EIGHTEEN

It's Friday. The day before Kate's wedding. And I still haven't told her that I love her – that she should sack Jerry off and choose me. I nearly said it to her on the phone at the beginning of the week, but then she started talking about needing to get the boys new uniform and the moment was gone, lost in the detritus of our everyday lives. And since then, whenever I think of calling her, I start thinking about the picture of the boys in their wedding outfits and everything I have to say seems stupid, like she'll just laugh at me. And it's like this dense fog's fallen over me, this odd lethargy that I can't seem to shift.

And now I'm stuck at school doing Show and Tell, aka the very worst thing about primary school teaching. And there's a fair amount of crap – reports, paperwork, parents' evenings, accountability, planning, assessments. But Show and Tell is the worst, and by a very large margin.

Darcy holds up a sparkly gel keyring and the class stare at it, as if it's a rare and precious jewel. The problem is she hasn't quite got the concept of Show and *Tell*. It works best if you actually speak.

'So what do you want to tell them about your keyring, Darcy?'

Nothing. Not even an acknowledgement of the question.

'Was it a present?'

Perhaps a slight twitch of the head. It's hard to tell.

'What do you put the keyring on?'

Darcy stares at me, and I realize my error. Only ever ask yes or no questions.

'Do you put it on your bookbag?'

Finally, a clear nod of the head.

'Wonderful. Well, it's lovely. You can sit down now, Darcy. Who's next?'

I look down at the list of names who didn't do it last week and, with a sense of trepidation, see that Harley is next.

'Harley. Come on then. Your turn.'

Harley comes up to the front and pulls something out of his pocket. I recognize it immediately as the stone he just picked up off the playground. I know because I told him to leave it outside, but he clearly ignored me and smuggled it in. I quietly admire the sheer audacity he has to pull out his contraband for Show and Tell.

'So what's this, Harley?'

'It's my special stone. I found it on the beach,' he lies. 'I went with Mummy and it's a magic stone and . . .'

Oh the irony, now I'm longing for the muteness of Darcy.

'Fascinating, Harley. Thanks for bringing in your special stone.'

But then he holds it to his face in a gesture that actually makes my heart hurt a little bit. 'I love it so much I'm going to sleep with it under my pillow.'

'I'm glad you have found something so precious to you.'

Mrs Watson looks at me in disbelief. Even I'm surprised by the genuine compassion coming from my mouth.

'And I'm going to read it a story,' Harley continues.

'I'm sure it will enjoy that.'

'And I think it might like Coco Pops for breakfast.'

I put my hands gently on his shoulders and give him my warmest smile. 'Sounds awesome, buddy. Now, who's next?'

I expect him to just keep talking, ignoring me completely, but instead he sighs, and then sits down. After (painfully) working my way through the rest of the children on the list, wondering how the hell I'm going to get them to perform in our upcoming class assembly in front of the whole school in a month or so when most of them can barely stand up in front of the class and string two sentences together, it's time for phonics.

'Right, everyone get a whiteboard and a pen and come and sit down ready for our Jolly Phonics.'

It's a clever marketing technique, I suppose, but there's definitely nothing jolly about doing phonics with my class. In fact, sometimes, as I'm pretending to be an aeroplane whilst demonstrating the sound 'n' or rubbing my tummy to show them 'm', I feel a deep and dark depression falling across me like the shadow from an annoyingly persistent cloud on an otherwise sunny day.

By the time they've all got a pen and a whiteboard and agonized over the fact their pen is a bit pale or not of their desired colour, it's nearly playtime, but like on *Mastermind*, I've started so I'll finish. It is the only valuable thing I teach them all day so I don't feel like I can skip it, as I do much of the rest of the curriculum.

'OK. Let's all have a go at writing the word "dog" – d, o, g.' I sound it out slowly multiple times, aware that even with this assistance, most of them won't get it. Then some of them start writing, others scribble on their shoes or legs, some just stare into space.

And suddenly, the fog lifts, and my head is bombarded with images . . . Kate in her wedding dress, the way we were both crying so much saying our vows that we collapsed into fits of giggles and had to force ourselves to continue. The same giggle, on our first date in McDonald's – the pivotal moment when our friendship became something more and she agreed to make it official and be my girlfriend. The look in Kate's eyes as she watched me cradling Gabe just after he'd been born – I still remember the feeling in my chest – first relief that Kate had survived what had turned out to be a very challenging labour – then fear, that I now had someone else to take care of, the feeling that I desperately didn't want to mess up this beautiful, innocent little creature I'd been blessed with – and then overwhelming love, for my son and the woman who helped me to create him. The photograph of my mum at the front of the church on the day of the funeral . . . the images just keep coming.

I'm about to lose everything. It's happening again. What am I doing sitting here when my wife is getting married to someone else *tomorrow*? My family is hanging on a rope and I'm about to let it go. They're about to fall.

'Mr Carlton? Mr Carlton?' It takes me a moment to realize it's Mrs Watson's voice and I look up to a sea of whiteboards being held up in front of my face. I know I am supposed to be talking but I have no idea what to say. My mouth feels dry, my throat tight. I loosen my tie to allow more air in, but it doesn't seem to help.

'Mr Carlton, I've done it.'

'Me too.'

'And me.'

All at once, there's a cacophony of voices and I feel like my head is about to explode. I push myself up out of my chair, steadying myself before stepping through the carpet of bodies.

'I'm sorry, Mrs Watson. Can you take over for a minute? I feel suddenly unwell.'

I don't wait for her to respond, just storm out the door and down the corridor, charging through the doors until I reach the open air, which I suck in in a desperate attempt to fill my lungs and stop my racing heart.

*

I'm not sure the night before her wedding is the optimum time to tell my ex-wife that I'm still in love with her, to ask her to scrap the whole marrying another man thing and choose me, but right now, beggars can't be choosers. It's like a lightbulb's gone on in my head, and now I can't believe I've wasted all this time waiting for Kate to say she still loves me when, Mimi was right, I should have been brave enough to make the first move myself.

The hotel is clean but corporate. It's not Kate. Not in the slightest. Just more ammunition for my gun. The receptionist tells me the room number (security's clearly not great either) and I take the lift to the third floor. If I'm going to deliver the speech of my life, I do not want to do it sweating and out of breath from climbing too many stairs.

I walk along the corridor until I find Kate's room. With a deep breath, I knock on the door and wait for Kate to open. She doesn't. Instead, it's one of her bridesmaids, Helen. She and her husband, Mike, were one of our shared 'couple' friends until we split up and they became one of Kate and Jerry's couple friends. I should've expected it. Mike never did have a backbone.

'Noah, what are you doing here?'

'I need to speak with Kate quickly.'

'Oh, please don't tell me you've come here on some misguided supposedly romantic crusade to try to win her back?'

Yes, that's exactly what I've come here for.

'No, of course not. I just need to talk to her for a minute. It's about the kids.'

The look of genuine concern on her face actually makes me feel a bit guilty for dismissing her as a hard-nosed traitor. 'Are they OK?'

'They're fine. I mean, they're safe. It's nothing like that. Please can you just get Kate?'

The door opens wider and Kate appears, in a white dressing gown with a blue facemask caked on her skin and holding two slices of cucumber that must've been adorning her eyes.

'What's up, Noah?'

I give Helen a look that says time-for-you-to-go and, with a glance that says don't-even-think-about-it, she takes the hint and goes back into the room.

'Can we go somewhere and talk a minute?'

Kate gives me a bemused look. 'Looking like this? I don't think so. Whatever it is you need to say, you're just going to have to say it here.'

It's not quite how I imagined it, but it's going to have to do. I close the door and sit down on the crappy dated carpet with my back leaning against the door. Kate does the same, putting her legs to the side of her and covering them with the bottom of her dressing gown.

Kate looks at me expectantly and suddenly all the words that I had rehearsed so clearly in my head abandon me and I'm left with only, 'You look nice,' which is a ridiculous thing to say when she looks like a Smurf.

'No, I don't. Come on, you did not come here to tell me that.'

I put my hands through my hair and lean my head back against the door. The strip lights on the ceiling give out a dull orange light. This is not how it was supposed to be. I wanted candles or fairy lights. Even the walls are painted a hideous green. I expect they were going for country house hotel, but it's more like pea soup.

'When did you stop loving me, Kate?'

She lets out a weary sigh.

'I mean, did you just wake up one day and realize you were no longer in love with me or was it over time? Did you gradually just love me less and less until there was nothing?'

'I didn't stop loving you, Noah. I still love you now. I just couldn't take being with you any more. I gave up on you, I guess. That's the best way to describe it.'

I clamp my bottom lip between my teeth. 'Right. Thanks.'

Kate turns her body towards me. 'Are you really going to do that? Are you going to play the victim?'

She doesn't let me answer the question. Instead, after the tiniest of breaths, she powers on.

'Do you remember all those messages I would leave on your phone? God, I'd be embarrassed to hear them now, so weak and desperate, begging you to call me, to just let me know if you were alive or dead.'

It suddenly dawns on me that this isn't exactly how I was expecting the conversation to pan out. That, in fact, I might have just opened a Pandora's box of resentment that Kate has kindly kept buried all this time.

'I wouldn't have even minded you needing your little blowouts, your escapes, but you didn't even tell me where you were going, when you were coming back, if you still wanted to be married to me or not.'

'I always wanted to be married to you. I'm not the one that went back on our vows.'

I know, as the words fall from my mouth, that they are like putting a kid's fancy dress costume near a flame.

'Don't you dare. I fought for us. I clung on for as long as I could. I worshipped you, Noah. I bloody worshipped you, but you broke me.'

At this, the tears come. Instinctively, I put my arm around her shoulder and pull her closer to me. To my surprise, she accepts my embrace.

'I'm sorry. I shouldn't have said that. I'm sorry.'

After a few moments, she releases herself from me and sits up, trails running from her eyes down her blue face like melted wax crayons. 'Do you think that I don't wish I could've been enough for you? That I could've mended you? I tried so hard, but whatever I did you just seemed to get worse. I thought having the boys might help, but even that wasn't enough.'

'I didn't need mending, Kate.'

'But you did. You did, Noah. Even now, you're still so furious with your mum but you won't admit it because it makes you feel guilty, as if you're being disrespectful, but you need to . . .'

'I think I should go. I'm sorry for coming here. It was a mistake.'

I expect Kate to apologize. To say she's overstepped the mark, but she doesn't. In fact, she looks free, like I've finally given her the opportunity to be honest and she's relieved by the release. 'So why did you come here? To upset me the night before my wedding? Was that the reason you came?'

I shake my head. 'I've never purposefully upset you. I came to tell you that . . .' *Why is it so bloody hard to just say it?* 'Honestly, I came to convince you that Jerry isn't right for you. That he's a knob and I'm much better.' I laugh and am glad to see the hint of a smile on Kate's face. 'I'm hotter, better in bed, funnier, obviously, we have more in common, we have two beautiful boys together . . .'

The more I list, the more the disguise of humour washes away, and what I really feel springs to the forefront.

Kate pushes a strand of blonde hair out of her eyes. She's had her hair cut into a shoulder-length bob for the wedding. It looks too neat, too ordered, and I feel a strange longing for her long, tousled surf-girl waves.

'Jerry's kind. He takes care of me. He loves those boys as if they were his own.'

'He doesn't even read.' It might not seem like a big thing to some people, but I see it as a fundamental flaw in his character. OK, it's not quite up there with 'abusive', but it's close.

Kate laughs. 'I know. I must admit that was the one thing that gave me pause for a while.'

I take advantage of her softening to press forward. 'You said it yourself, he doesn't know you like I know you.'

Kate shakes her head, as if having some kind of internal argument with herself. 'But he's trying to know me. He wants to know me. It takes time to build that stuff. It's not fair to mark him down for that . . .'

'I wouldn't do the bad stuff any more, Kate,' I say, noticing the desperation in my voice but not being able to disguise it. 'I'm sorting myself out, stopping the drinking. I'm doing so much better . . .'

'It's too late.'

'Remember all the good bits, the times we were so happy. We'd just have those bits. Think how amazing we could be.'

Kate starts fidgeting in a way that suggests she's drawing the conversation to a close. 'Soon, Noah, you are going to meet someone who you don't feel the need to run away from, who makes you feel happy and safe and secure, and you'll be glad this little plan to ruin my wedding didn't come to fruition.'

I shake my head, because I know the reason my marriage to Kate ended had nothing to do with her, and everything to do with me.

Sure enough, Kate pushes herself up and puts her hand on the door handle.

'He doesn't love you as much as I do. He couldn't. It's not possible.'

Kate turns and gives me the saddest smile I think I've ever seen.

'Don't go,' I grab her hand and try to pull her back.

'The girls are waiting for me.'

'Choose me. Choose our family.'

Kate appears to contemplate it deeply for a few moments and I wonder if she might actually say OK, whether I'm on the verge of victory, but then she drops her eyes and shakes her head. 'I'm sorry, Noah. I can't.'

Then she goes back into the room, leaving me facing a closed door.

As I walk back down the corridor, my legs threatening to give way beneath me, I hear a door open and look around to see Kate running towards me. When she catches up with me, she puts her arms around my neck and kisses me, on the lips, with a tenderness that breaks my heart.

'Thank you for loving me that much.'

Then she turns and walks back to her room and, to stop myself from breaking down the door, I head straight for the hotel bar.

*

I line the drinks up, methodically working my way through each one.

'Heavy night?'

I hadn't noticed the woman sitting beside me. She's in her forties, pretty, wearing a tight-fitting black dress and a bit too much make-up.

'You could say that.' I nod to her exceptionally large gin and tonic. 'And you?'

'It's my third. Just found out my husband's been cheating on me for three years with the nanny. I mean, what a bloody cliché.' She laughs, despite the fact she clearly doesn't find it in the least bit funny.

'Ex-wife is getting re-married tomorrow.'

She lifts up her glass and clinks it on to mine. 'To shared sorrow.'

'To shared sorrow,' I repeat and then down what's left in my glass.

The woman finishes her drink too and then she pulls her room keycard out of her handbag. 'You could come up and join me if you wanted? I'm putting the minibar on my husband's account.'

I know exactly what she's offering me and I can't pretend I'm not tempted. But I've come far enough to know that sleeping with this stranger, however lovely she may be, is not going to make me feel any better. In fact, it's only going to make me feel worse.

'I better get home. Got to take my children to their mother's wedding tomorrow.' I raise my eyebrows.

The woman nods, and I feel bad when I see the sadness of rejection in her eyes. 'Well, I hope it's not too unbearable.'

'Thanks.'

She climbs off the bar stool and turns away, and I feel the need to offer her some sort of reassurance.

'You're very beautiful, you know? And your husband is an idiot.'

It's a stupid thing to say – I've never met him and I have no idea of the ins and outs of why they really split up. But I can't just let her walk off without saying anything.

She turns around and offers me a sad smile. 'Just not beautiful enough, hey?'

I shake my head. 'Not at all. I've just been doing this long enough to realize that sleeping with beautiful strangers isn't the answer.'

She gives me a proper smile now. 'I'll try to remember that. Thanks.' And then she heads off to her room.

*

In the taxi on the way home, a message from Kate flashes up on my phone. It's hard to read with blurry eyes, but I just about manage it.

Why don't you bring Mimi to the wedding? We've had a couple of cancellations so there's spare food and I can make space next to you on your table. I know the boys really like her too. I think it'd be good for you to have a friend there x

I veer between feeling deeply patronized and oddly grateful, but she's right, the thought of going alone feels unbearable at this moment, so I text Mimi. I'm not exactly sure what my message says, but when I arrive at my door she is sitting on the step. When she sees me, she doesn't speak. She just takes my keys from my hand, opens the door and gently guides me through to my flat.

'Go and lie down. I'm going to make you a coffee and some toast.'

I shake my head. It feels heavy, stuffy, like I've got a stinking cold. 'Just get me a JD and Coke, will you? No need for the clean living any more.'

'Except the fact you have a wedding to attend tomorrow. You are going to go with your head held high. You're going to look after those boys and show them what a hero you are.'

I haven't got the energy to fight so I go through to my bedroom, kick off my shoes and lie on top of the cover. When Mimi comes through with a coffee and piece of toast slathered with peanut butter, I reluctantly prop myself up against the headboard and take them off her, putting the coffee on my bedside table and tucking into the toast. The smell of it reminds me how hungry I am, not having eaten anything since my cheese and ham sandwich at lunchtime.

Mimi takes off her trainers and climbs on to the bed beside me. 'So I'm guessing it didn't go to plan?'

'I don't want to talk about it.'

'OK.'

We don't say any more as I finish my toast. Then I put the plate on the floor and reach over for my coffee, taking a sip before putting it back on the bedside table. I shuffle down the bed and rest my head on the pillow, feeling suddenly exhausted.

And then I turn to face Mimi, saying the question in my head first, wondering whether to voice it aloud, before it slips out. 'Am I completely unlovable?'

I feel like a once-treasured teddy lamenting being tossed aside for the new, fluffier edition.

Mimi turns on her side and runs her hand through my hair. 'Not completely.'

I'm so drunk that my emotions threaten to overwhelm me and I feel my eyes filling with tears. 'I'm just so fucked up, Mimi. Why am I so fucked up?'

She reaches for my hand. I notice she looks tired, and it reminds me of how Kate would look at me near the end of our relationship, like she was bone-tired of *me*.

'The only thing in life you have control over is you, Noah. You will get past this and you will get over Kate, but what you do with the rest of your life is up to you.'

I know she's right but it feels like there's this invisible force constantly holding me back.

'I am trying.'

'I know you are.'

'Will you come to the wedding with me tomorrow? I'm not sure I can face it on my own.'

'Yeah, I'm sure I can quickly muster up a wedding outfit in the morning.'

'Thank you.' I want to go to sleep, but I'm suddenly scared to be alone, like I'm a kid again and I've just woken up from a nightmare. Having Mimi here is like clutching on to a comfort blanket and I don't want to let go. 'And will you stay with me tonight? Just fall asleep with me?'

Mimi seems to contemplate it for a few seconds and then, to my relief, she says, 'OK.'

She slips off her jeans and climbs under the covers, so I go and turn off the light and then copy Mimi and climb into bed beside her.

'Get some sleep, OK?' she says. 'You've got a big day tomorrow.'

I nod and she turns away from me and pulls the cover up over her shoulders, the street lamp from outside shining through the window and illuminating the side of her face.

On the windowsill, I notice the memory box she gave me and I guess she must notice it too, because she says, 'Have you put anything in there yet? Your memory box?'

'Things have been really busy, with Kate and everything. I will soon,' I lie. I don't see the point of dredging up the past, it's not going to change anything, but I don't want to upset her.

Mimi's head ruffles the pillow as she nods. 'I think you should try. When you get the chance.'

'I will.'

'Night then, Noah.'

'Night.'

I lie behind her, facing the same way but not touching, feeling a strange amount of comfort just to have her there.

CHAPTER NINETEEN

I wedge my fingers in the gap between my collar and my neck and yank, trying to loosen it, and pull at my woollen trousers, which are itching the skin on my thighs. I feel at once too hot and slightly shivery. I turn to Mimi, who is looking beautiful sitting beside me, dressed in a floral print dress, her hair adorned with a fake rose on a clip. She'd gone by the time I woke up, leaving me a note to say she was just popping home to get ready and that she'd meet me back at my flat. I was secretly relieved to wake up and find her not there. Without the haze of the alcohol, my outpouring of emotion last night felt embarrassing and entirely too much, and I was glad of the time to steady myself with several cups of coffee, paracetamol and a very greasy fry-up.

Now, in the ceremony room, the man on the keyboard in the corner begins the first few bars of his introduction and everyone stands up and turns to look at the back of the room. I can't look back. Instead, my eyes fix on Jerry, who looks like the cat who got the cream. When Kate passes our row I force my eyes to look up, following the length of her white dress, simple and stylish as could've been predicted; and then my eyes reach her face, but she's not looking at me, she's looking forward, at her husband-to-be. Mimi reaches over and puts her hand on my knee. I want to remove it, like when you're about to be sick and someone rubs your back. They mean well, but it just makes you feel worse, but I don't want to hurt Mimi's feelings.

At the moment the registrar asks the bit about whether anyone knows of any lawful reason that Jerry and Kate can't be married, I clear my throat and Kate looks over at me, her eyes pleading, but I'm not entirely sure if they're pleading with me to say something or not to say anything.

The registrar quickly scans the room and my hands feel heavy in my lap, too heavy to raise one in the air but too heavy to leave them there. The boys are sitting at the front of the room with Kate's parents, looking adorable in their suits, and I wish that they were sitting with me, anchoring me, telling me what I should do.

All too quickly, the moment passes and the registrar utters the typical, 'Well, that's the hard bit done,' and the congregation laughs.

And then it's the vows. I rub my palms together but the sweat just keeps coming. I take a deep breath and visualize Kate stopping at the critical point, realizing she's making a terrible mistake and running down the aisle into my arms, our two boys circling us, jumping up and down with excitement that their mummy and daddy are reunited, their once broken home stuck back together with super-glue, never to be broken again.

But she doesn't even look my way, her eyes firmly fixed on the man that she wants to share the rest of her life with. I had my chunk, my portion, now it's his turn. As she says the words 'I do', her voice falters, the emotion clear in the little giggle, the loving way she reaches up and wipes a tear from Jerry's cheek. And for the first time since she told me she'd met someone else, it dawns on me that she is really and truly in love with this man. She's not with him to get back at me, he's not a safety net, a plaster to cover the wounds I inflicted. I was so wrapped up in myself I missed it. Kate marrying Jerry has absolutely nothing to do with me.

*

During the meal, Mimi and I manage to knock back a bottle of wine each. I wouldn't say it makes listening to the speeches easy, but it makes it bearable. Kate's dad's speech is as gushing about her as it was at our wedding. I notice he cleverly uses different words, different examples, but the sentiment's the same. There's the addition of her being a wonderful mother and the noted omission of me, in my entirety, as if our children just appeared in her womb like she's the Virgin Mary.

Then the best man stands up. He's six foot, looks like he plays football, good-looking if you like that kind of obvious storybook-prince image. I hope he's going to reveal Jerry for the twat he is, but then he starts talking, and there's no mention of other women, stag dos, drunken escapades that end up with Jerry humiliating himself, no dark truths thinly veiled with humour. The only character flaw he reveals is that he's messy. I mean, seriously? That's not even a proper flaw. Your best man is supposed to tear you to shreds and hang them up for public scrutiny. When he's finished his speech, he and Jerry embrace in a manly hug with lots of back slapping, and then it's Jerry's turn.

I take a large sip of my champagne.

'Can we go and play outside, Daddy?' Gabe says, reminding me that he and Finn are sitting beside me.

'OK. Just stay by those doors though, yeah? I want to be able to see you at all times.'

'OK, Daddy.' Then the boys run through the room of crowded tables, adorned with lavish bright pink floral centrepieces and through the glass doors to play on the large lawn.

Jerry holds up his champagne glass. 'To my wife.'

The crowd cheer and clinking glasses echo around the room. Mimi touches her glass to mine, but I'm unable to lift it from the table.

'I knew from the moment I met Kate that she was the one.' Here, he turns from the audience to gaze into Kate's eyes. Jerry has what I would call weak eyes – an unremarkable colour, his eyelids hidden by the skin above. His face in general is quite unremarkable – not ugly, but not striking either – what one might call handsome or kind. He has a kind face – meaning what? That he's not attractive enough to break your heart? Pleasant, I think that's the word I would use to describe it. Like his best man, he's roughly six foot, but more rugby player in physique, although a rugby player who's not trained for a few years, softened around the edges.

Kate looks back at him in the way one might look at a well-loved dog, not like she used to look at me – there's no fire. Or at least that's what I tell myself. Because otherwise, I might smash my glass on the table, charge towards Jerry and stab a shard into his neck.

'She's kind. She's loyal. She's a wonderful mum. She makes the best cooked breakfast.'

It's a lie. She always burns the bottom of the eggs and overcooks the bacon so that it's too crisp.

'We started out as friends. We helped each other through some hard times . . .' (the implication being that I was the cause) '. . . but it only made us stronger, and now I know nothing will ever break us.'

More cheers from the crowd. I've had enough. I can't listen to any more.

'I'm going to go and check on the boys,' I whisper.

'Do you want me to come?' Mimi asks, and I can tell she wants me to say yes, but I just can't face the enquiry about how I'm 'holding up'.

'No, it's OK. I'll be back in a minute.'

'OK, if you're sure.'

The boys are playing rugby on the lawn, which has been set up with a range of activities for the kids. Giant Jenga, boules, croquet. Kate and Jerry are lucky. It's a lovely day. The sun is shining, there's only a gentle breeze.

'Can I play?'

'Yeah, you can be on my team,' Finn says, running up to me and jumping into my arms.

I swing him round. 'Come on then, let's show your brother what losing feels like.'

Gabe smiles and runs the ball past me whilst I'm lowering Finn to the ground and throws himself down between the two stones he's found to mark out the touchline.

'Hey, that wasn't fair,' Finn shouts.

'It's OK, go and get the ball. I'll sort your brother out.'

I run over and grab Gabe, lifting him up whilst Finn gets the ball and runs it towards the opposite end of the pitch.

The rest of the game morphs into something more representative of a wrestling match and eventually the boys decide to team up on me, grabbing my legs and pulling me to the ground and then both jumping on top of me. I tickle each one in turn until they're screaming at me to stop.

'Shh,' I giggle. 'We'll ruin the speeches.'

'They're boring,' Gabe says.

'I know, but they're important to Mummy.'

I gently manoeuvre the boys off me and we lie on the grass looking up at the clouds. Considering it's not very breezy, they seem to be racing across the sky.

'Look, Daddy,' Finn says, pointing at the sky. 'That cloud looks like a monster. See, there's the arms and the legs. And it has horns.'

'You're right, little man. It does.'

'I don't think it looks like a monster,' Gabe says, painfully honest, and I jab him in the ribs. He looks at me and rolls his eyes. 'Well, I suppose it does a tiny bit.'

I look over at him gratefully and touch his arm. 'You know, boys, just because Mummy is marrying Jerry, you know I'll still always be your dad, don't you?'

'Yeah. He's our step-dad now. You're our dad dad,' Gabe says confidently.

I nod, but hearing him describe Jerry as his step-dad sends a jolt of pain through my body. I don't want someone else to be anything that has dad in the title, even if it has an added prefix.

'And you know how much I love you and how much I want to see you, even though I don't see you as much as Mummy and Jerry do. It's not because I don't want to.'

'Why don't we live with you half the time?' Gabe says.

'We just thought it was easier for you to have one home where you spend most of your time instead of moving around all the time. And I work, so you'd have to do breakfast club and after school club, and I guess I worried you'd miss Mummy.'

'I want to live with Mummy,' Finn says, his face suddenly full of worry.

'Exactly. I know, little man. Everyone needs their mummy. It's OK, Daddy doesn't mind. I understand that. I just don't want you to think I don't want to see you. Or that I'm too busy. You two are the most important things in my life.'

'Look at the state of you lot.' Kate's voice travels across the lawn, but when I look up and see her face, she doesn't look angry.

I stand and pull each boy up, helping Kate to brush the grass off their suits.

'Congratulations. You look beautiful.'

Kate stands still for a moment, just looking at me. 'Thank you for coming. And for not ruining the day.' She smiles.

'There's still time.'

'Seriously. Thank you.'

I nod, any response frozen on my tongue.

'Right, boys, I was coming to get you because we have little gifts for you, to say thank you for being such an awesome page boy and ring bearer.'

'Yey!' The boys charge past us back into the hall.

'Right, I better go and help with the gifts. Jerry will probably give them the wrong ones, cue disaster.'

I smile.

'You coming in?'

I shake my head. 'I'm just going to take a walk around this amazing lake. I'll come and take the boys off your hands in a bit.'

'No problem. Take your time.'

She gives me a sad smile and I know it's an image I will always remember. Her in her wedding dress on the day she married someone else. She wore her mum's dress for our wedding. It was very simple, very plain, the key detail being the cut-lace arms. Today, her dress is a little more extravagant, but still beautiful and classy, as Kate could only be.

*

By the time I go back inside, it's Kate and Jerry's first dance. The song they've gone for is 'Better Together' by Jack Johnson. It's a bit of a cheesy selection if you ask me. Ours was this alternative song that no one at our wedding had ever heard of (which makes me ultimately cooler than Jerry and our relationship more authentic, of course). The basic premise was that we were both the luckiest people in the world to be born at a time and in a place that meant we would meet and end up together. That we were meant to be, for want of a better phrase.

I guess second marriage first dance songs are tricky when you come to think of it. So many love songs are based on finding 'the one' and never feeling that way before, but Jerry's not the one, he's two, and, despite the fact it didn't work out, I know what we had was a beautiful and intense love – that she *has* felt this way before, that it's not one of a kind.

I stand in the doorway and watch them for a bit, and then my eyes fall on Mimi, playing some sort of game with the boys and making them laugh. Then the DJ comes on the mic to invite everyone to join Kate and Jerry on the dance floor and, in dribs and drabs, couples wander over and start to dance self-consciously. I notice Mimi being dragged towards the dance floor by Finn and Gabe. When they get there, they stand in a circle, hands joined, and the boys pull Mimi around until she pretends to be so dizzy she can't stand up and falls to the floor, the boys erupting in fits of giggles and pulling her back up. She's so good with them and they're so happy – it makes me smile.

The song changes to Beyoncé's 'Single Ladies (Put a Ring on It)', met with much amusement from around the room. Gabe and Finn start swinging each other around and then flinging each other off to do body dives across the shiny floor and Mimi looks a little uncomfortable, wiggling her hips on her own, so I squeeze through the other people on the dance floor until I reach her.

'Come on, let's show them all how it's done.'

Mimi raises her eyebrows. 'I'm not exactly a dancer.'

'With that bum, I think you can give the rest of this lot a run for their money.'

She laughs and I put my hand around her waist. We jig around for a little bit, Mimi chuckling at my snake hips, and then, somehow (I'd like to say I didn't orchestrate it, but I'm not sure), we end up near Kate and Jerry and the atmosphere changes, suddenly feeling more charged and competitive. I'm not the world's best dancer, but I feel like Justin Timberlake next to Jerry's dad dancing, and to be fair to Mimi, she's shaking her bum like a good 'un.

We carry on this way for a little while, Kate and I occasionally catching each other's eye, and then I don't know why I do it, whether I'm trying to make Kate jealous or not, but I take Mimi's face in my hands and kiss her. And for a moment, the music seems to slow and I forget where I am, I stop caring whether or not I've got Kate's attention and just enjoy the feel of Mimi's lips on mine, but before I know it she's pushing me away and shouting in my ear.

'What are you doing? The mission's over, Noah. She chose him.'

Mimi strides off the dance floor and I notice Kate whispering something in Jerry's ear and then she's making her way through the crowds too and Jerry and I are left, awkwardly dancing side by side. We look at each other, both bobbing our heads.

'Think I need the toilet,' I say.

'Yeah, I'm going to check on my parents.'

But neither of us moves, we just stand there like two pathetic nodding dogs, until he makes the first move and leaves the dance floor and I follow, feeling like I'm at a crossroads, being torn in multiple directions and not quite sure which route to choose. I find myself scouring the bar area but neither Kate nor Mimi are there, so I search the little room next door where lots of the guests are gathered but I can't see either of them. I go outside on to the lawn – no luck – so I take a look around by the toilets and, just as I'm about to admit defeat, I spot Mimi, backpack on, heading out the front door of the hotel.

I follow her outside and watch as she sits down on the pavement.

'Where are you going?' I call, and then catch up with her and sit down beside her.

When she turns to look at me, she looks exasperated. 'I'm going home. I don't belong here. You need to sort stuff out with Kate on your own.'

I know she's probably right but I desperately don't want her to go, especially knowing that I've clearly hurt her.

'But I want you to stay.'

Mimi runs her hands through her hair. 'Why, Noah? So you can use me to make Kate jealous? I don't want to play that part. I don't want to be a pawn in your game.'

'That's not what you are. That's not how I see you.'

'Well, it's how you make me feel. And I deserve better than that. I might not be like Kate, the type of woman that men would change their whole lives for, but I still deserve respect.'

'That's not true. You *are* that type of woman . . .'

Mimi shakes her head. 'It doesn't matter. Look, I just feel that it's run its course. Our friendship, I mean. I think maybe it's best if we don't see each other any more.'

It's like being slapped. 'Is that really what you want?'

Mimi sighs. 'I know I don't want to feel like this.'

A taxi pulls in to the car park, kicking up gravel as it does.

'Just stay a bit longer. Give us more time to talk.'

Mimi stands up, opening the car door, throwing in her rucksack and then climbing in. 'I just want to go home.' She looks like a child, homesick on a school trip.

I want to say more, to stop her from leaving, but I have no idea what to say, and besides, I can tell she's desperate to go.

'OK. Well, I'll call you.'

Mimi nods wearily but I get the sense that she doesn't want me to and, as I watch the taxi drive off, I wonder whether I'll always end up hurting anyone who's stupid enough to get close to me.

*

When I walk around to the back of the hotel, I notice Kate sitting alone on a bench away from the crowd on the far side of the lake. I walk over and, as I sit down beside her, she looks up briefly and then back down at her wedding ring, which she twirls around her finger.

I offer her my jacket, but she declines so I put it on myself. It's starting to get cold, the sun sinking in the sky, emitting an orange light that seems to wrap around the world in bands.

'Are you OK?'

'Yeah, I'm OK. Just needed a bit of a breather. Weddings can get quite intense, especially your own.' Kate laughs awkwardly. 'Well, you know what it's like.'

I try to smile but my face feels tight.

'It's hard, isn't it?' Kate continues. 'This whole "moving on" thing. I thought it would be easier.'

I picture Kate saying her vows to Jerry, the thought of us doing the same all those years ago. 'Do you think the fact it hurts so much tells us something? That we still love each other? That it's not over between us?'

I'm not asking to convince her this time. I'm asking because I genuinely don't know the answers any more.

Kate shakes her head decisively. 'I couldn't sleep last night thinking about it. Worrying I was about to make a huge mistake. I still look at you and am stunned by how gorgeous you are. You still make me laugh. You know, every year, I look forward to our family day out. I mean, really look forward to it. And when it's over, I always feel ridiculously bereft.'

'Me too.'

'So I know that if there was any way I could put our family back together, I would. This is never what I wanted for the boys. Separate houses. A step-dad.' Kate's eyes start to tear up and I hate to see how much this is hurting her, how conflicted she is, and how I've probably only made things worse. 'But something died between us, Noah, a long time ago, and there's no fixing it. God knows I tried.'

The guilt feels all-consuming. I've made so many mistakes. 'I'm so sorry. For ruining our beautiful family.'

'It wasn't just you, Noah. I should've tried harder to understand. I shut you out, busied myself with work and then the kids. I got angry instead of trying to delve deeper.'

'You were a great wife, Kate.'

Kate shrugs. 'I could've been better. I don't want you to go through life thinking it was all your fault. It wasn't.

But, either way, what I'm trying to say is, I love Jerry and I'm sure I want him to be my husband. But I want you too. I will always want you in my life. Sitting beside me when our babies graduate, when they get married, have kids. I don't want to choose. I don't want to lose you. Am I just being greedy? Is there a rule to say you're only allowed to love one person?'

I put my hand on top of hers. 'You've always got me.'

Kate looks me in the eyes. 'Promise?'

I nod, the lump in my throat preventing all speech.

'What we had wasn't a waste, you know?' she continues, taking my hand in hers and squeezing it gently. 'And this isn't goodbye.'

It hits me all of a sudden – the relief. Because that's exactly what I've been so terrified about – that her marrying Jerry would make all the years we spent together pointless, that it would erase our past, that I was losing her forever, losing my family, just like I lost Mum. But it doesn't mean that. And Kate's still here.

We don't speak for a while, just sit there holding hands, until Kate lets go to straighten the skirt of her dress. 'So are you going to tell Mimi that you like her?'

I draw back my head in surprise and then shake it. 'It's not like that. We're just friends.'

'Oh, come off it. That kiss was *not* platonic.'

She's right. It didn't *feel* platonic. But it's a day of heightened emotions – things are bound to feel confusing.

'Well, you might not believe it but, for the past couple of months, she's been trying to help me derail your wedding.'

'What? Really?'

'She thought that if I became my best self, you might remember why you fell in love with me. Stupid, hey?'

Kate furrows her brow as if coming to a deep realization. 'So that's why you sorted the flat?'

'The flat, doing more stuff with the boys, cutting down the booze, my stunning new "do" . . .' I ruffle my hair. 'It was like in the films when they give the girl a makeover and then suddenly the dumb lead guy realizes how amazing she is.'

'So I'm the dumb lead guy in this situation?'

I smile. 'If the shoe fits . . .'

Kate looks out over the lake and then back at me. 'Well, I'm flattered. A bit shocked, but flattered. But for what it's worth, it wasn't necessary. I didn't need reminding.'

'It was my rock-hard abs, wasn't it?'

'Of course. You know me, Mrs Superficial.' Kate pauses, a wry smile forming on her lips. 'But, seriously, I think she likes you more than she's letting on. And I can tell you like her. She seems really great, Noah. And annoyingly beautiful. Is her bum even real? Surely it can't be real.'

I smile. 'We're just friends.'

'If you say so. But I'd be happy for you, you know, if you met someone. It'd be weird, of course, but I'd like to think we could be friends.'

'Like I'm friends with Jerry?' I tease.

'You know, if you got to know him, I think you'd quite like him really.'

'Never going to happen. Our relationship will never be *that* healthy.'

The song changes inside and I immediately recognize it. 'Kodaline.' It was one of Kate's favourites. She used to play it over and over again. I remember one time she put it on once the kids were in bed and we danced around the kitchen to it.

I stand up and hold out my hand. 'It's that bloody song again. Care to dance?'

Kate looks up at me, unable to keep the emotion from her face, and then she takes my hand and I pull her up and put my hands on her waist and we dance, a butterfly circling us like it's drawing an invisible rope before flying off towards the lake. And as I stand there, dancing with my ex-wife on her wedding day, I realize I'm surprisingly OK. The fight is up. Kate's married someone else and I haven't died. I don't feel like lying down on a train track. I can still see a future for me and it's not entirely black.

The words sing out from inside. '*A love like this won't last forever . . .*'

How apt, but how untrue. Because I know that this one will. Not in the way I'd once thought, but it will definitely last forever.

*

'Let's see who can get the most marshmallows on a stick,' Gabe says, starting his off. 'Daddy, are you playing?'

'Of course.'

We stuff marshmallows on to our sticks, pushing each other's hands out the bowl to prevent each other from winning.

'Hey,' Finn says, giggling. 'That's mine.'

He swoops over and takes a marshmallow off my stick.

'Oh, we're playing dirty, are we now?' I tickle Finn so that he drops the marshmallow and falls to the floor.

'No, Daddy, stop,' he says through splutters of laughter.

Gabe takes the opportunity to take the lead, squashing the marshmallows together so hard they scrunch up like an accordion. 'Come on, you two, I've finished. One more minute and it's time to count.'

I pull Finn up off the floor and we fill our sticks the best we can then all start counting.

'Ten,' I say.

'Oh, I've only got eight,' Finn says, so I squeeze two more on for him. 'There you go. Ten now, like me.'

We both look over at Gabe, who has a smile spreading across his face.

'How many?'

'Fifteen.'

'No way, let me see.' I count each marshmallow. He's alternated between pink and white for each one to make it easier to count. 'He's right. It's fifteen.'

'Yey,' Gabe punches his fist into the air. 'Come on, let's dip them in the chocolate fountain.'

So we do, repeatedly dipping back in as we eat the marshmallows, all of our faces covered in chocolate. When we've finished and I'm feeling sick, Kate comes over.

'Look at you lot,' she says, shaking her head but laughing. 'Good luck getting them to sleep tonight.'

'Oh, we're going to have an all-night party in the hotel room, aren't we, boys?'

'Yeah,' they both say together, their chocolate-covered faces beaming.

'You're going to regret saying that. You know Gabe will hold you to it.'

'Probably,' I say. 'It's a lovely wedding, by the way.'

'Thank you.' She kisses me on the cheek. 'Oh, and have you remembered about having the boys that extra Saturday, for Sarah's wedding?'

'Sure, it's on the calendar. Must be wedding season.'

Kate smiles and then I turn to the boys. 'Come on, let's go and tear up the dance floor.'

So we do. And, somehow, it turns into the sort of day I'll look back on with fondness when I'm old.

CHAPTER TWENTY

'Is Mimi around?'

The man at the door, who I deduce is Mimi's dad, looks me up and down and, from the look on his face, I'm not sure he's particularly impressed with what he sees.

'Who's asking?'

I hold out my hand, my palms suddenly feeling clammy. 'I'm Noah.'

Reluctantly, he shakes my hand, nodding slowly. 'I've heard a lot about you, Noah.'

'Don't believe a word of it.'

He doesn't laugh. 'No, I'm not sure I do.'

I think perhaps there's an insult in there, but I'm not quite sharp enough to work it out.

'Well, I suppose you'd better come in,' he says, opening the door and taking a step back to let me through.

As he shuts the door, Mimi appears from another door-way. She looks particularly cute in spotty shorts, a white T-shirt and flip-flops. 'What are you doing here?'

I look at Mimi's dad, a hint that I want to speak to Mimi alone. He doesn't take it, standing firmly in the hallway.

'I just wanted to speak to you.'

'You could've called me.'

I look over at Mimi's dad again, but it looks as if he's determined to humiliate me as much as possible. 'I thought you might not pick up.'

Mimi nods and I'm fairly sure I was right. 'Come in. I'll get you a drink. Dad was just about to mow the lawn, weren't you, Dad?' Mimi smiles sweetly at her dad and reluctantly he stands down and heads back through the house.

Mimi leads me to the kitchen. 'Coffee?'

'That'd be great, thanks.'

She gets a mug out of the cupboard and switches the kettle on. 'So how was the rest of the wedding?'

'It was nice. The boys and I ate so many chocolate-covered marshmallows we were nearly sick.'

'Had to be done. And Kate looked amazing.'

'She did. So did you.'

'I wasn't fishing for compliments.'

'I know you weren't. I just wanted you to know.'

Mimi's eyes drop to the floor and, when she looks up, it's like she's put on a mask. 'So what is it you wanted to speak to me about?'

I lay awake all last night thinking about how I'd hurt her and how crap that made me feel. How sad I'd be to lose her. So I know I have to try and make her understand.

'Look, maybe I did kiss you last night to make Kate jealous and I'm sorry about that. That was really shitty of me. But for you to think I've just been using you, that you don't mean anything to me . . .'

'Noah, it's fine. You don't need to explain.'

'But I want to explain. You know you said you're not the type of woman men would change their whole life for, well, that's not true. You're exactly that type of woman. And I'm so sorry that I made you feel that way.'

Mimi shakes her head. 'I was being silly. I shouldn't

262

have stormed off. I was just tired. Maybe I was going down with something.' She laughs self-consciously.

'You weren't being silly. I never should've made you feel like a pawn in a game. You've become my best friend, Mimi. And you were right, I didn't really have any proper friends before you. I *did* need you. I *still* need you, in fact.'

Mimi looks like she's about to soften but at the same time there's a sadness in her eyes, a reservation.

'Will you forgive me?' I ask, eyes wide.

Mimi hands me the coffee she's made me and I take it, nervously awaiting her answer.

'If I must.'

A glimmer of a smile crosses her lips and I put my coffee on the side and embrace her in a hug. 'Thank you.'

After a few seconds, she shrugs me off and starts busying herself with tidying away stuff in the kitchen. 'So what are your plans for the rest of the day, anyway?'

I take a sip of my coffee. 'The boys have made me promise to take them camping next weekend so I need to go and buy some stuff. They've been going on and on about it and the weather looks great so I've finally given in.'

Mimi clears the last of the things off the draining board. 'Oh, I love camping. Haven't been for years. I keep trying to persuade Dad but he says he's not sure he'd be able to get back up off the air mattress these days.'

'You should come.'

'Oh, no, I didn't mean that.'

'I know you didn't, but you should. The boys would love to see you and I've not put a tent up for years. I could do with the help.'

Mimi takes her phone out of her pocket and studies it, as if it might have the answer to what she should do. 'I'm just not sure . . . I . . .'

'I'll bring you all the snacks you want. And wine. And even buy you an ice cream with a Flake. Come on, you can't say fairer than that.'

Mimi smiles, and it feels like I've got my old Mimi back, before things started to feel so complicated. 'Oh, go on then. Dad's away on a fishing weekend anyway and I hate being in the house on my own.'

'I'm glad a weekend going to the beach with me *just* about beats sitting at home eating microwave meals for one.'

'It's a close call.'

'Pick you up about nine Saturday morning?'

'OK. I'll dig out my camping stuff.'

*

'I'm going to take Harley for his thrive session today, Mrs Watson. The rest of the children are doing free play so if you can just prevent them from killing each other, that'd be great.'

Mrs Watson rolls her eyes and I stifle a smile as I lead Harley to the nurture room for his thrive session. I mean, seriously, the semantics in schools are just brilliant. It's basically just some one-to-one time where we talk to him about his emotions in the hope he'll then learn how to control them. I'm not sure I really buy into all the supposed success stories, but it's good to get some time with him on his own to check how he's doing.

I look through Harley's thrive book at the activities he's done with Mrs Watson. My favourite is where he's drawn an incident that happened in the playground and then underneath drawn what would have been a better way to deal with it. What makes me laugh is his depiction – he's drawn himself punching another child and then blood squirting out of the child's face in every direction, like there's been some kind of massacre.

I look at the plan for today's session. *Paint pieces of paper different colours to show different emotions and talk about when child has them.*

'So, today we are going to do some painting.'

'Cool, can I paint Spiderman?'

'Well, no, we are going to paint the paper certain colours to try to show your different feelings.'

'Oh.'

I love how he doesn't even try to hide his disappointment. There's something to be said for the tactless honesty of little ones.

'So you're obviously feeling disappointed. What colour could we use for disappointed?'

'Grey?'

'Perfect. Great choice. Grey is exactly how disappointed feels.'

And then I suddenly realize that I am cheering when he is telling me he is feeling grey. Not even dynamic angry red, or sad blue, but grey. I squeeze some black and white paint into a palette and hand Harley a brush. He swishes the paint together and then starts covering the paper.

'Can I paint something grey like an elephant?'

'No, you just have to fill the paper with grey.'

Harley sighs and then continues painting, the blank grey page in front of us guilt-trippingly juxtaposed with the word 'thrive' written in capitals on the front of Harley's book. I look out of the window, and just outside, in the little garden the school uses to tick the box of involving the children with nature, I notice the overgrown vegetable patch, full to the brim with dandelions.

'Hold on one second, Harley. I'll be back.'

I rush to the science cupboard and sure enough, in the deepest, darkest corner, there's a plastic container with a load of seed packets in it. I pick out some radishes, carrots and onions and take them back through to Harley, who has started to paint his hands.

'Fancy going and doing some planting?'

'What about the painting?'

'It's a bit boring, isn't it?'

Harley looks stunned, like he can't believe a teacher is admitting to imperfection, and then he nods, a little anxiously, as if he's worried he still might get told off if he says he's bored out of his brain.

'Come on, let's go and get some fresh air.'

I lead Harley out into the little garden, find a trowel and a small fork stuck into the ground outside and hand the trowel to Harley. He begins digging straight away, jabbing at the soil and yanking out the weeds.

'Good job, Harley. You've obviously done this before.'

Harley shakes his head. 'We only have stones in our garden.'

'Well, you're very good at it. Just make sure you dig all the way down so you get the roots out too. Then the weeds won't grow back.'

Once we've cleared the patch, I show Harley how to make holes in a row a few centimetres apart then show him the packets of seeds.

'Which one are we doing first?'

He points at the radishes. 'Like Peter Rabbit.'

'Oh yes, he likes radishes, doesn't he? Right, just gently tip a few seeds into each hole.'

I rip the top off the packet and hand it to Harley. Of course, he's too heavy-handed and pours a ton of seeds into the first hole then looks up at me, and the fear in his eyes hits me right in the chest.

'I'm sorry. They just came out too fast.'

I ruffle his hair, immediately transported back to all the times I felt that fear. Like when I put too much coffee in when making Mum a drink and she screwed up her face and spat it out all over the table, or when I got a bit of shell in the cake mixture when I cracked the eggs and she threw the whole lot in the bin, or when I'd accidentally knock a cup over when we were having dinner and she'd scream the place down like there'd been a murder.

'It was an accident, Harley. It's fine. These things happen. Just use your fingers to pick some up and put them in the other holes.'

'Oh, OK.' Then he does just that, brushing the remaining seeds off his fingers with his other hand. 'Shall I make another row of holes now? Then we can put carrots in. I reckon Peter Rabbit would like those too.'

'Perfect. You're doing a super job.'

On hearing this compliment, Harley's face brightens from his smile all the way up to his eyes. Planting these seeds, he has not once argued with me, or got angry, or thrown anything. His body has been still, his features relaxed and content. He's just a kid – he doesn't want to be lashing out, getting in trouble all the time, constantly being told he's making the 'wrong' choice. He's just handling things in the only way he knows how. And watching him, I realize that while the whole self-improvement plan may have failed in its primary objective, I still want to be better. As a dad. As a teacher. As a friend. And I'm more determined than ever to get things right for Harley.

*

I strap Harley into Finn's car seat. Emma texted me to ask if I could bring him home because she wasn't well and everyone she'd asked was unavailable. Despite my initial concern about giving her my number, this is the first time she's been in contact so I agreed to help her out. I'm not sure what the general opinion would be of me giving Harley a lift home, so I slyly smuggled him out of school via the back gate and threw him into the back of the car. Once he's securely strapped in, I jump in the front seat and drive out.

'Can you take me home every day, Mr Carlton?'

'No, buddy, it's just a one-off today because Mummy isn't feeling very well.'

'But she doesn't feel well lots of days so you could take me all those days?'

I'm touched by his logic. 'The thing is, Harley, I'm supposed to stay after school to do boring work. I'm sneaking out today. Shh.'

I hold my fingers to my lips and Harley smiles, happy to be complicit in my disobedience.

'Well, can you stay for a little bit and play with me?'

It seems such a basic right – an adult who wants to play with you. But I remember a lot of times when Mum would wave me off and send me away. That feeling of rejection, of being a nuisance. I wonder if my boys have felt it too – when I've been preoccupied, too self-involved to engage. I don't want them to feel that any more.

'I'll see if it's OK with Mummy, OK?'

I'm conscious that I'm Harley's teacher and that it's not exactly normal to be going to his house and playing with him, but at the same time I don't want Harley to feel alone, like I'm just another adult that doesn't really care.

'Yey, thank you so much, Mr Carlton.'

When we get to the flat, Harley smashes the door with his fist multiple times until eventually Emma appears. Her T-shirt is covered in stains and she looks like she's not seen the light of day for weeks.

'Oh, thank you so much for bringing him home. I'm feeling terrible.' She runs her hand through her hair, which is greasy and tangled, while Harley scuttles in under her arm and rushes up the stairs.

'It's OK. I hope you feel better soon.'

'Thanks.'

Harley reappears at the top of the stairs, his eyebrows knitted. 'You said you'd stay and play for a bit?'

I look back at Emma. 'He wondered if I could play for half an hour. If you're feeling rubbish and need a hand?'

'Please, Mummy.'

At first, Emma looks like she's trying hard to hide her relief at the suggestion of help, but then her façade appears to falter. 'Would you mind? If I could just have an extra half-hour lying down, that would be such a help. As long as I'm not keeping you from something important.'

'Yey.' Clearly seeing it as a done deal, Harley skips back to his bedroom.

'Only planning your child's education. Nothing important.'

Emma offers a half-smile, like when someone makes a joke when imparting bad news, and then opens the door wider and steps back, allowing me to go in.

'Right, I'll go and see what he's up to. You get some rest.'

'Thanks.' Emma turns and shuffles along to the lounge, going in and closing the door.

When I reach Harley's room, he's sitting on his floor drawing a picture and, when he sees me, he covers it with both hands.

'Don't look.'

'OK, I won't. Do you want me to go back out of your room whilst you finish it?'

'No, you can sit on my bed as long as you close your eyes.'

'OK.' I clamber over the mass of toys splayed out on the carpet until I reach his bed, where I sit down on his Marvel Avengers quilt cover.

'Close your eyes then.'

'OK, boss.'

Harley smiles and I close my eyes tight so he knows I'm not peeking.

'Once I've finished my picture, can we go and play football? I've put two flowerpots for goals out the front.'

The space outside the flat is about a two-metre-square bit of concrete, but I don't have the heart to tell him it's not really suitable for football. And I guess sometimes you have to make the best of what you've got.

'Sounds good.'

'We'll do penalty kicks. Five each.'

'OK. I'm sure you'll beat me, I'm not very good.'

'I'm really good. I practise every day after school when Mummy is sleeping or making tea.'

'Well, practice makes perfect.'

Suddenly a piece of paper is wafted in my face. 'You can open your eyes now.'

I open my eyes and look at the picture he's drawn. It's of me and him (I know because he's labelled us) and I can just about make out two flowerpots and a football.

'It's amazing, Harley. I love it.'

'It's you and me playing football.'

'I know. I can see that. It's so good I could tell that's what it was straight away.'

A broad smile fills Harley's face. 'Shall we go outside and play now?'

'Yes,' I say, placing the picture on the bed.

Harley picks it up and hands it back to me. 'No, you have to take it with you and put it on your fridge.'

'I will, I promise. I'll put it in my car as soon as we get outside. Thank you, Harley. It's very kind of you.'

'It's because you're my best friend. And Mummy sometimes, when she's not being cross.'

It's surprisingly touching, but again I worry that I'm getting too close. I mean, reception children tell you all the time that they love you, they invite you to their birthday parties, draw you pictures . . . but this feels different, like I'm filling the role of his absent father or something. And I'm definitely not the right person for the role. I'm barely doing a good enough job with my own kids.

'Thank you, buddy. Does Mummy get cross a lot, then?'

'She gets cross if I ask her too many things or when I spill my breakfast or make a mess.'

'Well, it's hard being a mummy, you know? Sometimes I'm grumpy with Gabe and Finn. Usually because I'm tired or busy.'

'I don't have a daddy any more,' he says, very matter of fact. 'He decided he didn't want to see me and went away.'

Put in the simplistic language of a child, it feels like such a painful truth. I think so often we want to dress it up as being 'difficult' or 'complicated', but Harley's right. If his dad really wanted to see him, he'd move heaven and earth to do so.

'Sometimes mummies and daddies fall out and they find it hard to see each other, but it's not because of you, OK?'

Harley shrugs. 'I hope they make up soon. Daddy used to play football with me, but Mummy always says she's too tired and there isn't space.'

I place my hand on his shoulder. 'Come on. I think it's about time you showed me these amazing skills of yours, don't you think?'

I guide Harley out of his bedroom and follow him downstairs. As we reach the door, there's no sign of Emma so I quietly open and close the door so as not to wake her. Harley puts me in goal first and I soon realize his view of his footballing ability is greatly inflated, so have to allow the only two shots out of five he gets on target to roll past my foot. When it's my turn to shoot, it's hard to ignore my competitive drive, but I force myself to kick the ball right at his feet and send a couple past the post, meaning I score zero to his two.

'See, I told you I was the best.'

'And you were right.'

'Can we play again?'

I check my watch. It's five o' clock. 'OK, one more go each then we'll see if Mummy has sorted anything for your tea.'

I let him win again and then pick up the football. 'Right, I bet you're starving. Let's go and see what there is to eat.'

When we get in the flat, Emma is still asleep, so I sneak into the kitchen and open the fridge. Randomly, it's stacked full of Muller Rice but little else, so I open up the freezer and spot a packet of fish fingers.

'Fish finger sandwich?'

'I've never had one before.'

'What? You've never had a fish finger sandwich? Well, you've got to try one then.'

'But Mummy's asleep and I don't know how to make it.'

'It's OK. I'll do it.'

I put a load of fish fingers under the grill, get two plates out and cover four pieces of bread with ketchup. After a while, Emma comes in, yawning.

'I'm so sorry. I must've fallen fast asleep.' She looks over at the grill. 'Oh, you didn't have to cook. I was just about to sort him something now. We usually don't eat until about six.'

'He was hungry,' I say and then realize it sounds like a criticism. 'I thought I'd let you rest.'

'Thanks. I would've done it, though. I wouldn't have let him go hungry or anything.' She starts frantically tidying up the kitchen as if she wants to prove to me how 'on top of it all' she is.

'I know.' Although I'm not convinced. She has this vacant expression today that makes it feel like she may not have remembered that a child needs to eat at all.

The timer beeps on the grill and I take the fish fingers out and scoop them on to the bread, four for Harley, four for Emma, then squash the other pieces of bread down on top.

'There you go, buddy.' I give Harley his plate and he carries it into the lounge, and I give the other plate to Emma. 'I made you one, too. It's a culinary speciality – fish finger sandwich.'

Emma smiles, but again it's barely a smile, only given to acknowledge my joke but with nothing behind it. 'I don't need you to cook for me.'

'I know. But I was making one for Harley anyway.'

'Well, thanks.' She takes her plate through to the lounge and sits next to Harley. There's something almost child-like about the way she sits, her knees pulled up to her chest with the plate resting on top.

'Right. Well, I suppose I should get going.'

'OK. And thank you for all this.' Then just as I'm about to leave, out of nowhere, she bursts into tears. 'I'm sorry. I feel so useless.'

I stand still on the spot, unsure what to do. Should I give her a hug? Normally if I saw someone crying, I would, but she's the mother of one of the children in my class and it already feels like I'm way more involved than I should be.

'I just can't do it any more,' she continues. 'I can't even look after myself. How am I supposed to look after a child?'

I immediately glance at Harley, not feeling comfortable at him hearing his mum say this stuff, but he's intently watching a Spiderman cartoon, ketchup smeared around his mouth, seemingly numb to his mum's outburst. It makes me think perhaps he sees her like this a lot.

'Shall we go in the kitchen?' I nod my head towards Harley.

Emma follows my gaze. 'Oh, he's OK.'

The thing is, I know she's wrong. That just because seeing his mum like this has become Harley's normality, it doesn't mean the scar tissue isn't being formed.

'I think we should go in the kitchen.'

I don't give her a choice because I leave the lounge and, with a noticeable sigh, she follows me. Her clothes hang off her and she looks like she's got weights attached to every extremity. Her eyes are still brimming with tears and one escapes and rolls down her cheek.

'You're a good mum, Emma. I know it's hard, but I think you need to try to put some of the other stuff aside and focus on him.'

It's probably stupid advice, impossible for Emma to do, but I wish someone had said something similar to Mum when I was growing up.

'I do. I think about him all the time. I'm just no good at any of this. He deserves better than me. Maybe Mimi would take him for a while. Do you think she would? Just until I get my head straight. He loves Mimi more than me anyway. He'd be happier there.'

I shake my head. 'You're his mum. He loves you more than anything in the world and he needs you. I'm sure Mimi is happy to help out when you need it, but Harley needs to be here and he needs you to step up to the plate.'

Emma nods repeatedly, more tears falling down her cheeks and dripping from her chin.

'I do love him. I don't want you to think I don't love him. I just think he'd be better off without me.'

'He wouldn't.'

Emma nods, but I can tell she's somewhere else. That nothing I say is really going in.

'I better go now. Make sure you eat your sandwich.' I put my head around the door to the lounge. 'I'll see you at school in the morning, OK, little man?'

'Bye, Mr Carlton,' Harley says, but he doesn't take his eyes off the screen.

On the drive home, I can't stop thinking about them. I know I'm in too deep, but I just feel so responsible for Harley and I don't know what to do for the best. But, at the same time, being with Emma is like someone pulling the stitches out of old wounds. I'm still so raw about everything that happened with Mum and, if I'm ever going to make something of my life, I've got to start to face up to it.

*

I pick up the memory box from my bedside table, a beer in my other hand, locate a pen and some paper and sit on my bed with my back against the headboard. I try to think of some happy memories of Mum to write down. I write about a family holiday to Spain where she spent the whole time playing with us in the pool, even though I could tell she really wanted to read her book. About a trip to the circus. I remember the clown falling off his unicycle head first into a five-tiered cake, emerging with a face covered in cream. We all laughed until we had tears streaming down our cheeks – it was rare to see Mum so unashamedly happy and looking at the joy on her face just made me laugh all the more.

I try to conjure up more positive memories but I can't ignore the sick feeling in my stomach. I feel like a fraud. Because in Spain Mum also told me that she wished she'd never had children – that we'd ruined her chance of making anything of her life. And the thing that really sticks in my head about the trip to the circus is the walk home, the way Mum's demeanour changed completely like she'd just received terrible news. The way she refused to hold my hand. The way, when Dad was chatting to us about all the funny bits of the show and Ben and I were giggling, she said, 'I thought the whole thing was a bit immature, to be honest' and stomped off ahead of us. I rip the piece of paper into thin strips and push them off the cover on to the floor.

Then I pick up my phone and text Mimi.

What if the memories aren't good?

It's a few minutes before she replies.

Write them down anyway. x

I stare at the fresh piece of paper, doodling around the hoops at the top, then I push it to the side and lie on my bed, pressing the button on my biro so that the nib goes in, out, in, out, the clicking sound strangely hypnotic. It feels like a betrayal, to fill a box with all the times Mum hurt me, when I loved her so much, *love* her so much. But then I sit up and grab the pen and the words flow out of me like the water when you unblock a dam. I write about the time she told me that she thought Ben was better than me, the time I broke down in tears in front of her because Kate and I had fallen out over something and she shouted at me for being 'pathetic' and 'weak', the way she never let me have a birthday party because 'birthdays should be spent with family, not friends'. And then suddenly I'm able to write about the way she'd always sleep beside me when I had a bad dream, the time she took me for ice cream after school because I'd been kind to one of the boys in the class who was being picked on, the times she came home from parents' evening with an array of treats because she was 'bursting with pride', the time she taught me to paint, the stories she read, the way she'd sing to me for ages when I couldn't get to sleep.

And then, as if the pen isn't under my control, I start writing about Dad too. About the time he'd been out drinking all night (not unusual) and Mum had told us that the reason he was barely there was because he couldn't stand to be around us and then, later, I'd woken up from a bad dream and gone downstairs to get myself a cup of milk and he'd been there on the sofa, sobbing. At first, he'd shouted at me to go back up to bed, but then he'd caught up with me on the stairs, wrapped his arms around me and apologized. As a kid, I always wondered why he'd held me that night if what Mum said was true. But she could be pretty convincing.

I write about the time Mum was screaming at Ben and me because we'd got some paint on the table and Dad just stood in the doorway and watched. But I also find myself writing about the time Dad taught me and Ben to skateboard, how the three of us collapsed on the grass in fits of giggles after Dad was showing off speeding down a hill and then hit a piece of gravel and fell flat on his face. The trips to the beach. The games of frisbee. The nights sleeping in the tent in the garden because Mum wouldn't let us go 'proper' camping. Sometimes, I think it's easy to reach a point where all that's left is resentment, like the opposite of rose-tinted glasses, skewing all versions of events.

When I'm too tired to write any more, I stuff the pieces of paper into the box and close the lid, putting it back on my bedside table. And it's ridiculous how cathartic it is to shut it all away. Whenever I've read stuff about therapy or worry boxes or any of that stuff, I've always thought it was bullshit, that it's too simplistic, idealistic, but as I get undressed and climb under the covers I feel lighter, and when I rest my head on the pillow I manage to go to sleep.

CHAPTER TWENTY-ONE

Just as we arrive at the campsite, the heavens open and the rain starts hammering from the sky like the start of the great flood. It's just my luck. We've had the most unbelievable start to spring so far, and the day I decide to go camping, the British weather decides to revert to its usual dismal self.

'Can we go to the beach now?' Finn shouts from the back of the car.

'Do you have a window next to you?'

'What?' Finn says, not taking his eyes off the in-car DVD player.

'Look out the window.'

'The beach isn't there. I said I want to go to the beach.'

I bang my head against the steering wheel and Mimi laughs.

'He means it's raining, duh brain,' Gabe says.

'Soooo,' Finn says, 'we can wear our coats.'

'Well, I'd like to get the tent up first really, little man. Let's give it five minutes to pass. Just finish watching your film.'

Mimi looks over at me and bites back a smile.

'What?'

She leans forward and looks out the windscreen. 'Are you sure it's going to pass in five minutes?'

'The weather forecast said it was going to be sunny all weekend.'

'And we're trusting the weather forecast rather than the view outside the window because . . .?'

'They can see from their satellites. This is obviously just a minor blip.'

'Perhaps a flock of birds flew past and blocked the view for a while so they missed the ginormous rain cloud filling the sky.'

'Perhaps.'

We sit in the car for about fifteen minutes, watching the rain bouncing off the windscreen.

'The film's finished now, Dad,' Gabe says. 'Shall we just put our coats on? We can do the tent when we get back.'

I look at Mimi to gauge what she wants to do.

'Fine by me,' she says. 'I can't think of anything I'd rather do than head out into the torrential rain and battering winds with only a thin cagoule.'

'Seriously, though, is this OK?' I sweep my arms to encompass the car, the weather, the campsite, my two boys.

'It's great.' Mimi taps my thigh and I fight the desire to take her hand and hold on to it, instead smiling at her and then opening the car door. It's odd, but I felt this sort of nervous excitement picking her up, and I feel it again now, along with an almost desperate desire for her to have a good time on this trip.

'Come on, then. Coats on. Hoods up.'

As soon as we exit the car, it's obvious that putting on our coats is as pointless as listening to the safety instructions on an aeroplane, but, in a similar way, it makes us feel like we're doing something to protect ourselves against our impending doom. We head towards the beach path, running at first, and then, as if accepting our fate, we slow to a walk. Luckily it's not too cold, so although we may be drowned rats, we are not shivering drowned rats. Our clothes stick to us like they've been glued on with wallpaper paste and the rain drips from our hoods, our noses, our chins.

Eventually we reach the beach and the boys run straight towards the sea. I'm about to stop them with a ridiculous, 'Careful you don't get your clothes wet,' but I stop myself just in time and the boys charge into the white water, squealing at the temperature and running back out before turning and running in again.

'Shall we join them?' Mimi says.

'That's a whole other level of wet and cold. But you go ahead if you want.'

Mimi looks out to sea and then strolls over and sits beside me on a relatively flat rock that I've found. For a while, we just watch the boys, giggling and splashing each other, setting each other challenges for who's brave enough to go in the deepest. Over time, somehow I forget the rain pouring from the sky and just enjoy watching my boys so happy, getting on, not attached to a screen or badgering me for sweets.

'Thank you for inviting me.'

'Really? In this weather?' I hold my hands, palms up, to the sky.

'It's not your fault. And what's a British camping trip without a little rain?'

'Bloody weather forecast. I'm sorry.'

'Don't be silly. It's fun. And look how happy the boys are. That's what matters, right?'

'I'm really glad you came.'

'Me too.' Mimi smiles at me and there it is again, the weirdly charged atmosphere I've felt since I picked her up this morning. Then the boys come running back to us, their teeth chattering in tandem.

'Can we go and get dry now?' Gabe says, holding out his arms like a scarecrow, his clothes hanging off him, weighed down by the intake of water.

'I'm hungry,' Finn says, his default setting whenever there's a momentary break in proceedings.

'Come on then. Let's go and get the barbecue started.'

Mimi looks up at the sky. 'You're still going to do the barbecue in this?'

'I brought a load of sausages and burgers in the cool box. They won't keep until tomorrow. One way or another, I will get that barbecue going.'

'OK, if you say so,' Mimi says, a sceptical look on her face. Then she turns to the boys. 'Come on, you two, I'll race you to the top.'

And as I watch her, grabbing the boys to hamper their progress up the dune, making them giggle until their eyes run, I suddenly wonder why I've been fighting the feelings that now seem so obvious to me. When I kissed Mimi at the wedding, it felt right because she *is* right. And not just for me, but for the boys too. She's right for all of us.

I'm suddenly desperate to run towards her and tell her everything. But then it hits me that, only a week ago, she was trying to help me get Kate back – how can I ever explain how blind I've been? Plus she's going travelling in a couple of months, and despite the tension I feel whenever she's near me, who's to say she feels it too? Especially now I've wasted all this time chasing the wrong person.

They run ahead over the top of the dunes so I can no longer see them and I trail behind, my head a mass of questions. When I get back to the campsite, Mimi is getting the boys undressed, folding up their wet clothes as she goes.

When she sees me, she shouts, 'Open the car.'

So I press the remote and she bundles the naked boys into the car, then slips off her shorts, her jacket long enough to maintain her decency but not long enough to prevent my eyes being drawn to the tops of her thighs. Then she gets into the car. I slip my shorts off too and climb in with them. Mimi has found the bag of pyjamas and is helping Finn put his on, whilst Gabe does his own.

'Now, that's better. So, Super Dad, what's going on with this barbecue? We're starving.'

I'm not sure how the hell I'm going to get a barbecue going in the pissing rain when I struggle to get one going on a bright day with only a breath of wind, but I'm determined to make it work. To show Mimi I'm not completely useless.

I reach behind my seat and pull out a bag of Kettle Chips. 'Share these to keep you going. I'm going to go and set up under that tree over there. It should be sheltered enough.'

Mimi opens the crisps and gives a handful to each boy before offering one to me and then tucking in herself. 'Well, careful not to start any forest fires.'

'I'll try my best.'

I find some old joggers festering in the footwell in the back of the car, leave the others stuffing their faces, and carry the disposable barbecue in a plastic bag over to the shelter of the tree. I kneel down, put the barbecue on a rock and try to light it. It's at times like this I wish Mum had encouraged us to join the Scouts. She always said it was too regimented, that we were stuck in the institution of school for enough hours as it was without the added commitment of extra-curricular clubs, but looking back I think she was just lonely. With Dad always at work and no job of her own, Mum was alone all day and was always desperate to pick us up from school, despite the fact that by the time we'd walked home, she was often so tired she'd just go to bed.

So, without any Scout training, the best I can do is to use the lessons I've learnt watching series like *Castaway* and *Shipwrecked*, which basically amounts to turning my body into the wind (which has conveniently picked up just in time for our barbecue) and cupping my hands around the match in a desperate attempt to stop it from blowing out. It fails, of course, and after more attempts than I can count, I have to admit defeat.

I skulk back to the car with my disposable barbecue and bag full of wasted meat and open the car door.

Mimi tries to stifle her giggles but fails. 'Fish and chips?'

I push out my bottom lip like a toddler. 'It's such a waste.'

'Don't worry, I'll pay.'

'It's not about the money. It's just there are starving children in Africa.'

'The meat will probably survive until the morning in this wonderful weather. Burgers for breakfast?'

I sigh. 'Come on then, fish and chips it is.'

Mimi slips on some joggers too and we drive to the local chippie and bring our fish and chips back to the campsite, Mimi and I squeezing in the back with the boys, who choose to put *The Lego Ninjago Movie* on the tablet. I've not really sat down and watched it properly before, just heard and seen snippets whilst busy with something else, and it's actually really funny. When Mimi or I laugh, the boys do too, even though I'm pretty sure most of the humour goes over their heads.

'Can we always have movie night in the car with fish and chips?' Finn asks, ketchup splattered all around his mouth.

I lean over and kiss the top of his head. We watch the whole film, Mimi and I sandwiching my two boys, and I suddenly have a picture of what we *could* be. It's not the family I was picturing, the one I've been fighting for, but now I see it could be just as happy. Except I bet I've blown it by taking so damn long to realize.

When the final credits roll and Finn starts yawning. I look out the window, as if I hope the rain will have suddenly stopped, despite the fact I can hear it rhythmically tapping on the roof like an African drum ensemble.

'Right, boys, I'm going to put these front seats back as far as they will go and you two can sleep on them.'

'We get to sleep in the car?' Gabe says, as if I've just told him he can exist on a diet of only sweets for the rest of his life. 'But where are you and Mimi going to sleep?'

Mimi looks around. 'The boot?'

'Don't worry about us. It'll stop raining eventually and I'll put the tent up.'

'Are you sure about that?' Mimi asks, elevating her eyebrows as if she's had cosmetic surgery.

I find BBC Weather on my phone and hold up the screen to Mimi. 'See, it says no more rain for the rest of the weekend.'

'Yes, but it also says it's currently sun and cloud and seventeen degrees Celsius. I beg to differ.'

'It's slightly ahead of schedule. Trust me, ye of little faith.'

'OK, I'll trust you.'

As soon as I open the door, the wind and rain hit me and I run to the boot and open it. Of course, their sleeping bags are buried somewhere underneath all the other crap you need when you go camping and I wonder, not for the first time, what it is I actually think I like about the whole camping experience. It's like childbirth for women, I guess, the horrific reality gets pushed somewhere deep in your psyche so that you forget that actually camping is really quite painful. Not as painful as childbirth, I'm sure, but pretty bloody painful, and you fill your brain with images of being out in the wild, at one with nature, staring up at the stars, listening to the sounds of the birds and the foxes snuffling outside the tent, away from the distractions of screens and consumerism. Free. At peace. But, as I pull on the cord of Gabe's sleeping bag and inadvertently also pull out toilet roll, cutlery, burger rolls, and most annoyingly, my pillow, and they land with a thud in the thick, muddy tyre marks my car has made in the field, I promise to myself that I'll remember this moment the next time

287

I even contemplate going camping, for there is nothing peaceful about it. I stuff all the crap back into the boot, including my mud-covered pillow, manage to locate Finn's sleeping bag and both boys' pillows and then run them back to the front of the car, shoving them both in the front door before climbing in myself.

On the passenger seat, Mimi has lain down with both boys squeezed in on either side of her, reading them some of *The BFG*. When she gets to the giant, she puts on her best West Country accent and the boys giggle at all the made-up words. She's much better than I am. I always shy away from doing voices when I read to them, feeling too self-conscious and stupid, which is probably why they always end up fighting, distracted, but Mimi has them hanging off every word.

'Ah, just what we needed,' she says, reaching over, pulling Gabe's sleeping bag out of its carrier, unzipping it and draping it over them. Then she puts a pillow behind her head, wraps her arms back around the boys and continues reading. Before long, Finn is asleep and I carefully lift him out from under Mimi's arm on to the driver's seat, undo his sleeping bag and wrap it around him and then kiss his forehead.

'OK, I'm going to try to put the tent up. The rain is easing slightly. Just one more chapter though, OK, Gabe, no hassling Mimi to read you another one.'

'Promise.'

I leave them in the car and get the tent out the boot. The heavy rain has softened into a feeble drizzle so I wrestle the tent out on to the squelchy, waterlogged ground and start to put it up. When I'm finally pegging in the last of the guide ropes, Mimi appears, holding her hands, palms up, to the sky.

'It's stopped raining. You were right.'

'I'm always right.'

'You know, Gabe is super-smart. Some of his questions and comments about that book were so insightful, I was blown away.'

'He takes after his father.'

'Is that right?' Mimi smiles and then points to the tent. 'So, can I go in now?'

'Of course. Fill your boots.'

She crawls in and lies on the large groundsheet and I follow her in, lying down beside her. Without the boys being here as planned, the tension in my chest is palpable. I feel my pulse quicken, my breathing becoming more strained.

But then Mimi stands up. 'Come on, let's sit outside and look at the view. That's the whole point of camping, isn't it?'

She pulls me up then I get two camping chairs out of the boot and set them in front of the tent. From the cool box I take out the wine, feeling forlorn at the sight of the bag of burgers and sausages.

'Can I tempt you with a hot dog?'

Mimi laughs. 'I've only just started to digest my fish and chips. You're determined not to waste those sausages, aren't you?'

'I can't lie. It's eating away at me. I'm not sure I'll be able to sleep if I waste them.'

'Go on then. By the time you've got that barbecue going, I'll probably be hungry again.'

And as we sit on our camping chairs, the sausages barely sizzling over the meagre heat of the disposable barbecue, drinking our lukewarm wine, overlooking the sea with the sound of the waves crashing in front of us, I know that, like when you see your baby for the first time, I will forget all the pain that led to this moment and remember this as the definitive camping experience – relaxing, peaceful, the beauty of nature all around us.

'So how are you feeling about Kate now?'

I wonder, for a second, if she senses the shift between us too and is trying to gauge my feelings, but maybe that's just wishful thinking.

'I'm feeling really good. You know, I think maybe it was more about the fear of losing my family, of having wasted so many years, but now I realize I haven't lost them. Or Kate even. It's just different.'

'Change is hard.'

'Yeah, but good sometimes too.' I wonder if I should say more but I have no idea what to say, how, after everything with Kate, I'm going to manage to convince her that my feelings for her are genuine.

'True.' Mimi leans over to the barbecue, picks up a fork and stabs it into one of the sausages. 'Looks done.' She blows on the food and then takes a bite. 'Pretty good.'

I help myself to a sausage too and then find a plastic box to put the rest in for the morning.

When Mimi's finished her final mouthful, she starts shivering, her teeth audibly knocking together. 'It's getting dark and I'm actually pretty tired. Shall we call it a night?'

'Sure.'

I try to hide the nervous excitement I feel at sleeping in a tent with her and go to get our sleeping bags, pillows and a wind-up lamp from the car, suddenly noticing the memory box I put in the boot, just in case. I'm just about to close the boot and leave it there when I change my mind, pick it up and take it with me. Mimi is already in the tent when I get back, and I hand her her pillow and sleeping bag, putting the box in the corner of the tent and straightening my bedding out on the floor. Then I hang up the lamp, tying it on to one of the tent loops near the door.

Her eyes rest on the box for a second but she doesn't say anything about it. 'Right, close your eyes.'

'Why?'

'Because I'm taking my clothes off.'

I try to joke away the tightness in my throat. 'And? It's not like I haven't seen it all before.'

'So, that was different.'

I squeeze my eyes shut but then open one with a smile. Mimi pulls her top back down. 'Stop.'

'OK, sorry.' I close my eyes properly this time, covering them with my hands for good measure.

I can hear her slipping off her clothes and throwing them on the canvas and it takes immense willpower not to look or reach out and touch her bare skin.

'Right, I'm done.'

When I open my eyes, she's tucked up in her sleeping bag, her bare arms peeking out over the top.

'You can watch me if you want. As long as you don't get too excited.'

I take my top off and swing it around my head like I'm in *The Full Monty* and Mimi laughs. Then I climb into my sleeping bag in my boxers and, with a moment's hesitation, grab the memory box and hand it to her. I'm scared – because she might think less of me when she reads what I've written, but at the same time, I want her to understand. And I have a glimmer of hope that maybe it will help the rest of my feelings make sense to her.

'Will you read my memories?'

Mimi's unable to hide the emotion on her face. 'Of course. If you're sure you want me to?'

I nod, feeling my heartbeat in my throat. But it feels somehow easier to be open with her in the half-light from the fading camping lamp.

She opens the box and takes out one of the pieces of paper, squinting to try to read it. I reach over and take the Lego Batman torch out of my pocket and hand it to her. For about twenty minutes, she reads the notes, one after another. She doesn't comment on them and I lie silently beside her, watching the shadows from the trees flickering and waving on the roof of the tent.

When she's finished reading, she puts all the pieces of paper neatly back into the box, shuts it and hands it back to me. Then she leans over and hugs me.

'Thank you. For sharing that with me.'

'Thank you for making me do it. I think it was probably long overdue.'

After a while, we break apart and then we both lie back down, but Mimi is fidgety and I get the sense she has more to say, and I'm scared that she might be about to ask me more about Mum's death because despite letting her read my memories, I'm still not ready to talk about that.

Thankfully, after an extended breath out, she says, 'Do you think you should get back in touch with your dad? Even if it's just for closure.'

I've thought about it, particularly after writing all that stuff down. Ben gave me Dad's address a while back – 'Just in case,' he'd said, handing me the scrap of paper. At the time, I screwed it up and put it in my pocket, thinking I'd throw it in the bin when I got home. But I didn't. I kept it. But I just don't think any good would come out of me seeing him. How anything he had to say would make things any better. 'I don't think so.'

'It's just . . .' Mimi lets out a long breath and I get the sense she's scared to say what it is she's thinking. 'Well, I know it's not quite the same, but there was someone in my life once who really hurt me and sometimes I wonder if I could find him and tell him now, whether I would. Whether it would help.'

'The one from the song?'

Mimi nods.

I'm desperate to know more, but I'm conscious that I don't want to push her too far, so I don't say anything in the hope that she might continue, that lying here in the dark might make it easier for her to open up to me too.

'He was my manager,' she continues after a small pause. 'Saw me singing in a pub one night and said he *had* to represent me. He made me feel special, kept telling me I had this unique talent. He was older and I became besotted with him. He said he'd never felt that way about anyone before. And then a few months before my A-levels, I found out I was pregnant.'

Totally out of my control, I feel tears pricking my eyes.

'I was terrified but excited. It felt like this romantic adventure. I had visions of us on tour together, the baby with us. Stupid, I know. When I told him, he totally freaked out, said it was all too heavy. Turned out he'd been sleeping with another one of his clients behind my back. I lost it, stopped singing, flunked my exams, locked myself in my bedroom for months.'

'So what happened with the baby?' I ask, as gently as possible, because I'm guessing it's not easy for her to talk about.

'I had an abortion. And I've hated myself for it every single day since. Sometimes I even torture myself by imagining what he or she would be like. They'd be about the same age as Gabe now . . .' Mimi's voice starts to crack and she stops speaking.

It's a heartbreaking thought – that different circumstances, a different decision, could mean that Gabe wouldn't exist. And I can only imagine how painful it must be for Mimi.

'You shouldn't hate yourself. It's not your fault.'

The clouds must have finally cleared, revealing the light of the moon, because it's bright enough for me to clearly see the sorrow on Mimi's face.

'My point was, maybe it would help. To tell him the effect he had . . . well, I don't know. It was just a thought.'

'I'm so sorry you went through that.'

Mimi shrugs and pulls her sleeping bag up over her shoulder. 'I shouldn't have been so stupid.' Then she rolls over so that she's facing away from me. 'I'm actually pretty tired now. I think I'll get some sleep. Night, Noah.'

I pull my sleeping bag up over my shoulders too and lie facing Mimi's back. I can almost feel her vulnerability in the air and I want to show her that I understand, that there's no judgement here, but I'm scared of pushing her away, so nervously I reach out and take her hand, which is resting on the outside of her sleeping bag and, to my relief, she doesn't slap it away. Instead, she threads her fingers through mine and pulls my hand to her tummy, drawing me closer to her, and we stay like that, not saying anything further, until we fall asleep.

*

The following evening after the long drive home, the boys going straight to bed after giving in to the exhaustion caused by an unsettled night sleeping (or not sleeping) in the car, I pour Mimi a glass of wine and take it into the living room to her.

'I've been thinking and I reckon we should record that song you sang me.'

Mimi looks me up and down as if she can't understand what I'm saying. 'Why? So you can watch me when I'm not here?' she teases.

'Well, yeah, that. But, being serious for a second, I don't want to see you waste your talent. Let's put it on YouTube. It could become a huge hit.'

Listening to Mimi last night, I realized that she has done so much for me and I want to do something for her in return. I don't want that idiot that broke her heart to ruin her chance of achieving her dream.

295

'I don't know. What if people put horrible comments on there?'

'Oh, come on. You're a big girl, you can take it. And besides, why would they? It's great.'

Mimi looks like she's pondering it for a while. 'I just think putting it on YouTube is like saying, "Hey, look at me. Aren't I wonderful?" And I'm really not.'

I want to say *but you are*, but I'm scared if I start gushing about her too hard, it'll scare her away, just as it feels she is getting closer. 'You said yourself that you don't really want to be a barmaid, so take a risk. Give your dream a chance. What have you got to lose?'

'My dignity?'

'Come on, if I wasn't convinced it'd be a huge success then I wouldn't encourage you to do it. I'm not going to purposefully set you up for a fall.'

'Promise?'

I draw two lines across my heart.

'OK, go on then. But if people slate it then I am going to blame you.'

'Deal. I'll get my guitar and my camera.'

I go into my room to get what I need and when I return to the lounge, Mimi is looking in the mirror above the fireplace, playing with her fringe and then licking her finger and rubbing at the stray make-up underneath her eyes.

'You look beautiful.'

She turns around, looking embarrassed that I've caught her examining herself. Then she takes the guitar from me and sits on the sofa with it, plucking the strings and twisting the knobs at the end to tune it.

'Where shall we film it?'

'You look pretty good just there.'

Mimi scans the area around her and then shrugs. 'OK. But can you set the camera up and go?'

'Don't be silly. I'll be looking into the viewfinder the whole time, though, so you can pretend I'm not even here, OK?'

Mimi takes a deep breath and then nods her agreement. I position myself behind the camera and then she begins and her voice cuts right through me so I force myself to focus on the mechanics of the filming, zooming in to focus on her eyes, her fingers on the strings, then drawing back out to capture the whole of her.

When she finishes, I switch off the camera and join her on the sofa and she suddenly looks serious.

'Thank you. For forcing me to do this.' She holds up the guitar. 'I didn't realize it but I think I've been hiding for a long time. I needed the push.'

'That's OK. It's the least I could do after everything you've done for me.'

'I do appreciate it . . . appreciate you . . .'

It feels like a 'moment'. Like it's now or never.

'Look, Mimi. I need to tell you something.'

She looks concerned. 'What is it, Noah?'

I feel the nerves bubbling in my throat and take a deep breath. 'The thing is, I thought you were making me a better person with all the things you were suggesting to impress Kate. But it wasn't that. What was making me better was you. Just being around you. Does that make any sense?'

Mimi nods but doesn't say anything so I feel I have to continue.

'I've been a total idiot.' I shift my position on the sofa, sitting up straight. 'You make me happy, Mimi. And you make the boys happy and, yes, you're my best friend, but I also want you to be so much more than that.'

Mimi looks at me for a few seconds and I wish I could read what she's thinking. I get the sense that maybe she *does* feel something for me too, but then she shakes her head slowly and I feel my heart sinking into my stomach. 'I don't want to be someone's second best.'

She looks so sad and I'm desperate to hold her, but I can tell that she doesn't want me to. 'You're not. I was just blind. In denial.'

She shuffles a little further away and I can tell she's preparing to leave. 'I'm going travelling in a couple of months, anyway, and I meant it when I said I'm not looking for a relationship.'

I nod, my heart on the floor, wishing I'd figured it all out sooner. Maybe then we would have had a chance. But it's too late for 'what ifs'. And, besides, I've got a lifetime of those stacked up already.

Mimi stands up and puts her glass on the side. 'I'm going to go. But thank you for the trip. Please tell the boys I had a wonderful time.'

'Will do.' I see her to the door and she opens it and then pauses.

'If things had been different . . .'

Mimi tails off and I nod, then she kisses me on the cheek and leaves. And I go back to the sofa, torturing myself by picking up the camera and pressing play.

CHAPTER TWENTY-TWO

Once I've herded the class into assembly, I hurry to the office.

'Has anyone heard why Harley's not in today?'

Verity taps away at the computer and shakes her head. 'No, he's often late though, isn't he? Expect Mum just couldn't be arsed to get out of bed.'

I check my watch. 'He's not normally this late. Can you call, please?'

'I'm busy inputting data at the minute. Can you do it?'

'Of course. I've only got a class of thirty children in my care, how silly of me to suggest you do it.'

Verity sighs. 'They're in assembly, aren't they? That gives you ten minutes, surely?'

'You're right. I can't imagine how I was going to fill the time. Good idea.'

I find Emma's mobile number on my phone and ring that, but it's turned off so I root through the class files to find her home number. It rings for ages before I get to the answerphone so I leave a message. Then, for some reason, I try again. After a few minutes, it picks up.

'Hello, is that Emma?'

There's a muffled noise on the other end of the line and then it goes dead. I dial the number and try again. This time it picks up more quickly.

'Hello? Emma?'

I can hear a voice, but it's too quiet to make out what is being said.

'Hello?'

The same voice again and this time I can tell that it's Harley's.

'Harley? Harley, put the phone up to your ear,' I say loudly.

'She won't wake up.' This time, his voice is almost too loud.

'Mummy won't wake up? Have you tried to wake her, Harley?'

I can hear Harley crying on the other end of the phone and my heart starts to race. 'I've shook her and shook her but she won't wake up. I think she must be super-tired.'

A bolt of fear shoots through my chest. 'Hold on, OK, buddy. I'll be right there.' I put down the phone and turn to Verity. 'I've got to go. It's an emergency. Find someone to cover my class.'

'How?'

'I don't care. I've got to go.' I run out of the office, sneak back through the hall and run down the corridor to my classroom, grabbing my keys and then heading out through the back door. I buzz my way out the gate and run to my car, nearly crashing into someone coming through the school gates as I try to pull out. Whoever it is beeps at me, but I power through and race to Harley's flat. En route, I call Mimi, but it goes straight to answerphone.

As I get closer, I'm fairly certain what I'm going to find, but I'm hoping with all my heart that I'm wrong. When I get to the door I pummel it with my fist, and after what feels like forever, I hear Harley on the other side struggling to open it.

'Harley, it's Mr Carlton. I think the door is bolted. Can you reach up and there should be a little switch that clicks?'

'I can't reach.'

'Get a chair from the kitchen and climb up on it.'

'OK.'

I can hear the chair scraping across the floor and then, finally, the door latch releases.

'Now move the chair back so I can get in.'

I hear Harley jump off the chair and then pull it back along the floor. Then the door is free. When I enter the flat, Harley is still in his pyjamas and I notice that his trousers are wet and he smells of wee.

Harley follows my line of sight. 'I didn't reach the toilet in time in the night, but I didn't want to tell Mummy because I thought she might be cross.'

'It's fine, Harley. We'll get you cleaned up in a minute. First, where is Mummy?'

'She's in her bedroom. She won't wake up. That's why I'm late for school. Am I going to have to miss my playtime?'

I run past Harley up the stairs and call down. 'Of course not. You're not in trouble, Harley. I need to check on Mummy, OK? Can you go and put the TV on?'

'I want to help Mummy with you.'

'I need you to just stay down here for a minute so I can make Mummy better, OK?'

Harley nods and I rush to Emma's bedroom, praying she's just taken a super-strong sleeping tablet and Harley's touch hasn't been firm enough to wake her. But as soon as I see her, I know my fears were founded. Her mouth is open, her skin pale. I slap her face, but she doesn't respond. I put my hand on her chest; she's still breathing, but her breath is shallow. For a moment, I'm catapulted back in time. Opening the shed door to find Mum lying on the floor, the smell of sick hitting me immediately, then finding it all over her face, in her hair. Shaking her over and over again, but her body feeling heavier than normal. More stiff. Colder.

I focus on Emma, call an ambulance and frantically search the room for clues that might help the paramedics, but there's nothing. Once the ambulance is on its way, I call Mimi again. This time, she answers.

'Hey, Noah. What's up?'

'It's Emma. I think she might have tried something stupid. I'm with her now at the house.'

'What the fuck? What do you mean?'

'Just come now. I'll stay with Harley. You can go in the ambulance with Emma.'

'Ambulance? Bloody hell, Noah. She's OK though, isn't she? She's not going to die?'

I don't want to give her false hope, but I don't want to panic her either. 'The ambulance will be here soon. I need you to come now.'

Mimi seems to switch into action mode. 'Of course. Give me five minutes and I'll be there.'

In less than five minutes, I hear Mimi charging through the door and up the stairs and then, seconds later, two paramedics follow.

'She's in here,' I call out and they appear at the door.

The female paramedic pushes past us to get to Emma. She feels for a pulse and then checks for various things, making comments to her male colleague using terms that I don't understand, and then he hurries downstairs and comes back moments later with a stretcher, which he squeezes on to the minimal floor space, and then they both lower Emma on to it. Just as they do that, Harley appears at the door.

'What's happening to Mummy? Why are they carrying her?'

'Can one of you please get the boy out of here?' the male paramedic says.

I hold out my hand to Harley but he doesn't take it. 'Come on, Harley. Let's go watch a film.'

Harley throws himself on to the stretcher, resting his head on Emma's chest, before the female paramedic gently lifts him off and passes him to me. I pick him up, cradling him in my arms tightly as he fights to escape, and carry him into his bedroom so that the paramedics can get Emma out of the house and into the ambulance, followed by Mimi.

I place Harley on his bed and he tries to run away so I grab him and wrap my arms around him, trying my best to hold him back.

'I want to see my mummy. I want to see my mummy.' Tears that seem too large for his face begin to fall from his eyes.

'I know you do. But the doctors need to take her to the hospital to make her better and Mimi is going to be there to look after her too.'

'I want to go with her.' He elbows me in the stomach and I tighten my grip, then he does it again as the door slams downstairs.

'I promise I will take you as soon as they phone and say she's ready for visitors. I promise. The second they call, we'll go to the hospital.'

'But I want to go with her now.'

'I know. I'm so sorry, Harley.'

And then, almost without realizing it, I am crying too and Harley stops fighting and climbs on to the bed beside me, kneeling up so he can wrap his arms around my shoulders.

'I'm sorry. I didn't mean to hurt you.'

I shake my head. 'You didn't. It's not your fault. None of this is your fault, Harley.'

'So are you crying because Mummy is poorly?'

'Sort of. But mostly because you're sad. I don't want you to be sad, little man.'

'Perhaps we could look after each other?'

I wish all the parents from school who have written Harley off could see him now. That they could see the sweet, caring boy hidden beneath the difficult behaviour, and I feel guilty that I was just like them at the start, judging him and wanting rid of him.

'I think that sounds like a plan. How about you go and choose a story whilst I quickly ring school and then we can make a cosy den and I'll read to you in it?'

'A den? Yeah.' In a transformation of mood that is only possible when you are a child, Harley rushes off the bed and starts piling pillows and cushions in the corner of the room. 'Do I have to go to school, though?' Another rapid transformation in mood.

'No. Neither of us is going to school today. I just need to ring them to let them know. Oh, and grab some clothes out the cupboard, buddy. I'll put those in the wash.'

Harley goes straight to his cupboard and I go out into the hallway and ring school, explaining, much to their annoyance, that I won't be in for the rest of the day. I don't tell them exactly why, just that something's come up, and Verity takes great pleasure in informing me that the head has had to cover my class for the morning and isn't going to be impressed that she now has to put aside all her other more important and pressing jobs to cover the class for the rest of the day. But I figure, when it all comes out, she'll get over it.

When I re-enter Harley's room, he's draped his quilt across the top of his chest of drawers and piled several boxes on top of each other to support it at the other side, creating a canopy over the cushions he has placed in the corner of the room.

'I've made a den.'

'I can see. It's great. Have you chosen a book?'

Harley holds up one of the Albie adventure stories Finn loves. I notice from the sticker on the side that it's the one he chose from class on book-choosing day.

'Great choice.'

He nestles in amongst the cushions and I get down on my hands and knees and crawl in next to him. I lower my head on to one of the cushions and my legs protrude out from under the canopy. I loosen my tie and pull it out from my collar and then take the book off Harley and begin to read.

He's transfixed, as if I'm the world's best storyteller and it's the most exciting story he's ever heard. When I finish, I close it up and put it on the floor but he lifts it up and hands it back to me.

'Again. Please.'

'OK.'

As I'm reading, I notice him slipping down until his head is resting on one of his pillows and his body is curled up like a millipede. I lower my voice and slow my words, and sure enough, his eyes start to close until he's breathing loudly, almost snoring.

When I'm sure he's definitely asleep, I sneak out from the den and go back into Emma's room, opening cupboards and drawers in the hope I might find something to explain what's happened. I must see the note, but not really take it in, because I close the drawer with it in, but then open it again, reading the words on the front. 'For Harley – when you're old enough to understand.' I feel a wave of panic wash over me, first as a kind of sickness in my throat and then as hotness in my cheeks and across my forehead. I take the note out of the drawer and sit on the bed. I know I shouldn't read it but I have to see what it says. Opening it up and looking at the page, I feel so dizzy I can barely make out the words. As they fall I wipe the tears from my face, like I'm trying to tear off my skin. I remember Mum's note word for word, even though I've tried so hard to forget it. Dad scoured the house for ages looking for one. He tore through her shed, smashing her canvases against the wall, but they wouldn't break, launching her paints at the door, ripping the hairs from her brushes. I was the one that found it, as I meticulously put her paints back where they belonged, her canvases in the exact position she'd had them in on the walls, her work in progress propped back on her easel, which I reassembled. It was in her 'special box'. She'd shown it to me once. It had Grandma's wedding ring and her favourite gold brooch inside. Mum had thrown the rest of Grandma's stuff away. They'd never been close anyway. In fact, the only positive thing Mum ever said about her was, 'She was excellent at darning socks so the seam didn't feel uncomfortable in your shoes.'

When I found it, I opened it with trembling hands, read it and then took a lighter to it right there in the shed, tempted to drop it to set the whole bloody place alight, but instead I threw it outside and stamped on it until it was just a smattering of ash on the gravel. I never told anyone what it said.

I stuff Emma's note in my pocket and feel my phone buzzing so I answer it without looking at who it is.

'She's going to be OK. They've pumped her stomach. Suspected overdose.' Then Mimi starts to cry, loud splutters crackling down the phone. 'How did I miss this, Noah? I knew she had her lows, but this?'

I remember the conversation I'd had with Emma when I last came over. The weird way she was acting. If anyone should've known this was going to happen, it was me. But I didn't take enough notice. I was too wrapped up in how uncomfortable she was making *me* feel. How she was unearthing emotions I didn't want to face up to.

'It wasn't for you to spot, Mimi. We all missed it. It's not your fault.'

'I really thought she was doing better. Why didn't she feel she could talk to me?'

Again, the guilt. Because she did talk to me. And what did I do about it?

'Is Harley OK? Poor baby.'

'He's fine. I read him a story and he fell asleep so I'm just letting him rest.'

'Thank you. I'll come and stay with him tonight. I just want to wait for Emma to wake up so that she has a friendly face to look at and then I'll come back. Is that OK?'

'Of course. Take your time.'

'Thank you so much, Noah. For looking after Harley. For noticing. For caring enough to ring her to see where he was. Without you . . .' Mimi sniffs. 'Well, I can't bear to think about it.'

'Don't. She's going to be fine. Do you need me to pick you up from the hospital?'

'No. I'll get a taxi. I don't want Harley to come here. Not yet anyway. See you later.'

'OK. See you soon.'

I put the phone down and go back into Harley's room. He's still asleep in the makeshift tent so I take up residence on his bed and wait for Mimi, my head a garbled mess of images and words and emotions. Looking at Harley asleep, he looks so innocent, and, despite it not being her fault, I feel so angry with Emma for risking tainting that. Because finding your mum lying on the floor dead is not something you ever get over. And knowing that she *chose* it, that leaving you was better than staying with you, well, that's enough to ruin a whole life.

I'm not sure how much time it is that passes before I hear the door open and footsteps on the stairs. And then Mimi's there, red-eyed and pale. When she sees me sitting on the bed, she smiles, but I can see the effort behind it, how utterly sad she's feeling. She comes in and sits beside me, looking over at Harley still asleep on the floor.

'Thanks so much for staying with him.'

'Of course. No problem.'

'Have you had anything to eat? Do you want something?'

Although I haven't eaten all day, I know I couldn't stomach anything. 'No, I'm fine. Actually, I thought I might get going.' My voice sounds almost robotic, like it doesn't even belong to me.

'Oh, OK, unless you fancy a walk? I thought I might take Harley to the park when he wakes up. Take his mind off stuff. And you could probably do with the fresh air after being stuck here?'

I could. I feel like my lungs are shrivelling and fresh air is exactly what I need. But I know that I can't find it with Mimi and Harley. Not right now. I need to get out of here. I need a drink.

'Thanks, but I might just go home and have a shower and stuff. If that's OK with you?'

Mimi nods, but I can tell that she's not just looking out for me – that she wants someone to look after her, and I hate myself that I'm not man enough for the job. But really I'm doing her a favour. I failed to help Emma when she tried to reach out to me. I couldn't save Mum. Mimi's so much better off without me. I don't deserve her. Like I didn't deserve Kate.

'Of course, you go. Harley's much better company than you anyway.'

I know she's just putting on a brave face but I stand up ready to leave, feeling wobbly as I get to my feet. 'OK. Well, call me if you need anything, OK?'

'Will do.'

I bend down and gently stroke Harley's hair. 'I hope he's OK.'

I'm not sure if it's because Mimi notices the emotion in my voice, or whether she's feeling bad for turning me down the other night, but she reaches out for my hand to hold me back. 'Are you sure you're OK?'

I nod, desperate to get away, desperate to get home and drink myself into a mindless stupor.

'OK. Well, I'll see you soon, yeah? And thanks again, for everything.'

I force a smile and then leave her snuggling in next to Harley.

*

On my way home, I make a misguided stop. I can smell the hand sanitizer all the way down the corridor. It's bitter, but underneath it there's something much worse. The smell of rotting, of misery. When the nurse, a ruddy and exceptionally smiley-faced lady, shows me into the room, Emma's awake but drowsy and, perhaps I imagine it, but the first thing I see on her face when she notices me is a strange sort of fear. But then, although I can't see my reflection, if any of the intense rage that is swirling inside of me is apparent on my face, it's probably a perfectly natural reaction.

'Noah.'

'Emma.'

'Apparently I have you to thank, or scream at, for not letting me die?' She smiles weakly, but I don't.

'I read your note.'

Emma looks confused and then it's clear the penny drops. 'The one for Harley?'

I nod and then put my hand in my pocket and pull it out. Emma turns her head away, as if it hurts to look at it.

'My mum committed suicide.'

Emma looks up at me in surprise and a single tear slides down her face, as if someone had dropped it there with a pipette.

'And do you know what?' I continue. 'If she hadn't succeeded, if someone had got to her in time, like I did to you, do you know what I would've told her?'

Emma focuses on her hands, one of which has a tube protruding from the top of it.

'I'd have said, "Don't be so fucking selfish." How dare you write that note to your son pretending you were doing him a favour? You think his life would be better if you killed yourself? Try living in my head. I wish you could, just for a second. Don't you dare do that to Harley. Do you understand me?'

More tears meander down her cheeks now and she wipes them with her knuckle then nods.

'I want you to rip this up.' I hand Emma her note, which she takes, her hand shaking.

And then, slowly, she rips it into strips. 'I'm so sorry, Noah.'

She shouldn't be apologizing to me. My outburst is completely unjustified and I loathe myself more than ever. But it feels like I'm possessed and I've got no control over myself.

The nurse puts her head around the door and I realize I've been shouting. 'Is everything OK in here? Emma, are you OK?'

'Don't worry, I'm leaving.'

Before I can do any more damage, I ignore Emma's cries for me to stay and storm past the nurse, who eyes me with the disgust I deserve, and then march out to find my car. Before I start the engine, I call school and leave an answerphone message to tell them I have a sickness bug and won't be in for the rest of the week. Then I drive home, stopping to get some alcohol, and then take it into the flat, drinking the Jack Daniel's straight from the bottle until I'm so off my face that I must fall asleep.

CHAPTER TWENTY-THREE

The rest of the week is a blur of drinking, sleeping and calling in take-out food. I only leave the house to buy more alcohol. I don't shower. I stream box set after box set from Netflix but don't watch any of it, or if I do, I don't remember what I've seen. The sofa becomes my bed, my cocoon, it takes on the scent of me, becomes like a second skin.

For the first day or two, Mimi calls a lot. She sends several messages, some to tell me how Emma is, others asking if I'm OK as I'm not picking up. I don't text her back, even though I should be writing messages to her that say the exact same thing. It's been a couple of days since her last message now and, although I miss them, I'm glad she's given up on me. It's for the best, for her anyway.

I'm supposed to be going back to work in two days' time but it feels like an impossible feat. The thought of me wearing a shirt and tie, of not smelling like booze and sweat and shit food, of being able to string a coherent sentence together – it seems like that version of me is a very distant memory and I'm not sure how to find him again. If he even exists any more.

My phone starts buzzing. I'm not sure where it is but I can feel the vibration somewhere nearby and run my hand along the back of the sofa. Sure enough, it's there, pushed deep down at the back of the cushions. When I hold it up and squint to try to make out the name, the light of the screen causes the backs of my eyes to throb. It's Kate.

Reluctantly, I press answer and hold the phone to my ear. 'Hello?'

'Where are you, Noah? You promised you'd have the boys whilst we went to Sarah's wedding. Please tell me you're just running very late and not that you've forgotten?'

I search my brain for the memory of the agreement and it's there, but I hadn't realized it was today.

'There was an emergency. I'll be there in half an hour.'

'We're going to miss the service, Noah. We don't have half an hour. Can I just drop them off? It's out of the way, but at least we'll be on the move.'

I look around the flat. 'Well, uh, I'll meet you outside then you don't need to get out the car.'

'OK. Fine. We'll be there in ten.'

'Sure.'

I know I need to clear the flat of the rotting pizza boxes, the bottles of Jack Daniel's thrown across the floor, the filthy quilt and pillows stained with tomato sauce and grease, but it feels insurmountable. So I go and throw some water on my face, slightly disturbed by the grey-faced man staring back at me from the mirror, and then throw on some joggers and a T-shirt before heading outside to meet Kate. I sit on the pavement whilst I wait for her, standing up feeling like a challenge too far, until I see Jerry's car and force myself on to my feet and wave.

Jerry pulls the car into a space a few doors down and I watch as Kate bundles the kids out the car before grabbing their rucksacks out the boot. When she reaches me, she looks red-faced and not at all happy.

'What the hell is going on with you?' she says in a lowered voice, the boys trailing behind her.

'What?' I shrug and then stand up tall, trying to disguise how terrible I'm feeling.

Kate ushers the boys up the path to the flat. 'You look a right mess. And you smell like a brewery.'

'I had a fun night. Just because you don't have them any more now you're married to Mr Boring Pants, don't take it out on me.'

Kate opens her mouth and I prepare myself for the barrage of abuse, but then she closes it again and shakes her head. 'I have to go. The sun is shining. Get the boys outside, please. And have a shower. I'll collect them tomorrow around lunchtime.'

'Have a good time.'

'You're not going to drive them anywhere, are you?'

'Kate, I'm fine.'

She runs her hand through her hair. 'Please just promise me you won't go out in the car. Please, Noah.'

'Fine, whatever, I won't go out. Now go, you're going to miss the service.'

'Thank you. Bye then, boys,' she calls out to the boys who are nearly at my door and blows them both kisses. Adorably, they both blow her kisses back.

Then Kate looks at them wistfully, as if she's worried this is the last time she'll see them as innocent beings before I corrupt and ruin them for good.

'They'll be fine. Relax and enjoy yourself.'

Kate smiles, but looks less than convinced, then she heads off down the road to Jerry's car.

*

'Can we go to the park, Daddy?' Finn says, climbing on to the sofa to lay his body on top of mine.

They've been watching TV for the past hour or so whilst I've lain on the sofa drifting in and out of sleep. When I force my eyes open, I can see they've both helped themselves to bowls overflowing with dry Coco Pops and numerous Fruit Shoots.

'Daddy's still tired, buddy. Why don't you just watch another couple of episodes? We'll go to the park tomorrow morning, yeah?'

I attempt to close my eyes, but Finn holds them open by pushing up my eyebrows.

'I'm bored of *Spiderman*, Daddy. I want to go to the park now.'

'Just a bit longer, OK?'

I gently move Finn off me and turn to face the back of the sofa, quickly drifting off again, but it's not long before I'm awoken by him poking my eyelids.

I move my head away. 'Finn, stop.'

Finn puts his hands on my cheeks and turns my face towards him. His palms feel clammy, like they did when he was a toddler, the skin still squidgy. 'Why are you sleeping all the time, Daddy? Are you poorly? Do you want me to get my doctor's kit and check you over?'

'No, I just want you to let me sleep.'

Finn climbs off the sofa and goes and sits beside his brother on the floor and then, just as I'm about to apologize for sending him away, there's a thump on the front door. Who is it *now*?

Before I can stop him, Finn runs over to the door, reaches up and opens the catch.

'Hey, little monkey.' It's Ben's voice and soon he's in the flat – horrifyingly followed by Claudia. Just what I need.

I sit up and run my fingers through my hair in a poor attempt to look more presentable. When Claudia surveys the state of the flat, I can see her nose physically turning upwards, like she's just driven past a field where they've been muck-spreading.

'Boys, get your shoes on. We're going to the park.' Claudia picks up the remote and turns the TV off, the boys staring at her in shock.

'Hang on, who says we're going to the park? They're my kids, not yours, Claudia. Talking of which, where are the two little Miss Perfects?'

'Don't be an arse, Noah,' Ben says. 'Anyway, they're with Claudia's folks. We thought it'd be best to come on our own.'

'Didn't want to expose them to me, hey?'

'Truthfully, no,' Claudia says and then she ushers the boys over to find their shoes and starts helping them put them on.

Then it suddenly dawns on me why they're here. 'Kate sent you, didn't she?'

'She's worried about you,' Ben says.

'She doesn't think I'm capable of looking after the boys, more like. I'm a good dad, you know? I don't need help with them.'

'You *are* a good dad. Don't be mad at Kate. She just cares. Come on, let's get out and blow off those cobwebs.'

Part of me wants to shout, 'I don't bloody well need looking after', but the other part wants to hand over complete control of myself – *just tell me what to do*. With a dramatic sigh, I go into my bedroom and change into a clean T-shirt and then locate my flip-flops by the door and follow them all out. On the walk to the park, my head feels heavy and my limbs ache, as if I've spent the past week over-exerting myself, when in reality I haven't moved from my sofa. I don't talk to Ben or Claudia and instead they focus on the boys, each holding one of the boys' hands and chatting away merrily about something or other I can't quite hear. I feel shivery even though it's not cold and I wish I could have a drink to stop the throbbing in my head.

When we arrive, I take up residence on a bench and Ben sits beside me, whilst Claudia follows the children closely as they traverse the climbing frame.

'So, what's up?'

'Nothing. What is with everyone? Nothing's up, OK?'

Ben holds up his hands in surrender. 'I'm just asking, Noah. You don't need to bite my head off.'

'I'm just sick of people always thinking the worst of me.'

'People *care* about you. There's a difference. And you stink of whisky, you look like shit and your flat looks like you've got squatters. What do you expect people to think?'

I rub the sleep out of my eyes and then look directly at Ben. 'Why did you get back in touch with Dad without talking to me about it first? I thought we had a pact. Us against him.'

Ben sighs. 'Not this again. Come on, Noah. We're adults now. Surely after everything you've been through you can see it's not that simple? That people make mistakes?'

'What's that supposed to mean?'

Ben shakes his head. 'Let's just talk about this when you're in a better mood.'

'You betrayed me, Ben.'

It sounds sort of stupid as it exits my mouth, particularly as my voice is strained and almost whiny, like we're kids again and he's taken the opposition's side in a playtime brawl.

'I didn't betray you, Noah. I just wanted a family. A proper family, like Claudia has. I wanted that for the girls.'

'But he ruined that, don't you see? He ruined our chance at a happy family.'

'No, he didn't. He made a mistake. He was heartbroken when Mum died. He didn't know how to cope with it.'

'*He* was heartbroken?'

My voice must be raised more than I realize, as everyone in the park turns to look at me and I notice Claudia saying something to the boys before hurrying over.

'Do you think maybe you should save this conversation for another time? A better place? I think you're scaring some of the children.'

I laugh bitterly. 'I bet you love this, don't you? Having to swoop in and rescue my boys from me?'

Claudia looks at me and I'd like to say the look she gives me is patronizing, but actually she just looks sad. 'I'm only trying to help, Noah. I'm not quite the bitch you think I am, you know?'

Ben stands up and puts his arm around Claudia and it makes me feel crap that he thinks she needs protecting from me.

'Do you want us to take the boys to ours for bit?' Ben asks. 'Just until you're feeling a bit better?'

'I'm fine. Thanks for checking on me. But you can go. I'd like some time alone with my boys.'

Ben and Claudia turn to walk off, hand in hand, but I can tell they're reluctant to leave. After a few seconds, Ben turns back. 'Call us if you need us though, yeah? Don't be too proud.'

I nod, feeling shit that my loved ones no longer feel I can be trusted with my own children. But as I sit watching them clambering up the cargo nets, smiles spread across their faces, and yet all I can think about is when I can leave, go back to my flat and have a drink, I realize that everyone's right. I am a terrible father and my amazing boys deserve someone so much better. Someone like Jerry. And for the first time in my life, I'm glad they've got him. I know he won't let them down, won't disappoint them, won't damage them in ways that last a lifetime. He's what they need and I am not.

*

When Kate arrives to pick the boys up the next day, they are playing on their tablets and stuffing themselves with Haribo.

I put my arm across the open doorway to discourage Kate from coming in, but she ducks her head and steps under it.

'Flat's looking good,' she says, surveying the chaos.

'We can't all live in a show home, Kate.'

She storms over to the boys and grabs the nearly eaten packet of sweets from in between them.

'Hey, we haven't finished,' Gabe says, indignant, looking up from his tablet briefly.

'You have now.'

Gabe begins to protest, but when Kate glares at him he soon stops.

Kate heads towards the kitchen and, as she passes me, she takes my hand and pulls me along. Like a slightly confused child, I go with her.

'Right, tell me what's going on,' she says, as her eyes flick around the room, and then she starts picking up various bits of debris and throwing them in the bin.

'You don't need to do that. I'll tidy once the boys are gone. I just wanted to spend the time with them rather than sorting out the flat,' I say, even though we both know it's a lie.

Kate shakes her head. 'I can't bear the thought of you living like this.' She starts running a bowl full of water, squirting in the dregs of the Fairy liquid left in the bottle on the side.

'Stop. I'm fine.'

Kate begins to pile dirty plates and bowls into the soapy water, bubbles flying out as she throws the things in.

'Please, Kate. Just stop.' I don't mean to shout it as loud

as I do and feel guilty as I watch Kate's shoulders jolt in shock.

When she turns around, slowly, there are tears in her eyes. 'I really don't know what's going on with you, Noah, but please don't slip away from us again. The boys need you.'

I look to the floor so that she can't read what I'm thinking. 'Work's been full on. I've not had a chance to tidy. I'm not slipping anywhere.'

'Then look me in the eye.'

Slowly, I raise my head and look directly at her. 'There's nothing wrong. When you next come over, you won't recognize the place. I'll even buy some potpourri, how about that?'

Kate smiles, but it's just a fledgling smile, still unsure and not fully formed. 'Please just let me do the washing-up for you?'

'Why?'

'Because everybody needs looking after sometimes.'

I have a sudden intense desire to fall into her arms and let her cradle me like a newborn.

'I'll do it as soon as you leave. Let's go and get the boys' stuff sorted. It's your turn to do some parenting now, slack arse.'

Kate nods, but I can tell she doesn't really want to leave. 'OK. You pack their bags and I'll be bad cop and drag them off the tablets.'

'Sounds like a good deal.'

Once the boys are all packed up and ready to go, I give them both a cuddle and Kate ushers them out to wait by the car. They look so tiny walking down the path, their backpacks nearly sending them off-balance. And the fear I felt yesterday at the park comes rushing back, making me feel sick, and I know that my boys will be better off if I just let them go, slowly fade from their lives until I'm a distant memory.

'I'll see you next weekend then. Call me if you need anything, OK?' Kate says, resting her hand on my arm.

'Actually, I was wondering if you could have them next weekend. I've got loads of reports to write and having them this weekend as well has set me back quite a bit with them,' I lie.

'Oh, OK. Sorry.'

'It's OK. I agreed to it. I just didn't realize quite how much I had to do.'

'So, do you want them the following weekend then? I think I'm supposed to be taking Gabe to a birthday party that weekend, but you could always take him.'

'Oh no. Let's just keep it as it was before. I'll see them in three weeks.'

Kate furrows her brow. 'Are you sure that's OK? It seems a long time.'

As I'm speaking, I know that the road I am now travelling on is a dark one with no happy place at the end. 'It'll give me the chance to get this work done.'

'OK. If you're sure. See you then.'

*

As soon as I've shut the door I go into the kitchen, retrieve my bottle of Jack Daniel's from the cupboard, unscrew the cap and drink it neat from the bottle. I pull the plug out of the kitchen sink and watch the water swirl down it. I pile all the dirty crockery, now dripping wet, back on to the side and head into the lounge, settling back into my cocoon on the sofa and willing myself to just sleep.

CHAPTER TWENTY-FOUR

I'm not sure what time it is when my phone starts vibrating, but I pick it up and strain my eyes to read the name jigging up and down on the screen. It's Emma. I ignore it and it stops, but then it immediately starts again and I know I have to answer. I owe her that.

'Hi, Emma. Are you OK?'

'Oh hi, Noah. I wasn't sure you'd pick up.'

'To be honest, I wasn't going to.'

'Right. That's what I thought.'

The guilt I've been feeling since I went to visit her rears its ugly head again and I know I have to apologize, even though I still feel so angry, because I know it's not her fault. It was never about Emma. 'Look, I'm sorry about how I treated you in the hospital. I was totally out of line.'

'It's OK.'

'It's really not. I should never have come to see you. I'm sorry. Anyway, I'm sure that's not what you were calling me about. What's up?'

'I just wanted to talk to you. Harley's staying at Mimi's for the night. I wasn't sure who else to call.'

It's the kind of honesty I've been looking for from the outset so I know I can't shut her down.

'OK. What do you want to talk about?'

'Could I come over? I'm sorry to ask, I just really don't want to be alone.'

'Um, well . . .' I'm so torn. The last thing I want is to have Emma in my flat, but she's doing what I asked her to, she's reaching out instead of doing something stupid. And I couldn't live with myself if I sent her away and something terrible happened. 'The flat's a bit of a state, but if you can put your blinkers on, I'll be here. I'll text you my address.'

'Thank you, Noah. I really appreciate it.'

'No problem.'

And when she arrives, it's odd but her presence in the flat makes me realize that I don't really want to be alone either. She looks tired but pretty, her hair swept into a messy bun, no make-up on, wearing cargo shorts and a sporty vest. Unlike when I saw her in the hospital, ghostly white, her eyes sunken and red-rimmed, she has some colour to her cheeks today, a slight glow to her skin.

She sits on the other end of the sofa and nods her head towards the half-empty bottle of Jack Daniel's. 'I hope none of this has anything to do with me. Mimi says she's not heard from you since, well, since, you know.'

I shake my head. 'Work's been busy.'

Emma offers me a sad smile. 'Harley says you've not been in.'

I nod slowly. 'Right. Can't get away with that lie then.' I stand up. 'Do you want a drink? I can get you a glass and some Coke if you want to help me get through this.' I hold up the bottle of JD.

Emma shrugs. 'OK.'

I go through to the kitchen, fill two glasses with ice and carry them through to the lounge, tucking a bottle of Coke underneath my arm. At first, the conversation is stilted between us, both of us avoiding the 'big' topics before swiftly realizing that those are the only things we really have in common. We talk about Harley for a bit and she tells me he's doing OK at school, that he misses me. But then the conversation teeters on the edge of why I'm not at school again, so I change the subject.

Once we're making our way down to the bottom of the bottle of JD, things start to feel easier.

Emma leans against the arm of the sofa, putting her legs up on it and drawing her knees to her chest. 'I am so sorry for what I did. I know you think it's just a poor excuse, but I honestly believed Harley would be happier in the long run if I wasn't there.'

'I know it's not an excuse. Like I said before, I'm sorry. I shouldn't have said what I said.'

'No, I really thought about it and you're right. Even if I'm not the world's best mum, as long as I'm trying and I love him, it has to be better than him growing up thinking I didn't love him enough to stay with him.'

I nod, biting my lip to stop the threatening tears.

'I'm sure that what happened with your mum didn't have anything to do with the way she felt about you, you know,' Emma continues and I shrug, as if to say, *of course I know that, I'm not stupid, everyone knows that*. But then I'm a kid again, wondering why one minute Mum's smothering me with kisses and the next slapping me round the face.

'You're so special, Noah. I wish you knew how special you are.'

And then, suddenly, Emma's right next to me, running her hand through my hair, and then she puts her hands underneath my T-shirt. And before I can really contemplate what's happening, her nails are running down my back, setting my hairs on end, and she's kissing me on the neck and then on the lips and I'm so drunk that I can't figure out how to stop her, and in a way her lips are like some strange sort of reassurance, and for a moment their soft warmth is a comfort. But then her fingers scurry towards my trousers and start pulling at the button and it comes with a bolt of clarity that this is in no way what I want.

I grab her hand and hold it still. 'Stop. We can't do this.'

I release Emma's hand, thinking she'll move it away, but she doesn't. She returns to my button.

I shuffle back as far as I can. 'What are you doing?'

'What? We're both single. You do realize my sister doesn't want you, don't you? I know I don't quite measure up to her perfection, but I'm actually pretty good in bed.'

I shake my head, but the motion makes me feel dizzy and I lean on the coffee table with both hands to steady myself. 'We're both drunk. When you're sober, you'll realize you don't want this.'

Emma gives a bitter snort. 'Of course, unhinged, neurotic Emma. I couldn't possibly know what I want.'

A strong wave of nausea comes over me. 'I need to lie down. I'm sorry. There's some money on the side in the kitchen. Use it to get yourself a taxi.'

'Right. Get what you want from me and then throw me out.'

'I didn't want anything from you, Emma. You kissed me. I just didn't push you away soon enough.'

Emma chews her bottom lip, her eyes angry and tearful. 'So you're going to tell Mimi it was all my fault? Make her hate me even more than she already does?'

I'm not sure what Mimi would think about Emma and me kissing, maybe she wouldn't even care, but I don't think it's worth potentially causing problems between the two of them, or us, especially as it meant nothing.

'No. I won't tell her anything. We were both drunk. Let's just forget about it, OK?'

Emma looks me up and down, slowly. 'I can see why she turned you down.'

Underneath the façade of anger, I can hear the pain of rejection in her voice, but nothing I say is going to have a positive outcome at this point so I leave her on the sofa, stumble through to my bedroom and collapse on the bed, my head spinning. I think I must fall asleep because it's pitch-black when I wake up and I feel delirious. I drift off again, lost in my dream – Mimi's there but then she turns into Kate and she pushes me off a cliff and I'm falling, falling, and instead of jerking awake like I usually would, I feel every second of the fall, my stomach lurching up to my throat, aware that death awaits. Then just before I hit the ground I'm snapped awake and it's light. My head is pounding and there's a banging coming from somewhere, I'm not sure if it's in my head or if it's external. But then it's there again and I realize it's coming from the front door.

I force myself up, retrieving my glasses from the pillow, and as the world comes into focus, I suddenly remember what happened with Emma and hope beyond hope it's not her knocking. Shuffling through the hallway, I reach the door and open it, preparing for an argument, but I'm surprised to see it's Mimi, a paper bag with some kind of pastry or something similarly greasy in her hands.

'Can I come in? I've brought croissants.' She smiles her beautiful smile and for a second, I feel better, but then I'm scared that Emma's told her what happened and that this friendly introduction is just a pretence before she starts shouting at me.

I glance back into the flat. 'It's a bit of a state.'

'That's OK. I don't mind.'

I hold the door open wider and step back to let her in. 'OK, if you're sure, but you're entering at your own risk.'

I quickly gather together a few of the dirty plates, wrappers and bottles and take them through to the kitchen then brush off the sofa cushions and sit down.

'How are you? I've been worried about you,' Mimi says, sitting beside me. She doesn't look angry, just tired, her eyes missing their typical sparkle.

'I'm sorry I've not been in touch. I've not been in a good place. It's complicated, but I'm sorry.'

'It's OK.'

'It's not. Your sister tried to commit suicide and I just sank into myself. I should've been there for you.'

'Probably.' Mimi offers me a sad smile.

'How's Harley?'

'He's doing well. They've been assigned a family support worker who's going to make sure they both get the help they need. And Dad and I have been taking it in shifts to look after Harley and give Emma some respite time. Dad's going to stay over there for the next week or so, but they don't think Emma's at risk of trying anything again. I think it really scared her.'

I picture what Emma was like last night and hope that external agencies might be able to give her the help she needs. 'Well, at least one good thing's come out of it then.'

Mimi nods and then she looks like she might cry and reaches over and grasps my hand. 'Emma told me about your mum, Noah. That she didn't die of cancer.'

I feel something tighten in my chest. 'Oh.'

'I hope you don't mind her telling me. I told her I was worried about you and she said maybe that was why you'd gone AWOL. I'll go in a minute and give you the space you need but I just wanted to say I'm so sorry, Noah.'

I bite down on my thumb. I can't speak so I just nod.

She puts the bag of croissants down on the coffee table. 'I'll just leave these here. Call me anytime if you want to chat.'

I put my head in my hands and then look up at her. 'You know, sometimes I hate my mum for killing herself, like *really* hate her.'

Mimi settles back into the seat, clearly sensing my need to offload. 'I can understand that.'

'Really? You're not just saying that to make me feel better?'

'No. Your mum was clearly unwell. And the way she acted, her choices – they weren't her fault. But that doesn't mean you shouldn't feel angry and hurt. What you went through, it wasn't fair. No child should have to go through that.'

'I was nineteen. I wasn't exactly a child.'

Even though I still felt like one.

'I'm not just talking about the suicide, Noah. I'm talking about all the things you wrote down. And I'm sure many other things that you didn't. You have every right to be angry. But be angry at the disease. Not your mum. Not your dad. And not yourself. Nothing that happened was your fault.'

I feel a stray tear meandering down my cheek, then my breathing quickens and an odd noise forces its way out of my mouth, followed by more tears.

'I don't want to ruin my boys like my mum ruined me.'

Because she did, that is the stark reality, even though it makes me feel guilty to think it. It feels like a betrayal of the woman I loved more than anything else in the world for such a long time. But she broke me, not just by killing herself, but by the heart-wrenching pattern of withdrawal and then total immersion and love, repeated over and over so that it left me desperately seeking the glimmers of the good stuff like an addict desperate for their next fix. It's been easy to just blame Dad all these years – for not making her better, for leaving us when she died – but I have to accept Mum's part too.

'You won't ruin them. You're amazing with those boys.'

I shake my head. 'I told Kate I couldn't have them this weekend. Maybe I should just move away. Leave them to be a happy family.'

Mimi takes my face in her hands. 'They wouldn't be happy without you. You have to stop thinking like that.'

'But I'm scared I'll never get over stuff. It feels like one step forward, two steps back all the time. I thought I was getting better. That I was dealing with everything. But then seeing Emma . . .'

'Of course it set you back. It was bound to. You can't see it, Noah, but you are so much better than you give yourself credit for. The way you are with your boys, Harley, the way you saved Emma, even the way you love Kate . . .'

Mimi pauses but I can tell she has more to say. She begins twisting her bracelet around her wrist, her eyes focusing on the movement rather than looking at me. 'In fact, I've been thinking about you a lot this week. Well, for longer than that actually, but then nearly losing Emma . . . it just made everything seem so much less complicated than I thought it was.'

'What do you mean?'

'After everything that happened with James, I've always been really cautious when it comes to men. Too cautious, probably. And you, well, you've always felt like this huge, terrifying risk. Sorry, no offence.'

I smile. 'It's OK. None taken.'

'But then it suddenly dawned on me that you're one of the good guys. You're not who I thought you were.'

'Thanks, I think.'

'I mean, I always thought you were funny and interesting and relatively attractive . . .' Mimi smiles. 'But I thought you'd break my heart.'

'And now?'

'Well, now I think you might be the one to mend it.'

It's the moment I've been waiting for. And I know that I should feel elated, and for a few moments I do, but then I look around at the state the flat's in and think about this past week, Emma, the way I treated the boys, and I can't help it – my stomach drops.

'But what if I mess this up like I've messed up everything else?'

333

Mimi moves towards me. 'I won't let you. We'll take it slowly, OK?'

'And what about the fact you're going away?'

Mimi shrugs. 'I don't have to go for too long. We'll figure it out.'

And then I'm not sure if she kisses me or I kiss her, but one way or another we're kissing and all the shit and the pain start to melt and it feels like returning to somewhere you've not visited for twenty years – simultaneously foreign and somewhat familiar.

CHAPTER TWENTY-FIVE

The return to school is almost as hellish as I imagined it was going to be. I get lots of sympathetic looks and comments about my 'horrendous stomach bug' (why is it with a stomach bug people feel the need to over-share their own gruesome experiences?). When I bump into the head teacher, she's not so sympathetic – more sceptical – *What a coincidence that you developed a bug right after you ran out of school to visit the Thomases.* I'm not sure what she's implying. She doesn't know how Mum died, so she's not joining up the dots. I'm not sure if she thinks I'm making the whole thing up – that I fabricated the suicide attempt and spent a week having a jolly with Emma – but either way, she doesn't seem convinced that I was really ill.

Today, we have to practise our class assembly. It's kind of like a surgeon returning to work and being faced with a mass traffic accident on his first day back. Assemblies are basically just a way for the head to check that you're actually teaching something and for teachers to outdo each other. I usually go for the standard hold up a few pictures, sing a song, perhaps act out a little story number, but, after watching a few videos on YouTube, this year, for some unknown reason (maybe because I'm feeling guilty for having the week off, maybe because I'm trying to prove something to myself, who knows?), I've decided to go the whole shebang. A proper production – costumes, instruments, props. I'll show the rest of the staff not to rule me out as 'the one whose assembly will always be shittier than theirs' in future. It's a retelling of *The Three Little Pigs* called *The Three Little Wolves* – it's basically exactly the same story but the pig is the bad one and the wolves are the goodies. Should be fairly straightforward – or so you would think.

I assign the parts first. The only two children in the class who I've actually managed to teach to read are given the job of narrators. The middle-of-the-road kids form the chorus (plus set creators so they don't feel they've been given an unimportant part – which they have). The ones who wouldn't be able to learn the words to the songs if they had headphones permanently attached to them for the next month are given the role of percussionists. How hard can it be to bang a drum or shake a tambourine roughly in time to the music? Very hard, it turns out. And the bright, slightly obnoxious ones are given the roles of the three wolves. Last but not least, I give the role of naughty pig to Harley. It might feel like he's been a little typecast, but the decision's based more on the fact that this way I can see him at all times, he's not holding a beater that he can use to smack someone else on the head, I'm ticking the inclusion box and I have this (probably misguided) vision of him proving everyone wrong – of this being his 'moment'.

The practice doesn't start well. There's a lot of confusion over the fact the wolves are kind and the pig is the baddie, and I mean A LOT. I'm tempted to just switch it back to the original, but I think that'll just make matters worse, so we stick with it. None of them can get their lines, the narrators keep making the microphones squeal, cue covering ears, screams and tears from all the weedy ones, the percussionists might as well not even be there (they just stare at me blankly when I demonstrate keeping a steady beat) and one of the wolves wets himself all over his costume. In fact, the only one who's any good is Harley, who snorts and shouts his way through his part like someone out of RADA. Oh well. I will not admit defeat. It's only day one. The only way is up.

*

'Can I be a total pain and change my mind about not having the boys this weekend?'

I can hear Kate clattering around on the other end of the phone, emptying the dishwasher or something similarly noisy. 'It depends. Are you going to change it back again in the meantime?'

I shake my head vehemently even though Kate can't see me. 'No. I can promise you that.'

There's a pause, as if Kate is considering my response, and then she says, 'So what's changed? I thought you had reports to write.'

I take a deep breath. 'Emma, Mimi's sister, tried to commit suicide. Her son's in my class. I found her.'

'Oh, Noah. I'm sorry. Is she OK? Is Mimi OK?'

'Yeah, they're both doing OK.'

'I knew something was up when I came over.'

'I'm sorry I couldn't tell you at the time.'

'It's OK. I've just been worrying about you. How are you holding up?'

'As you can expect, it brought up a lot of stuff to do with Mum. You were right when you said I was angry at her. I think maybe just admitting that was half the battle. And realizing that I couldn't change it – what happened, you know?'

'Good for you, Noah. I'm really glad you're finally dealing with it. But why weren't you going to have the boys?'

'I panicked, I think. About messing them up. Like Mum did with me.'

'You won't mess them up, Noah. Well, no more than all parents do with their kids.'

'Thanks. I'm doing better. I know I've said that before, but I think I really am this time. Mimi and I have decided to give things a go. And I was hoping to take the boys to meet Dad at the weekend, if that's OK with you?'

'Of course.' I was expecting Kate to gush about how wonderful it was that I was finally going to go and see Dad, but there's no mistaking it, she sounds sad.

'What's up?'

'It's nothing.'

'Come on, Kate. I know you well enough to tell when you're upset about something.'

Kate sighs. 'I'm just sorry I couldn't help you like Mimi clearly has, that's all.'

I suddenly get it. I've inadvertently made her feel like she wasn't enough.

'Hey, don't say that. It's not like that at all. I just wasn't ready before. It has nothing to do with you.'

Kate sounds like she's doing something again, moving to a different room or tidying something away, the sound of doors closing, her breathing suggesting more exertion. 'I'm sorry. I'm being selfish thinking of me in all this. I'm really happy things are starting to work out for you, Noah. Honestly.'

'Thank you. And I'm sorry I didn't do it all sooner.'

'Don't be sorry.'

I tuck the phone between my ear and my shoulder whilst I pour myself a glass of apple juice. 'So is it OK for me to still have the boys at the weekend?'

'Of course. They'll be thrilled.'

'Thank you, Kate. Really. I know not all ex-wives would be so understanding.'

'Yep. You lucked out with me. See you Sunday.'

*

I pull back Mimi's chair and she does a little curtsy before sitting down. It's our first proper date and I'm actually quite nervous. I didn't go too posh as it didn't seem very 'Mimi', but I wanted something that felt special enough, so I went for a nice gastro pub by the water. It's a warm evening so we sit outside, and it reminds me of our drink after the art gallery and how far we've come.

'Well, this is very nice.'

'Only the best for you, of course.'

When the food arrives, it's delicious and I'm chuffed that I made a good choice. The benefit of having been friends first is that the conversation flows effortlessly, there are no awkward silences and it's hands down the best first date I've ever had. Mimi looks beautiful in an unusual patchwork denim dress, her red hair glowing in the candlelight.

Once we've finished our mains, the waiter brings over the dessert menu and I know better than to suggest sharing. She orders a hot fudge sundae and I go for the chocolate cheesecake. We talk about a new song that she's working on. The one we uploaded to YouTube has had some really positive feedback so far and it seems to have spurred her on to keep writing, which I'm really glad about. I tell her some amusing tales about the horror that is my class assembly, and she puts the date into her phone so that she can come along and laugh at my misfortune. Before long, the waiter brings over our desserts and after he's placed them in front of us and left the table, I decide to broach the subject of my plans for the upcoming weekend.

'So,' I say between mouthfuls, 'I thought I might take the boys to meet my dad this weekend.'

Mimi's face immediately lights up. 'Oh, Noah. I'm so pleased.'

'You were right. I think the closure would do me good. And I wondered if you wanted to come with me?'

'Of course,' she says, looking like someone who's just been asked to be a bridesmaid. 'I'd be honoured.'

'Great. And I thought I'd tell the boys about us on Friday night. If you're OK with that?'

'What about us, exactly?' Mimi asks, her eyes teasing, as she looks at me over the top of her wine glass.

'Well, that we're, you know, going steady.'

A burst of wine flies out of Mimi's mouth. 'Going steady? What century are we in, Noah? Surely nobody uses the term "going steady" any more?'

I find myself laughing with her until we're both giggling like schoolgirls. 'I'm not sure where it came from, to be honest. I've never said it before in my life.'

'Well, I'm glad you're going to tell the boys. Shows it's more than a mere dalliance, darling,' Mimi mocks.

'I'll tell them you're my bitch. Is that better?'

'Much.' Mimi sips the last of her wine and reaches across the table to hold my hand. 'Thank you for an excellent first date.'

'You're very welcome.'

The waiter comes over and takes our bowls away, not speaking, as if he senses he might be interrupting a 'moment'.

'So do you want me to drop you home after this?'

I've not touched a drop of alcohol this week and it's amazing how much brighter I feel. People always say alcohol is a depressant but I really believed it was making me feel better – now I wonder if it was a big part of what was dragging me down.

'Actually, I told my dad I wouldn't be home until the morning.'

'Well, that was very presumptuous of you, wasn't it?'

Mimi smiles shyly, her cheeks just slightly blushing.

'I'll go and pay the bill.'

*

When we finally reach the end of an exhausting week of rehearsals, I pick the kids up from school and take them to their favourite café (they love it because it has the best selection of cakes you've ever seen). We haven't been for a while so I wanted it to be a treat, somewhere special to announce my 'news' that Mimi and I are now together.

But when they walk in, they go straight to their usual sofa and sit down, fighting over who sits by the window.

'Do you want to come and order, boys? To choose something?'

'Oh, I'll just have a hot chocolate and a brownie, same as usual,' Gabe says, taking a stack of Pokémon cards out of his pocket and scrolling through them.

Finn doesn't even bother to speak, just nods, which I take to mean he wants the same as Gabe.

They used to rush to the counter, gaze up at the menu wide-eyed, take ages deliberating about which cake to choose. *It's like Willy Wonka's chocolate factory in here, boys. Come on, give me something.*

I order the hot chocolates and brownies (choosing the most impressive slice of chocolate cake I can find for me, covered in Smarties and marshmallows) and take them over. That'll show them. Unfortunately, my plan backfires as they then start arguing over my cake and I end up having to buy another piece and get stuck with a chocolate brownie.

Once they've stuffed their faces, I begin my announcement, feeling unexpectedly nervous about the news I'm about to impart. At first, it didn't seem like a big deal telling them that Mimi and I are now in a relationship. I mean, she spent a fair bit of time with them when we were just

342

friends – the fact that we're now sleeping in the same bed at the end of the day doesn't really have much bearing on them. But then I realized that this is the first woman I've cared about since Kate. All being well, I want Mimi to be in the boys' lives for a long time. I want her in a leading role. And them being happy about that is hugely important to me.

I adopt the third person as a kind of distancing technique. 'So, boys, Daddy's got something to tell you.'

'What? Are we going on holiday?' Gabe says, eyes lighting up.

'No, it's not like that . . .'

'Have you got us the new Aquaman Lego film?'

'Well, no, I . . .' Now I'm worried my news is going to be a disappointment. 'It's something about Daddy.'

'You're turning into a woman?' Gabe shouts and the whole café turn to look at us.

'No, no. Where have you heard about stuff like that?'

'One of the boys in my class, Timmy, well, his dad said he was born in the wrong body so he's turning into a woman so Timmy's going to have two mums.'

Finn screws up his face as if Gabe's just imparted one of his particularly delightful stories about one bodily function or another.

'Right, OK, well, no, I'm not becoming a woman. I've got a girlfriend. Like Mummy has Jerry.'

'Are you going to get married too?' Finn asks enthusiastically.

'No, nothing like that.'

'Oh,' he whines. 'I wanted another chocolate fountain.'

'Sorry about that. Anyway, it's Mimi, you know, my friend Mimi. She's my girlfriend now.'

Gabe looks like he's wondering how what I'm telling him is 'news'. 'I thought she was your girlfriend anyway. You're always with her.'

'I like Mimi,' Finn states, matter of fact. It looks like he's got a beard with the chocolate icing all around his mouth.

'Good. So you're both OK with Daddy having a girl-friend? You don't mind Mimi spending more time with us or staying at Daddy's sometimes?'

'Of course not. We're happy for you, Dad,' Gabe says and, for a second, I can picture him as an adult, joining me for a pint at the pub, and the thought makes me simultan-eously happy and sad.

'Great. Well, I think she might come over tomorrow, if that's OK? In fact, I thought we might go to see your granddad.'

It feels weird calling him Granddad. When you picture a granddad you visualize someone warm, cosy, with per-manent sweets in his pocket. I can't imagine my dad like that.

'But I thought you said Granddad lived in another country?' Gabe says with furrowed eyebrows.

When Gabe reached an age where he started asking questions about Dad, saying he lived abroad seemed like the easiest lie and I've not really had any reason to change stories since.

'I did. But he lives here now. So is that OK if we go and see him tomorrow?'

'Yeah, fine.' The boys don't look particularly bothered either way, but I can't expect them to understand the sig-nificance of it.

'But tonight it's film night with Daddy. I've decided it's time to introduce you boys to the world of Percy Jackson.'

'Finally,' Gabe says, jigging excitedly in his chair, but Finn's too busy licking his finger and using it to pick up the crumbs on his plate to engage in the conversation.

CHAPTER TWENTY-SIX

The satnav says we're only ten minutes away and my insides start churning as if I'm on a loop-the-loop roller-coaster. I'm sorely tempted to press the 'stop guidance' button and turn around, but I just keep following it, robotically, hoping that going through the motions of changing gear, indicating, steering will start to calm my racing heart.

As we get even closer, it feels weird seeing the area that I've avoided for such a long time. We pass a shop where I'm guessing he buys his milk, his bread, his whisky. And then I hear 'You have reached your destination' and slow the car down until I see the number twenty-three. It has a red door. A small front garden with no plants, just gravel. The paint is chipping off the window frames. It's quite a depressing house really.

I sit there for a moment, in two minds about whether I want to go and knock on the door. Maybe he won't be there? There's no driveway, just a row of cars parked along the road, so it's impossible to know if his car's here. I'm not even sure what car he drives these days.

'Do you want to go in?' Mimi uses a gentle voice, as if asking if I'm ready to identify a body in the morgue.

'Sorry. Yes.' I turn to the boys in the back. 'Come on, boys. Let's go and see if Granddad's home.'

'Have you not called him first?' Gabe asks, incredulous.

It's a reasonable question. It's probably crazy to drive for an hour without even knowing if he's going to be in, but every time I thought about picking up the phone, I didn't know what to say.

'Do you want me to wait in the car?' Mimi asks. 'I don't mind.'

'No. I'd like you to come in. If that's OK?'

Mimi reaches for my hand. 'Of course it is.'

We get out of the car and I walk, nervously, towards the front door, Mimi just behind me. The boys run ahead, pushing the metal gate open and running up the path, slamming on the door before I can tell them that actually I'm not ready for this, I want to go home. Dad doesn't answer and I feel a strange mixture of relief and disappointment, but then the door opens and he's standing there, in jeans and a lumberjack shirt, his hair still thick, a little greyer at the sides but mostly dark, like mine. And he's looking at the boys with confusion, as if he's going to shout at them for knocking on his door for no reason, but then he lifts his head and sees me, and he looks so overwhelmed with emotion that I don't know what to say, how to feel, how to act. Finn has no such problem, hurrying straight over to Dad and hugging his legs, and I'm scared that Dad might start crying. Because if he does then I know I will too.

'Please, come in,' Dad says, his voice strained.

He opens the door wider and the boys and Mimi go through into the small hallway. When I go past, Dad grabs my arm with both hands, squeezing it, and says, barely audibly, 'Thank you so much for coming.'

I just nod and Dad guides us all into the lounge. It's bare, nothing on the walls or the surfaces except for two photos in brown frames. One of him, Mum, Ben and me at the beach when I was about six. I think I remember it, but maybe I just remember a generic trip to the beach rather than this specific one. The other photo is of Ben's two girls – it's the same one he gave to us one Christmas. They'd had a professional family shoot done so we all got the treat of cheesy, airbrushed photos of them all.

Dad must follow my gaze because he says, 'I didn't have any photographs of your boys.' He pauses before turning back to me. 'I'd love one though, if that's OK?'

'I'll see if I can find something and send it over to you,' I reply coldly. I so want to be OK with everything, to forgive him, to give him what he clearly needs, but the anger and resentment in my gut is so strong, so toxic, that I don't know if I can.

'Thanks, that would be great.'

I can hear the vulnerability in his voice but can't quite bring myself to warm to it.

Gabe comes over to me and tugs on my arm until I bend down so he can whisper in my ear. 'Can we have a drink and a biscuit?'

Dad must hear him because he looks embarrassed. 'Sorry, I haven't offered you anything. I don't have a lot of visitors. What would you like?'

'Go and help your dad out, Noah. I'll look after these two toerags,' Mimi says, ruffling each boy's hair. 'And I'll have a cup of tea, please.'

I know what she's doing. Trying to force me into a conversation I'm not sure I'm ready to have, but I reluctantly follow Dad through to the kitchen. It's strange at first, neither of us knowing what to say. He turns the kettle on and gets out three mugs and I look in the fridge for some sort of juice for the boys. It's odd to see the contents. A few carrots, a half-eaten tomato. The usuals – milk, bread, butter. Beer. A couple of microwavable meals. In fact, it's not unlike mine, which is a depressing thought. I take out the apple juice and Dad passes me two glasses to put it in.

'Thanks.'

'The boys are gorgeous. Ben's shown me pictures on his phone but they're even more stunning in real life.'

'Must take after Kate.'

'I can see a lot of you in there too. When you were little.'

'I'm surprised you can remember.'

Dad tries to secure eye contact with me. 'I remember everything.'

He pours hot water into the three mugs and, standing in the silence, wanting equally to wrap my arms around him and punch him in the face, I wonder if I can do this.

'And is that your girlfriend?' Dad continues. 'She's very beautiful too.'

I nod.

'I'm glad. I was really sorry to hear about you and Kate. I always thought you two were so well-suited.'

'We were. But there's only so far you can push someone before they break, you know? I drove her away.'

It sounds more pointed than I mean it to. Or maybe I do mean it to sound that pointed, I'm not sure.

'Well, I'm sure it wasn't all your fault. Try not to be too hard on yourself.'

Is he excusing himself? Or just being kind to me? Either way, I feel myself bristling and try to breathe it away. I didn't come here for a fight, but at the same time it feels like this forced politeness isn't going to get us anywhere. That I'll just walk out feeling the same resentment, the same rage. I wonder if Dad feels it too – the need to face the elephant in the room – because he says, 'I'm sorry that I wasn't the best dad, Noah. And that I just left after your mum died. I thought you boys were better off without me. That you hated me, resented me for what happened to your mum.'

I take off my glasses, cleaning them with my sleeve, hoping the everyday action might calm me. 'I think I should go.'

Dad reaches out to touch my arm but I move out the way. 'Don't go. Look, I'm just trying to explain.'

I put my glasses back on and look directly at him. It feels weird really looking at him after all this time. The ways he's changed. The ways he hasn't. 'Better off without you? Our mum had just killed herself. We *needed* you.' It's hard to say this last bit and the words catch in my throat a little.

Dad lets out a long breath. 'I'm sorry. I don't know what else to say. I didn't know how to cope with the grief. I felt guilty *all* the time. I felt like I'd failed you, failed her; because I'd buried myself in work, I'd not been around as much as I should've been, but I didn't know how to help her. How to make her happy. And then when she died, I just wanted to hide away.'

'So you just left us there? To take care of ourselves?'

'You were nineteen, Noah. Ben was twenty-one.'

'So you'd done your job, had you? A pretty shitty one, but we were grown up. You'd served your time. Time for us to stand on our own two feet?'

Dad leans against the worktop, as if he's struggling to stand on his own. 'It wasn't like that. I thought I had nothing to offer you. That I'd done enough damage as it was. But I came to my senses, Noah. I tried fighting for you boys but you wouldn't have me.'

'Do you blame us?'

'No, I don't blame you for anything. Not a single bit of it. I deserve every second of the heartache and loneliness and regret that I have endured all these years. But I can't change the past, however much I want to. All I can do is try to be a good dad now. A good granddad. But it's up to you if you want to let me.'

The reason I came is because I thought that I could, it felt like I was ready, but now I'm here I'm not so sure. I still want to. But it feels like the past has got its arms around me and it won't let go.

'Let's just go and play a game with the boys. We can talk about this another time.'

'OK. Except I don't really have any games. Sorry. Ben usually brings stuff with the girls.'

'It's fine. I've probably got some in the boot. I'll have a look. You go and have a chat with the boys, if they let you get a word in edgeways.' I try to lighten the mood, but the air still feels thick and heavy, like it does just before a storm.

Dad smiles, but it feels a little forced. 'Thanks. I'd love to.'

We take the drinks through to the lounge and then I leave them and go out to the car. It feels good to inhale a deep breath of fresh air and I take my time walking to it. When I get there, I open the boot and prop myself on the edge, allowing myself to take a moment before going back inside. I wonder what the boys are making of Dad, what he's making of them. Then I notice Mimi out of the corner of my eye and she comes over and sits beside me on the edge of the boot.

'Gabe's got your dad playing hangman.'

'Sounds about right. Are they OK?'

'They're having a lovely time, giggling away.'

A strange mixture of emotions fills my chest – relief that they're all getting on, sadness for all the years they've missed.

'I'll come back in in a second. Just needed a breather.'

'Of course,' Mimi says, standing up.

'I didn't mean for you to go.'

She sits back down. 'OK.'

I let out a long breath. 'I'm not sure I can do it.'

'Don't be silly. You're here. You're doing it.'

'But how do I forgive him? Even now I've accepted that it's not all his fault, that Mum hurt me just as much, more, even. I still feel so angry with him for abandoning us – not just when she died, but for not being around more when they were still together, for not helping us with her.'

'So tell him that. Tell him how much your mum hurt you. And that you're sad that he let her.'

It's not that easy, but I know that sitting on it all isn't doing me any favours either.

352

'Come on. Let's go back in.' I grab Uno and Jenga and Mimi follows me back to Dad's house. He and the boys are gathered around a piece of paper, Gabe jumping up and grabbing his forehead every time he guesses a letter wrong and Dad draws the next bit of the hangman. When Dad sees me, he looks up.

'Is hangman OK? The boys wanted to play it.'

He looks frailer than I remember him, not so much physically, but less sure of himself. He always seemed so confident when we were growing up, like whatever he said was gospel and we had no right to question it. But now he seems desperate to seek my approval and I'm not sure if I feel flattered or sad.

'Of course. It's one of our favourites, isn't it, boys?'

The boys don't respond to me, whispering in each other's ears about which letter to guess next, so I sit down on the sofa and let them get on with the game.

We stay for about an hour. The boys teach Dad how to play Uno and have lots of fun correcting him when he gets things wrong. We all play a fairly competitive version of Jenga, Mimi being the one to eventually cause the tower to collapse. And for a while it seems normal, a typical family get-together, but then I start to feel tired and decide it's time to leave.

When we're at the door ready to go, I avoid any over-emotional goodbyes or physical affection by loading myself up with the boys' games and promising to come back and see Dad again soon. I don't yet know if I will but it's definitely not out of the question either, which is progress of sorts, I suppose. The boys do hug him and I notice he holds on longer than would be expected for a casual goodbye, perhaps scared he'll never get to do it again. Then he kisses them both on the tops of their heads.

'It was so brilliant to see you,' he says to them, his face beaming. Then he looks at me. 'And you.'

I nod.

'And if you could send me a photo of the boys, that'd be great. Or bring one over. Or I could come and see you.'

He looks like he's trying to be casual about it, but I can sense how much he wants to see us again and I wish I could give him a guarantee.

'We'll sort something.'

Dad's shoulders fall but he nods, seemingly accepting that I'm not ready to commit to anything just yet.

Mimi leans in and kisses Dad on the cheek. 'It was lovely to meet you, Mike.'

'You too, Mimi. I hope to see you again soon.'

Mimi smiles and then I start the procession down the path, unable to ignore the sadness I feel at walking away, pressing on my throat like a swollen gland. When I turn back to shut the gate, Dad is still standing at the door and he waves, and I wave back and manage a half-smile, and then Finn starts hassling me about having one of the cakes in the back of the car, but I'm too distracted to respond.

'Go and tell him,' Mimi says, her hand placed gently in the small of my back.

I look at her, contemplating what she's said, and then I hand her the car keys and she leads the boys to the car whilst I walk back to Dad's door, knocking on it firmly, despite my hand shaking.

When Dad opens, he looks surprised. 'Did you forget something?'

'Can I come back in for a second?'

'Sure. Come on through.'

We go back into the lounge and I sit down on the sofa, Dad sitting beside me, looking slightly scared.

I take a deep breath and then begin, because if I don't say it straight away then I'm going to end up not saying it at all. 'When she shouted at us for nothing, or made us feel guilty for having friends, when she told us we were useless, that it was our fault she was so miserable . . .' I swallow down the lump in my throat. 'Why didn't you stop her?'

Dad puts his head in his hands and then rubs his eyes before looking up. 'I did try. I did talk to her about it but she didn't get it. I'm so sorry, Noah.'

There's no point trying to stop the tears from coming now. It's beyond my control. 'I loved her so much but I always seemed to disappoint her . . . I never understood what I'd done wrong.'

Dad puts his hand on my cheek and it feels like something inside me is breaking down. 'Oh, son. You didn't do anything wrong. I'm so sorry I let you go through that.'

Dad wraps his arms around me and I don't resist. I hug him back, feeling like a kid again, needing the strong arms of my father to make me feel safe.

*

On the way home, at the boys' request, we take their bikes on to the Downs. Once we're out the car, Gabe cycles off ahead and Mimi patiently helps Finn, holding on to the saddle and running alongside him.

'I'm doing it, I'm doing it,' I can hear Finn shout as I trail behind them all.

When he starts to lose his balance, Mimi runs in front of him and grabs the handlebars, helping him to stop safely and climb off. I catch up with them and shout Gabe back, and he starts pedalling towards us at speed.

'I was riding on my own, wasn't I? You weren't holding on to me,' Finn says, his face beaming, his voice out of breath.

'You were,' Mimi lies and I reach over for her hand and squeeze it.

When Gabe returns, he throws his bike to the ground and slaps Finn on the back.

'Hey,' Finn says, his face scrunched. 'Daddy, Gabe just hit me.'

'I'm playing tag,' Gabe says, although we all know he just wanted a free shot at his brother. 'Come on, Finn, you're it. Are you playing, Mimi? Daddy's always too slow.'

'Right,' I say, grabbing him and just about managing to pick him up and dangle him head first above the ground. 'I'll show you.'

I gently place him on the ground and he, Mimi and I run off whilst Finn chases after us. We play tag for a while, and then when I'm worn out, I suggest we find an ice-cream van, so Gabe cycles off in search of one and we follow behind, me pushing Finn's bike and him holding Mimi's hand.

When we reach the ice-cream van, we join the queue, whilst the boys chase around nearby. Mimi links her arm through mine and rests her weight lightly on me.

'I'm really proud of you for today. In fact, I feel like a proud teacher watching my student graduate.'

I smile. 'Because it was all down to your excellent guidance?'

'I'd like to say I played a part.'

I kiss the top of her head. 'You did. A huge part. Thank you.'

Once we've finally reached the front and bought the ice creams, I call the boys over and we sit on the grass like a row of skittles, Mimi and I in the middle with one boy either side of us. The sun is out and there is only a gentle breeze. In fact, it is a perfect late spring day. Summer always feels time-pressured, like you have to make the most of it because you know it'll soon be over and the sky will return to its usual soul-destroying grey. But spring is full of anticipation, of hope. If it's hot, it's a bonus, you can just relax and enjoy it. So that's what we do. My two boys and this woman who feels a lot like spring herself.

CHAPTER TWENTY-SEVEN

Kate and Jerry have invited us over for dinner. Kate decided it would be nice for the boys to see us all together so we could show what a happy, united extended family we are. I'm not entirely convinced. There's no way I'm ever going to be friends with Jerry. Not because I'm bitter that he's now married to Kate. In fact, I haven't thought about Kate in that way for ages now. It's just that he's a boring fart who only wants to talk about sport or gadgets, like his new lawnmower that, guess what, mows lawns. But here we are. And despite having to endure Jerry's fifteen-minute demonstration of how to use his new egg peeler, I'm actually having a pretty good time.

The boys have got pizza on their laps in the lounge and are watching a film, so they think it's the best party ever. Jerry has cooked steak and chips (very manly) and I hate to admit it tastes great. Of course he can cook to restaurant standard, unlike me, who struggles not to ruin a microwaveable meal.

'This is delicious,' Mimi says. 'I can see why you left Noah for Jerry, Kate.'

Kate and Jerry start wetting themselves and Mimi looks over at me (I'm not laughing).

'Too soon?' Mimi gives me a cheeky wink and I can't help but smile.

'I like you already,' Kate says to Mimi. 'I told you she was a keeper, Noah.'

'You were right,' I say and, when I look at Mimi, she looks like a kid whose teacher just told them that their work was the best in the class.

'So what else do you like to do when you're not cooking delicious meals, Jerry?' Mimi asks, charm personified.

'Oh, I'm a simple man. Football on a Saturday, beer and a take-out, a walk followed by lunch in a country pub. That sort of thing. Noah thinks I'm a boring bastard.'

'I don't know where you get that impression.'

'Probably because every time you saw Kate for the first year we were together you said, "What are you doing with that boring bastard?"'

I glower at Kate.

'A relationship can't work without honesty. Sorry, Noah,' Kate says with a shrug.

And there it is – the recurring pressing guilt. It's been about a month now since the kissing Emma incident and things with Mimi are going fantastically, but it's often there, niggling at me like a tickly cough. Sometimes I wonder if I should just tell her and be done with it. But things are going so well that I don't want to complicate them. I'm finally happy. And I've been unhappy long enough to know that this isn't something I want to jeopardize.

'So which team do you support?' Mimi continues. 'I can't believe Noah's not into football. I tried to take the boys for a kick-about when we first met but they were having none of it.'

Jerry laughs. 'Sheffield United. It's my hometown. And, I know, they must be the only two boys in the world who don't like football. I always find it fascinating, the whole nature versus nurture thing. Shows nature wins out, doesn't it?'

'Except I nurture them too, Jerry. So it's not exactly nature versus nurture, is it?'

'Oh, I know. Of course you do,' Jerry says, waving his hand. 'I just mean them spending the majority of their time with me doesn't seem to have had an effect, that's all.'

Kate starts clearing the plates and pouring us all more wine, clearly picking up on my slightly sour feelings at being pushed out as the minority parent. 'Dessert, everyone? I cooked this bit, so it'll probably be terrible. That's one trait Noah and I share, so the boys'll probably be shocking cooks, their poor wives.'

Whilst Kate is away from the table, we all tuck into our wine, and then she brings over a chocolate cheesecake, greeted by oohs and aahs around the table. As Kate serves up, Jerry takes a bottle of Shloer from the fridge and pours some into Kate's wine glass.

It takes me a while to take it in, to process it, and what I'm suddenly fairly sure it means. I know that Kate sees me staring at her glass and then at her even though she avoids eye contact, because when our eyes do meet, she's unable to hide the truth in hers.

'Well, thank you, Kate,' Mimi says. 'This is delicious too. Trust me, you're a much better cook than Noah.'

Kate's eyes plead with me and I can tell she thinks I'm about to start catapulting my chocolate cheesecake across the room.

Instead, I raise my glass. 'Well, I suppose a toast is in order.'

Mimi and Jerry look over at me, confusion crinkling their features.

'Congratulations. Looks as though you might get your footballer after all, Jerry.'

Mimi glances at me and then at Kate, and I can tell she's beginning to join up the dots. 'Oh, congratulations. That's wonderful news.'

Jerry taps my glass with his. 'Well, thanks, Noah. I didn't realize Kate had told you yet.'

'She hadn't. I worked it out.'

Kate puts her spoon back into her bowl. 'Excuse us. Noah, please can we go and have a quick chat outside?'

'Honestly, Kate. I'm really happy for you.' I smile at her so she knows I mean it. I think I'd be inhuman if it didn't sting a little, the thought of this new adventure my boys are about to embark on that I'm no part of, but it's all part of moving on, I guess. And I'm OK.

'I'd still like to have a chat alone for a minute, if that's OK with you, Mimi?'

She turns to Mimi, who is trying her best to look like she's perfectly fine with it, but I'm not so sure that she is.

'Of course.'

'I'll be back in a minute.' I place my hand on Mimi's shoulder and then follow Kate outside, grabbing my jacket on the way. We sit on their swing chair on the decking.

'Honestly, Kate. I'm fine. You don't need to explain.'

'I know it would feel odd if it was the other way around. I didn't want you to find out like this. I wanted to tell you.'

'So how far along are you?'

'Thirteen weeks. We wanted to wait until we'd had the scan. We were going to tell you tonight. That's one of the reasons we invited you over.'

It did seem a little out of the blue. I should've guessed she didn't just want to play happy families.

'Have you got a picture?'

'Of the scan?'

I nod.

'Yeah. Do you want to see it?'

I nod again, momentarily lost for words. I do want to see it, but I'm not sure why.

Kate goes inside and comes back out with the small rectangular image in her hand. When I look at it, I feel my heart constrict, as it takes me back to us cuddling on the sofa, poring over the scan pictures of Gabe and Finn. It's strange to think of her and Jerry doing the same.

'I expect you're hoping it's a girl?' I force a laugh.

'Actually, yes. But only because I can't imagine a boy that's not part of you, like Gabe and Finn. It sounds silly, but I just think I'd find it easier if it was a girl.'

I'm not sure which would be worse for me. A couple of years after we had Finn, I suggested trying for a third. I always wondered what it would be like to have a daughter, a 'daddy's girl' to balance out our two boys who would clearly push me into the path of an oncoming car if it meant saving their mum. But Kate kept avoiding the conversation and continued to religiously take her contraceptive pill. I guess she knew earlier than I realized that our marriage wasn't going to stand the test of time. And now she may be having a daughter. But it won't be mine.

'Congratulations.' I don't mean for it to sound so sad, but it does.

'Would you have any more?' Kate asks, cutting through my thoughts.

'I don't think so. I'm not exactly great at all this relationship stuff, am I?'

'I don't know. You and Mimi seem great to me. I really like her, you know? I'm glad you've found her. For a while there, I worried you'd always be hung up on me.' A slow smile spreads across Kate's face.

'Oh, because it's such a hardship having a hot thing like me pining over you?'

'You can't imagine how horrible it's been.'

For a while, we sit and swing, Kate pulling a blanket from her outdoor storage box and draping it across our legs – the gentle rhythm strangely soothing, probably tapping into some subconscious infantile memory.

Whilst she's not looking at me, I feel confident enough to approach the subject that is never far from my mind. 'Can I tell you something and you promise you won't hate me?'

I feel Kate turn her head towards me but I continue looking straight ahead. 'Of course. You know you can always tell me anything.'

I pause, take a deep breath and then say it. 'Mimi's sister kissed me.' I feel better the second it shoots out of my mouth, but then the guilt seeps back in.

'What?'

'Shh. She might hear us.'

'What did you do?' Kate sits up straight.

'I stopped her, but not straight away. I was pissed. Depressed. For a moment, I felt she understood, about Mum, I don't know. It was just before Mimi came over and told me she wanted to give things a go, so we weren't together, but even still . . .' I lean my head back and look up at the sky. 'It's such a mess. I finally find someone I want a future with and I fuck it up. Why do I always do that?'

'Is her sister going to tell her?'

'I don't think so, but she's hard to predict.'

'Well, I would've thought as she kissed you, she wouldn't want Mimi to know.'

'Yeah, that's what I'm hoping. But maybe I should tell her anyway. Like you said, a relationship needs honesty.'

Kate shakes her head like she's trying to create enough momentum to take off. 'Ignore what I said in there. That does not apply to this situation. You'll lose her and it'd be for nothing.'

'So you're encouraging me to be a lying bastard?'

'No. You weren't together at the time. Your head was all over the place. You're a lot of things, Noah, but you're not dishonest.' Then she pauses, and looks at me quizzically. 'Did you ever cheat on me? All those times you stayed out all night and I didn't hear from you? You know, you could tell me now and I'd forgive you.'

I look her straight in the eyes. 'Never. I swear on my life.'

Kate nods slowly, her eyes appearing to contemplate something deeply. 'Don't tell her, Noah. You've got something good there. A chance to be happy. You deserve that.' She taps me gently on the leg and I feel faintly reassured, like Kate giving me permission not to tell Mimi makes my dishonesty somehow acceptable. 'Right, we'd better get back inside before they start to think *we're* up to something.'

'Thank you. For still being my best friend.' I take Kate's hand in my own, linking our fingers together.

She lifts my hand to her mouth and kisses it. 'Always.'

'And congratulations about the baby. He or she is one very lucky little thing to have you as a mother.'

Kate smiles, her eyes welling up. 'Thank you.'

*

In the car on the way home, Mimi is particularly quiet and I wonder if, in her eyes, I've failed some sort of am-I-still-in-love-with-my-ex test. Because I no longer see Kate in that way, I forget that it might still be strange for Mimi. But she needn't worry. I never thought it would happen again, and she's definitely the only woman I want to be with right now and, if it didn't sound so dramatic, I'd say 'ever'.

'You OK?'

She looks wistfully out of the window, making patterns on the glass with her finger. 'Are *you*?'

'Of course. Why wouldn't I be?'

'Oh, I dunno. The fact your ex-wife is having some-body else's baby?'

I place my hand on her thigh. 'It was a bit of a shock, I'll be honest. It's strange to think of the boys having a sibling that shares no more with me than a stranger on the street. But it's not because I'm still in love with her, if that's what you're worried about?'

Mimi shrugs, twiddling her hair around her finger – the picture of someone who is trying to pretend that's not exactly what they're worried about. 'I'd understand if you were. She's stunning, and lovely, and makes a cheesecake like Nigella.'

I smile. 'Trust me, that's the best she has ever cooked. It wouldn't surprise me if she bought it and then just bashed the edges a bit to make it look homemade. And you are stunning too, and lovely, so you have nothing to worry about.'

As I say it, Emma's face flashes through my brain. Mimi and I weren't together. She'd be hurt, but she'd understand, wouldn't she? And I'd be rid of this guilt. It could make us stronger, couldn't it?

'Actually, there's something I wanted to tell you.' The words stumble out of my mouth without me having prepared what to say. I flick the indicator to pull into my road and the tick-tock is like a woodpecker hammering into my skull, preventing me from thinking straight.

When I don't continue, Mimi says, 'What is it?' Her voice is a mixture of concern and anticipation.

'Well, the thing is . . .' I manoeuvre the car into a space and pull the handbrake on, turning the ignition off.

Then I look at her, her beautiful face, her kind, expressive eyes. And I just say what I'm feeling. 'I think I've fallen in love with you.'

She looks back at me and I expect to see surprise, perhaps even a stray tear meandering down her cheek, but instead she's smiling. 'About bloody time. I've known that you're in love with me for a long time, Noah. I was just waiting for you to realize it so that I could tell you that I love you too.'

'Oh, is that so?'

'You didn't keep coming back to the scuzziest pub in town for the atmosphere now, did you?' Mimi reaches for my hand and then leans across the handbrake and kisses me. 'But, thank you, it's really lovely to hear.'

'It's OK. I mean it. I never thought I would, but I do.'

Mimi pulls back. 'So you never thought you'd fall in love with me? Should I be offended about that?'

'No. I don't mean that you're not amazing.'

'Irresistible?'

'Yes.'

'Inspiring?'

'Maybe.'

'Beautiful in an almost other-worldly sense?'

I give her my best I'm-well-aware-you're-taking-the-piss glare. 'What I mean is, I just didn't think I'd ever love anyone again. I know that sounds dramatic. I'm only thirty. But it just felt so impossible. And then you came along and everything seems possible again.'

Mimi pinches my cheeks. 'Who knew you could be so adorable? Right, come on. I think you've earned a shag with all that.' She opens her car door.

'Glad to hear it,' I laugh, getting out of the car and meeting her on the other side. Then I pick her up, struggle with the front door key and carry her to the bedroom, knowing that the time for me to tell her about Emma has passed and that, if I want to be happy, I need to stop letting it eat me up and just move on.

CHAPTER TWENTY-EIGHT

It's the morning of my class assembly. Although I'm trying to hide it behind a laissez-faire demeanour, I'm shitting myself. I attempt a little bit of joviality with the parents, laughing and rolling my eyes when two of the children walk in having a fight over a drumstick, one trying to grab it off the other and getting a swift smack over the head with it.

'Save that for the performance,' I joke, loudly enough for everyone to hear, even though the two children involved are not acting in it and the play doesn't involve any fighting.

Once they're seated along the benches at the front of the hall, some of the children start waving to their parents, but most of them haven't turned up despite the fact they don't work and have been sent multiple reminders. Harley's waving like a madman and I search the crowd to see both Emma and Mimi sitting together, Emma giving him the thumbs up and Mimi blowing him kisses. I wink at Mimi, who gives me a cheeky wink back, and Emma gives me this look – I can't really work out what she's trying to say, but it makes me feel unsettled. Like she's holding a detonator in her hand and if I do or say anything that she doesn't approve of, she's going to press it. I smile at her, trying to win her favour, but she just drops her eyes to the floor.

The head appears beside me and whispers in my ear, 'I've been really looking forward to seeing this.' She says it in such a way that I sense it's a warning, more *Your job is on the line* than *It'll be so lovely to see what the children have been up to*. I smile, but don't say anything, keeping my hands gripped behind my back, my nails digging into my skin, my eyes facing out towards the rest of the school lined up neatly in rows, with the smattering of parents on chairs behind.

Once everyone's in, the head claps her hands, and like robots, all the children clap back, sitting up straight then putting a forefinger to their lips. My class, sitting behind her, wriggle and whisper and I try to give them the evil eye, but it doesn't work. When the head turns around with a face like thunder though, they all fall silent. Creeps.

'Right, today, we have the wonderful reception children. I can't believe their first year with us is nearly coming to an end. Well, I can't wait to see what the children have been learning. I'll hand over to you, Mr Carlton, and the reception class.'

I stand up, giving a sickly smile. 'Thank you, Mrs Jackson. Well, I know the children are a little bit nervous (*get the excuses in early*) but I hope you enjoy our performance, as they've worked so hard on it and I'm really proud of them (*guilt-trip everyone into thinking it's better than it is*). Take it away, class R.'

Nothing happens and I feel myself breaking into a cold sweat.

'Darcy, remember what we practised?'

Darcy stares at me blankly. I gave her the 'welcome to our assembly' line as I figured it was fairly impossible to forget it. It seems I was wrong.

I creep along the line of children and take her hand, pulling her up off the bench and over to the microphone. I whisper 'Welcome to our assembly' in her ear, but she says nothing. So I say the words, feeling like I should be putting my hand in the back of her head and moving her mouth like a puppet. I smile at her and gesture for her to sit down, but she doesn't. I'm not sure if she's realized that she suddenly likes the limelight or whether she has no idea why there is a man stood next to her waving his hand, but in the end I have to manoeuvre her back to the bench, at which point luckily she sits down.

With a bit of off-stage prompting, the next few children manage their lines and then the full production kicks off. It's going well; the first little wolf builds her house using the bales of straw I managed to cadge off one of the parents who happens to be in the farming industry. The audience look impressed. And then Harley comes bounding in, shouting his lines so loud the rest of the children cover their ears and then, rather than huffing and puffing and gently pushing the straw bales over as he's supposed to, he blows in the first wolf's (Annabelle's) face, smattering her cheeks with spittle, making her cry, and then karate-kicks the straw bales so that one falls off the other and knocks into her, causing her to topple over like a domino. Of course it had to happen to Annabelle (why did I choose her to be a wolf?) and her mum comes rushing down the side of the hall and picks her up, cradling her in her arms like she's been shot. She carries her offstage and I whisper in Harley's ear, pleading with him to try to stick to what we practised. He looks at me and I can't quite tell if the smile he gives me is one of agreement, or one that says I-am-in-control-here-and-no-one-can-stop-me. He charges off towards the second wolf (James) and, after taking a quick glance at me, launches into 'Little Wolf, Little Wolf, let me come in.' And, thank the Lord, this time, after James has said his line, Harley starts huffing and puffing and kicks the stick house (made of painted wrapping paper rolls) a little over-zealously but not enough to cause harm or upset.

The play continues without further incident and ends on a high with an out-of-tune but fun song (with dancing or at least something that resembles dancing) and soon, much to my relief, the ordeal is over and the parents start clapping. Mimi gives me a great beaming smile, blows a kiss to Harley and then to me, and I smile back. But then I notice Emma just watching us with a face that doesn't say 'happy' and then she whispers something in Mimi's ear and all of a sudden Mimi's face falls too and she stares at her sister and then at me, and my whole world turns black, as I have a pretty good idea what Emma's just said.

*

Once all the other classes and their teachers have returned to their classrooms, the parents are welcomed up to take photographs of their children. Mimi heads over to Harley, avoiding any eye contact with me, and I try to get over to her, but parents keep stopping me to pat me on the back and congratulate me for such an 'entertaining' assembly. I can't focus, my brain working overtime to think up a way I can escape from school long enough to talk things over with Mimi, but I know there's no way I can get out before the end of the day.

As Mimi walks past me, head down, I try to hurry the conversation I'm having with another parent along, but by the time I get away, Mimi and Emma have gone.

*

I try calling Mimi what feels like a thousand times but she doesn't answer the phone. I know she's working at the pub tonight so I wait until the end of her shift and then stand outside waiting for her to come out. I watch the last few punters leave and then open the door.

'Sorry, we're closed,' Mimi shouts, her back to me. And then when I don't respond, she turns around, her face falling as soon as she sees it's me. 'Please leave, Noah. I have nothing to say to you.'

'So let me speak. You don't have to say a word. And then I'll go if you want me to.'

'I want you to go now.'

I take one of the stools down off the table and sit down.

'Noah, I'm serious. Leave, or I'm going to call the police.'

'What did she say to you? She might not be telling the truth, you know.'

'So you didn't kiss her?'

'She kissed *me*. There's a difference.'

'And you stopped her straight away?'

I let my head hang, unable to hold it up, unable to look at her. 'I was drunk, my head was all over the place with the whole suicide thing.' Then I look up at her. 'We weren't together. It was before you came over to say you wanted to give things a go, did she tell you that? I didn't cheat on you. I'd never cheat on you.'

I mean it as a reassurance, but it comes out like I'm excusing what I did.

'So you spend the evening getting it on with her and the following morning fucking me? That makes me feel much better.'

'It wasn't like that. I realized it was a mistake and stopped it.'

'And how long did it take for you to realize that, Noah? Once you were almost in the bedroom?'

An image of Emma grabbing the button on my jeans flashes into my head. 'No, of course not.'

'And you're sure about that? You weren't too off your face? Because there's no coming back from this if you lie to me. You do realize that?'

I rack my brain for the memory of that night. I know I was drunk but I'm sure about what happened.

'What did she tell you?'

'*You* tell *me* what happened.'

'She kissed me, but I stopped her. I have no interest in Emma. I wanted to help her, that's all.'

'So why didn't you tell me? If you're so innocent, why didn't you just tell me when I came over?'

I run my hands through my hair. 'I wish I had. I've thought about it so many times since, but I just didn't want to hurt you, or ruin things between you and Emma.'

'So all this time we've been together you've just been pretending? Keeping things secret from me?'

'No. Not pretending. I'm so sorry I didn't tell you. I thought it was for the best.'

Mimi grabs a key from behind the bar. 'Well, Emma has a very different version of events so I'd like you to leave now, please. I gave you the chance to finally be honest with me, but you decided not to take it.'

'I *am* being honest. I promise you. Emma's the one who's lying.'

Mimi shakes her head. 'Emma's a lot of things but she's not a liar. She's my *sister*, Noah. She wouldn't do that to me.'

I can see how horrible this is for her. Either her sister's lying to her or I am. There's no winning here for her.

'I don't know what to say. How to convince you.'

Mimi starts walking towards the back door but then turns and heads back to me. 'You know, it took a *lot* for me to let you in after everything with Kate. I took a huge punt on you and I *never* do that. I knew there'd be times you'd need your space or whatever, but I always thought I could trust you.'

'I was protecting Emma. And you. I knew if I told you about her kissing me, it'd ruin your relationship. Over nothing.'

'It's not nothing to me.'

I stand up and try to wrap my arms around her, but she pushes me away. 'Please, Mimi. We can get past this. I promise you can trust me. I'd never do anything to hurt you.'

Mimi picks up my stool and puts it back on top of the table. 'I'm sorry. This just made me realize you're not the one for me. I made a mistake. I hope you find whatever it is you're looking for.'

'*You're* what I'm looking for. I love you.'

Mimi bites her lip and her gaze lingers on me for a few seconds before she looks away. 'It's not just about Emma. That just made me see things more clearly. We're going in different directions.'

'So let me come with you.'

'I'm sorry. I just don't feel what you want me to.'

'But you said you loved me?'

'I was wrong, I don't. Not enough.'

Unless my emotional radar has been completely off the past month or so, I'm pretty sure this is a lie and I hate that she doesn't feel she can trust me with the truth.

'Well, I'll be here if you change your mind.'

'I won't. Move on, Noah.'

I want to say that after taking over two years to even contemplate feeling anything for anyone new, the likelihood of it happening again is minimal, but I sense that she's had enough. She's said her piece. I've hurt her enough already. As much as I don't want to, it's time to leave.

'I want *you*. I love *you*. But if you're sure you want me to leave then I'll respect your wishes.'

'I'm sure,' she says, eyes looking directly into mine, and it's like being stabbed.

'OK. Well, have a wonderful time on your travels. And keep going with the singing. I'll listen out for you on the radio.'

Mimi looks like she's trying to smile but that her face is caked in plaster and she can't make it move. 'Thanks.'

CHAPTER TWENTY-NINE

'So, we've called this progress meeting today to bring all the different agencies together and see how things are going for the family. People present are: Harley's mum, Emma; the family support officer, Janice; Harley's teacher, Mr Carlton; the health visitor, Lucy; and me, Harley's head teacher, Mrs Jackson. Janice, shall we start with you?'

'Well, as we are all aware, Emma has been having some difficulties with her mental health and ten weeks ago she tried to take her own life . . .'

I try to block out the thought of her lying there motionless. The fear. But my sympathy for her has gone. All I feel for her now is anger.

'. . . we're really impressed with how Emma is engaging with all the support we have put in place. She is attending regular counselling appointments and a weekly stay-and-play session after school with Harley, and she has joined an online support group that was suggested to her for help with her depression. So, really, I have to say well done, Emma.'

Emma smiles shyly.

Mrs Jackson taps her papers on the table and then picks up her pen again. 'Well, from the school's point of view, I have been into a couple of the stay-and-play sessions and Emma seems to interact very positively with Harley. She uses lots of praise and has clear boundaries when he needs them. Mr Carlton, do you have any comments about Harley's behaviour in class?'

I force myself to be professional. 'We have a number of interventions we are using with him. Thrive. Tactile time. He's a good kid. He's doing much better, learning to share, to take turns, and he seems less angry.'

'And how about Emma? Is she doing Harley's reading with him? Is he fed? On time? Does he always have a coat?'

I look over at Emma and her eyes plead with me. This could so easily be a time for me to take revenge. But this is about Harley. And he is doing really well, and I'm happy about that.

'Things are much better. She listens to him read regularly, he's on time, he can tell me what he had for breakfast, he's well turned out. I have no further concerns.'

Emma glances at me again and smiles and I know she's trying to say thank you, but I don't smile back, I can't bring myself to, and I'm happy when the meeting is over and she has left the room.

Just before I head back to my classroom, Mrs Jackson taps me on the back. 'I just wanted to say well done. You've done a super job with Harley this year. Given him a much better shot at succeeding than he would've had without you.'

The rush of emotion I feel in my chest is unexpected. 'Thanks. I was just doing my job.'

Mrs Jackson rests her hand on my arm. 'Accept the praise, Noah. I know we don't always share the same *methodology* . . .'

I know what she's saying – your classroom is a shithole, you look like you've been dragged through a hedge backwards, you're always late, your class sometimes bears a closer resemblance to a farmyard than a group of children.

'. . . but whatever you're doing clearly works. And you went above and beyond for that boy. Thank you and well done.'

I attempt a nonchalant shrug while wanting to collapse on the floor in shock. And it makes me realize that this is why I went into teaching in the first place. The chance to actually make a difference in a child's life. It's still an amazing feeling. 'Thanks.'

'Oh, and one other thing I've been meaning to talk to you about . . .'

Surely she's not going to give me the sack straight after doling out such praise? 'What have I done wrong this time?'

She smiles. 'Nothing. It's actually an opportunity I thought you might want to take up.' She rifles through her bag and pulls out some paperwork. 'I was supposed to be spending the summer working in a school in Tanzania but my mum's really not well . . .'

'I'm sorry to hear that.'

'I think she'll be OK, we're seeing this amazing doctor. Anyway, my point is, I need to be here with her and so they're looking for someone to fill my place and I immediately thought of you.'

She hands me the paperwork and I take it with what I'm sure is a sceptical expression on my face. 'Because I'm the only one who has nothing to stay around here for?'

'No. Of course not. No, because you're great with kids. I think you'd be a huge asset to the team.'

'Really?'

'Absolutely. Take a look at all the information and see what you think. I've written George's number on there somewhere. He's the guy that organizes it all. I don't want any money for it. I've raised it all through cake sales and sponsored stuff. I'd just hate for it all to go to waste. Just think it over. No pressure.'

I'm strangely touched that she's thought of me. 'OK. Thanks. I'll have a look at it.'

'Yeah, see what you think. Like I said, no pressure.'

I take the paperwork back to class, shoving it into my bag with the knowledge that I'll be giving it back to her tomorrow with a polite 'Thanks but no thanks', but still undeniably chuffed that she thought I'd be any good at it.

*

The boys charge into the flat after school. Kate had a midwife appointment so she asked if I could hold on to them for a bit, and it feels really nice seeing them in the week, breaking up the time that we're apart. Apparently, they are frantically searching for something (they won't tell me what), but after a few minutes they come running into the kitchen, Gabe clutching his iPad.

'Come on, Gabe. Remember we said we were going to try hard to limit the screen time. Go and grab a board game and I'll play with you both.'

'No, I don't want to play on it. I need to show you something,' Gabriel says, short of breath. He starts tapping away on the screen and then holds it up for me to see. 'It's that video you did of Mimi. It's got three thousand likes.'

I look at the screen, Mimi's face staring back at me. 'That's not three thousand likes. That's thirty thousand.'

I scroll down through all the comments. A few wankers have put 'Hey there, sexy' type stuff but most of them are raving about the song and Mimi's voice and asking where they can buy it. And then I spot it, a comment from an actress. I recognize her name because she was on *Strictly* last year. I'm guessing she's gone on to talk about it somewhere and suddenly Mimi's name is on the map.

I wonder if Mimi's been checking it. If she knows that she's gone viral. I want to call her, but I know she wouldn't answer. And then I notice that she has replied to some of the comments so I decide to put a comment on there myself.

Told you you could do it x

Then I make the boys turn the iPad off so that I no longer have to see Mimi's deep green eyes or hear her voice gnawing into me.

'Do you think she's going to be on the radio, Daddy? Like Taylor Swift?'

'Maybe. One day.'

'Can she come over tonight, please?' Finn says.

I rest my hand on his head. 'Remember Daddy said we're not really seeing Mimi any more, buddy?'

'They split up, duh,' Gabe says. 'Like Mummy and Daddy.'

Hearing it like that makes me feel like such a failure. Is that how my boys are going to remember me? The man who messed everything up? Everyone else is moving on and making something of their lives and what am I doing? Festering in a pool of regret.

'Go and get a game set up, boys. I'll be there in a minute.'

The boys run off and I search in my bag for the paperwork from Mrs Jackson. Scrolling through, I locate George's number, pick up my phone and type it in.

*

After I've dropped the boys home, I'm just about to put a pie in the oven when the phone starts ringing. I ignore it at first, but when it stops it starts up again right away. With a flash of hope, I wonder if it's Mimi so I follow the vibration and eventually locate my phone in my school bag. When I pull it out, I see Emma's name on the front screen. I'm so tempted to blank her, but I wouldn't be able to forgive myself if it had anything to do with Harley.

'What is it?'

I can't hear what Emma's saying because there's so much noise on the other end of the line. Banging and shouting. A man's voice, I think. I can hear Emma's breathing – hurried. Then the banging and the shouting are more muffled, as if Emma has covered the phone with her hand.

'It's Doug, my ex. He's trying to break down the door.'

I feel a sudden panic. 'Where's Harley? Is he OK?'

'I made him go upstairs but he's terrified, Noah.'

I can make out the sound of a child's voice, crying and shouting.

'Go upstairs with Harley and keep the door locked, OK? Whatever you do, do not open the door. I'm on my way.'

I put the phone down, slip my shoes on and grab my keys. I drive as if I'm on a racetrack until I reach the house and see Harley's dad smashing his fists against the door then opening the letterbox and begging Emma to let him in. He's a big bloke and I'm suddenly a little scared and unsure about what I'm going to do. He doesn't look like he's in the mood to listen to reason.

'Hey, Doug. Hold up.'

He turns, momentarily startled. 'Who the hell are you? How do you know my name?'

'I'm a friend of Emma's.'

'Oh yeah. Another friend. She's such a fucking slut. I should've known to wear something on the end of it with that one.'

'It's not like that at all. I'm Harley's teacher.'

He looks a little wrong-footed. 'So what are you doing here now?'

'You're scaring her. And Harley.'

'Well, if she just let me in, I wouldn't need to cause all the commotion, would I? I only want to see my son.'

'Well, I'm sure that could be arranged. We could try to sort something at the school where you could come and see him with one of us.'

'I don't need a supervised visit.'

'OK, but you can't see him in this state. You need to calm down.'

Doug strides over and squares up to me. His mouth is so close that I can smell the alcohol on his breath.

'And who the fuck are you to tell me what I can and can't do?' he says, pushing me in the chest and causing me to stumble backwards.

I just about manage to stay on my feet. 'I don't want any trouble.'

'Then fuck off.'

He pushes me again, this time with both hands, and I crash back on to the ground. Then I hear the door latch being removed and Emma opens the door a crack.

'No,' I shout to her, but it's too late.

Doug has reached the door and has his foot wedged in the little gap she has open. He reaches through and grabs a handful of her hair, pulling her face into sight.

I force myself up and run towards him. When he turns to look at me, I punch him straight in the jaw, causing my fingers to throb. He punches me back, just below my eye, sending my glasses flying and blurring my vision. Then before I can hit him again, he hammers me in my stomach and then pushes me to the ground. After that I can't keep track of whether he is kicking or hitting me; the blows just keep coming until everything goes black.

CHAPTER THIRTY

When I wake up, everything hurts. I've never been in a car accident, but I imagine this is how it would feel. My bottom lip feels like it's swollen to half the size of my face and my vision is limited, so I'm guessing one of my eyes is similarly disfigured.

'You're awake?'

I'm not sure where the voice is coming from or who it belongs to, but as I turn my head, it's Kate's face I see first, then Ben's. Scanning the rest of the room, my neck feels stiff and my head pounds. In the corner, I spot Claudia, and I can't be sure but it looks to me as if she's in floods of tears.

'Claudia, is that you?'

Ben and Kate come and stand either side of the bed, Kate reaching to hold my hand.

'You're OK.' Kate is crying and laughing simultaneously.

'I'm OK. Claudia, are you seriously crying over me?'

Claudia wipes her face and then sticks her middle finger up at me.

'Did I have to get beaten up for you to realize you cared about me?'

Claudia's face breaks into a smile. 'Something like that.'

'You scared us,' Ben says, sitting down in the armchair beside my bed. 'Fucking hell, Noah. We thought you weren't going to wake up.' His voice catches in his throat and I pray to God he's not going to start crying too as I'm not sure I could take it if he did.

'Oh, so that's why you're crying, Claudia. I had to go and bloody wake up, didn't I?'

'That's not funny, Noah,' Claudia says, her voice regaining its usual disappointed-with-me tone.

'You can't go doing things like that, do you understand?' Kate says, squeezing my hand. 'We need you. We love you.'

'Do the boys know I'm here?' I say, suddenly feeling sick at the thought of them worrying about me.

'No. We haven't told them. They're with Jerry.'

'Good. I'm glad.'

'So what the hell happened anyway? Do you remember? Who's Emma?' Ben says.

'It's Mimi's sister. Her little boy's in my class.'

'So why was his dad beating the shit out of you? What have you done this time?'

'Nothing. I haven't done anything. She called me because he was trying to break down the door.' The memory of what happened is quite blurred. I remember blocking his way. I remember throwing the first punch. But why? Then I suddenly remember. 'Is Harley OK? Did he hurt him?'

'The police wouldn't tell us much,' Kate says.

'Then we need to ask. We need to find out.'

'Calm down, Noah.' Kate reassuringly strokes my hand. 'We'll find out, I promise.'

Then, through the glass panel at the end of the room, I spot Mimi.

Kate must follow my gaze because she stands up and kisses me on the cheek. 'We'll come and see you again later, OK?'

'OK. Thanks.'

She gestures for the others to follow her lead and they do. Outside the room, I see Kate giving Mimi a hug and then Mimi opens the door, comes in and sits in the seat that Ben has just left.

'Is Harley OK?'

Mimi nods. 'He's fine. The police arrived pretty much straight after he knocked you out. Apparently one of the neighbours heard the commotion and called 999.'

The relief feels like a warm blanket being wrapped around me. 'I'm so glad he's OK.'

'Thanks to you.'

I start to shake my head, but stop when it hurts. 'Anyone in my situation would've done the same thing.'

'Oh, I'm not praising you. It was a stupid thing to do. He's a nasty piece of work. It wouldn't have surprised me if he'd had a knife. You're lucky he didn't kill you.'

'So you're mad at me?'

Mimi extends her hand and touches my cheek. 'Furiously.' Then she smiles.

Seeing her soften, I'm desperate to say all the things I've been keeping inside since I last saw her.

'I'm so sorry that I didn't tell you what happened with Emma. I never ever wanted to hurt you, you have to know that.'

'Actually, I need to talk to you about that.'

There's a flicker of emotion in my chest – hope? Fear?

'Emma told me that she lied about what happened. That *she* kissed *you* and you told her you weren't interested. I'm sorry I didn't believe you.'

I can't keep the excitement from my voice. 'So is there a chance? For us?'

Mimi shifts uncomfortably in her chair. 'I booked the rest of my trip. I decided to go for four and a half months in the end.'

Disappointment is a strange sensation. You can almost feel the tug downwards. Like all your organs are being pulled to the ground.

'Sounds amazing.' I manage to muster a little faux-enthusiasm. 'I'm actually going away myself this summer. The head asked me to do this placement at a school in Africa. I figured it was about time I did something positive with my life.'

'Wow, that sounds incredible, Noah. Good for you.'

I hate the way the conversation is going – as if our lives are quite happily travelling in different directions when that's not what I want. Not one bit. 'I'll be here when you get back, you know?'

Mimi pushes my hair off my forehead and then stands up and kisses it. 'I'd better get to work. I'm really glad to see you're OK. Now get some rest.'

She turns and heads for the door.

'If you'd give me the chance, I'd spend my whole life trying to make you happy. You know that, don't you?'

When Mimi looks back, her smile is sad. 'Try to get some sleep.'

*

Kate appears to have pulled out all the stops for my leaving party. When Ben parks up in the driveway (on Kate's request giving me a lift over), I see a huge clump of balloons attached to the front door, bunting draped down to the front gate, little solar-powered lamps lining the path. Inside, there's more bunting leading through to the back of the house and towards the garden. As we pass the kitchen, there are bowls of salads and nibbles lining the worktop along with rows of glasses and copious bottles of soft drinks and cider. Through the patio doors, I can see the boys chasing around and Jerry stood at the barbecue whilst Kate appears to be setting up some games.

It's not until I'm outside that I notice him, standing in the corner of the garden as if he's not sure whether he should hide, jump over the garden fence or come and greet me.

When Kate notices us, she comes running over, hugging Claudia first and then Ben before lingering for longer on me.

'Is it OK? Your dad?' she whispers in my ear.

I nod, my chin rubbing her shoulder. 'It's OK. Thanks for all this, Kate.'

We move apart. 'You're very welcome.'

The boys charge over, smashing into me. 'Hey, Daddy. Come and play tag.'

'I will. Just give me a minute, OK?'

The others start chattering in a little circle and I go over to Dad, who is looking lost standing on the periphery on his own. It feels weird seeing him after the last time, when I broke down in his arms. I'm not sure how to act.

'Hi.'

'Hey, son.'

I nod to his nearly empty bottle. 'Do you want me to get you another drink?'

'No, I'm OK. I'm driving.'

'Soft drink?'

Dad puts his hand on my arm. 'I'm fine. Enjoy your party, Noah. You deserve it. The Africa thing is amazing. I'm proud of you.'

It's funny how those words always mean the most coming from a parent, regardless of how disconnected you may have been.

'Thanks. It's just an excuse for a free holiday really.'

Dad smiles. 'Perhaps when you get back you could bring the boys over and I'll cook for you. Don't laugh but I've been taking cookery lessons. Sad really, but it gets me out the house.'

I don't like the thought of him being lonely, especially considering I may have contributed to it over the years. And to my surprise, I actually really want to see him.

'Sounds good. I'd like that.'

'Great. We'll get a date in the diary.'

The boys start calling me to catch them and then run away.

'I'd better go and play tag for a bit or they'll never stop going on at me.'

'Of course. Go.'

I wander off towards the boys and notice Ben going over to Dad, ushering him into the circle. I chase the boys for a bit until I'm out of breath and sweaty then go inside to get myself a drink. As I'm grabbing a cider out of the fridge, I sense someone in the room and look up to see Kate standing on the other side of the worktop.

'Is this OK?' She gestures to the food, the garden.

'Are you kidding me? It's amazing. Thank you so much. I really didn't expect a leaving party.'

'Well, I couldn't just let you leave, could I?' Kate takes some bags of crisps from the cupboard and empties them into bowls. 'And you're sure you're OK with your dad being here? When Ben told him you were off on your travels, he really wanted to come and say goodbye.'

'It's fine. It's nice. Thank you.' I look at my watch and then glance across towards the hallway. 'Did you invite Mimi?'

Kate nods, her face falling. 'She said she thought it was best as just a family thing. Sorry.'

I shake my head. 'No worries. It's fine.'

'I still think she'll come round, you know? Give her time.'

'It's OK. She's right. She's better off without me anyway.'

Kate holds her hand up. 'No more of that.'

I try my best to put on a brave face. 'Actually, I've been meaning to talk to you about the boys.'

'Go on.'

'I was wondering if I could see them a bit more often once I'm back. Maybe have them stay on a weekday each week as well as every other weekend? I know it'll mean booking them into breakfast club, but it's only one morning a week and it might be a help when the baby comes. And I promise I won't let them down any more. That I'll always be there when I say I will.'

'I know. And you don't need an excuse, Noah. They're your boys too. I mean, I'll miss the little pains, but I think it's a great idea. You can do some of the mundane stuff like the dreaded spelling homework and reading journals.'

I smile. 'I'd like that.'

'So would they.'

I look outside. 'Right, come on, that barbecue smells like it's almost ready. I expect old Jamie Oliver out there has made his own burgers, hasn't he?'

'Actually, he has. He won't let me eat anything processed since being pregnant. I could murder a dirty hot dog.'

'Glad to hear he's looking after you.'

'He is.'

We go out to the garden and join the others. We play quoits (I win) and giant Jenga (I don't, sending the whole thing toppling to the ground and nearly breaking the boys' toes). We eat Jerry's delicious food and drink cider (Kate swigging on a non-alcoholic one and the boys drinking Appletiser, all proud that they get to drink it out of a bottle). The sun shines and the birds sing and if it wasn't for the Mimi-shaped hole, it would be a perfect afternoon. Even Claudia doesn't irritate me too much for once.

But all too soon, it's time to leave. And saying goodbye to my boys for six weeks feels like a task I will never be ready for. But first it's time for Dad to go, so I walk him to the front door, contemplating the awkward 'do we hug or don't we?'

'Have an amazing trip. Take care of yourself.' Dad puts his hands in his pockets and then takes them out and holds them in front of him, but then he drops them again, as if they're heavy and he can't keep them up.

So I hug him. And he hugs me back tight.

'I'm so glad we're back in touch,' he says into my ear and the emotion in his voice hits me in the chest.

'Me too.'

I tap him on the back and then we separate and he leaves. And I go back outside to find the boys, noticing that the others head indoors to give us some space.

We sit on the swings, Finn on my knee and Gabe on his own swing beside us.

'Promise you'll email me every day?' Gabe asks.

We recently set him up an account and he loves getting messages. (I'm well aware a huge part of it is giving him an excuse to go on his tablet, but it's still nice, seeing his words written down, imagining them said in his voice, and whilst I'm away I'm going to need them more than ever.)

'Every day. And I'll put a message on there for Gabe to read to you too, buddy.' I move Finn's unruly fringe off his face and kiss his forehead.

'I can read too now, you know, Daddy?' Finn gives me an incredulous look.

'I know. Sorry. You can read it yourself then.'

Gabe sneaks me a smile, knowing as well as I do that Finn is still very much at the c-a-t level of reading, and it shows how much Gabe is growing up because not that long ago he would've tactlessly put his brother straight about it.

'I'm going to miss you both every single day, you know that, don't you?'

'Do you have to go?' Finn asks, turning his head and peering up at me with watery eyes.

'He's going to help other kids. Ones that don't have as much as us. It's important, Finn.'

I smile at my eldest son and imagine Kate sitting down and explaining to them why I'm going away.

'But *we're* important,' Finn says, his face screwed up at Gabe.

I stroke his golden hair. 'You two are the *most* important things in my entire life and always will be. The other children are just borrowing me for a few weeks, but you get to keep me forever, OK?'

'I s'pose.' Finn gives me a grumpy look and I kiss the top of his head then lift him off me and stand up.

'And Mummy and I decided that me just seeing you every other weekend wasn't enough. So when I get back, you're going to stay with me for a night in the week too.'

'Every week?' Gabe asks.

'Yeah, every week. Is that OK?'

'Of course. It's awesome.'

I smile. 'Good. Come on then. Give me a hug.'

I crouch down and both boys wrap their arms around me and I wonder how long I can get away with staying here for because I'm not sure I can let go. But eventually both boys start wriggling and I know I need to get up and go home.

I ruffle their hair. 'I love you, boys. See you very soon.'

'Bye, Daddy.'

And then they both return to the swings as if it's just another day and I force myself to turn and go inside.

'Ready?' Ben says, holding out his keys.

'As I'll ever be.'

I say my goodbyes and thank yous to Jerry and Kate and then Ben drives me home. I sit in the back, quiet, watching as Ben and Claudia giggle about something one of the girls did. I'm not sure how I missed it before – how well they get on – maybe I was too busy seeing what I wanted to.

When we pull up outside, I lean through the gap in the front seats and give Claudia a kiss on the cheek, trying not to laugh at the shock (fear?) on her face.

'You're a good couple.'

Ben looks confused. 'What's got into you?'

I shake my head. 'Nothing. Just an observation. Thanks for the lift. And everything . . . you know?'

Ben reaches down to undo his seatbelt.

'Don't worry. I'll see myself in. Now don't do anything too crazy whilst I'm away, will you two?'

'Sod off, Noah,' Claudia says, but she's smiling.

'Take care of yourself out there, OK?' Ben says.

'I will.' I tap him on the shoulder then get out and walk into the flat.

CHAPTER THIRTY-ONE

I always find something sombre about airports. I don't know what it is. In the main part, they're full of people going on exciting trips, adventures, holidays, but they always feel like goodbye. Always make me sad for everything I'm leaving behind. And today, of course, they feel that way more than ever. The thought of not seeing the kids for six weeks feels like something's lodged in my stomach. Constantly prodding me. And knowing Mimi's flying off any day now in the opposite direction doesn't help matters much.

But, at the same time, I finally feel like I'm doing something important. That, in the tiniest of ways, I'm making a difference. A lot of times at work it feels like I'm going against the natural order of things, dragging kids who would rather be running around in the woods through a list of unrealistic and unnecessary requirements, trying to teach them about when to use a capital letter when they need to be learning which foot which shoe goes on, or making them stand in a straight line or sit with crossed legs when they should be charging around and jumping and climbing. But with the children in Africa, I might actually be able to make things a bit better for them.

I sit in the airport bar, not wanting to go through security yet. Kate always used to tease me about it. She wanted to go through and get settled as soon as we'd checked in, but I always felt there was something final about it. Something claustrophobic. Like once you were through you couldn't escape. You could never come back.

It's only ten o'clock in the morning but I've ordered a beer. I'm by no means the only one. Time doesn't seem to apply in an airport. People eat burgers at five a.m, porridge at teatime, start drinking before it's even got light. The alcohol goes to my head fairly quickly, which is a good thing, as I'm a bit of a nervous flyer (understatement), and I start to relax into the whole thing, allowing myself to look forward to the adventure ahead.

Then, out of the corner of my eye, I spot them. At first, I think I'm hallucinating. But then Finn sees me and starts running towards me and soon he's jumping up on my chair and nearly knocking over my beer.

'Daddy!' He wraps his arms around my neck and I hold him tight.

'What are you doing here?' I position him on my knee so I can look at him, still not quite able to take in that he's here.

'We've come to say goodbye. We brought you a present.'

Gabe comes up beside him, flicking his brother on the arm. 'You weren't supposed to tell him yet, Loserface.'

Finn puts on his best frown.

Then Kate sidles over, her skin glowing, her bump starting to show beneath her T-shirt. 'See, I told you he wouldn't have gone through,' she says, putting her hand on Gabe's shoulder. Then she turns to me. 'He was worried you'd have gone through security and we wouldn't get the chance to say goodbye, but I told him I knew you too well.'

I smile. 'And you were right. But you didn't need to drive all this way. You already threw me a party.'

'I know, but the kids said they had a present that they'd forgotten to give to you.' Then she lowers her voice. 'I wouldn't get too excited.'

Gabe shoves Kate in the side. 'I heard that, Mummy. It's actually really cool, thank you very much.'

'Yeah, it's to stop you getting eaten by a lion,' Finn says.

Kate bites back a smile. 'I think they think because you're going to Africa, you're going on safari.'

Gabe pulls Kate's handbag off her shoulder and rummages inside, taking out his favourite orange purse he's had since he was a toddler. Then he hands it to me.

'You want me to take your purse?'

'No, silly, look inside,' Finn says, laughing.

I open it up and pull out two one-pence pieces, shiny from rubbing around in the boys' pockets all this time, and I feel my breath catch in my chest.

'It's our magic coins, Daddy,' Gabe says. 'To keep you safe. Hopefully we'll be all right without them for a few weeks.' Gabe begins to look a little concerned, as if he's only just considered this potential problem.

I rub the coins with my thumb and then put one back into the purse. 'You guys share that one and I'll take the other. That way, we'll all be safe.'

Gabe crinkles his nose in contemplation. 'Yes, I think that should work.'

I laugh and pull Gabe into a hug, wrapping my other arm tighter around Finn, who is still sitting on my lap. 'Thank you so much, boys. I'll keep it with me the whole time.'

Gabe shuffles away and looks up at his mum. 'See, told you it was special.'

Kate ruffles his hair. 'You were right, as usual.' Then she looks at her watch and I look at mine. 'I suppose you'd better be going through.'

I scan the airport, realizing from the disappointment in the pit of my stomach that I was hoping Mimi might turn up. That maybe she'd appear at the airport with a declaration of love like they do in the movies.

I push the last of my pint across the table and lift Finn down off my knee. 'Yep, I guess I better had.'

As I stand up, Kate comes over and kisses me on the cheek, her firm bump grazing my side. 'We're really proud of you, Noah. Aren't we, boys?'

'Yeah. I told everyone at school that you were going to help children who didn't have as much money as us and they said you should come and do an assembly when you get home. Will you do that, Daddy?' Gabe asks.

'Of course. I'd love to.'

'And I'll be able to see you because I'll be in assembly too,' Finn says.

'That'd be awesome.'

I pick up my case and start to go, but Kate stops me, wrapping her arms around me. Then the boys follow, grabbing on to a thigh each. I'm determined not to cry, but it's not easy, especially as when I pull away, I can see tears in Kate's eyes.

'Take care of yourself and come back to us safe and sound, you hear me.'

I nod. 'I've got my magic coin to protect me now, so I'll be fine.'

The boys smile proudly and I crouch down so I can look them both in the eyes. 'When I come back, as soon as I get off the plane, I'm going to drive straight to your house to see you both, OK?'

'Will you bring us a present?' Finn says.

'Fiiiinn,' Gabe says, elbowing him in the ribs. 'You're not supposed to ask that.'

I smile at my eldest son, so full of pride I can feel it coming out my pores. 'It's OK. Yes, of course I will bring you presents. Now, give me one last hug, please.'

I wrap my arms around both boys, squeezing them together, trying to bottle the feeling so that I can take it with me. Then I let go and stand up. 'Now be kind to each other and look after Mummy. I'll see you really soon.'

Forcing myself to turn and walk towards security is almost impossible. I have to do it in one swift movement and not look back. But I can hear the boys cheering, 'Daddy, Daddy, Daddy,' like football supporters, as I walk towards the gate.

CHAPTER THIRTY-TWO

On the plane, I'm stuck in the middle seat, in between two young guys. Both of them stocky, the sheer width of them making me feel both squashed and insignificant. How do blokes even get that big? I reach into my bag for my headphones and happen across my mobile phone, which I pull out to turn off. I always worry – what if other people don't turn theirs off, or at least switch them to aeroplane mode? Do some people just idly ignore the warnings – and could that cause the flight systems to falter? Shouldn't someone be walking along and checking?

I try to keep calm and then, just as I'm about to turn it off, my phone starts ringing, my heart doing somersaults as I see Mimi's name on the screen.

'Hey, I was just about to turn my phone off. They're going to close the doors any minute.'

'I'm so glad I caught you in time.' Mimi sounds breathless, like she's just been out for a run. 'I was going to leave it until we both got back, but then I thought, what if your plane crashes and you never get to hear what I have to say?'

'You do realize I'm a nervous flyer, don't you?' I whisper, conscious of the two very masculine lads sitting beside me.

'I'm sorry. Your flight will be fine, forget I said that. I mean my flight, what if my flight crashed?'

'Not helping.'

I can almost hear Mimi smile. 'OK, forget about flights crashing. I just realized that when you have something to say to someone, you should just say it, not sit on it hoping for a better time. Because what if you wait and then the moment's passed and if you'd just said it in the first place then things would've turned out differently?'

'So are you going to say it, then? This thing that you have to say?'

'Yes. Sorry. Right. I love you. That's what I need to say. And that if the offer's still there, I'd very much like you to spend the rest of your life making me happy, because without you I'm not happy. And I don't want to be not happy forever.'

It feels like I'm floating, like I'm about to take off myself. 'The offer's still there.'

The bloke to my right coughs loudly and then turns to me to apologize. I shake my head and wave my hand.

'You're not sat on your own, are you?'

'No. I have a middle seat.'

'So come on then, tell me that you love me too. In fact, say, "I love you so much, babycakes, and I can't wait until we get to snuggle-wuggle."'

'No.'

'Oh, go on, you know we're not going to see each other for months. You'll regret it if you don't.'

'I love you,' I say under my breath, glancing over at the lads next to me, who are both pretending not to listen.

'Babycakes?'

'The stewardess is going to be along in a minute asking me to turn my phone off.'

'OK, OK, I'm sorry. Have a wonderful trip and call me lots, won't you?'

'Of course.'

'And you're sure you want to wait for me? I should be back around Christmas. I'll understand if it's too long.'

'I'll be there. Christmas present and all.'

'I'm going to miss you so much. I don't even want to go now.'

'Don't say that. You'll have an amazing time. Enjoy it.' Then I look from side to side and lower my voice. 'We have the rest of our lives to spend together.'

This time when I look at the guys beside me, they're smiling. Then I spot the air stewardess walking up the aisle towards me and I know she's going to tell me to end the call. It feels like there's so much I should say, so much I want Mimi to know, like how grateful I am to her for lifting me out of the gloom, for being willing to love me despite everything, but it's so hard to put it into words without it sounding trite or contrived and I've only got seconds before I have to go, so I say, 'I love you, babycakes.'

And Mimi laughs her deep, throaty laugh, just like she did when we first met in the bar, and I know that she knows, that she could see straight through me from day one, that there's no need to explain.

I put the phone down just before the stewardess reaches me, turning it off and putting it in my bag. And once the safety demonstrations have been performed, we taxi towards the runway and it feels great to be finally moving forward.

ACKNOWLEDGEMENTS

I've been lucky enough to work with a number of wonderful editors on this book – all who have helped to make it what it is today. So thank you to Tilda McDonald, Maxine Hitchcock, Clare Bowron and Clio Cornish for all your insightful comments and pointers.

Thank you, as always, to my wonderful agent, Alice Lutyens, for your endless support and belief in my writing, and for always making me laugh.

To my publicist, Olivia Thomas – publicity events never feel like work with you around!

To Sarah Bance – my copy-editor – for making the process so painless and for your kind words about the book.

To everyone at Michael Joseph – cover designers, marketing, sales – I'm so lucky to be part of such an amazing team.

To David Nicholls and Kodaline for the wonderful words/lyrics quoted in this book.

To all the big-hearted men in my life that helped me to write Noah – I'm not suggesting any of you are as flawed as him (!) but I feel very privileged to be surrounded by men who aren't afraid to cry or express their emotions, who show me the type of men I want my boys to become – Dad, Pete, Carl and my late Granddad, I'm talking about you.

To my parents – I really struggled to write the dedication to this book because it's impossible to express in one line how having you as parents has helped me. You are my biggest supporters, my best friends, my confidantes. Thank you for loving me so fiercely.

To my 'village' who keep me sane on a daily basis – you know who you are and I love you all.

To my writing friends for the coffees and the lunches – there're some things only fellow writers can truly understand.

To all the bloggers and reviewers who supported my first book – I hope you enjoy this one just as much and thank you so much for sharing the love and helping to get the book to as many readers as possible.

To my husband, Carl, for loving me despite my flaws and putting up with me when I moan at you. I do love you to bits really.

And last but not least, to my children – Jacob, Dylan and our latest addition, Coco. You are my reason for everything and make me happier than I ever thought possible. In the words of Jerry Maguire, you complete me.

Page TURNERS

Great stories.
Unforgettable characters.
Unbeatable deals.

**WELCOME TO PAGE TURNERS.
A PLACE FOR PEOPLE WHO LOVE TO READ.**

In bed, in the bath, on your lunch break.
Wherever you are, you love to lose yourself in a brilliant story.

And because we know how that feels, every month we choose
books you'll love, and send you an ebook at an amazingly low price.

From tear-jerkers to love stories, family dramas and gripping
crime, we're here to help you find your next must-read.

Don't miss our book-inspired prizes and sneak peeks into
the most exciting releases.

**Sign up to our FREE newsletter at
penguin.co.uk/newsletters/page-turners**

SPREAD THE BOOK LOVE AT

To celebrate the publication of
Until Next Weekend, we've teamed up
with CoolStays to offer one person the
chance to win a £500 voucher to
"Stay Somewhere Extraordinary!"

CoolStays showcases unique and unusual places to stay
across the UK, Europe and worldwide. We have made it our
mission to find you that special place with a difference, and
now have a growing portfolio of over 2000 hand-picked,
extraordinary places to stay.

From treehouses to lighthouses, cave houses to penthouses,
cabins, cottages, boutique hotels and B&Bs - Coolstays is
the definitive collection of amazing places to stay.

To enter the competition, simply visit:
www.coolstays.com/penguin

Terms and conditions apply

He just wanted a decent book to read ...

Not too much to ask, is it? It was in 1935 when Allen Lane, Managing Director of Bodley Head Publishers, stood on a platform at Exeter railway station looking for something good to read on his journey back to London. His choice was limited to popular magazines and poor-quality paperbacks – the same choice faced every day by the vast majority of readers, few of whom could afford hardbacks. Lane's disappointment and subsequent anger at the range of books generally available led him to found a company – and change the world.

'We believed in the existence in this country of a vast reading public for intelligent books at a low price, and staked everything on it'
Sir Allen Lane, 1902–1970, founder of Penguin Books

The quality paperback had arrived – and not just in bookshops. Lane was adamant that his Penguins should appear in chain stores and tobacconists, and should cost no more than a packet of cigarettes.

Reading habits (and cigarette prices) have changed since 1935, but Penguin still believes in publishing the best books for everybody to enjoy. We still believe that good design costs no more than bad design, and we still believe that quality books published passionately and responsibly make the world a better place.

So wherever you see the little bird – whether it's on a piece of prize-winning literary fiction or a celebrity autobiography, political tour de force or historical masterpiece, a serial-killer thriller, reference book, world classic or a piece of pure escapism – you can bet that it represents the very best that the genre has to offer.

Whatever you like to read – trust Penguin.